SILVER CROWN

ARABELLA ROSIER

Silver Crown
Book Three

Find me at: www.arabellarosier.com
Instagram: @rosierarabella
Tik Tok: @rosierarabella

Printed in Australia.

First edition: June 2023

Paperback: 978-0-6453965-5-3
Hardback: 978-0-6453965-6-0

Special thanks and acknowledgement to:
Editor – Chloe's Chapters,
Cover artist – Gab Nao Designs,
Formatter – Author Services Australia.

This book is written in British English.

*To the girls who feel trapped in the world
they're given, and choose the stars.*

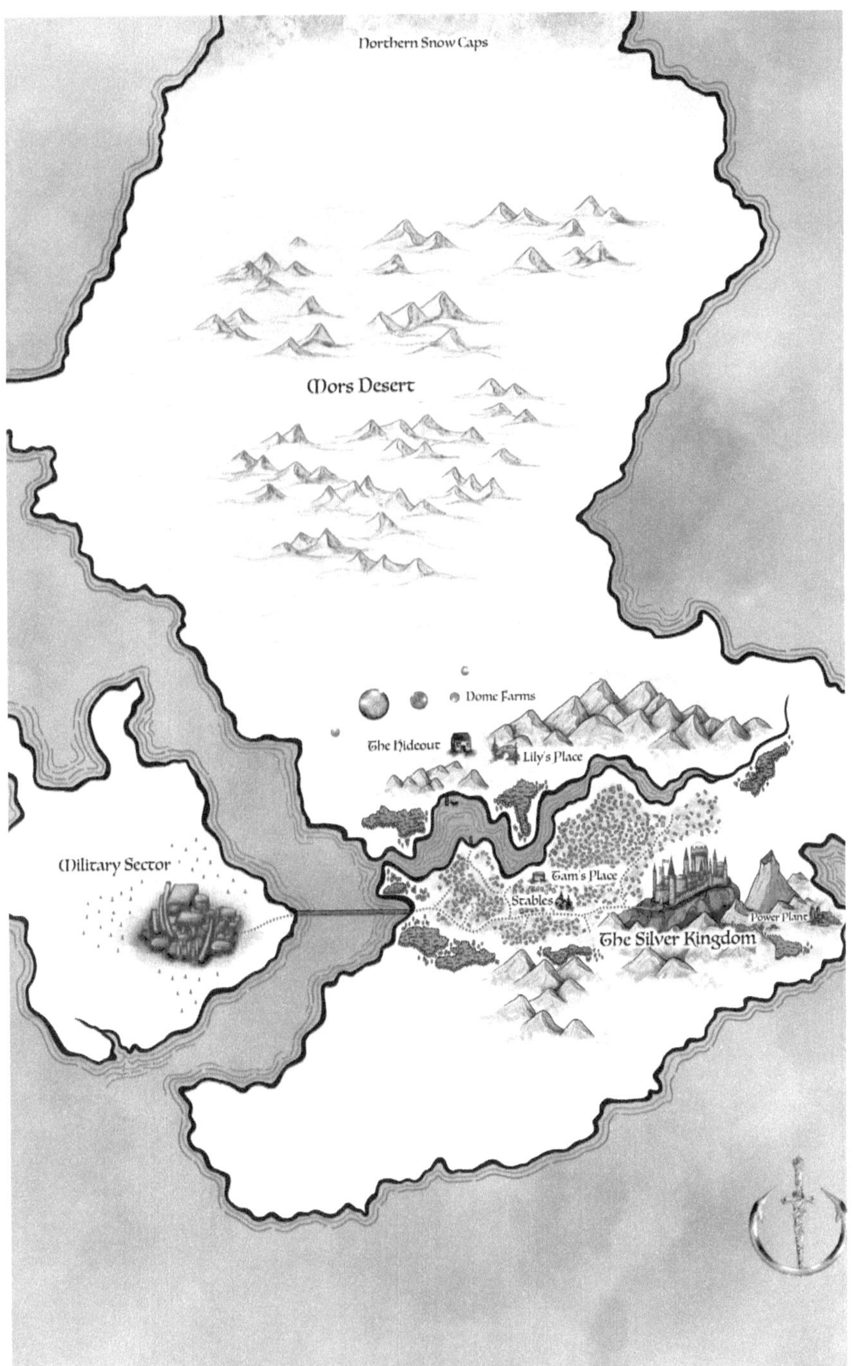

Northern Snow Caps
Mors Desert
Dome Farms
The Hideout
Lily's Place
Military Sector
Tam's Place
Stables
The Silver Kingdom
Power Plant

ELIJAH

"Landing gear locked. Preparing for touchdown on Umbran soil."

A boy, recently turned a man, grips the edge of his seat like a vice and takes a long, steadying breath to ease the acid rising in his stomach. The world is bright and full of colour, but he can barely see it as the guard beside him pilots their ship onto a landing strip outside the Silver Kingdom.

"Please tell me you're not going to puke," a guard sneers beside him, his blond hair shining in the lights. Jackson Mann isn't a friendly man by nature, but he knows how to get the job done.

That doesn't stop Elijah Brookes from disliking him.

Since a squadron of guards took Melanie to Umbra, forever sealing her fate, he hasn't been able to function. Sweat pools across his brow nonstop, his body wracking with shivers. It only took several hours of pacing around the ship before Jackson screamed "Enough!" and readied a plan to follow her.

Andrea was no better, with her endless pleas.

But the rest of their army, floating around them in invisible ships among the stars, unwittingly agreed. One thing was for certain: Melanie Beckett secured her position as the leader of the Terran fleet—since sacrificing herself to save Jasmine Spark's ship from being overrun—and now no amount of resistance would stop the Terran army from getting her back.

She had been taken down to Umbra, as a hostage, along with the rest of the crew on Jasmine's ship. Our orders were to wait, but waiting be damned. And since one of the ships in the fleet had an escape pod attached, Eli and Jackson immediately volunteered to be on the retrieval team.

Now they're whirring towards Umbra without a second thought, a plan, or any backup. It may be suicide, but the two of them was all the Terran army was willing to sacrifice for now.

But if they trying, the army will just send another team.

And another.

And another.

Until they get Melanie Beckett back.

Eli schools his shaking, tempers his breathing, and stares at the beauty of the planet rushing towards them. It feels off that the Umbran sky above the military base is void of ships, but the fading streaks of gas tells Eli the area hasn't been empty for long.

Melanie's arrival must have caused a disruption.

"Focus. On. Landing," Elijah spits, breathing deeply between words.

The sun is setting on Umbra, poignant and orange as it splits apart the sky, basking the clouds in gold. It's been less than a day since Melanie left their ship to save Jasmine. Less than a day since Eli lost her.

"Calm down, Brookes. For stars' sake."

Eli barely bats an eye at him. His heart feels like it's in his throat, pounding incessantly as their pod approaches the landing pads. Their speed decreases, thrusters pumping and lights blinking as Jackson splits a joyous grin and brings them home.

No one stops them. Which, again, feels off.

Where is the military? Where are the Umbrans?

"Something doesn't feel right," he mutters to Jackson, his eyes flitting back and forth between the window and the man pointedly ignoring him.

The landing pads glitter in the setting sun, yawning wide open for their arrival. Not a single guard patrols the space, leaving the expanse free for the taking.

Jackson maneuverers them down deftly, the humming engine beating in tandem with Eli's erratic heart. His hands strain against the armrest, readying to lunge him from his seat, but he stays still nonetheless, his body frozen.

"Melanie must have cleared the way. That's why they're letting us through," Jackson mutters, just as the ship settles smoothly. The entrance stays open just long enough for the sleek vessel to park.

"She was a prisoner, she didn't do jack all," Eli growls, his eyes taking in every detail.

"You want to go back?"

"Not without her," he says immediately.

"Then shut up."

Melanie's ship arrived via the Sector 2 military ports, as all ships do. But was it the best course of action for Eli and Jackson to follow?

Blackness engulfs them, save a small red light flickering several metres away. In the dim space, it highlights a few ships, as well as their guards. The light keeps flashing, over and over, like morse code or something.

Jackson curses, slamming on the gears of the ship.

"Ambush," Eli chokes out, out of his seat in seconds and scrambling for his sword. He's only had a few weeks to practice with the thing, but how hard can it be to skewer a man?

"*Stars*, Brookes, maybe we should have—"

"Listened to me? Oh yeah, that would have been a neat idea," Eli says hysterically, his chest inflating. "Maybe then we wouldn't be trapped. Maybe then—"

"Brookes? Shut up."

Their ship hums quietly as the engine dwindles to a standstill. All Eli can hear is the slamming of his heart in his ears as he stands by the window, shakily gripping his sword.

"Plan?" he asks Jackson.

"Not get caught?"

"Awful plan. Do you have another?"

"All involve getting captured," Jackson says, rising from his seat to squint out of the window. The guards converge outside, their silhouettes outlined by that flickering red light.

"Might be a fast way to get to Mel," Elijah muses.

"It's also a fast way to die. Your pick."

Eli groans, his body shaking even more as a loud voice splinters from the speakers, "*Disembark immediately or we will have you executed.*"

Jackson swallows loudly, his eyes glazing over. "Well, damn."

"So much for not being captured," Eli says.

"Okay, new plan. I stay on the ship and distract them and you sneak out the back. Try and find an exit towards the Ocean Train. Can you do that?" Jackson asks, turning his stormy eyes onto Eli. The tips of his blond hair are wet from perspiration, his breathing shallow.

Eli sucks on his lips and tries to still his beating heart. "And what will you do?"

Jackson frowns and turns slowly.

"*What will you do*, Jackson?" Eli insists.

"Whatever is required of me." His voice is flat. "Just go and get Beckett."

Outside the pod, the lights in the hangar beam, then blacken, then beam again.

Eli squints, the light hurting his head.

Each time it comes on, he can see the guards in all their glory—about 30 of them, give or take. Eli stands still, watching them all.

"Do I *really* have to argue with you?" Jackson sneers.

Eli blinks rapidly and shakes his head. "No, sorry, I'm going."

Without thinking too deeply about it, Eli repositions the sword and heads for the back of the ship, just as Jackson leans forward so the guards can see him.

"Disembark immediately or we will have you executed."

The threat repeats as Eli gets the exit shaft open and slides through it. Behind the ship, there are only a few guards, most of them having swarmed to the front to face Jackson.

"Go to hell!" Jackson shouts.

Eli trembles as he slips outside the ship, flattening his body against the side.

None of the guards see him, but he sees them and, more specifically, the crate of small metal disks they lug into the building. They gleam bright silver, reflecting in the pounding lights that flicker repeatedly in the cavern. One of the guards grabs one and turns some dials.

"Hold your fire," a voice shouts so loudly that Eli's head begins to ache.

The voice sounds female and static; unrecognisable as it blares through the speakers.

The guards rustle at the sound, glancing at each other. None seem to recognise the voice.

"Disembark immediately or we will have you executed. You have 30 seconds."

Eli can almost picture Jackson cursing at that voice, but he takes a breath and steadies himself.

He will need to make a run for it. Perhaps distract a few guards.

There are 4 standing around the back of the ship—he can handle running away from 4. It would avert them from Jackson and give his comrade the chance to flee.

The Ocean Train. He must find the Ocean Train and meet up with Jackson there.

Eli is just about to run, but a whoosh of sound distracts him.

"Time's up."

The voice hasn't even finished speaking when one of the guards lifts the metal device, aims directly at Jackson, and launches it at the front window.

There's barely a sound or a flash. One second, the ship is there, the next, it combusts entirely. Time seems to warp and elongate as fire sucks inwards, lapping at Eli's back.

His scream dances through the hangar, bounding off the walls as the implosion eats at him, tearing his flesh. Heat engulfs him, and all he can focus on is pulling himself away.

His hands slam onto concrete, his mouth wide and blubbering as pain takes over.

Time stretches, feeling endless, until the implosion has ended.

The ship behind him is gone—exploded into nothingness from a wave of fire and heat. There isn't even a mark on the ground to indicate the ship ever existed. Nothing remains, except for the young man howling on the floor.

His back still burns, the flesh peeled back by fire. His body feels like it is being eaten alive.

This is how your parents felt. You will die by fire now. Just like them.

Eli screams as the guards approach. The one with the crate of explosives lowers it to the ground with shaking fingers. All of them seem unsettled as their gazes flicker from side to side.

It takes Eli much too long to realise why.

"Did you *not* get my message?" a female voice shouts.

She stands over him, one cyborg hand wrapped around some

sort of comm. He doesn't recognise her immediately. His world is shattering, splintering away.

"Stand down!" the familiar female voice shouts.

And then Eli realises why none of the guards have taken him. Around the edges of the hangar, oozing from the shadows, is an army. They converge on the guards, swords still dripping in blood, their gazes unrelenting.

Eli tips his head to the female standing above him, the motion hurting so much that acid rips up from his stomach and burns his tongue. The fixture that was flickering now bathes the entire space in light, highlighting her every feature.

"Did you not get my message, Elijah?" Melanie Beckett repeats, squeezing the comm in her hands.

The lights. It *was* Morse.

As if I'm supposed to understand what it says. That damn girl.

She tilts her head to him, silver eyes flashing.

Melanie Beckett is here.

"What's going on?" a guard shouts.

The words ring in Eli's head as he, too, tries to figure that out.

"Melanie Beckett has taken over Sector 2," someone broadcasts. *Jesse?* Eli can hear his voice, but cannot see him. He must be standing behind him. Or in the shadows. Or both.

Melanie grunts. Her light hair is orange under the lights, her brows scrunched as she kneels towards Eli, still in the same clothes she wore back on their ship.

"I'm going to be sick," Eli says with a gasp.

Her fingers brush his cheek before she spins away. "Someone find a medic!"

Stars glint in Eli's eyes, the lights from the ceiling pounding in his skull. The fire eating his back does not relent, and the fleeing form of the girl he loves is the last thing he sees before he succumbs to death.

Fire takes over, and Elijah Brookes feels himself slipping away.

Dying hurts.

PART ONE

THE CASTLE

SAVANNAH

The world is a riot of colour and pain.

"Move," a guard barks.

Dread lashes me as they push me forwards. They sink their fingers into me, bruising the skin beneath my tattered garb with the strength of their silver armour. I stumble higher and higher up the castle stairs of the Silver Kingdom, chest splitting with each forced, laboured breath.

"She's moving, idiot," an Argenti man says with a laugh at the guard.

My heart stumbles. And then my feet. I try and forget *he's* there, but it's impossible.

Marcellus Hart takes the stairs first, his fingers playing with the hilt of Jesse's sword. When he turns back to see me struggling after him, he smiles.

The warmth in his face mocks me, as does the devilish twitch to his lips as he rakes his eyes up and down my dirty, bruised body.

"Struggling, sunshine?"

"Go to *hell*," I pant.

Umbra, a planet so alike our own, is ruled by a coalition of Georgian Elders—a people who have not aged a single day since they stepped foot on this planet circa 1700. These people have tortured me, humiliated me, and killed people close to me. And now, they herd me like cattle into a prison high up in the sky.

I huff loudly, my breath clattering around the small stairwell. The stone rings from our footfalls, echoing up and around the small, rotating space. My gait slows with each step.

"*Move*," one of the guards grunts again.

Acid burns in my mouth as I turn and fight the urge to spit in his face. "Say that again."

My feet stumble, breaking the intensity of my statement. But my hand twitches to the pocket in my tattered dress where I have my switchblade, eyes scanning the supple place under the man's jaw…

Marcellus reaches back and grabs me, his slender fingers brushing my skin as he hoists me up the stairs ahead of him. "Fury looks good on you, little mouse. But not here."

I grit my teeth as the breath lodges in my throat.

His scent of fresh air and mountain springs flutters around my face. Next to him, I smell putrid—dank from a dungeon cell and dried blood.

My dead brother's blood.

Bile churns up my chest and I crumble a little. With shaking fingers, I stare at the residue coating my skin.

Mason.

"*I will watch this castle crumble. I will watch the Elder's heads get spiked along the walls.*"

I will *take* their crown. I will make Umbra *mine* for what they all did to me.

Marcellus touches my shoulder. His body is so close, the freshness of his scent and the heat of his chest envelops me. Teeth chattering, I lower my hands, staring directly at the spiralling stairwell ahead of me.

"Alright, Your Highness, if fury is what you wish…" He trails off with a laugh. "But first, a few more flights."

I swallow sharply and ball my shaking hands into fists. Venomously, I say, "If anyone touches me, rushes me, you'll regret it. I swear."

With that, I storm up the stairs like a phantom.

"Atta girl."

᠑

I sleep. I eat. I drink.

I wake, hiss at the guards who try and move me, and then resume the cycle.

No one shifts me from my place in bed.

The room they keep me in a tall, isolated room in the castle, full of lace, candles with dripping wax, and glass… everywhere. The window circulates from floor to ceiling like a bracelet, just tall enough I can't reach it. On the other side of the room, facing the bed, is a hatch where guards come and go from the endless spiralling staircase.

This place is a gilded prison, but I can't begin to comprehend the context of this specific type of torture yet. One day soon, I know the isolation will drive me to tears, but for now, it's a gift on a silver platter.

It's a beautiful place to mourn.

Every day I watch the sun rise and fall through the endless window. The golden light fills the entire room, plastering the space in an array of colour. I stay awake, watching in wonder with my hands wrapped around my knees and the frilly blanket on the bed spilling past my shoulders.

"I miss you," I mutter. "Mason, *I miss you*."

I can see him in the purples that brush the sky—the same colour as the wildflowers in the village. I can see him in the moon and stars, like the twinkling in his eyes. I can see him in the spiralling village beyond the window, coming alive and going to bed like clockwork. It's a place my brother always dreamt about. A promise of the future.

"*I miss you, I miss you.*"

As the blanket slips past my thin shoulders, cold air hits my back and I shudder.

"Mason. *Come back.* Please."

The solitude doesn't affect me until the fifth sunset. I shiver as the sun disappears.

Mason is gone. My mother *killed him*, reducing him to dust with an S.P. gun.

He's gone, and I'm stuck here alone in a cold room with no one and nothing.

My brother would not let me stay here, suffering alone. He would come up with a plan to storm the castle and free me. He would sit by me, shivering just the same with his head on my shoulder. He's the only goddamn person in this universe that is—was—*mine*. I brought him up as both sister and guardian.

And now he's gone and I'm alone.

When I arrived, they gave me a nightgown, which I gladly took, given my old dress was covered in sweat, dirt, and blood. At some point they must have taken the mangled slip away, but I still haven't showered. My skin feels hot and the buildup of dirt has begun to itch. Over the last few days, even the clean nightgown has grown infected.

I trail my fingers over it, boredom making me overly observant.

My mind is screaming.

He's been gone 6 days. 6 sunsets and 6 sunrises that he has not seen.

The orange sky meets pink clouds. My eyes burn. I don't deserve to see it. I can't look.

He's gone.

"Mason…" I rock back and forth in bed with my arms tied around my legs.

A creaking fills the small room, but I ignore it. Someone's loud footsteps echo through the room, but I squeeze my eyes shut and pointedly ignore that, too.

This time, the person doesn't drop a tray of food—they walk towards me.

Rough hands grab my blanket and gently coax it back over my shoulders. The scent hits me first. Coffee.

Someone brought me coffee. *Stars. Yes, please.*

I don't lift my head, but a chill skitters down my back at who is visiting… Until he speaks.

"Your mother is going on trial in 3 days. I requested you there as a witness, which was granted."

Marcellus.

I swallow the knot in my throat but don't lift my head. I don't give a damn what happens to my mother. She killed my brother.

"Mason," I whimper breathily.

"His death might have turned the tide." Marcellus doesn't soothe me, but waits until I take the cup he's offering. I see him standing over me between the swaths of my hair. "I'll be back in 3 days. Maybe try and eat something before then. It could be good for you to build up your strength, little mouse."

He leaves the coffee on my bed. The trap door creaks and with it, Marcellus vanishes. I squeeze my eyes again and resume my rocking.

The coffee goes cold.

↭

Three days can be agonisingly long when you're left alone with the face of your dead brother haunting your dreams.

You cannot stay awake, because the silence of being alone splits your skull.

You cannot sleep, because he is there.

I can barely look at the strewn blankets spilling over the mattress like milk, clumped with knots and crumbs from breakfast. Instead, I pace. My fingers are sticky from the honey on my food and my throat raw from the dry bread. I lift one of the candles on my bedside table—the ones they never light—and toss it against the window. It lands with a heavy thump.

The annex room is beautiful, but it's crafted to drive a person insane.

And so, three days tick past like a growing shadow.

My mother might die… I might be able to watch it. So, I need to use this time my advantage. It's not like there's anything better to do in this goddamn room than plot.

My lips tilt into a small smile, just before I lift the second candle and toss that against the window, too. "Ugh!"

Another soft thump.

No one is guarding the hatch door, but they wouldn't hear anyway. The hatch is lined with claw marks and dents, as if previous occupants had bashed it to pieces.

I will not be that person.

Even if the Umbrans break me, they won't see it.

The sunrise above me disperses as the soft pinks stretch out until the blue sky is gone.

Any moment now.

The golden sunlight begins to touch the roofs of the village, casting an ember glow upon the trees and the roads twisting among the houses. Farther down, the glittering river snaking through glistens like a silver pendant.

I cannot see the sea from here, where Sector 2, military, is. I can't even see the Ocean Train that takes you there. But that's okay. Over a week ago, I gave myself up to the Elders so that my friends and father can be safety released. They'll be there.

The hatch opens. Marcellus clears his throat behind me, but I don't turn. A part of me yearns to ask about my friends, despite his escorts waiting below the hatch, who will absolutely overhear and bring all news to the Elders

Then again, I don't have to.

I'm an Argenti—a mythical, silver being with Terran and Occupant DNA, given the ability to use Silver Magic on this planet. Mine allows me to find my friends. I can locate their minds, their emotions, from any distance.

Appropriate, for a girl who hates the idea of losing them. A girl who gave up her life for them and would do anything for them.

I know they're still on Umbra, because I can sense them in my mind, like a constant ticking. When I track them with my Silver Magic, I can feel them all over in Sector 2.

Melanie. Jesse. My dad. Jasmine. Eli.

No one knows what I'm doing, too lost in their own minds to notice my presence, but I swear I feel Marcellus smile whenever I fork out my Magic.

Marcellus Hart can harness power from other Argentis, sucking them dry like a vampire and fuelling himself with their abilities. Lately, it feels like he's been doing that a lot.

Every time I touch his mind, he's harnessing something... Or someone.

I shake my head, wiping my clammy hands down my night gown. Heat spirals up my neck and my frustration reaches a cresting point.

Why him? Why is he so intriguing to me?

I still my mind, losing myself to the view before me in a bid to forget him. At least my Silver Magic means I don't need to rely on anyone.

I stand with my back to the hatch, keeping my posture solid. I do not twitch when the sound of footsteps echoes up behind me.

Marcellus chuckles. "Like a queen overlooking her kingdom," he observes.

Coolly, I turn to face him. I try and keep the emotion off my face, but my eyes meet his sparkling silver ones, and a smile quirks on my lips.

Once, I may have rebutted him.

I am not a queen.

I am not a revolutionary.

I am not the girl from the prophecy.

So many claims were made—all of them semi-true, but also utterly false.

I can, and will be, whatever people believe I am. Because at the end of the day, their opinion doesn't matter. To them, I'm just a figurehead.

The real Savannah Shaw is the person I am only in private. So, if Marcellus wants to make me his queen, so be it.

I will be anything or anyone so long as it gets me Umbra.

"Let's go," I breathe, brushing past him.

His lips quirk and he gestures to the trap door. "After you, Your Highness."

SAVANNAH

"Savannah Shaw."

My name rings through the throne room, dancing past the wide windows and the herds of Argenti. Lights twinkle against their skin like stars. I almost forgot the way the room looks like space, with light beams glistening all around us.

"Where's my mother?" I enquire.

They place me in the middle of the room, right before the podium on which they sit. 7 thrones for 7 Elders.

No one breathes as my words shatter the room. Behind me, I swear I hear Marcellus miss a step. He scoffs quietly, and many Argenti whisper amongst each other.

I fork out my Silver Magic, tasting it thick in the air. No one detects me using it with the scent of Magic already so heavy in the room.

My mind touches Marcellus's sister, Amadea, before skimming over the Elders. I pause on my grandfather and Sixth Elder, Alexsandre, then Evaline, the Seventh, before landing on the sharp mind of my mother.

Venus Collins is far away, seemingly under our feet. Concealed. Broken. Hurt. She's in the dungeons, most likely.

Behind me, Marcellus drifts towards Amadea before the Third Elder stands.

His auburn hair is bright under the starry lights, standing out among the crowd of silver-haired Argenti. He rises above all Elders, overlapping his ring-covered fingers in a careful display. The Elders are a coalition and will appear as such to the public but in this room, everyone knows the truth.

The Third Elder is in charge. They don't even try to hide it from me.

"Venus Collins will not be present for her trial. You, Savannah Shaw, will speak on her behalf today."

Bile rises in my throat as I stare up at him. He levels my stare, a soft smile brushing his lips.

I will not react. I will not give him that satisfaction.

Next to him, the Fifth Elder stands. She's a fragile thing, older than the others, with hair nearly the colour of milk. She usually hunches in her chair and never raises her voice. The whole room stops breathing as she helps herself out of her hair.

"I am Eleanor," she announces. "The Fifth."

I blink. Names are earned here. People do not give them away freely.

She dips her head, then continues. "And I will not be present while Savannah Shaw condemns one of our Argenti children."

Huh?

Her lips seem to tremble as she steps off the dais, her soft hands patting down her white skirts. Quietly, she walks out of the room.

The Argenti move for her, the grand doors opening before swallowing her away. From outside, I spot Melanie's uncle.

My breath hitches as he grins at me—a small flicker of spite before the door closes on him.

I barely have time to collect myself as another Elder stands.

This one I know—the Fourth. A dainty man with glasses and a flighty nature. He was the one who spoke for the Third that fated day my brother died. I'd wager he's firm under the Third's thumb.

"I am the Fourth, and I will also not be present for the trial of one of our children."

Like Eleanor, he drifts through the room, dispersing through the grand doors. When they open, Melanie's uncle smiles at me again. He isn't important enough to be let inside, but he stands right by the doors to mock me.

I allow myself a long, even breath, and stare up into the face of the Third Elder. He avoids my eyes and scans the room with cool indifference.

He's playing with me.

My fingers tick by my side as I stare at him until Evaline, the Sixth Elder and Lythia May's mother, stands. She's one of mine, and he has her.

"I am the Sixth, and I will not be present."

She doesn't meet my eyes as she walks through the room, her sapphire gown hissing against the marble floor.

I stare deeply at the Third, twisting my Magic into his head. His lips twitch, as if he senses it. He tastes like an open flame.

Something cracks in my chest as he steps back and lounges in his seat, his eyes still scanning the crowd of Argenti.

Venus, a leech desperate to climb the ranks, is one of his most loyal soldiers. What's to say he ever intended to kill her?

This is just a power play. A way to ridicule me and show how unimportant my brother's death is to him.

I suck on my lips. Stars, he weaves a complicated web… but not complicated enough.

"What is this trial, if not a game to keep your soldiers entertained?" I demand.

The First Elder is the only one paying attention to me. His long hair is clasped back with a metal silver band, and the sun from the window bounces off it, blinding me as he whips his head to the others.

When the Third doesn't look over, the First finally speaks.

"We do not condone murder," he says firmly. "Venus will be given a fair trial, but that doesn't mean we have to sit here and approve of it."

"Hmmm," I muse.

I hold my hands behind my back and tilt my head at the Third. Behind me, I can feel amusement rippling off Marcellus in waves, his mind clashing with mine due to my Magic.

"What are you implying?" The Third finally asks me.

"Is this display, this waste of time, worth playing out? Maybe we can sidestep the dramatics and get to the point of all this."

Amadea's mind is flinching. It matches the tempo in my own.

The Third Elder opens his mouth to speak but I cleanly interrupt, "Or is this all intentional? Perhaps Venus was merely following your orders to kill her son. I do suppose the loyalty of soldiers should be tested from time to time. Maybe we should announce that to your Argenti children now, so that I can go back to bed."

The mention of Mason cleaves something in my chest, but I hold it down.

From across the dais, Alexsandre pops his mouth a little, his frantic eyes latching onto me. The room is dripping in silence so thick it cloaks us more wholly than the scent of Silver Magic.

And then Marcellus laughs. A long, rough peel that splinters the room.

The Third Elder stands abruptly, "Argenti, you are all dismissed. The trial of Venus Collins and the murder of her son will be postponed."

The frenzy that ensues behind me is comical. Everyone rushes for the door, trying to maintain order, yet too energised to remember where to place their feet. Hushed whispers circle, nearly impossible to hear over the resounding footsteps.

Above them all, Marcellus is still laughing. It's like lightning in my veins.

I turn briefly to look at him. He finds Amadea, slinking his arm around her shoulder casually, his silver eyes dancing like starlight. He feels my gaze and quickly winks before dipping out of the room like the rest of them.

My stomach twists in waves, but I do not follow. Instead, I turn and face the Third. The other 4 Elders appear frozen. Alexsandre squeezes his hands together as I make eye contact, as if unsure what to do.

"Ready to spin some more bullshit, or can we finally speak plainly?" I ask directly, my voice steady.

The Third Elder leans forward in his chair, his hands knotted before him. "Speak," he says harshly.

I take a quick breath. "I'm not here to petition for my mother. Her verdict is inconsequential in the face of the greater game. Truth be told, I don't care for your Argenti politics."

"And what game may that be?" he asks plainly. He doesn't once let his mask of cool indifference drop. But as I stretch my mind out to him, I can feel him raging.

I give him a gentle smile. "Tell me, why do you try and undermine your people at every turn? What about Umbra's loyalty? What about your people? Are they still congregating, yelling over my death or my freedom? Surely you would want to placate the people who run your planet."

The tension in the room is thick. Every nerve in my body is on fire.

My words could get me killed or thrown in the dungeons again to be tortured. But none of those things scare me the way they used to. Death doesn't seem so bad when you've already faced it, countless times.

Besides, this is worth the risk. Umbra is worth it.

"Are you suggesting," he says quietly, rising up to his full height in his seat, "that the Commoners are more important than the Court?"

I got him.

I try not to smile. *The game is in my hands now.*

"I'm suggesting there is power in masses, there is power in the people, and there is power in owning them all." I tilt my head, smiling sweetly. "Wouldn't you agree?"

He lets out a short breath, tightening his lips. He already knows this, of course. But before this moment, he didn't know I knew.

He doesn't see me as anyone dangerous.

He doesn't see me as a powerful player.

Before now, I was a figurehead and a pawn. As of today, I can be a threat or an ally, depending on how we leave this throne room.

"Give me a proper room with a large bed and a million cushions, and a coffee machine. I miss coffee. A lot." I chuckle a little. "Give me that and full roaming rights of the castle. I'm allowed into every room, I can direct any guard to do anything I say. Give me the rights to the castle and then and only then, will I help you fix this mess."

His façade breaks abruptly.

The Third Elder laughs, his face cracking as tears build in his eyes. Alexsandre startles, gripping his seat, and the other Elders sink further into their own.

I stand steady, still, letting him get it all out. It takes him a moment.

I almost roll my eyes when he wipes a tear from his eyes, his face creased.

"And why"—he scoffs between coughs—"would I possibly grant that?"

He is so, so cocky. And blinded.

I need to remind myself that no matter my bargaining power, I am still in his domain. He can offer me the castle, but for now it remains his. At any moment, he can flick a finger and a guard will rush in to take me.

But I have to trust that won't happen, so long as I keep his interest.

I need to stay interesting. And I need to stay powerful enough for him to think he can *take* my power.

"You have the Argenti, but I have the people. And the people have Sector 2 and Sector 3. There are more numbers down there than within this castle. Do you really want the crowds to storm your gates?"

He looks at me like I'm insane. He knows all this. He's smarter than I'm suggesting and puts on a careful act of seeming totally unbothered by me.

He doesn't even care to rebut what I'm saying.

I need to lay my plan out now, before I lose him.

"Let's appear united to the public," I begin, causing him to blink. "It will take some time, as no one will believe it if it happens immediately. Certainly not after that stunt you pulled by nailing me to a Hover and parading me through their streets. But over time, we can integrate it. Slowly. We let them digest the new future—one where the prophesied gets the crown not by stealing it from existing rulers but by working with them."

They all stare at me, unblinking.

I still my body and stand with my hands behind my back. I let my offer stew before softly adding, "Let's make the prophecy come true, once and for all."

The Third Elder swallows sharply.

I win.

He doesn't smile at me, doesn't blink. The inferno surrounding his mind has reduced to embers, burning quietly in the back of his head.

"This concept seems too simple, too jarring, especially for our Court," Alexsandre says plainly. "If you get full rights to the castle, people will talk."

"Let them," I say.

The Third Elder smacks his lips. "Hmmm."

"What will *you* say to the Court if they question you?" the First enquires, eyes locked on me.

"I wouldn't need to say anything," I admit truthfully.

"And what about you mother?" he presses.

I blink. A rush of pain floats through my chest, catching me off guard. My eyes move toward the window, where the sunlight spears into the throne room. The shafts of golden light pull at my skin like daggers, brushing my feet and hitting the marble.

Two meters to my left, right under the light… *That* is where Mason died.

My chest heats as my blood pumps furiously. I lift my head and return the gaze of the remaining Elders, still waiting for my answer.

I say it plainly. "Kill her."

Before they have the chance to respond, I turn around and leave.

The grand doors open for me, the sound splitting through the room. They do not stop me, and I keep walking.

The great game has begun.

May the best player win.

MARCELLUS

The truth is, I was the first person to find the prophesied.

Long ago, when Venus sent the child to Terra, I knew.

That's the thing about immortality. You get bored, you fill the hours, until spying on others and playing games becomes a pastime.

Until recently, I didn't give a rat's ass about the girl.

Being Argenti is a repetitive, constant slur. Finding Savannah was merely something to fill the hours, only, it didn't give me the same level of excitement it would have centuries ago.

Until I met her.

The day I met Savannah Shaw in the Mors Desert was the moment I felt my life begin to shift. She was pure power, but not in the way I had grown to know. She looked Common, but she was not. She looked hopeless, yet she was anything but. I became addicted to what she could mean for Umbra. And, achingly so, I needed to be a part of it.

No one—not even my father—could begin to comprehend it.

The second time I met Savannah Shaw, I was no longer the same man.

You see, when you live your entire existence following the scent of power and listening to your father lecture you about Argenti supremacy, it becomes a default. *Only the power of the Argenti will help me. Only the power of the Argenti will save me.*

And yet, there she was. Savannah Shaw.

She was no ordinary Argenti, but she radiated like none other. She had over half of Umbra blindly following her before she was even born. She continuously puts herself in the line of fire, just to protect people who will never be worthy of her protection.

She learnt how to harness her Magic in weeks, under intense duress in the dungeons, when it takes most Argenti years to do so.

Power.

I nudged her towards Amadea, using my own sister to spy on her. I planted seeds in my father's mind to lock away Venus and destroy any of her ambitious plans. I even went as far as to tell my spies in Sector 2 to flee, so that Savannah's friends could stand a chance at taking the base. I trust Beckett is capable, but it's a variable I shan't leave unchecked.

All is in place, so now, I wait to see what new turmoil Savannah will cook up. Stars, she never disappoints. The chaos of it all is intoxicating.

She leaves the throne room with her head high, the Argenti parting for her. My stomach flips at the sight. I inch towards her like a dog to a bone, but my sister's small fingers whisper against my skin. A pulse of her Magic spills through me. It's her way of saying *careful, Marcel.*

So instead of following Savannah, I turn back to my father. This needs to be official.

My knee lands on the marble floor in front of him. None of the Argenti follow me.

My status isn't exactly above theirs, but years of fighting to stay my father's favourite has given me some level of right. It's hard to say if it's respect or fear that shines in their eyes, but the distinction never bothers me, so long as I stay on top.

"Father." My voice carries with the unspoken question.

His voice is slightly gruff, but he tries to cover it as he says, "Follow her, Son."

I dip my head. *Wonderful.*

All Argenti watch me leave, their eyes like cannons aiming for my back, whispers dancing among them.

If I had stolen Venus's Magic, I'd hear their thoughts about me in my head. But that's enough to drive a man insane. I've stopped taking her Magic years ago—to hell what they think of me.

They want what I have. My standing in court.

It's sickening.

The Argenti are all hungry for power. For legacy. But they do *nothing* about it. No risk, no reward. I, on the other hand, live for the thrill.

I let a smile melt on my face. My father departs his throne as I make my leave—my idiot father, who let me walk out of the throne room freely, giving me exactly what I wanted: Savannah.

I don't let the satisfaction melt over my features until I leave the throne room. My feet carry me past the lush lounge outside and down the spiralling stairs, faster than I should be allowed. No guards stop me as I practically lunge my way down, like a dancer or a happy-go-lucky idiot carousing the castle.

My face twitches. My heart is in my chest, screaming at me to slow down, but I all I can think of is the viciousness in Savannah's words when she said, "Kill her." That announcement surprised every damn person outside the room as the door opened—including me.

Power. I'm sick with the idea of it. I'm sick with the idea of *her.*

I catch up to her by the seventh spiral. While I'm frolicking, she's practically falling, rushing as if her life depends on it. No wonder the guards haven't caught up.

I swing my arm over her shoulders, nearly knocking us both over. "Little mouse."

She doesn't gasp, or trip, or look alarmed at my presence. She just holds herself against the wall and stares.

The silence stretches for a long beat, the faint light on the stairs slashing across her dirty face. The scent of her skin fills the space between us. She smells sour and looks awful, yet I've never seen someone look more regal.

After what feels like a century, she finally speaks.

"Marcellus."

The sound of my name on her lips is like a vice around my chest. I want to ingest the sound of it. I want to feed off it like air.

But I don't twitch, nor show my emotions. They have never done me any good, anyway.

I've spent years pushing them down, yet the thrill of Savannah resurfaces them. What a bitter fate, to be tempted so easily by a powerful woman.

Do you realise how much you stir me, Savannah Shaw? I want to say. Instead, I throw the ball back in her court.

I purr, in a voice I use to get what I want, "Savannah."

I expect her to shiver at the sound of it, or to bristle. She does neither, her gaze flat as she stares at me. And that is why she intrigues me so much—she never does what I expect.

It heats my blood. I always want to see what she does next.

"I'm going to my room," she says authoritatively, even in the tight space between us.

I offer a cocky smile. "Ah, and here I thought you didn't know the castle well, considering your prior sleeping arrangements. I'm merely here as an escort, unless you wish to wait for the guards you so blatantly left behind?"

She swallows but says nothing. Something thickens around us—Magic. Her Magic. Instinct makes me want to steal it from her, with my arm still around her shoulders, but I force it down. She will feel that. Maybe once, I could have gotten away with nipping at her power, but Savannah Shaw is a fast learner and I'd bet on my sister's life she would know exactly what I'm doing.

Instead, I pull my arm back and lean against the staircase, ankles crossed, as if to solidify a point.

"Hmm, I'd think you, at least, would understand," she says, then turns her back on me to continue her descent. Not a single muscle in her face gives away her thoughts.

With her back turned, I furrow my brow. And then it clicks.

She's been using her Magic to trail people around the castle.

The realisation is like a tidal wave of shock to my system, because *of course* she has. What else would you be doing when locked in the dungeons, except finding more ways to best your rivals? I would have done the exact damn same.

From behind me, the clatter of footsteps sound. Guards.

I call down to Savannah, "Argenti rooms have cameras in the white whorl lamps. Oh, and an Argenti on floor 2 has a penchant for coffee. In case you're ready to hunt, little mouse."

I don't know if she hears or understands, but shortly after, two guards drift by me on the staircase, avoiding my gaze and trying to stay as far from me as possible. They *heard*, which meant she heard, as she wasn't quite so far away. Good.

She may have won this round with my father, but he will always land the final blow. Soon, she will find her new chambers empty. No clothes. No bedding.

It's a blow he offers all Argenti. He gives them a place in the castle, but little else, just to test their resilience. When he did it to me, I just stole money from his personal stores and bought the most expensive goods Umbra had to offer. Silk underwear and all. Surprisingly, he never asked for the money back.

With a pattering heartbeat that hasn't been this nervous in years, I smile in the darkness. And, because I'm a gentleman, I decide to give her space to settle in for a few hours.

"I'm going to get bored." I sigh. "Let's do something fun while we wait."

After some rash deliberation, I flex my hands and make my way to the dungeons.

Down to Venus Collins.

JESSE

The burning scent of metal and blood fills my nose as I lunge towards Melanie, sweat dripping down both our backs as we parry under the fluorescents.

Sector 2 is loud and bright and never sleeps.

I suppose it shouldn't surprise me how quickly Melanie Beckett adapted.

We have the training room to ourselves. I stole a captain's key card on the night we took over the Sector and, despite the fact Mel disabled all higher authority key cards, she made sure my stolen one still had access for anything. As the name suggests, the captain's private training room is one of few places only a captain can enter. It's decked out with hundreds of weapons—swords, knives, maces, spears, bows and arrows—among other things Melanie is too terrified to touch.

Tonight, we train with the long sword. Melanie can barely heft the damn thing with her normal hand, but thanks to her cyborg one, she keeps up well enough. The stubborn streak in her only makes her want to try harder.

I've never met anyone else in my damned life who needs to be the best at everything.

She wipes the sweat from her brow, her pink lips parted as she sucks in air. I slow a moment, stepping back and giving her a second to collect herself. I don't usually allow my opponent the luxury. Even Savannah was never given this sort of reprieve, but this is Mel.

She's softer than most; harder on the surface, but more fragile deep inside. A harsh, aggressive sort of protectiveness overcomes me as she buckles down, lowering to her knees.

"You're brutal, Jesse Hayes," she gasps out.

I shrug, the corner of my mouth twitching against my will. "Hey, you wanted to train with me, you idiot. If you wanted someone disabled you should have asked Brookes."

Her silver eyes immediately flash up at me. *Ah yeah. Whoops.*

"Sorry," I offer.

Brookes is currently incapacitated in the hospital wing, right beside the always squirming Jasmine Spark. They moved him there the same day we left the castle—the same day he landed on Umbra. The same day Jackson Mann died. His back looks like a patchwork of mottled skin, his breathing laboured even in sleep.

Melanie firmly instructed them to keep him drugged up until he's entirely healed. It's been nearly two weeks.

"I'm bad at this, Jesse," Melanie mutters, shoulders tight as she lifts her heavy long sword. She favours her metal arm, so I've been forcing her to distribute the weight.

"You're not bad," I admit slowly.

She softly lowers her eyes to her sword, her lips parted in exertion. "I want to be good. Better. Savannah picked this stuff up so quickly."

She's jealous, I realise.

I huff a little, then lower my sword. Behind Melanie's head, a digital clock tells us the night has turned. We're in the midst of the Second Night, where the temperature outside turns so cold, it's nearly impossible to step outside without dying.

Most of the compound is asleep. But not Mel. Never Mel.

Coming here helps me get out of my head and lets me sweat it out. Since Mel's and Tamaz's army took over Sector 2, the place has never felt so alive, yet so empty all at once. Turns out, when we put together Tamaz's army, others followed. Those on ships from Terra had allies here, and even a few guards from Sector 2 turned when they saw us.

It all happened so fast.

We didn't make it far from the castle before our people converged, stole the guard uniforms, and entered the compound without anyone noticing until it was too late. Mel hijacked their security, blocked all access, and baled all guards into whatever room they were in. Then our army went through, room by room, picking through the people. Those who didn't turn were offered exile or death. If it were up to me, I would have killed them all. Even the turncoats, I don't entirely trust. But Mel does. It's part of her charm.

We just need to pray we have enough numbers to hold out against an attack, should one ever come. I crunch the numbers every night, nervous for such a thing to happen.

But Mel has doubled down on our firewalls, tacking on extra safety measures and security. The place is nearly impossible to breach. But if it is, we have a constantly rotating schedule of heavily armed men and women—both ours and the turncoats—on duty simultaneously.

I slide my sword onto the rack, the sound of clattering metal echoing through the room.

"You don't have to be good at this," I clarify without turning, acutely aware of her eyes burning into my back. She doesn't return her sword to the rack or move from her spot. And, when I turn, her silver eyes are swimming. "Because I am, and you have me."

She holds herself like a stone, staring at me. I once said something similar to Savannah, but only because she favours that ridiculously impractical switchblade. With Mel it's different.

With a curt nod, she finally moves, crossing the space towards the weapons rack. When she brushes past me, the scent of her lemon shampoo wafts through the room, mingling with the intense scent of metal and sweat.

She's changed. Melanie Beckett has changed.

She packs away her sword and heads to the exit without lifting her eyes back to mine, as if unsure what to say to me. My stomach curdles as I watch her shoulder the door open.

"Mel," I say, a nervous tilt to my voice.

The fluorescents flicker above our heads as I dart forwards. As the door opens, the whistling howl of wind fills the space. The corridor in this section is long and narrow. One side is filled with doors to training rooms. The other is a never-ending floor-to-ceiling window. No one else fills the space except for a group of young guards—children, practically—who stand by the window, talking amicably.

Beyond the window, the world looks like doom.

The guards must be some of the turncoats, considering how used to the sight they are.

Mel shivers when she makes eye contact with the Second Night, but bundles her shoulders and keeps walking.

I'm not used to it anymore, despite growing up with it, and it makes me shiver too. It's like I can feel the cold, even protected behind the walls.

Sector 2 is on an island barren and void of all life. The dirt around the compound has been stamped down from training drills, footsteps and spaceships alike. The only thing spanning as far as the eye can see are stumps from cut-down trees and stones large enough to twist your ankle if you aren't careful.

It was out there, among those ruins, where I lost my sister.

Or thought I had lost her.

As it stands, she is now in the compound with us. She hates it here and one can barely tolerate being near her. She prowls the halls like a storm, her three cats always on her heels. She comes and goes often, scouting on my behalf, but since it turned dark, she returned. Sometimes, she spends the Night back in her cave, but several hours ago she returned with a report, and Mel insisted she stay tonight.

"They still hold Savannah in the castle, but there's little else to report. This is good news, though. It means they haven't decided what to do with her yet. I did hear musings that Venus went on trial today for the murder of her son—the Argenti are gossiping about it like old hens. Word hasn't reached the Commoners yet, but Argenti business hardly ever does."

Heat surged in my chest and my hands had felt numb. Mel asked my sister to take her assigned room for the night, and then I grasped Mel's hand and whisked her into a training room. Pushing my body to its limits takes my mind off other pains.

"You know," I say calmly, sliding my hands into my pockets as I follow Mel down the long corridor. "If you want a new apprentice, there's a large pool of acolytes here who would happily oblige."

Mel stills. Her training leathers glisten as she turns smoothly to face me.

"I didn't even want to train Mason in the first place, Jesse. Why the *hell* would I want another starry-eyed kid interfering with my work?"

Her words echo like a thunderstorm, deadlier than the whistling wind beyond the window. None of the guards turn to acknowledge us, too lost in their own conversations.

"You cared for him. I know you did." I try for soft, but my tone comes out accusing.

"Doesn't matter. He's dead."

She turns on her heels abruptly, continuing towards the exit at the other end.

A pang hits my chest and I blink it away, a knot forming in my throat as I force myself to follow her. For weeks, I've wanted to ask her a simple question about Mason.

For weeks, I've been selfishly reliving an insignificant memory.

But everyone is hurting, and no one is listening. Mel has changed so much. Months ago, she knew my heart inside and out, but now I can barely tell her what's in it. And she's breaking, too, perhaps more than me.

She's breaking, and I've been too wrapped up in my own memories to notice.

I might have lost Savannah, but I can't lose her, too. So, I push on and don't say a word.

When I fall asleep, the stupid memory comes back. Again, and again, and again.

Savannah. On the floor in the throne room, the sunset beyond the windows dancing in her matted hair, bringing out ribbons of red among the brown. So beautiful, even in disrepair.

The S.P. gun that killed her brother clatters to the ground and she stares at the red dust lining her pale fingers. I stand by Mel, who's shaking so strongly it feels like my world is breaking. And then Savannah's eyes touch mine for the briefest of seconds.

Her eyes touch mine and then dart away. Her face contorts. Her lips tighten.

Why does looking at me causes her more pain than the red dust on her hands?

As my heart shatters, the question that has been haunting me for weeks makes its first appearance: Does the love of my life blame me for her brother's death?

It doesn't matter, really. I want to know the answer, but I don't feel like I deserve it.

My pain doesn't begin to compare to everyone else's. I can shoulder it and I can drown in it. Because no matter the answer, I do know this: I've lost her forever.

Savannah Shaw, the girl I came back to Umbra for, will never love me again.

Because when she looks at me now, all she will see is her brother's death.

I push the pillow into my face and try not to cry myself to sleep again.

SAVANNAH

My new room is filled with soft greens, whites and browns. I stand back from it all, feeling too dirty to be in this beautiful space.

"Welcome home," I say with a gentle quirk of my lip, and walk through the threshold. The guards barely know what to do with me, and the one with orange hair whooshes air from his lungs when I close the door on his face.

They will stay there on alert. Do I trust them? No. Am I glad I have them? Yes.

It means I have won.

I turn slowly within my new room, drinking it in with a pounding heart. It's an exquisite mix of Georgian finery that's dainty and gold, with frills on the beds and an ornate chandelier, meeting a place of futuristic beauty. The room is half open, the rounded front breaking into the sky, with thin curtains barely veiling the rolling kingdom under the starlight. It never rains in the Kingdom, ever. So why have walls and windows?

My face feels flushed as I recall what Marcellus said.

Ugh. Fine, I'll bite.

The first thing I do is locate the hideous white lamp on my bedside table and walk onto my balcony. The thing seems to be made of pottery and is cold and heavy to lug. I have no clue if Marcellus was kidding, but I'd be damned if I didn't listen.

I drop it over the edge of the balcony, not waiting for the telltale *crack* of it smashing before turning back inside to properly explore. With trembling fingers, I follow the curtains to a large, heated pool.

I have my very own hot spring.

In my bedroom.

Immediately, I start ripping my clothes off with haste.

Half of the hot spring faces the far wall, with waterfalls trickling into it. The other is boarded off by stones. The room is circular and bordered with swooping arches and thin white curtains that dance in the breeze.

I sink my toe into the water, the heat almost warm enough to be scalding, and then submerge myself entirely. As my face sinks under the surface, weeks of grime melt off my pores and disappear into the filters lining the edges of the hot spring.

I'm too high up in the castle for the spring to be naturally made, but I wouldn't go as far as calling this thing a bath. It's too mind-blowing to be anything short of magic. Perhaps it's Argenti-made?

I blow bubbles underwater, letting my body sink to the bottom of the spring. It isn't deeper than the height of my chest, but I fold my legs and let myself drift down.

Mason would lose his mind over this, I think.

Despite the warmth of the water, my blood goes cold, and I rise.

Mason is dead, I remind myself. *Your mother killed him. You will never hear his laughter again. See his smile. See the stars in his eyes.*

I scrub myself until my skin is raw, weeks of dirt and grim on me. But there's no soap to help me. And when I pull myself out of the spring, no towels, either.

Despite the water, I don't feel clean.

Hair plastered to my face and pattering droplets of water on the ground, I walk back to the bed, where a large dresser spans the space of one wall. I thumb the doorknob, swinging it open.

It's empty. My face heats and teeth clench as I scan the room to get a better look at it. There's nothing that make this space personal. No bathrobes by the spring, no pyjamas to sleep in, nothing to brush my hair with.

The Elders are taunting you.

"Fine. If you want to be petty, be petty," I growl and storm towards the curtains separating the room from the world outside. The floor merges into a stone patio that juts out of the castle, the sun warm and soothing above my bed.

I sit against the golden railing no higher than my waist and close my eyes. My body is still as the warm breeze breathes over my skin and licks water off my face, chest, and hair.

I close my eyes and breathe slowly.

Somehow, I sleep through the Night, protected from the hazardous cold thanks to the Kingdom's Dome, sleeping blissfully outside among the tepid air. Until there's a pounding knock at my door.

ᔌ

I grab the frilly piece of fabric that serves as little more than a decorative blanket and wind it around my chest, knotting it so that it swoops down to my ankles.

I wasted the entire Night sleeping.

The knocking at my door is excessive, drilling into my skull. I make way to open the damn thing, but the person on the other side beats me to it. I'm seconds shy of being naked when Marcellus storms into my bed chambers, his hair windblown.

I would have *felt* him coming and locked onto that damned man like a bee to honey with my Silver Magic, but I was sleeping.

"Want to know what I did last Night, my dear?" he asks, his face inches from mine.

There's not a hint of emotion on his face, but the intensity of his words is hot and heavy. My Magic cascades over his body, drinking in the taste of him, the feeling radiating from him. He almost seems…breathless. This close, I can practically feel the fast pounding of his heart.

My skin still feels hot from the sun—not burnt, if skin even burns on Umbra—but warm enough that the frilly thing covering my body suddenly feels scratchy and sticky as I take him in. I knot my hands over my chest, limbs loose as my gaze wanders over his face.

My hair has dried strangely, sticking out at odd angles and, as he leans over me, so close I can feel the warmth of his breath, I'm acutely aware of a tuft of my hair tickling him.

"No," I say, deadpan.

He blinks, as if suddenly realising how close he is standing to me. He smiles softly, backs up and begins scanning the room with quiet trepidation.

"Mother dearest says hello," he muses. "Well, she would have, if she wasn't so busy cussing me out for a solid 20 minutes."

Ah.

I tilt my head at him, analysing the way his body ripples as he moves about the large space. He's not wearing the silver robe of the Argenti. Instead, he's donned fighting leathers.

The sight of it reminds me of Jesse. Yet the way he looks over me, silver eyes rippling with promise and death, feels nothing like Jesse. My Magic splutters as he notices it wrapping around him, his own filling the space to join mine.

I don't really want to talk about my mother, but it feels like his main mission in life is to annoy me.

"She will forever want me dead, you know. In the same way she wants you dead now, too. And you know why, little mouse?" He waits a beat, relishing the way I sigh deeply and squirm in irritation. "*Power.* She wants it, we have it. It's been an ongoing battle with her, for my entire existence. Perhaps next, I will steal you, just to vex her."

"You are all sick with need," I say, immediately regretting it. I shouldn't have said it.

Anddd here comes another monologue.

"We are all sick with *want*, my dear. It's what keeps the planet spinning. We flock to power and we make love to our successes. Your mother is vexed. You are the cause of all these power shifts. Although, she would never admit it, I'm afraid. She created you, a ruler, yet has no idea how to rule over *you*. My father, on the other hand? Now *that* is a predictability she can work with. And Beckett's uncle. The Court. She has them all wrapped around her finger. Impressive, really."

"Melanie's uncle is a worm."

His composure breaks as laughter cracks around the room.

"That he is. But his importance shouldn't be missed, sunshine," he coos. "He will do anything for Venus. Question is, will his orders make an impact before she dies…"

The way he trails off, appearing contemplative, is such a freaking fake display that I have the urge to shove him off the balcony. He wants to know why I want her dead. It's sickeningly obvious.

I cock my head and smile. *Try and guess.*

I withdraw my Magic, losing touch of the guards posted outside my door and the comings and goings of people around the castle, and lean back against my bed frame.

"Savannah," he purrs, prowling towards me. "My little mouse, my queen, for the love of all things good in this world, why do you wish death upon your poor mother?"

Poor mother, my ass.

His finger brushes my chin, tipping my face up to his. I let him
see the unveiled expression and smile.

This man knows the great game better than I do. He's lived it all
his life and, for all I know, considering people don't age on Umbra,
that could have been hundreds of years.

I need him. And maybe that means I should let him in a little.
Weeks ago, his little sister Amadea gave me a list of names: *Evaline ;
Alexsandre ; Roman ; Celestine ; Marcellus.*

He's on it, as are Evaline and Alexsandre—the Sixth and Seventh Elder respectively. The others, Roman and Celestine, are yet to
be discovered, but that's on my long agenda of things to learn. And,
in order to learn anything, I need access to the castle.

"I have a question for you."

"Hit me."

Allowing the Elders to portray me as an ally is simply a façade—
one that neither of us really believe in—but it's just the first step.
The first chess piece in a game that's just beginning.

"What is your father thinking right now?"

He smirks. "A question for the ages, I'm afraid."

I force down a sigh of irritation. Step back from him, and snap,
"the point isn't about my mother. It's about playing on their level.
Besides, at least I get a cool room out of it."

He snickers.

Then just because he's annoying me, I add with a large dash of
fake cheer, "I mean, have you *seen* that hot spring?" I pull myself
from him and swing my arms out before the entrance to the bathing chamber. "I can't wait to see the rest of the castle!"

His eyes track me, glittering in a devilish sort of way, before he
allows himself the slightest of smiles. "If you're wondering whether
my father will grant you roaming rights, the answer is yes and no. I
put Amadea on the case to see why he accepted your truce."

I can feel his Magic coating me, wrapping around my body

as I move around the room. His Silver Magic is never his own. Instead, he sucks the Magic from others and uses it for himself. He could have any sort of Magic right now, but I don't allow that a second thought.

"Excellent, Marcel."

The words feel bitter for some reason.

"Marcel?" he enquires with a tilt to his lip.

I tilt my head at him. Turn away. My pulse shudders down my body, chilling my skin. In a great heave, I push past the white curtains and hide out on the patio. I wish I could see the ocean from here. I wish I could see my friends.

I lower my hands onto the railing and curse myself internally. *Stars, I'm so out of my depths.* My skin feels itchy, my stomach rolling as I turn over my words. Why did I call him that?

He's Marcellus. Marcellus Hart. Son of your biggest enemy. It doesn't matter that he's on that stupid list of names, I cannot trust him entirely. And yet… I must.

Stars.

I fork my Magic out across the Kingdom. It tumbles over thousands of souls—faceless people I cannot connect to without knowing them well enough to understand or feel. It tumbles across the water, towards Sector 2, where I feel Jesse.

And then I feel Melanie. I feel all of them. My father. Jasmine. Eli.

All well. All alive. All much too far from me.

With my awareness branched out, I notice the precise moment Marcellus takes a step towards my patio.

"By the way," I say evenly, "have you ever heard of waiting for a lady to allow you into her bedchambers? I don't remember ever inviting you in."

His eyes flicker to my empty bedside, where the lamp once was. "Just wanted to see if you trust me yet."

I have nothing to say to that.

He pauses. I can feel his anticipation and apprehension. His energy feels like it's on fire, like he's excited to see what I'll do next. He wants to watch the world burn. I can *feel it*.

"Little mouse?" he enquires, as if waiting for me to elaborate.

I'm not in the mood. "Get out."

To my surprise, he does. Quickly. But amusement pounds off him in waves.

I let the irritation sink into me. *Ugh.*

I need to distract myself. And I need clothes. Immediately.

So, I storm off my patio towards the door to my bedchamber. My guards startle when they see me. The redhead gasps while the one with the trimmed beard reaches for his weapon.

"Relax," I say, "I'm just going for a walk."

Both jostle and glance quickly at each other. They seem untrained and nowhere near as deadly as other guards I've had the displeasure of knowing.

I walk until it grows dark again. I walk and I walk and I walk.

Only when the sun lowers in the sky and my mind has settled, do I turn around. Time to get back to business.

I hunt for Amadea Hart.

AMADEA

The very last thing I expected today was to find Savannah Shaw tapping on my door.

But there she is, wearing a blanket. Her hair is matted but clean, fluffing around her face in all sorts of angles. She tips her head at me, cheeks flushed and a casual grin on her face, then steps into my room before I have the chance to invite her in.

My heart skips a beat as she passes me, and I catch my breath. She frightens me a little. I shiver, pulling my arms over my chest, feeling awkward in my skin.

"Oh, Dea, this castle is beautiful," she exclaims, throwing herself on my bed.

I avert my eyes as the blanket splits up her leg, revealing her thigh. My pulse skitters in my chest like a bird as she trails her eyes over my silver hair and the small frame dressed in a pale pink nightgown. She *looks* at me. Like, really looks.

Usually, people miss me.

It's become too easy to lie to everyone, but not Savannah. When I'm wearing a pretty skin, or an ugly one, they brush their eyes past me and see what they want to see. But when my hair is silver and I'm completely Amadea, they avoid me even more.

That's the thing about being a powerful shapeshifter. I've never had a friend.

My teachers, my brother, even the Commoners I find on the streets in other skins… they are my closest friends. But Savannah looks at me like she sees something new. Like she might just like me for me.

"What are you doing here?" I ask, rubbing my arms and feeling naked as she takes me in with her keen grey eyes. Her Silver Magic dances around me, picking at my skin and taking me apart. She's been following me with her Magic for a while now, but it doesn't bother me.

I already know why she's here. Marcel asked me to spy for him and ask around about her. She must be curious as to what I've learnt.

I don't like giving information up easily. She will need to prove she deserves it.

As expected, she doesn't. She answers me with a gentle smile before speaking, then lifts her eyebrows, as if my question was obvious.

"I have no clothes."

I guess that explains the blanket.

"I'm smaller than you," I say. "Seems weird to come here for clothes."

"But you, my friend, have a million forms."

I crack a smile. "The workers will tend to any of your needs if you ask them nicely. They are usually frightened of the silver ones."

She blinks at me, slowly. As if not realising we *have* workers.

"I'm not quite an Argenti," she mumbles, drifting her eyes from mine to take in my room, her attention fleeting. She drinks in the pink walls, the curtains that bridge the gap to my open patio, and the large bath resting behind the far wall of the room. Her gaze hovers on my amenity table, over all my hair clips and ribbons.

My room isn't special. All Argenti have the same. Yet, she lingers.

"You know you are, considering you track me with your Magic."

Those grey eyes flash at me. Humour dances within their depths. "Okay, we'll get back to that," she says, brushing away my comment.

I knot together my eyebrows. I don't know what she's implying.

"Was there something else you needed?" I supply.

She brushes the air again. I've never seen her look so playful. So… happy. Maybe, because of my younger age, I remind her of her dead brother. Perhaps she doesn't see me as a friend at all. Good thing I'm not just Amadea. I'm everyone. I can be *anything*.

"Mmhmm," Savannah murmurs.

"What are you doing here?" I ask her again.

"I must admit, Amadea, you are very well spoken and smart for your age. Even with your mighty powers."

My heart flips a little. I fight the urge to squirm again. "How old do you think I am?"

She blinks at that. Takes a long look. "Eight?"

I don't smile. I don't even move. She's wrong. I'm young, but I'm not *that* young.

The question seems to trouble her. She heads to my closet, finger skimming on the knobs to throw it open. The thing is large and spans most of the room.

"Your father doesn't seem to care about me seeing you," Savannah says with narrowed eyes. I tilt my head, a part of me wondering if I remind her of Mason. Is she here because she's trying to be a big sister, or is she just here to speak nonsense? She sounds so innocent and harmless, but I know she's carefully trying to pry information from me.

It's so *Umbran* of her. She suits court, even if she doesn't realise it.

"Mhmm," I mutter, scared to say more.

She looks so normal, with her skin peppered in freckles and her dark hair tufting around her face, but her eyes are so keen, her movements so deliberate. She can choose to be anyone—an invisible girl or someone with the potential to be great—which is a trait I thought only I had in this castle.

Everyone on Umbra pretends to be someone they're not, but Savannah isn't pretending, she simply *is* everything. Can be anything.

This girl is infinite. It makes my skin crawl with nerves.

"The deal you made with him was a falsehood. He will not follow through on it."

She floats away from my dresser, hands knotted behind her back casually, and dips her head out of my curtains to take in the setting sun. "I figured as much."

Before she has time to spew more half-questions at me, I quickly splutter, "Have you found the others from the list?"

She turns and looks at me, smiling slightly. "And here I was thinking you see everything that happens in the castle."

Her eyes shine like stars, glittering with humour. I lower my gaze, pulse shuddering.

"If you don't want to ask the workers for clothes, go take some from the laundry room on the bottom floor of the castle."

My words are dismissive, but she doesn't balk.

"Oh, I know. I walked past it earlier," she says, turning back to the sunset. "But thank you."

I blink at her back. Slowly. With a clumsy breath, I settle on my bed, pulling my knees up to my chest. I can feel her Silver Magic thick around this room. The silence in the space between us yawns as she continues to dissociate, eyes glazing as she takes in the setting sun. With a heady breath, I let my restraint release, pouring Silver Magic through my pores. I feel connected to the space around me, rooted to my spot on my bed, as I yank the strands of Magic out of the core of the planet and through my skin.

My entire body tingling, I turn my head towards a mirror against the wall. The thing is large and gilded, decorated in swirling membranes of silver. My brother bought it for me last year, for my birthday.

From within, a girl with brown eyes and auburn hair smiles back at me. Her hair tumbles down her waist, curls messing against the sheets. Her eyes look large and terrifying due to her impossibly light eyelashes and brows.

It's a girl I saw on the streets several days ago. A shy thing with her hair tied in a scarf and many years older than me as she nursed a bulging stomach heavy with child. My hand flattens on my own stomach in trepidation, exhilarated to find it flat.

When Savannah turns her head back to me, she goes immobile for a moment. The gesture is small, hardly noticeable, but there all the same. She quickly masks it with an expression of neutrality.

"I'd best go find some clothes. Let me know if you hear anything of note in the castle."

I probably won't. But okay.

She picks herself up and glides back towards my door. My heart skips a beat watching her. The moment her chocolate-brown head vanishes through my door, I fall back into my bed and sink into my pillows.

Exhaustion pounds at me, nagging at my skin. I hate this castle and the rules that govern it. Why lie and play games when you can hide behind someone else's skin? Is it worth losing yourself?

I fall asleep trying not to think about it.

JESSE

My sister smiles at me through the glass of my allocated bedroom.

Daybreak. I always loved daybreak in Sector 2.

From here, I can see the ocean and the train when it lumbers forwards. From the assigned chambers from my childhood, I used to be able to see a slip of the pilots' landing ports and would wake every morning to watch my father and his men launch into the sky.

I would sit there, grinning, until my mother pulled me from the window and told me to get dressed for classes. Lily would always sleep in. I would go to basic training, where a man named Carter—whom I later killed—would always say "Morning little Hayes" with a smile. Those days were simple, before everything went to hell. I often wonder... if my father hadn't died and I actually said good morning back to Carter and had a decent relationship with the man, could things have been different?

I squeeze the lip of the windowsill, forcing myself to smile as my sister waves at me from the Ocean Train—whenever she spends the Night here, she takes her cats out early to do their business. Behind her, Tamaz follows, a grim smile on his scarred face, having just got off the Train from the mainland. Tamaz mentored my father, but I only saw him occasionally. I always liked the man, though I'm not sure if he ever liked me. Because of the scandal that broke his family, he relocated to the mainland soon after I began my training. Tamaz's daughter, Lucille, had an affair with my father before I was born, and was sent to the African base on Terra to do her penance. I only saw Tamaz during graduation ceremonies after that, when he was conscripted as an official Umbra guard.

The man grew rougher with each year. If I didn't know better, I'd fear him now.

I push away from the window, shaking the memories free. Mel probably pulled an all-nighter, which means she needs me to whack some sense into her. I quickly dress, making sure to deck my body with an array of carefully polished knives, and slink out my bedroom.

The barracks is basic, with nothing more than a bed, communal shower, and lavatory at the end of the corridor—the exact place I would have been assigned had I ever graduated as a guard. I would have hated it, but worked through my year of service before training to be a pilot like my father.

It was all I ever wanted.

"Little early for you, isn't it, Hayes?"

My body freezes on impulse, and I turn around to face Laurence. The man is a legend in Sector 2. His father was a talented general who was training him to one day take his place. He never finished that training, but people still speak of him. With valid reason.

Both him and Tamaz are the ones I need to watch out for.

Because both are wildly dangerous and both can barely tolerate my presence.

I'm sure they don't quite know what to make of me—a rogue fighter with connections in high places, a sister for a spy, and an ex-girlfriend who's the infamous usurper.

The real question is: who exactly *is* Jesse Hayes?

"You were meant to be scouting last Night," I respond, ignoring his jab.

He shrugs on a thick jumper, as if that was the reason he went to his room. I let him fumble with it, a nerve ticking on my temple.

The man doesn't waver under my intense gaze. He just smiles, his peppered whiskers bristling as he does. He places his hands in the pant pockets of his stolen guard uniform and nudges his head towards the break room. Each barracks has them, but this one is always the busiest. Even at this time of day, I can hear voices drifting from within.

"You look like death, son. Follow me, I think we both need a coffee."

My nerves kickstart and my skin prickles, but I do as he says.

We walk in silence until we enter the breakroom, and only then does he break it by asking, "Sugar? Milk?"

I don't listen, because inside, his men are talking, not yet realising who Laurence has brought with him. A man I don't recognise whispers, "But what does it mean, Samael? 'The chocolate-haired princess is alive and well, and negotiations are underway in the castle. An official statement will be provided by the Elders in the days to come'. Honestly, what a load."

Samael snickers. "That girl just doesn't want to die, does she?"

I whip towards him, fingers edging for a knife. All conversation instantly drops.

The men from the Safe Holds stare at me and then lower their heads, slumping against their seats. Laurence sighs loudly at it all. "Black coffee seems like your kind of poison, eh, Hayes?"

The coffee here is bland. I don't really care for it, but I grunt, my eyes hazing under the sharp fluorescents. The men and women from the Safe Holds all linger by the meagre coffee machine now, trying to catch wind of my response. They do a good job of looking unbothered, with their heads resting on metal tables and their eyelids drooping. All of them went on recon with Laurence last Night, so it's believable. From the back, Samael is whistling an irritating tune while nursing a bowl of cereal. He's probably doing that just to irritate me.

Laurence sighs again when I don't answer him, and just pours me the coffee black. My body naturally backs away from him then, because there's a familiar voice bubbling down the hall. Lucille. I'd recognise Tamaz's daughter anywhere.

"—Spirit hasn't broken. And her ideas are beautiful, my dear."

I move away from the coffee station, hands twitching by my knives, and head towards the exit. A metallic door shuts behind her as Lucille pockets her key card.

"Jesse," she breathes, seeing me in the shadows. Her frail hands lift to her heart and she smiles. "Good morning, my dear."

I swallow, eyes darting to her friend. Andrea wasn't on patrol with Laurence, and her eye dart away from me as I try to catch them. Her cheeks are rosy, her hair slightly mussed as if she slept in a fit.

"What are you doing with Andrea?" I ask, stepping out of the break room.

Lucille dances towards me, her soft hands grabbing my shoulders delicately. "You must ask Melanie Beckett to give more clearance to our new friends. Perhaps then I'll get a decent sleep sometime."

She leads me back to the coffee machine, her white dress fluttering and bright under the lights. Laurence smiles softly at her as she enters and holds out the steaming cup of coffee he originally intended for me. She takes it gladly, blushing a little.

"Andrea, why do you need clearance?" I insist, trapping the girl under my gaze.

She sways a little before me, trying hard not to look at me.

Instead, she says to Laurence, "Jasmine is okay, but I worry for her. She's bored in the med ward and is constantly awake planning for Savannah. All she does is grill me with questions."

It feels like a chilled breezes wafts through the room. The urge to run to Mel and inform her of this overcomes me, but I stay and listen.

"I have reason to believe the Elders are planning a fight soon," Laurence says darkly. "Unfortunately, that's taking up all our time, but I will speak to Tamaz about finding her a way to walk again. I leave to the Kingdom again soon."

Andrea smiles and lowers her hand. "Thank you. She would like that, I think."

Okay, enough.

"Andrea, *why* are you seeing Jasmine?" I blurt against my better judgement.

Finally, she turns those frightened eyes on me, her jaw tightening. "She's my friend."

Irritation swells in my chest and I fight the urge to shake the girl's shoulders. "You sure about that?"

"I'm making you and Melanie a coffee, my friend," Laurence says, trying to intercept.

We both ignore him.

"She's the reason my sister and I got out of the Safe Holds on Terra, you know. She found us after the Elders bombed the island, then brought us food and stories from above. She was our lifeline. I owe her everything."

I try not to groan. Lucille squeezes my shoulder, as if she senses that.

All around me, the men have started to come alert. All of them were in the Safe Holds. And all of them now hate me. Some glare, some even smile. Samael, the brute, is cracking his neck as if hoping I'm going to fight him.

"She also got your sister Cassidy killed, I hear," I remark with deadly calm.

Andrea throws every ounce of venom into the look she gives me.

"Enough, Hayes." Laurence slams a coffee into my hand. "You're exhausted. We all are. Please don't hurt this sweet girl just because *you* are hurting."

My hands wrap around two scalding cups, both sloshing with liquid. I stare at him, my heart pounding. The knives strapped to my body feel hot, but I don't allow myself the pleasure of releasing them. Perhaps that's why Laurence gave me the coffees, not that I couldn't splash hot liquid in his face instead. But what would that achieve?

"Fine," I hiss.

I turn out of the room silently, but my ears are ringing.

Everything in me is angry and hurting, and these jabs just make me want to hit something. I need a release, a chance to breathe, but throwing my coffee in their faces will only make me more agitated.

Lily is in Sector 2 somewhere. I can find her—go with her to escape for a little while.

But first, I need to find Mel to clear my head. At least I can vow not to tell her about Andrea's stupid requests. At least there's some sort of victory in that.

Ugh. What a coward I've turned into.

JESSE

"Jesse, get inside. That coffee better be for me or—"

"It's for you, love."

The twin cups of coffee in my hands burn my fingers as I stand in the entrance to Mel's new and improved office. It's grand, because she stole it from one of the military's captains. The space between the door and her desk is swimming with bookshelves and military memorabilia. The Umbra insignia—a silver crescent with a sword impaling it—has been stamped into the enormous carpet at our feet.

"Inside. Now, please."

I make my way towards her, eyes scanning for her familiar ashy blonde-brown head. A window has been blacked out with a heavy curtain, and holograms and glass screens fill half the office space. I must navigate around four holographs of maps and faces before I find her among it all, head buried above a metal desk where glass panels seem to have been welded into it, shining blue and red with lights and code.

"Laurence is back today. Told me I looked like death the moment he saw me, then forced these monstrosities in my hands. I think I might actually hate him," I say lightly, handing Mel one of the coffees.

Mel grabs the coffee without lifting her head from the computer.

"Be nice. He's done a lot for us," she says.

It's true. Since he came to Umbra with Mel and I gave him my only weapon, allowing him to escape, he's been ever loyal. Stars, Laurence might just be our most loyal fighter. He's also nice. A peacekeeper through and through.

Stars, he's a pain.

"He annoys me."

Mel waves her hand, nearly finishes the burning coffee in one go, then winces at the way it scalds her throat. She points to the chair beside her without lifting her eyes off her screen.

"Yes, ma'am." I roll my eyes and take my seat, lifting my feet up on her desk.

I do it simply to get her attention away from the screen.

"Hey, feet *off*," she says right on cue, head whipping up and her metal hand thrusting my boots away. I grin as she settles her silver eyes on mine in a huff.

"Want to know what I learnt?" I say, leaning back in my swivel chair. It spins a little as I quirk my lip at her.

"That you're rude and imposing and callous?" she says, her lip twitching as she turns back to her screen.

"That I'm handsome and brilliant and my presence is holy to be around?" I finish. Mel scoffs. "No, not that. I already knew all that. I just learnt that Savannah's alive."

Mel's head whips up. "What?"

I take a long sip of my coffee. *So bland.* "Mmhmm."

"Jesse," she says, staring at me. She's tugged her hair into a rough updo. Strands of it brush out and tickle her cheeks and, as she watches me, a lock brushes into her eye, which she makes no move to push away. I stare at that strand, a fight starting in me, and quickly realise that I'm staring at her.

I lower my head, clearing my throat. When I lift my eyes again, my heart misses a beat when I realise her face is red.

"Laurence and his men spent the Night in the Kingdom. This morning, before they left, the Elders made a statement: *"The chocolate-haired princess is alive and well, and negotitaions are underway in the castle. An official statement will be provided by the Elders in the days to come."* They broadcast it along the screens outside the castle gates, to stop the mob. Considering you do *not* know, I'd wager they've blocked your access to the castle's firewalls. You might want to get onto that, love."

She stares at me, unblinking, and I take her moment of confusion as a chance to lift my legs back up on the table. For the first few seconds, she doesn't notice, then she breaks from her stupor and slaps my leg. As expected.

"Jesse, for *stars' sake*."

I lower my legs with a grin. Immediately, she comes back to herself and her mind begins to whir. I watch her eyes flickering with interest and the way her fingers tap a little against each other as she contemplates plans.

"I hadn't thought to check the castle security in the last few days. I've been too consumed with defending our own. They must have noticed me prodding and thrown me out. I was scouring the Kingdom's security this morning and nothing seemed amiss—it must just be the castle itself they have blocked me out of. The question is why? What are they planning?"

"Atta girl," I utter, rising from my seat. "Happy hunting."

I'm halfway through the massive office, scaling around holograms when Melanie breathes, "Jesse, wait. One second."

I turn, unable to see her from this far away. With a pounding heart, I sip at my coffee. It tastes too milky and burnt all at once. Yet I still drink it.

"I planned to check on…" She clears her throat. "I won't be able to leave the office today, most likely. Can you check on Elijah for me, give me a status update?"

His back *would* be healed by now, considering the copious amounts of *Velox* in our med ward, but a fragment of metal from the imploding ship had sunk into his back, near his spine. If we were to inject him with *Velox*, the metal would become trapped and mended around his heart, which is a problem in itself. Since arriving in Sector 2, Melanie has been scouring the planet for a surgeon capable of fixing him. Turns out, no one of that calibre was on Sector 2 when we took over.

So Eli was put into a forced coma, with nurses catering to him and Mel urging the recon teams to bring back a surgeon. So far, no luck.

I stare at her, my eyes glassing over. A sour taste fills my mouth, my stomach rolling. Since she can't see me, I let my dissatisfaction show. "Sure."

The poor man is half-dead in the hospital wing and yet I still can't bear the thought of him. He's so *happy*, so *excitable*, and never leaving Mel's side.

In the last weeks, she has wanted him there. She cares for him. Might even love him. And he's perfect for her. He's good. He will follow her to ends of the world and back and I. Can't. Stand. It.

Jealous. The bitter word fills my chest. *You're so freaking jealous. Get over it.*

"And can you re-con with your sister? I have a feeling something is coming other than planned assaults from our end. I'd like to have her on the field, as she's the most affective with her cats." Mel pauses for a second too long. "Just don't… don't tell Laurence I said that."

Planned assaults from our end. That's the first time Mel has used those words, and I tuck it away for later.

I snicker. "Damn, I would have loved to rub that in his nose."

"Don't, Jesse."

"Of course not. How could I dare insult the sweet old man?" I smile.

I finish the rest of my coffee and straighten, about ready to leave, when I say quickly, "I might go with Lily this time. I need to get back on the field, get some fresh air and do something hands-on."

Mel doesn't respond. I give her a few solid beats to say something, but she doesn't.

Planned assaults from our end.

Could our people be planning more than recon? And if so, why hasn't Mel told me? I suck on my lips to prevent from asking. She knows I'm good at scouting. Right now, I need it more than anything. I need to escape the hell space of Sector 2 and the painful thoughts and memories spiralling in my goddamn head. Even if leaving is dangerous.

The office feels cold, the silence pressing, so I clear my throat and turn to the door.

"I'll try and be back as soon as I can," I say in farewell.

I think I hear a soft, "Okay" before I shut the door.

ᔓ

Elijah Brookes looks helpless.

I'm glad I'm here today and not Mel, because this would break her heart.

The med ward on Sector 2 is quite possibility the most sterile place from my memories and, if I'm being honest, it hasn't changed one bit, no matter how lively they've tried to make it. As a child, the long space seemed endless to me. Rows upon rows of beds, holographic screens, syringes, test tubes, and a blue light imbedded into the white walls that doesn't flicker or move. Everything is still and dead.

There is no official site where medicine is tested or created on Umbra, so Sector 2 became the main hub. Of course, within the Kingdom and the castle particularly, they have sub-units for medicinal testing. So, considering we have taken over this place, I have no doubt they will become the primary grounds for healing.

I stare down at Eli. Someone gave him a red blanket, which stands out starkly against the white-washed background. On the metal table beside him drip the dying petals of roses that patter down onto the floor.

Besides Eli, Jasmine is humming to herself and lighting an array of candles on her own metal bedside table.

"Fire is banned in the ward," I say, without taking my eyes off the sleeping Eli.

"So are guards, unless they are injured, so go and—"

"I'm no guard," I interrupt, flashing my eyes to her.

"No." She cocks her head. "You're not really anything, are you?"

My breathing feels heavy and too loud in this small space. Her eyes are rimmed with red as she takes me in, her lip shaking slightly. My head aches as I stare at her, fingers inching for a sword that is not there.

"If I'm not anything, then what does that make you?" I bite.

My eyes lower towards her limp, sprawled legs. The healers in the Kingdom have been testing ways to heal paralysed spines. Alas, that is across the ocean. The healers here are trying to learn what they can, asking Mel to break into the castle's files.

To my satisfaction, Mel has not. She will eventually, but there are other more concerning matters than the fact the blonde cockroach cannot walk.

"Forgotten," she exclaims with a whoosh of breath. "I *hate* this place. It's so bland and gross and plain. I want to get out of here and help Savannah, Jesse."

"Maybe you should walk out then?" I rock back on my heels, sneering.

If you asked me to explain in vivid detail why I can't stand Jasmine Spark, I wouldn't know what to say, just that I do. I have a low tolerance threshold with most people, I'll admit. Human beings can be so infuriating, but Jasmine Spark takes the cake. Even Eli, breathing shallowly next to her, his body all bandaged, I can feel partially sorry for.

"Fire is so cleansing, don't you think? I wonder if that's why they used it to banish evil, back when the world was medieval. Fire can cleanse the soul." She's staring at the candles, her gaze distant.

"Perhaps you should light yourself on fire, then."

Her blue eyes whip towards me. "You'd love that, wouldn't you?" She stares at me, and I stare stubbornly back. After several beats, she sighs. "Can I ask you a favour?" she asks, attempting to pull herself into a sitting position with her arms. Behind her, the candles make the space smell like jasmine flowers. It makes me want to gag.

I scoff. "Why?"

"Because you're here. I don't get visitors often, just reports from Laurence and the occasional ghost of Melanie hovering in the corner with the nurses. She can barely look at me. Did you know she's the reason I'm paralysed?"

I know exactly why she's paralysed, and it's not because Mel threw a knife into her back. No, it was because Jasmine went against orders and made contact with an Umbran pilot while they were hovering around the planet, jeopardising everyone, killing one of her teammates, and getting the rest captured.

"Mel is busy. She's running Sector 2 *and* breaking into Umbran networks *and* training with me."

"Defensive, much?" Jasmine says, tilting her head. The glow of the candles makes her curls look orange when she does that, adding warmth into the sterile space. But the smell… it makes me feel sick.

"Vain, much?" I counteract, nodding at the candles.

"I happen to like the smell of jasmine flowers." She pouts.

"I don't," I admit.

"Clearly. You know, you're not that cute when your face is all crumpled."

"I'm always cute. Get to the damned point."

She rolls her eyes and leans against her pillows with a deep sigh. Her jaw is tight when she says, "Can you ask Mel to give Andrea and my other friends clearance? Or at least, find me someone else to talk to while Elijah is napping? I'm so bored. I'd like to find someone to help me plot my master plan to help Savannah win Umbra."

Heat roars in my ears, but I keep my face cool. "To *plot?*"

She bats her eyes at me innocently. The mere insinuation of Jasmine Spark plotting sends my blood roaring. Last time she did that, I almost lost Melanie.

She folds her arms behind her head, gently closing her eyes with a soft smile on her lips. I could *strangle* her.

"You know, you and Mel aren't the only ones with ideas on how to help Savannah," she says, sighing a little. "Mason always said the people on Umbra are too focused on what's inside the Dome. Savannah is now, too. And the people that fought for her and got sent to Terra for it... we all agree."

Stars, I hope Lily is nearly ready to go. I really, *really*, need to get out of here. I checked in with her before coming here and, after a couple choice words, she decided to let me join her. Her massive cats were prowling the perimeter of the food hall when I left, eyeing the array of military food the turncoats had placed out for us.

Tamaz had been staring at them, a hungry quirk in his lip. It was his idea to enlist the cats. When this was brought up with Lily the day we first met up with his army, we lost her for a solid few days. I had no clue where she was, or if she would even return.

But she did.

She came back with Cerberus, pain lining her face, and nodded at me. *"I will help. But only because of my little brother. No one is allowed near my cats unless they say you can. You can try, of course, but they'll probably take off your face."*

And that was that. Our army gained some spies.

Stars, what does she even mean by them saying one can approach, anyway? The snow cats are wild animals. For my peace of mind, I just avoid them. They have their own way of doing things.

It began with only Cerberus, but eventually he went home and another cat took his place. Now, she has at least three snow cats always following her.

I believe the cats make her feel at ease and put a smile on her face, even when she needs to be back in Sector 2.

"I'm leaving today for a scouting trip. Ask Mel yourself," I snap, spinning on my heel. I need to get out of this wretched room.

"Did you hear anything I said, Jesse?"

Yes. No. Honestly, I don't care.

"Figure it out, Jasmine."

The smell of jasmine flowers is making my skin itch, so I shift quietly but quickly to the exit. Then I freeze, take a long, long breath, and turn back to face her. She doesn't know why I turned back, but she's smirking at me, as if she won.

My eyes rake Eli next to her, laying straight and immobile, that red blanket covering half of his body. He has blue patches on his skin, tracking his vitals and displaying them in holographs behind him. My eyes trace the life-size holograph of his slowly beating heart.

The next breath is pained. The girl he keeps in that heart is *mine*. Mel is *mine*.

"You're so self-centred, sometimes."

I turn back to Jasmine with tight lips. Be that as it may…

"Can you give me a quick update on Eli? Mel wants to know," I say stiffly.

She bites her bottom lip to stop herself from grinning. "Only if you ask her to bring me a friend. Preferably someone who knows the castle."

I turn on my heel, slam through the door, and leave before she has a chance to say anything else.

"Wait!" she calls out, her voice distant.

I don't. I need to leave before I strangle her.

My feet take me back to Mel. I hide in the shadows of the compound as I go, where people barely lift their heads as I pass them. My head throbs as I think of all the ways I can make Jasmine's life more awful in that med ward, but truth be told, I don't really need to do anything. She's already in enough pain.

Stars, do I *want to,* though.

I round the next corner sharply and nearly slam into someone, turning my body at the last moment. Tamaz, as well as a turncoat. I've caught them mid-argument, and Tamaz almost looks ready to kill the young man. He grunts when he sees me, eyes widening in surprise.

Tamaz's scarred face looks ugly under the throbbing fluorescents.

I nod at him but don't stop. I don't particularly care what the turncoat has done or said to tick him off, and I don't want to stay and watch Tamaz beat him senseless either.

The turncoat's face looks red and terrified as I push past them.

My breathing feels short and rapid. I can't stand this place.

To my left, windows occasionally come into view, highlighting the barren land and the harshly cut tree stumps in all their glory. It was the same view I stared at as a child after I thought my sister died in the Night. And not long after, the barren lands reminded me of my mother's death too, when she voluntarily went out there to end the suffering.

I try now to look at it in a different light, considering my sister survived.

But even so, Sector 2 is still so full of bad coffee, blood, and pain. I blink the images away. I need to get out of here.

My body slams into Mel's office door, louder than any noise I feel like I've made in my life. Melanie spins to face me. She's moved from her desk, circling one of the holographs that outline the castle.

"Jesse?" Her eyebrows rise, her breathing rapid as she takes me in.

I must look flushed from running, but I don't care.

"Eli is the same. Nothing's changed." With that announcement, I turn on my heel, dashing away from her office like it's suffocating me.

Sector 2 seeps into my soul, sucking me dry. Pain fills my lungs until I can barely breathe. For the first time, I realise why Lily never returned, despite the hurt it caused me.

We are the same, she and I. This place suffocates us both.

I need out. I need air. I stop by the cafeteria, scanning for snow cats. A trembling guard turns and looks at me, eyes wide at the sight of me.

"I need my sister," I say to him.

With a nervous hand, he points down the hall, towards the Ocean Train.

I don't even thank him as I head out to where Lily is waiting for me.

9

AMADEA

"**W**ake up little bird."

"Go away," I grumble at my brother.

He stands above my bed, frowning at me in his Argenti finery. I hate the clothes, with their harsh lines and blinding silver. My brother's suit looks painful on him—too clean cut, too sharp, too impossible to move in.

The mere fact he's wearing his finery tells me I'm expected to wear my own.

It's still dark outside, but it's always dark in the mornings. Night and day on Umbra are long, and people sleep throughout both periods. Long naps fill the void of their endless lives.

"Father requests us," he says in a monotone voice, twisting one of the silver rings he places on his finger. Umbran crests. Family crests.

He hasn't worn his jewels in a while, opting instead to carry the new sword he acquired when chasing Savannah. Today is a different kind of fight. Another game to be played. Today, he looks less like my brother and more like the soldier my father wants him to be.

I open one eyelid, look at him groggily, and groan. His face is as sharp and hard as his suit, which tells me he already knows what father wants from us. It isn't good.

With a long, long sigh, I slowly lift myself to a sitting position. My silver hair tumbles past my shoulders as I sit and, as it does, I feel my Magic wrap around me.

It can be difficult to control the Magic when sleepy and dis-jointed, and my brother watches the strands of my hair turn brown with a dissatisfied look.

"Ugh," I huff, grabbing my sheets and tossing them off me.

The ceiling lights pound down on me as I stalk for my closet and brush my small fingers over the many dresses. I hunt for one of the grandest silver ones I can find, which usually means the itchiest.

Being small sucks. I can barely reach the clothes rack.

So, I shift myself into an approximation of our mother. My body soars up, legs extending and turning the colour of cream. My silver hair shortens, as soft as silk around my shoulders, and my hands bear burn marks. I wrap those wrinkled, injured hands around the hangar of the silliest dress in my closet and turn back to my brother.

"I hate when you do that," he growls, his eyes glowing like a storm.

"Dress like Mother?" I say, lips tilting.

"*Be* Mother," he counteracts, knotting his hands carefully over his chest.

"I can't *be* her. I can only try to look like her." I roll my eyes then turn to the bath chamber to change.

He grunts, "*Stars*, Dea. It's the same to me."

Marcel never judges my shifting because he knows it's just Magic. Our voices, our movements, our soul doesn't change. The only time he flinches is when I shift into our mother.

I was barely a year old when she died. But Marcel remembers her.

She was one of the Occupants, but she died during the Moon Blitz. The last memory I have of her is one of fire.

I have dreams of her holding me, encasing me with her body, as the sky rained down death. I nearly died, but my brother found me and put me in a suspension tank made from the sap of a Tenere tree, keeping me in suspended animation for over 200 years, along with some other Argenti who barely survived the fires. It was centuries before our science developed enough to save me. Most of my vital organs were failing, but *Velox* wasn't a thing yet. We'd only just started developing *Prius*—a drug that takes days to heal a person—but I needed something stronger as I was already on the brink of death. If it weren't for the Tenere tree and my mother's inherent knowledge of her planet, I would be dead along with her.

Or so, that's what my brother says. He stayed with me for over 200 years, fighting not only to keep himself alive, but me too.

I owe him everything, yet he never tells me anything about her.

I shift my body into the version of her I know, or assume to know, but it's near impossible to know if I'm accurate. There are vague drawings and memoirs describing the appearance of the Occupants, but only the Elders and the original Argenti know for sure.

I glance down at my mottled hands, understanding that my mother would have not looked like this, for she never survived the fire that came with the Moon Blitz. My mind always gets carried away with these things. I dress in the zombie version of her.

A walking nightmare, Marcel had once described this form of mine.

But it's the tallest form I know to take, because the Occupants were taller than traditional homosapiens. If I want to reach something from a high shelf, it seems logical to become one.

"What does Father want?" I ask from the bath chamber, dropping Mother's hands and letting them merge back into my own so that I can fit into my dress.

"Savannah," he says. "Unsurprisingly."

My brother always stills when he mentions her, and even more so when he looks at her. Usually, he is always moving, always planning, always playing games with our father. But as soon as she enters a room or her name comes up in conversation, it's like he forgets everything.

Father made him track her when she first landed on Umbra, chasing her through the desert and riling up scenarios to scare her, but he always did it on his own terms. She was delivered to Father, as requested.

Many of the Argenti speculate it's because he wanted to scare her a little—play with her and taunt her by showing exactly how much power they hold here. But I know my brother better. He never plays my father's games entirely.

"So their truce is over?" I ask, stepping out of the bath chamber.

This silver dress has a slight poof to it, trailing to the floor in sheets of silver. It hugs at my chest and squeezes my lungs, too itchy and tight and impossible to move in. But Father came from a time when gowns were a sign of power and respect. Appearing in front of him, dressed like so, usually makes our interactions better.

"It never began," Marcel insists, turning his head towards me and taking in my dress. He sucks on his lips, oblivious to the terrible itching in my corset.

"She would have worked with him," I whisper.

Marcel lifts his eyes from my dress, his eyes glittering. "Would she?"

No, he's right. Her appearance in my rooms yesterday proves as much.

I roll my eyes. "What is it that Terrans say? Keep your enemies close?"

"They do, but that's not what I'm implying, little bird. Savannah understands her role and position in the castle. She made that abundantly clear when she stepped into the throne room the other day and played her hand. Father has been doing all he can to keep me from knowing the technicalities of her position, but I doubt that a half-empty bedchamber and the freedom to roam the castle ensures she has officially agreed to work with him. Father wants more. And he will use us to get it." Marcel's eyes are half on me, half glazed. I barely feel him slip into his Silver Magic, but the glassiness of his eyes tells me whose Magic he sapped.

"You're sniffing her out?" I say, folding my arms over my chest.

"She was in your room last night, wasn't she? Along with every other inch of the castle, it seems."

Celestine's eyes glaze over just as strangely when she sniffs out other people.

"Did you spend the night with Cece again?" I ask, the taste of bile filling my mouth.

I hate when he flirts and sleeps with people in order to leech Magic off them whenever he pleases. Celestine is an Argenti who can track people by smell—an ability my father loves to use. The *Bloodhound*, the Commoners like to nickname her.

I wonder how terrified Savannah will be when she discovers that the Bloodhound is a women on her list… if Savannah even gets scared these days. Besides, Savannah is a tracker, too. And arguably better. Giving her that list was a stupid idea, really. By putting my brother on it, I wonder if she will even figure out the real purpose of why I gave it to her…

Stupid.

Marcel told me he ditched Cece's Magic for Savannah's back when he was tracking her through the desert and was overwhelmed with the possibilities of what Savannah could do. Cece can physically smell people and the paths they've walked, noting how long ago they walked it depending on how depleted their scent is. But

Savannah? She can locate people instantly, just by connecting to their minds. Not only that, she can *feel* them in her soul.

They are similar, in so many ways. But where Cece is all blood-lust, Savannah is all love. That's why Cece's Magic is that of a hunter, I guess, whereas Savannah uses her Magic to connect to the people she loves.

"We spoke over a drink, Dea. Don't assume the worst of me." He grins and raises his eyebrows. "Now, your hair looks stringy and awful, but if you're satisfied to let Father grill you about it, I suggest we get a move on before he hacks both our heads off."

With a huff, I shove past my brother to the door. I should probably brush my hair or twist it into a braid, but being late fills me with more dread than my hair does. At least I put the dress on.

"Hacking heads off isn't what Father does."

With a monotone voice, he deadpans, "Not unless there's a statement to be made."

I don't allow myself to be afraid, though. Not as we move through the castle, Argenti and workers shifting out of our way as if we're royalty.

My brother hovers his hand over my lower back, guiding me and helping me to stay steady in this stupid dress, and I swallow the twisting feeling in my stomach and put on a pretty little smile.

JESSE

The overwhelming smell of sea salt is ripe within the Ocean Train. It's heavy in the air and sticks to the soles of our feet from where some idiot decided to lug fish into our carriage. The drum came directly from the water, which now leaks.

Our people do not control the Kingdom, but we do control the Train.

The Kingdom flowers around us as Lily and I step out of the carriage. I nod at our soldiers manning the station, feeling unnerved. There's not a single Argenti in sight, nor any resistance to us claiming the station.

Something feels off, as if we will only have access to the Ocean Train for a short while longer. Any day, the Argenti could get wind of us infiltrating it and retake it. We are powerful enough to hold back men, but don't have the strength to hold back the Argenti, should they come. Not here, at least.

"Do we have farmers bringing us fish?" Lily asks, tilting her head at me.

"No. No, we do not."

"We apprehended the fish trawler," a soldier says ahead of us. He climbs up the stone stairs leading into the fields. The trees are plump with fruit.

"Hmm," I muse.

Lily sucks on her lips from where she stands beside me, her fingers still behind the ears of one of her cats. I don't recognise this one. It's hackles are constantly raised and it hisses at everyone coming in and out of the Train.

The cats hate the water. They hate the heat. But more than that, they hate people.

Tamaz had convinced Lily to use her cats as spies, but she never brings more than one with her across the water, and she always picks the largest and angriest cats for the job.

I glance over at my sister, whose eyes are narrowed on the drum of fish still within the Train. I know exactly what she's thinking, because it's on my mind, too.

A slim soldier with dark hair reaches for the fish with a glint in his eyes. I don't recognise the man, but I turn to him anyway.

"Dump it," I say immediately, watching his fingers still on the handles as he shakily turns to look up between Lily and me. His hands shake a little when they finally notice the snow cat snarling at him.

"It's food," he says apprehensively, almost in question.

"It could be poisoned. Dump it."

Lily's eyes flash towards me, breaking her glare with the fish. Humour dances there.

The soldier nods, pulls the fish from the carriage and lugs it towards the far end of the Station so that the open end of the barrel can tip back into the sea.

"Not back into the water, you idiot!" I exclaim, my heart pounding as I stalk over.

My feet slap against stone, loud in my haste. The soldier turns and looks at me, dark brown eyes blinking in confusion. With a thrust, I yank the barrel back before it has a chance to tilt over. Water slips out of it, the smell of fish and sea slopping over my fighting leathers. I hiss, heat travelling up my body as I glare down at him. He blinks up at me, his face going red.

"Jesse, leave the poor man alone," Tamaz calls.

I turn slowly, reluctant to take my eyes off the idiot. My old friend stands a way away, his hands deep within his pockets. He never wears fighting leathers anymore, and his dark grey tunic billows in the ocean wind.

I inhale deeply, sucking in the tang of the ocean as I turn to face the man.

Below, waves pound against the shore, muffling my grunt as I release the drum of fish.

"I'm going on recon. Deal with this for me, would you?" I ask a little abruptly before striding towards the stone stairs leading off the station.

"Recon? That's a bit above your pay grade," Tamaz says with a sneer. He behind me as I walk away, planting myself besides my sister but far enough from the hissing cat who eyes Tamaz like he's dinner.

Tamaz is oblivious, leaning against the stone railing.

"Bite me," I say evenly.

Last time I was in the Kingdom with Tamaz's army, I went to the castle to free Savannah, after the Argenti captured her. We tried everything. In the end, it was Lily who made the difference, not me. She joined us with her cats and, through her, we learnt that Mel had come to Umbra and was captured. Once again, I didn't have a choice.

Mel needed me. I didn't think—I just acted and, in turn, was captured, too. I was foolish and not thinking straight. If it wasn't for Lily, her cats, and Tamaz's men, I'd probably still be a captive and have been sent back to Terra by now.

"Try and think with your head, Hayes. Not your heart."

What would he say if I told him my heart was broken and incapable of making decisions?

"You're not my mentor."

As I thump down the stone stairs, pushing past countless soldiers, I swear I hear him hissing at me. My sisters cat hisses too as I pass them, so the sound is swallowed.

She follows wordlessly, and the soldiers part for her and her cat with wide eyes. "He poses a good question, though. Why are you here today, little brother?"

I need air. I need space. I need to feel happy again.

"Does it matter?"

I run my fingers through my tangled hair. I can't remember the last time I cut it.

Lily looks at me with raised eyebrows.

I roll my eyes at her, turning towards the fruit trees. Eyes press on us from the guards around the platform, but when I turn, I can't see who or where the gazes are coming from. I feel claustrophobic, and my breathing grows deeper as I try and clear my thoughts.

"Come with me where no one can hear," I say softly.

She clicks her tongue in response, signalling the cat to walk with us. Soft sunlight dances across our backs as we pass under the trees, following a path that cuts directly through the village and up to the castle.

I can feel my sister bristling beside me, her head moving as she analyses the space around us. The farther we walk, the less our soldiers are present. We move into a place unoccupied by soldiers on either side, and 15 minutes later we find ourselves on the outskirts of the village where anyone can spot us.

I move off the path. My body merges into the tree line, and my sister immediately follows, her face relaxing.

"We need to destroy the Ocean Train," I say the moment we're out of view.

My sister tips her head at me, her fingers knotting around her cat's fur. "I agree."

Damn, that was easy. I blink at her, then look away.

"Any ideas how?" I drag my eyes over what appears to be an apple tree, still too young to bear fruit, then towards an Umbran native, lush with what looks like orange bananas.

"Before we get to the idea portion of this conversation, perhaps we should discuss whys and whens," she says calmly.

"You know why." I turn back at her, eyes narrowing. The dark blue of her eyes, so alike mine, are glittering as she analyses me. "The fish is suspicious. It might mean nothing—might even be a sign of the people showing their support and wanting to keep ours fed—but it could be a warning from the Argenti. They can easily descend on us and retake the Train. That would give them the chance to advance on Sector 2."

Lily purses her lips and twists her wild hair around her fingers. "Laurence has been saying the same thing about the Train whenever he goes on recon. It's too dangerous to keep the line open. We need to block off the mainland entirely, build a different route to the Kingdom only we know about and use that for transport. Your idea isn't revolutionary, Brother."

My skin feels prickly and I twist away from her, fingers tapping on my weapons belt. I reach for my sword out of habit, before remembering Marcellus Hart stole it weeks ago.

I take a knife out instead and slam it into a nearby tree. The blade sinks into peach. I stare at the damned thing with a pang in my chest.

"Okay then," I say contemplatively, "the thought is mutual. Good. Can we get back to brainstorming ideas?"

"The question of *when* stands. We can't just destroy it without making contact with Sector 2. We need to bring supplies first— food, medicine, people—and time it accordingly."

I suppose I could bring some medicine over for Jasmine. Capture a few medics for Elijah, then smuggle them to Sector 2. But it feels like so much effort.

"That will waste time. And communicating our movements just means that our plans can be discovered by the wrong people. What if the Argenti catch wind of what we're doing and attack before the Ocean Train is destroyed?"

I flick the peach off the blade of my knife with a long sigh. The scent of the fruit sticks with me, its juices dripping down my arm.

"Tamaz will throw a fit if you do this alone."

"I'm not alone," I say, looking at her pointedly.

"Tamaz will still try and kill you for this."

"And? If you have a proper point to make, I suggest you make it."

Lily stares at me. Then, slowly, devilishly, she grins.

If there's anyone who would ever go rogue with me, it's my wildcard of a sister. She wears a miss-match combination of leathers, furs, and stolen cotton pieces in shades of greens and browns that bleed into the scenery around her. We *could* do normal recon. We *could* stick to information-seeking jobs.

But there's teams of people already doing that. And it's not like Mel expects me to return without getting the job done. She will expect me to discover something, act on it, and take care of it.

If that includes blowing up the Ocean Train? So be it. I'll deal with the fury of Tamaz after. My heart settles as I look at her, my chest warming.

"Alrighty, little bro. Let's blow the damn thing."

I sheath my knife, breathing my first proper breath since coming to Umbra.

Finally, action.

It takes us several hours to pinpoint the location of the Elders' weapons manufacturing centre. Lily's cat—she calls this one Wrath—had already discovered the general whereabouts of it last week. Tamaz knows, as does Laurence, which tells me Mel has sent many units to find the centre before.

"They always get deliveries from the back of the castle. Food and wares go through the main ports above ground, but weapons and guards enter through tunnels under the castle. We found a Hover carrying wares down there, so Laurence and his men followed it back. They only made it so far before the damn thing went invisible, though," Lily explains as we hide in the bushes outside of the castle, staring up at the stone turrets.

Somewhere, Savannah resides in there. Unless they took her back to the dungeons.

"Have your cats followed the trail yet?" I ask.

"Not yet," she says with a sheepish smirk.

It takes 30 minutes for a Hover to enter the tunnels below the castle, which is lucky, really. It could have taken days. Another 15 minutes later and it remerges. With Wrath following it home, there's nothing for us to do but wait.

The bushes itch my skin long before the beast returns, prowling on silent feet. Lily scratches its ears, then it proceeds to hiss at me.

"Get on," Lily says, swinging her legs over its body.

"Stars no," I grunt.

"*On*," she demands.

I get on. Damn her. The bloody thing slashes its paw at me. But I get on.

We arrive at our destination quicker than it took for Wrath to discover it, slipping through a nearly undetectable forcefield that makes him squirm. When we slip out the other side, we immediately stop and stare.

I twist my fingers around Wrath's fur, another hand firmly on my sister's shoulder as she clings onto the beast and stares up at the spectacle with a shimmer of fear. A cold dread settles in my stomach, washing through my chest as I stare up at the enormous mountain.

"The volcano," Lily breathes. "Of course."

I immediately scurry off Wrath, fingers brushing a nearby sapling as I sink down to the floor, hiding my face among the leaves. Lily does the complete opposite, grabbing a nearby branch of a higher tree and swinging herself up into the canopy for a better look.

The volcano is seemingly endless. Grass sways at our feet, but it's thin and spindly, blending into a rocky terrain that travels up the tall mountain peak. Dirt and stone meet the apex, where a constant swath of steam disperses into the clear blue sky.

But it isn't the volcano that twists my stomach, it's the facility surrounding it. It's metal, harsh, and more sterile and sharper than even Sector 2. A rippling forcefield circles it, but something tells me this isn't the only line of protection encasing what's within.

I stand from my spot among the bushes. There aren't many guards around, and we are so close to the forcefield. Like a curious idiot, I hover my hand over it.

"It's standard. It might let us through since we're Umbran." My words are quiet and get swallowed up by the breeze before they make it far, but Lily hears.

She leaps down from her tree. "There's no guards on rotation, meaning they must have more defensive measures to prevent access. Also, I doubt being Umbran is the key to get us through this one, little brother," she whispers from my shoulder.

I let go of a long breath and turn to face Wrath, who has taken to rubbing his raised hackles against the bark of the tree Lily was in.

"If they have anything to blow up the Ocean Train, it will be in there," I insist. "We have to get in."

Just as I say it, Lily's hand grips my elbow like a vice, yanking me down.

I hold my breath, sinking my head breath the leaves. Wrath doesn't seem to care, but he makes a disgruntled sound at our fast movement. My sister nudges me, head nodding back towards the volcano.

From within the depths of the compound, another Hover emerges. It's impossible to say what it carries, but I'd wager weapons. Only one guard is on the damn thing.

My sister is grinning when I turn back to look at her. And she utters the exact same thing I'm thinking. "Why get inside, when they can bring it out for us?"

I'm grinning with her before my mind completely catches up with the words.

AMADEA

My father's office is a sterile little thing.

Once upon a time, Elias Hart was a scientist. It seems funny, imagining him leaning over vials and inhaling fumes without his rings, the slicked hair or stern posture.

The heavy oak door whispers shut behind us, locking us in the tight space overlooking the Kingdom. A green, magical fire crackles in the corner, easing no heat into the space because under the Dome, the temperature is always regulated. It sheds light across the grey carpet, our father's cream wood desk, and the many holographic screens that play in the air.

He stares impassively at me with dead eyes and gestures for Marcel and I to take a seat.

"Father," we both say in synchronisation.

"Sit," he insists, as if his gesture wasn't indicative.

I inhale a long, quiet breath, taking in the scent of Silver Magic that has been following me like a ghost since I left my bedroom. Savannah is keeping tabs on me, as per usual.

I keep my eyes locked on my satin shoes, my hair slipping over my face. He scans the silver strands brushing my pale cheek and the way I suck on my bottom lip. I can feel him picking me apart. I'm in my original, Argenti skin. My father would destroy me if I stepped into his office wearing anything else.

"The Collins girl has acquired clothing, books, and has somehow manged to steal a coffee machine from an Argenti room, all in the time since I offered her a room within this castle," our father says, cutting immediately to the chase. "Can you tell me how?"

In his chair beside me, Marcel coughs to hide his laughter.

I flash my eyes to his, and we both give each other a brief look that says, *Savannah stole a coffee machine?*

I feel her Magic stall a little around my heart, as if trying to squeeze out which emotion I'm feeling. It's enough to make my head spin.

"Shaw," Marcel says.

Father turns to him, an eyebrow raised. "Excuse me?"

"Savannah Shaw. Not Collins."

Father levels him with a long look, then lowers his head to his desk where a holographic screen flashes with security. Savannah's friend, the Beckett girl, infiltrated all of it. It took Father days to notice. Apparently, his secret group of hacker courtiers—ironically, trained by Beckett's own father, back in the day—had been instructed to block her out of our systems. I haven't spied on them since the order was put out, but considering Father has security running in his office, I'm betting they've successfully blocked Beckett's attempts once more, or she has become more trouble than they expected.

Probably the latter.

"Collins will be terminated tomorrow," Father tells us absently. "To make a statement that we still have control."

Marcel stops breathing next to me. I focus on him without turning my head away from Father, and we give each other the briefest of sidelong looks.

"Savannah?" he asks attentively.

"No, her mother. But I require the Shaw girl to be the one to do it, considering all the Argenti heard the kill order when she stormed out of the room."

It takes everything for me to not wipe my clammy palms down my stupid dress.

I must warn Savannah.

Her Magic feels thick and hot now, lapping me like warm honey. Despite how much I feel her around me, I know within my soul that she will not understand why my heart is racing. She will need to be told. I doubt I'll have to chase her down after this. She will come to me.

With my head hazy from the heavy tang of Magic sticking to me, I barely think before speaking. "Why would you listen to Savannah?"

Marcel blinks, his silver eyes flashing to me. My heart skitters.

I shouldn't have asked that.

My pulse trembles in my throat like a little bird as Father lifts his head to me. He knows I spy, but I try to never make a point of it.

"I have reason to believe she won't do it. I want to see how broken she is."

Oh. He's afraid of her display in the throne room.

He's worried she has more power than she lets on. Hilarious, really, because that's exactly what Savannah wanted him to think.

Father is the type of man who worries about everything. Becoming immortal has made him paranoid, and losing his Occupant wife and donning the title of Elder has only made that worse. He's skittish. Nervous.

He may appear composed and regal on the surface, but he's still that young scientist at his core. Father will never kill by his own hands, nor take the blame for anything. He will undermine anyone he sees as a threat. His wit is his shield, his brain, his weapon.

On Terra, he worked for others in a Georgian empire. He built fancy machinery and experimented with fancy ideas. He nearly turned down going to Umbra, sick with dread over the unknown. But he did it to prove a point—weak men do that when threatened.

The thing is, Umbra made him feel worse. For the first time in his life, he didn't know anything. He wasn't the smartest person in the room and he certainly wasn't the bravest. He had to climb his way back up. He bred with this new race, learnt their ways, and fought to be the smartest in the room once more, as if starting from scratch.

And then, it was all stolen from him again. Umbra was destroyed, and he was nothing but a frightened man at the mercy of a greater power.

Elias Hart is a feeble man, but that's what makes him dangerous. He will do anything to anyone that threatens his power. It's the only way he can feel strong again.

"You don't have to unveil your position to her. She knows you're the one pulling all the strings," Marcel reminds him.

Father gives him a fragile smile. "Does she?"

He tips his head at Marcel. I watch my brother stiffen and hold himself upright.

"Children," Father says, shaking his head, "remember, this girl may unravel everything we have. We have already lost so much, yet still have more to lose. We are a small people, with a long, treacherous history. We take pride in knowledge, in our safety, in our home. Yes, it's selfish to keep what we hold dear locked behind bars, but what will happen should Terra discover us? What happens when the universe knows what we have? This girl… she will always be a threat to our lifestyle. We must eradicate that."

I stiffen my jaw, locking my teeth together to prevent myself from saying anything.

Marcel and I both know this. This is the reason Father bombed the base on Terra, and why he is working at bringing Savannah down to his level. Ultimately, his end game is to cut all ties with Terra.

We will issue warnings, of course... I hope. Father tells me he always issues warnings.

"Us first," Marcel murmurs. "Our people first. Always."

"And if there are any leaks—anyone willing to *risk* leaks or connection to Terra—they must die. You both know this, do you not?" Father asks.

I know, in my heart and soul, that he's about to reveal why he called this meeting. The silence between us all is deafening as he stares, a slight tremor on his lips.

He always reminds us of our positions, of our loyalties, before asking something of us. And the way he stares at me... I shiver. My entire body wracks and I have to physically force myself to stare into my father's depthless eyes. Usually, he stares at Marcel like that. Usually, Marcel gets the jobs and I stand by as collateral.

But not today.

"Amadea, you will be sent to Sector 2 to spy on Beckett."

Ice leaks down my veins, immobilising my body. Marcel doesn't speak for a beat, appearing to have frozen too. I turn to look at him and, jaw tight, he nods slowly at our father.

You're kidding.

Movement flushing back through my veins, I finally build up the courage to say, "Will I be Amadea or someone else?"

Father turns back to his security feeds. "Someone else. I'll expect a report from you every week. You're both dismissed."

Still not breathing correctly, Marcel nods again and grabs me by the elbow, yanking me out of the room. I stumble a little on my feet, struggling to walk in this impossible dress as he hoists me down the corridor. Everything aches. My feet, my chest where the stupid dress hugs me, my pounding heart and my blooming headache.

Savannah's Magic is still thick around me, and I feel it pulling off my skin in waves, telling me she's also coating Marcel, who guides me like a maniac down the corridors.

I don't know how to spy for other people. How do I pretend to be someone's friend, show my face around Sector 2, and then get letters out across the Train to Father?

We aren't even in control of the Train anymore; Savannah's people are.

I suppose that may just be a matter of time, though. First, Father will want to get spies across, then he will limit their access to our side. We will have people in enemy territory, but they will be shut off completely.

There are too many variables in play. If I were him, I would have taken the Ocean Train already, which can only mean he's thought of it and is planning something else.

"Are we heading to Savannah?" I ask my brother as soon as I focus and realise where we're going.

The castle is grand and tall enough to echo everyone's voices. Its white marble towers above us, occasionally yawning open into the sky, where flowers and vines blossom along the pillars locking us in on either end. We pass through an inside courtyard, where eyes follow us closely. Argenti, in gowns and battle attire alike—one of them even wears an EXO Suit—stop speaking to watch Marcel haul me past. I hold my breath, still my heart, and keep my face expressionless. In the courtyard, a breeze trickles over us, tickling my hair across my cheek. It sounds like their whispers as it passes over me, disrupting my skirts.

I can barely hear them over the loud slapping of my satin slippers.

I lower my head and try not to look annoyed. "We don't need to go to her, she will come to us."

Marcel's lip twitches. We exit the courtyard, slipping through an archway to a place much more secluded. The moment the smaller space swallows us, his grip on me eases.

Her door is just ahead, plain and seemingly unnoticeable

among the many other Argenti bedrooms. There are no guards before it, which means she isn't there.

"Should we wait for her, then?" I ask.

Marcel shakes his head.

"Seems like she went towards the kitchens, nosing into food like a mouse, I'd say. We can't wait for her to come to us. We need her. Now." He does a good job at looking unbothered, but his eyebrows are pinched a little.

I furrow my brow. "Cece?"

He must still have her power in his veins if he knows where she is. Marcel glances over at me and winks. We turn around the next corner abruptly, and there she is.

I almost stumble upon seeing her. She slows down, her feet whispering down the hallway. No one would ever hear her.

Stars.

Her gown is exquisite, like liquid diamonds trailing down to her feet in a waterfall of glittering satin. It breathes as she moves, fluttering around her legs like wings. Her chest expands when she sees us, rippling the gems that creep up her neckline.

A god. Savannah Shaw looks like a god.

Her lip quirks as she studies us, her fingers nestled within her dress, as if she's clutching a weapon there. There's no one else here, yet she analyses us as if we are a threat, her face expressionless except for that slight curve of her lip.

Behind her, way down the corridor where white pillars soar into the sky and meet the open air, a singular worker stops in their tracks, stares at us, then immediately scurries away.

We have minutes until the gossip spreads.

"In my bedroom. Now." Her voice is barely above a breath.

She slips past us, incredibly silent, the curls of her hair barely dancing as she sails forward like a wraith. Savannah unlocks the door with a large metal key. I haven't seen a key like that in years, with most people's bedrooms being locked by Magic and DNA sensors.

Marcel chuckles when he sees the thing. "Don't you trust us, little mouse?"

"No," she says plainly, shouldering open her door.

"Where did you ever find such a thing?" he enquires.

She levels him with a cool look as we pass her threshold, and I throw my feelers out to sense the distant ripple of Magic spread over me. So she hasn't disabled the Umbran-approved locks then. She must just want extra security.

"I found a room filled with stolen and broken things," she says simply.

"Stars, you've been busy, little mouse," my brother purrs, closing the door behind him. Savannah grunts, then hoists up her dress to reveal a long array of knives strapped to her legs.

I stumble, my breath catching, as she works at unlocking them. Several bruises pocket her pale legs, unhealed by the *Velox* they pumped her with in the dungeons, which tells me they are relatively new. Marcel busies himself with a hair brush on her nightstand to avoid looking at the long stripe of pale skin she is flashing as she unbuckles those knives.

They don't look comfortable. Something tells me they aren't the only ones she's carrying.

"Interesting," Marcel murmurs, dropping a hair pin into a trinket dish on her nightstand, which is filled with all sorts of accessories. "You've been collecting things, little mouse."

And there, across the room on her vanity, vials upon vials of liquid shine in the light. Rouge and face paints fill the space, along with jewels—so many jewels. Most of them are simple and a sign of lower wealth, but plentiful considering she is not their rightful owner.

"I'd wager your bathroom is equipped with towels and soaps, your wardrobe is filled with dresses and battle attire, and you keep a nightgown under the pillow on your bed?" Marcel muses as Savannah loosens the last knife on her thigh and throws it on the pile on her bed.

Marcel lifts her pillow and a slip of a blue nightgown peers out from under it. Savannah reaches over, impossibly fast, and slaps his hand. Hard.

He pulls it back, rubbing it with his other hand.

They both stare at each other for a long and furious breath. Fire rages behind Savannah's eyes, ice and humour behind Marcel's.

"Dea, what were you were doing not long ago? Why were you so frightened?" Savannah says, her Magic swelling with her words.

"Father wants me to spy on your hacker friend in Sector 2."

Savannah's eyes darken and she clamps her jaw. "Why?"

I flick my eyes to Marcel, who has turned back to analyse her. He answers for me.

"As you likely know, your friend has taken over Sector 2. They occupy and have full control of the Ocean Train… for now. They have been battle ramming our security, blinding our security team and eating away at private information. On top of that, scouts have been drifting in and out of our Kingdom." He pauses for a moment, letting her digest, before adding: "It's within my knowledge that your… what do you call him? Your boy toy, Hayes, was sighted at the Ocean Train not long ago. Father doesn't know this yet, and I plan to make sure he doesn't until we get Dea out safely."

Savannah sucks on her lips, flinching at the mere mention of Hayes, and turns abruptly to face the window. "Get her out safely?"

"At the risk of revealing my heart, my priority has been and always will be, my sister. So yes, I plan to get her out safely." He pushes my shoulder playfully, but makes the error of actually looking annoyed when he glances at me, which tells me it's been eating at him.

"She won't be bothered if she looks unrecognisable. If she goes to Sector 2 to spy for your father, no one will suspect a thing."

"I don't know how to send information to the castle. I don't—"

Marcel interrupts me to respond to Savannah, "Except, I don't want her to change her skin. I don't want her to appear as anyone but herself when she goes to Sector 2."

"Which is why you want Jesse. Because he can ensure she is protected," Savannah says.

I peek up at my brother, trying to get his attention despite how determinedly he's staring at Savannah's back.

"I'm safer as someone else. They won't want an Argenti there, especially one told to spy on them. But I don't know how I can get letters to the castle—"

"You won't send letters to the castle," Savannah says with a steely expression as she turns. "We'll keep your father preoccupied and think of some excuse if needed."

I blink at her slowly, and suddenly everything starts to make sense.

"I'll be going to Sector 2 as a refugee."

"You'll be going to Sector 2 as a friend of the prophesised queen," Savannah confirms, as if she plans to take me there herself.

"Father will kill me if he ever learns of this."

Marcel is smirking, satisfaction pouring off him in waves. "As Savannah said, we will keep him too busy to remember to kill you."

A muscle ticks in my forehead. This is too risky. As if sensing my doubt, Marcel places a gentle hand on my shoulder.

"I'll come up with a deterrent. He will be so busy with me, he won't bother questioning what you're doing," Savannah adds, sensing my uncertainty as well. My brother's eyes glitter at the girl before us.

"Glad we're on the same page," he says.

Savannah palms the back of her neck, shivering a little under the weight of his gaze.

"What sort of deterrent?" I ask.

She simply shrugs. "How will we get her to Jesse?" she asks instead, her eyes suddenly unseeing the moment she breathes his name. I feel Magic forking out of her, ripping through this room.

It gives me whiplash as it spirals out the window and down the Kingdom. "Right now, our priority is getting her out of the castle."

We. Our. As if we have always been a team.

"Just tell me where I can find him," Marcel says. "I can deal with it from there. Your position in the castle right now is too delicate to risk anything until she's out."

Savannah tightens her lips, then slowly, reluctantly, sighs. Hastily, like she's already regretting it, she holds her hand out to him. "Take some of my Magic with you."

My brother's eyes soften, light up, then catch fire all at once. He gently places his hand over hers, the hairs on his arms standing up as he does.

Tension plays through the room and I shiver at the feel of it.

"Ah," Marcel says as the Magic dances over him. Savannah blinks, yanking her fingers back as if shaking the feel of him away. "You beautiful, brilliant thing," he whispers.

Savannah glares at him with the entirety of her power in those steel-coloured eyes, and then turns her gaze from his as if burnt.

"He's… he's here. Jesse. Behind the castle someways. By the…"

A whoosh of air scoffs out of her in amusement.

Marcel raises an eyebrow. He doesn't attempt to try the same thing she did, knowing the Magic he took from her is limited.

"By the volcano," she finally says.

Beside me, Marcel's smile widens. His fingers curl a little on my shoulder as he laughs. "The idiot is planning to destroy the Ocean Train," he exclaims.

"*What?*" Savannah says.

"We keep all our weaponry hidden under the mountains. The Ocean Train is becoming a hindrance to both parties. Who will claim it? And what will happen when the Elders make their move? Your people must be frightened and ready to take action. They have all the weapons they need at Sector 2—more than we have. The *only* reason they would be by the volcano is if they need something impressive to happen. Considering the looming question of the Ocean Train, I'd wager that's what they're doing."

"Interesting," Savannah remarks, her eyes clouding over. "And if you're wrong?"

"Then your boy toy is just a greedy rat chasing after weapons that very well might kill us all," Marcel says dully.

A slash of pain crosses her eyes. "He is… he is not my boy toy."

A light flickers behind Marcel's silver eyes as he smiles at her. "Interesting."

I exhale loudly. Both turn to look at me.

"Should I go to the volcano or should I meet them back at the Ocean Train?" I enquire.

"I want you nowhere near an explosion, little sister," Marcel says hurriedly.

Savannah scoffs. "It's one or the other, Marcel. Either she goes with Jesse and risks the potential fallout of whatever he's planning, or she goes alone under a false face. It's up to you."

His eyes flicker a little at the use of the nickname, just as she flinches immediately after saying it. Neither comment on it, choosing to look away from each other and to me.

I groan. "You're not really going to make me choose, are you?"

I swing the balls of my feet against the bed, hitting the soft cotton with quiet thuds.

"Do you want to choose?" Savannah asks, her face melting as she glances down at my swinging feet. Her bottom lip trembles a little and she sucks it in with a long, strained breath, her eyes travelling back up to my face as if trying to compose herself.

I wipe my sweaty hands down the length of my silver grown.

"Just… tell me what I need to do."

Marcel stands, pulling me with him.

A little smile works its way to my face, then my heart shudders as I remember something: I wanted to find Savannah for a different reason than my brother.

Before Marcel has the chance to herd me out the door, I stop and spin, my eyes locking on Savannah's.

"I need to warn you," I begin, pushing away Marcel's fingers as he reaches for me. He pauses immediately at my words, as if recalling the same thing.

"Ahh, yes. That." His words seem far away to me. All I can see is Savannah as her face slightly sinks, preparing for the worst.

"Father plans to execute Venus tomorrow."

The words come out in a rush. There is no subtle way to say it.

Savannah's lips quirk. "It's okay, Dea. It's okay."

I shake my head. "No. It's not. He's going to make you do it."

Marcel sucks in a lungful of air. A tangle of pain crashes over Savannah's face, but she quickly schools it. It's no secret she despises her mother, but making her the executioner? It's disgusting. *Wrong.* No child should ever be sentenced to do such a thing to their parent. Ever.

"I just... thought you should know," I say pathetically.

Savannah nods and swallows sharply, not quite able to get a response out.

Marcel finally opens the door to leave, his face sombre. "I'll be there," he assures her. "I'll be there with you."

She nods. "In some way or the other."

As I leave, I realise the sight of her haunted face could mean more than she lets on. For some reason, I don't think Venus will be dying tomorrow, now that Savannah knows about it.

The idea of that is a little unsettling.

JESSE

"You have no clue what you're doing. None."

The heavily equipped man on the Hover stares down at me with a searing gaze.

I'm surprised it's me he looks at and not the snow cat's vicious maw full of teeth.

"Oh, trust me. I know exactly what I'm doing," I tell him as I scan the Hover hungrily.

It's loaded with S.P. guns, explosives, toxic chemicals, advanced medicine—even black strips of fabric that look like mechanical tech suits of some sort. We could destroy the freaking castle with what the Hover is carrying. I swallow sharply, but don't look too long and hard, because this man could alert backup. We need to kill him first, then get the hell out.

"Jesse?" my sister asks, her wild eyes darting up at the sound of Hovers.

Wrath knocks the man to the ground, taking Lily's worried tone as a command, his teeth baring the man down. He tries to scurry away, but knows he won't get far.

Bile climbs my throat and I step away. "Wrath, just take him off the main road."

There's no way I'm leaving a blood trail for them to follow. Only, the damn cat just stares at me, hissing gutturally as a long drop of saliva splatters on the quaking man's face. I watch him swallow sharply and drag himself away from the cat.

Lily hisses, stamping her boot down onto the man's throat. His fingers grab her ankle. Pure, unyielding muscle ripples down his arms and, if it weren't for the presence of Wrath, he would have knocked Lily flat on the ground by now.

"What are you going to do?" Lily asks as she tears her gaze from the man.

I contemplate my next step. The obvious choice would be to go with Lily and take the Hover, but something tells me there's a reason the vehicle is so heavily loaded. Why are the Elders sending so many dangerous weapons to the castle?

I reach to the ground and lift a hefty rock from the footpath. The guard immediately drags his eyes to me and, in one solid motion, he grapples Lily. She stumbles off, her wild locks whipping around in the air as she spins and regains her posture, sinking into a stance before him. At the same time, Wrath lunges onto the man.

"Help!" he yells, spinning from the cat.

I slam the rock into the side of his head. A large whack resounds as stone meets his skull, splintering the bone. I curse as the man falls to the ground. Blood spills from the indent in his skull, leaking a crimson trail across the road.

I curse again. Loudly.

The sound of his call for help tingles in the back of my skull. The Hovers are too damn close—they would have heard it. Hands shaking, I propel the rock into the treeline out of frustration, sweat spilling down my brow as I lean over the dead man.

"I take it that wasn't what you planned," Lily says with a sneer as she rises from her stance. Her fingers curl around Wrath's ears. The cat tilts its head, sniffing at the blood.

"No," I grunt, sliding the man's jacket off his shoulders. "Get him off the road."

"What about the blood?" she asks.

"I'll spin a lie."

Her lips thin, but she goes to retrieve the man, hoisting him over Wrath's back with a strength I didn't know she had. *Stars, my sister is a force.* She only stumbles slightly under his weight, supporting his bloody head as she slides her arms out from under his armpits.

"You're going to take the man's spot?" she asks.

I don't nod. I just shoulder the jacket and jump onto the Hover decked with supplies. The sound of the closest Hover is just around the bend.

"I'll meet you back at the Ocean Train," I say, starting the vehicle.

She grunts but manages to slip between the trees just as the Hover rounds the corner.

My sister, the phantom.

↶

One Hover down. He didn't look at me. Didn't look at the blood on the road. The guard simply stared straight ahead in what seemed to be a mixture of anger, determination and fear.

I'm in deep trouble.

I sweat in the guard's jacket, pulse pounding in my ears as I steer the Hover down the path to the castle. There's another one ahead. I can't hear it over the whir of my own engine, but I know it's coming. Someone will see the blood or call for help, and then a storm of Umbran guards—maybe even Argenti—will rain down on me.

We left too many clues behind for it not to happen.

Stars, Jesse. Why are you going to the castle? Just take this Hover to the Ocean Train and go. The voice of reason in my head sounds exceptionally close to Mel's voice. And I know she would be right. Why am I doing this? Why do I care?

I tighten my fingers around the steering. The castle won't be far now. I just need to make it there before anyone raises an alarm.

A storm is coming, Mel. They are coming for us, and I need to discover how and when while I have the upper hand.

I say it in my head as if she can hear me. As if I'm an Argenti telepath, much like Savannah's mother, Venus Collins. The woman who killed Mason. Who nearly killed me.

My stomach churns, ice sliding down my back. She wanted to kill me. I was the reason she rose that gun. Instead, Savannah lunged for me, just as her brother lunged for her. Then he went up in red dust. Which means, in a way, Savannah's hatred for me is valid—I will always be the one who was meant to die, no matter if she ends up forgiving me.

I want to tell Mel about it. I want to share my pain with the girl I gave my heart to all those years ago in the shuttle going to Terra. But Mel has blocked herself from me and hidden her soul away in her work. I wonder if that's because of me, too.

A breath of air spins past me and I hold my breath as I whoosh past a Hover. I tighten my back, lock my eyes ahead, and listen to the sound of my heart pounding and the whir of my engine until it's far enough behind me that I can breathe.

That's two.

Each Hover exiting the castle is empty, void of supplies. And each one that heads to the castle is so stocked with explosives and guns, you can barely see the person driving.

The only thing they'll be able to see of me on my Hover is the

guard's uniform across my shoulders and my shock of dark hair—
which isn't unusual. The disguise isn't perfect and would have been
finetuned if Mel were here, but it should be enough to get me to
the castle.

I don't need to go *in*, I just need to get close enough to see
what's happening, then make my way out.

The castle looms up ahead. I'm just about to turn my Hover
into a group of dense trees to my right when someone calls for me
up ahead. *Damn, damn, damn.*

If I lose these weapons, I will kick myself.

"A moment, if you will," the captain says, standing at a hastily
assembled outpost. I swallow, nodding at him.

Keeping my body straight and my head turned toward him,
I quickly let my eyes drift, taking in as many details as possible.
The road around the tunnels leading into the castle is worn, but
not as much as I'd expect with frequent travel to and from the volcano, which tells me this hasn't been going on for long. The guards
walking in rotation are few and far between, and the outpost I've
stopped at has little more than a table covered in supply lists. It's
covered in a camouflage-brown sheet covering it, attached to trees
by ropes.

They don't want to draw attention to this exercise, which I
expect will be over within the next few days. This is in preparation
for a plan they have yet to enact, which also tells me it's incredibly under-guarded and will be quite easy to get access to if handled right.

"Your commute is behind schedule and there's been signs of a
skirmish reported from Base." The captain gets right to it, his eyes
lowered on a paper. He whistles, indicating someone behind him to
check my vehicle. "We will just be a moment."

His voice is rough and strained but sounds familiar. I don't
know where, but I must have encountered this man before.

My body is frozen. I don't allow myself to breathe while they pick apart my supplies, fingers brushing every item. Every second feels like a ticking bomb.

"I did not see anything, sir. May I ask where this skirmish took place?" I enquire.

The captain keeps his gaze lowered on his paper and taps it with his finger. I avert my eyes immediately, hoping he doesn't recognise me.

Stars, I'm done for.

"The Terran unit from Sector 2 was sighted not far from Base. We believe they have accumulated weapons."

The captain's eyes drift to me, enquiring. I can feel them searing into me.

No captain would say these things to a low-level guard. I blink slowly, carefully taking in the man before me.

His eyes land on me. Mine land on his. We both stare.

But I'm the first one to speak, my voice cracking. "*Laurence?*"

13

MARCELLUS

I wonder if Amadea knows Savannah is following us? It's the first thing I noticed after stepping out of her chambers.

She follows us back to my own quarters, which delights me in ways I cannot quite put a finger on. I walk slowly as we traverse the castle, so as not to rouse suspicion. We could go back to Dea's rooms, but I wouldn't be surprised if Father is keeping tabs on her chambers right now. Besides, I have getaway bags stashed in mine.

I cannot read Savannah's thoughts, but through Cece's Magic I can smell her coffee-and-lilac scent as though she has her head pressed to my chest, hugging me.

"Marcellus," an Argenti greets me as we walk.

The area around here is always teeming with Argenti and, right now, they are all dressed for combat. Some are in EXO Suits, others in comfortable garments. Both are in high contrast to their usual dress clothes.

I tune out their voices, but something sour turns in my stomach at the brief sight of Cece practically blowing someone off mid-conversation to make herself look pretty for me. She smiles with teeth that look like fangs.

I look past her, Magic begging to crack at my fingers.

Cece sniffs, using her Magic. I hold my breath, as if that will damn make a difference. I push my sister into my chambers gently, and she squirms under my touch.

"I can walk myself, Marcel."

I know you can, but I'm scared like hell for you.

It's a damn big risk I'm taking, and it will only be a matter of days until Father expects a report from her. Though, I suppose I could forge something if needed.

My heart is electric as we enter my chambers and I close the door, activating wards I instilled with Magic years ago to lock them out and keep sound in. But even then, I still can't breathe well. I haven't been able to breathe well for days.

The castle is in turmoil, as if holding its breath, too. It makes nerves tick under my skin, the desire to act teeming in my soul. *What is Father planning? And why hasn't he told me?*

Forces have been rallying under our noses both in the Kingdom Sectors 2 and 3. My father has spies everywhere, which means *I* have spies everywhere, which means I'm anxious as all hell right now. A fight is coming, from all sides. Everyone is readying for slaughter and no one but my father and I seem to know why. And yet… he's keeping me in the dark about it.

I slather my clammy palms down my dress pants and put a calm smile on for my sister.

My space in the castle is lavish, excessive, but utterly sterile and void of any sign that makes me… well, me. I burnt anything personal centuries ago and instead hoarded riches from my father to extend my rooms and deck it in a thick veil of finery. The entire space is a museum of power. Because why not?

My bedsheets are pure silk, with emeralds twisted into the golden bed frame. I picked gold because it is a Terran substance and impossible to find on Umbra. Our people prefer silver, but I like to stand out. My clothes, all pressed and cleaned, hang from a crystal case. I had the floors replaced with white marble, with animal furs to cushion my feet. Wine stands ready to pour on countertops and stolen weapons from fights I've won hang from a case that stretches the far wall. The only thing in this room I can call my own is a book on Umbran plants that my mother wrote centuries ago, which I memorised and burnt. Its ashes rest in a pretty, silver box next to my bed. A final memory.

The room is everything anyone could ever want, but it's nothing I care about. Just another game. A way to flex my reach over the people of Umbra.

It isn't until Dea tugs a little leather satchel from under my bed, tumbling the contents on the marble floor, that I let the smile fall from my face.

"Be quick," I advise.

Somewhere outside, Savannah has moved from the castle and begun scaling the outside walls to get closer to my chambers. Weird. Beats me why she would strain herself so much, when she could just do what the rest of us do and don a fake smile. Confidence is the best way to walk the castle unbothered. Exerting herself this way is so… Terran of her.

"Should I just bring clothes?" Dea asks me.

"Unless you plan to travel in the nude," I respond absently.

She rolls her eyes. "No weapons or food then."

I trail my hand down my bed. I haven't slept in it for so long. Sometimes, I sleep away the Night in another Argenti's room, flirting until they give me a sufficient serving of their Magic. Other times, I spend it in the kitchens, drinking and chatting with the staff and learning gossip. Other times, I merely find a daybed outside in a courtyard and comb through correspondence from my father's spies until I'm so tired I pass out. All this, to find out information about and for Savannah.

I live and breathe Savannah Shaw at this point.

"Dea." I sigh, my blood fizzling as she combs through the satchel and pulls out a pretty little bow and ties it into her hair. "I adore how meticulous you are, but for the love of all things pleasant, hurry the hell up."

"Does standing still bother you, Brother?" she teases.

It always has. I want to *move*, to plan, to act at all times. It's why I barely sleep. It's why I'm addicted to Savannah's zest like a drug.

And yet, my entire life is one long wait—standing and smiling for backstabbing courtiers and filling their ears with words instead of knives. I've been raised a courtier and I'm good at it, but inside my body is always humming and craving *more*. More action, more excitement, more games.

I reach over and tear some jeans, an ugly hooded jumper, and a plain singlet out of the satchel and throw them into my sister's lap.

"One minute." I storm onto my balcony to give her the privacy to change.

My chambers are *infinitely* larger than most, and my balcony stretches twice the size of Savannah's. The railing shines gold in the sun, and daybeds surround the freshwater pool that drifts out onto the balcony. Sparkling wine sits on tables with ice wells beside them and towels and spare swimming trunks flutter over cushioned chairs that float suspended in the water.

I squint and search along the castle walls for the girl I can't stop thinking about.

I sniff a little, more inconspicuously than Cece, and find her somewhere above. I twist my head, but the balcony above blocks my view. She's there, though. I can feel her standing on it, like she's burning a hole through to me. The sound of her shoe brushing the ground above is hardly audible.

Heat surges in my chest. Magic floods me, crackling my fingertips.

I click with my mouth, unable to stop smiling, and go back to my sister.

Inside, Dea's hideous dress is on the floor, and she's just pulling the hooded jumper over her head. I lean against the weapon cabinet. Silly, pointless things, weapons are. Useless hunks of metal given to people with no real power. The case opens for me. It will open for no one else.

The day I stole the power to ward from an Argenti was the best day of my life—second only to the day I killed him. In doing so, I ensured no one else could steal that power. As it stands, I'm the only one alive who has working protection wards.

I lost the ability to make new ones roughly 120 years ago, but I spent about half a year warding things across the planet, high as I was on Magic. There are many buildings and places that only I can enter to this day.

It was a fun year. Shame that I've forgotten where over half the wards are.

I wrap a hand around Jesse Hayes's sword, then close the case. Magic sizzles as it slides shut, then I push the blade against my sister's chest.

"Be a dear and hold my favourite toy for a moment."

She blinks at me. "You're planning on bringing Jesse's sword… on the way to meet Jesse? Like an exchange, of sorts?"

I give her a blank smile. "Be smart, Dea. I don't exchange. I taunt. And perhaps a blackmail a little, you know, for funzies."

Her eyes roll. For a man that looks to be no older than 20, that probably sounds ridiculous coming out of my mouth. "If you ever say 'funzies' again I will stay with Jesse Hayes and never come home. I'll let him bury me under Sector 2."

"Naw, you love your big brother too much for that, little bird."

She huffs. Or laughs. I don't know.

"I'm ready," she says.

I open the door to leave immediately. The Magic keeping my room in a sound bubble snaps, like a pop that only I can hear, and I tense at the nearby Argenti.

Stars. It's like they're waiting for me.

Irritation rises in my chest like a fire and I snap out against my better judgement.

"You lot are wasteful, just standing around with clearly nothing better to do. I shall let my father know you are squandering the day by lingering at my door. I hear he was looking for an Argenti to assist with interrogation in the dungeons, if anyone fancies that? We should all learn the importance of pitching in."

They all stare at me. Cece practically glares.

If there's one thing the Argenti hate, it's being placed in my father's line of sight. The only thing they hate more than that is the stinking rot of the dungeons.

They all vacate the hallway, some faster than others. Cece continues to glare as she leaves, irritated that I looped her in with the rest of them. I wink at her, then turn to my sister.

The Bloodhound is a force who probably enjoys the dungeons. She wears power in a way that many others around here do not, but she is also an underdog by nature. She used to be no one, until she became a test subject. Nothing vexes her more than being reminded of the fact that she is still a nobody. No number of deaths at her hands will truly rise her to the ranks of Pureblood Argenti.

It's why I keep her around.

I leave my door open, take Jesse's sword from my sister, and feel Savannah lower herself onto my balcony, still obscured. It's impressive, how easily that little mouse can hide.

"Corridor is free," I gloat, my voice singing. "Close the door on the way out, Your Highness."

Amadea furrows her brow, thinking I'm talking to her. When I lead her out and leave the door open behind us, I notice it click in her brain.

I'm clearing the path for Savannah.

I walk bristly through the castle, Jesse's sword bouncing against my back. We wasted way too much time. I fork out Cece's Magic, aiming for Jesse, but her Magic isn't like Savannah's—I can taste everyone around me. *Yuck…* the scents of some people.

My head spins and nausea churns in my stomach. I consider using up Savannah's Magic just to avoid the feeling. It's no wonder Cece is a certain level of crazy.

It takes us about 10 minutes to make it to the ground level of the castle, given the Argenti rooms are close to the armoury. Many think the weapons belong to the Elders, but they belong to the Argenti. The guards, too. We distribute the weapons and we control everything. Then the Elders control us.

My heart pounds a crazy tempo, my cheeks flushing as warmth spreads through my body in anticipation. A part of me wonders how Savannah will get through, but I don't sense her lingering by the guards for long before continuing. Whatever she's doing, it's working.

She pulls her own weight. The though lurches something in my chest, fluttery and heavy at the same time. I'm grinning by the time we reach our destination.

Dea looks at me, drinking in my expression. I recognise the curiosity on her face, as if she's trying to spy on my thoughts. I slap a mask on, sinking back into the courtier.

I slow. And then she slows, too. Before us is one of three secret doors in the castle. Top secret and very exclusive. It's heavy, wooden, and locked firmly. A large silver Umbran crest glints on it, practically humming with the Magic imbedded in it.

As we wait for Savannah to catch up, I stare at the upside-down crescent moon with the flimsy sword slashing down into it. The symbol of how our people bested the planet, survived the Moon

Blitz, and created a feral mockery of society in place of one once beautiful.

It's a symbol of everything I dislike about Umbra. It reeks of helpless men who relied on weapons and bloodlust to win. I loved the planet my mother loved—the planet that was pure balance and power, not because we made it so, but because it was born to be.

Some people are born to wield that kind of power. Others never will.

I miss her wisdom. I miss the way she beautified the world and the sound of her laugh.

The way she would cradle me with such love and say things like, *"Marcellus, my young warrior, you are the passion in your father's veins mixed with the core root magic of the planet that birthed me. You will always hold home in your fingers—fight for it, and always be the best of both our worlds."*

I will forever spend the rest of my existence remembering those nonsensical words.

I grip my sister's hand as we stare at the door until Savannah is a breath behind us. I feel her cloak me like an embrace, her scent searing my mind.

Take a good, long look at that door, little mouse. We might soon need it.

I tighten my lips, calmly let the air drain from my lungs, and release the hold of Magic I have on Savannah. Immediately, I feel blind. Then my skin begins to itch as I fork the Magic out and search for Hayes. I can't trace him into the castle yet.

"He's still outside. Come, Dea. We will find a place, and we will wait."

We leave the door and Savannah and find a place on the outer edge of the cavern of weapons. The Elders have drastically started mobilising troops and supplies as I expected.

War is coming.

My eyes drink it in, but my muscles are utterly relaxed. War doesn't matter. The Argenti are untouchable anyway. *For now.*

The trick is getting my sister out and bringing Savannah into the thick of it.

Somewhere behind us, she has slipped among the crates of weapons.

I don't for one second search for her with my Magic. Not when I know she has it handled.

Yet, I can't help but let my mind drift with her a little. I can't help but wonder what wicked new plans are entering that mind or what our next game is.

It's intoxicating.

SAVANNAH

I stand in the shadows like Jesse taught me, and stare at him.

Jesse is here.

It feels like a dream. Like being picked up and thrown back to a time and place where nothing mattered but him. Only now, everything matters. And it *hurts* to see him.

My fingers dig into the stone wall of the castle, my body plastered against a nook where no one can see me. I rake my eyes over the entrance leading outside. It would be so easy to flee, to jump on the stolen Hover Jesse occupies, but I do not.

What's behind me is much more important. This cavern is filled with guns, ammo, and explosives, with guards strolling past it all and counting the goods. Between the piles, I see the face of a little girl.

Amadea's eyes land on my hiding place, as if sensing the Magic I have forked out. Her small hands wrap around a crate of guns, her silver hair slipping over her shoulder as she leans forwards. I can sense Marcel next to her, thanks to my Magic, but I cannot see him.

I shouldn't be here. if I'm caught surrounded by all these S.P. guns and explosives, I could revoke my rights to stroll around the castle. And yet, where else would I be? I've been separated by my friends and family for so long. I haven't even been able to console my father after the death of Mason. He would be in agony right now, knowing his daughter is stuck in the castle surrounded by the enemy. Being here feels like the closest I will ever get to them.

And, by some miracle, I've been given the gift of seeing Jesse's face.

He stands on a Hover decked with explosives, his face downcast and his expressions unreadable. But I don't need to see them to know he is tense. His knuckles are fastened around the steering, his back locked and strong. His exchange with the captain by the entrance is quick, then he's hurriedly rushed forwards.

What in the world is he doing? Why is he entering the weapon loading dock?

I pull myself forward and peer out from between crates of explosives. I drag my finger over the crates, lips pursed in concentration as I watch him enter the chamber.

"Hayes," Marcel's voice peels throughout the chamber.

Jesse freezes.

I hold my breath. If either man knows I'm here, they don't show it. They just stare each other down with glares that could raise hell.

"You," Jesse utters.

"I didn't peg you as a delivery man, but that works out nicely for me." Marcel lazily rakes his eyes over a seething Jesse, then gasps. He places a hand over his chest in mockery. "Are those *bombs*? And *EXO Suits*? Oh Hayes, my panties are falling."

Amadea, concealed behind him, stays silent. But I can feel her heart racing and nerves tingling down her back thanks to the bond of my Magic between us.

I even my breathing, still my heart, and pull myself back into the shadows to watch. There are no guards around them. Yet.

"You have my sword on your back," Jesse growls.

Marcel leans back on a crate, crossing his feet. His eyes are twinkling.

"All will be returned in due time. You'll find I have little need for beaten metal when I have"—Marcel raises his pale hands—"these at my disposal."

Electricity cracks at his fingertips and Jesse physically recoils.

I swallow bile as I watch the Magic he stole from another Argenti light up the space between them. Marcel still leans on the crates, Jesse still stands upon the Hover, but both lean forwards as if they want to reach out and snap each other's throats.

"That electricity lost me Savannah."

I hear the words spiral and tumble. They hit my heart, cause my lungs to still.

"Was it *really* the electricity?" Marcel taunts. "Or was it just *you*, Hayes?"

Jesse flinches. Maybe he has been asking this question himself.

"Savannah," Mason cries, trying to get my attention. "Savannah!"

I blink the stars out of my eyes, just as the Argenti with the lightning slaps her hand down on Jesse and the S.P. gun behind me redirects onto him too.

Lightning forks up his body, wrapping him in light.

The Argenti behind me steps forward, prepared to end him entirely. Prepared to shoot him.

Jesse arches in the air and I lunge towards him on instinct.

The memory slams into me.

I stumble backwards as Jesse jumps off the Hover, eyes burning.

My back slams into a crate, stinging my thigh and drawing blood. The pain is enough to centre me and bring me back to the scene at hand. My ears ring as Jesse stalks towards Marcel. He angles his head, teeth bared as he lowers his head to Marcel's neck, as if he plans to sink them deep into his skin.

Marcel crosses his arms, douses the electricity, and laughs. It takes me a beat to realise Jesse whispered something to him.

"Let's make a deal, Hayes," Marcel says, loud enough for me to hear.

"You're in no position to make a deal with me," Jesse hisses, his face inches from the other man.

"Oh," Marcel exclaims, his face alight with laughter, "but I am. You see, you took your Hover into *my* castle, filled with *my* supplies. And for what, exactly? To discover why we are collecting explosives?"

The desire to lunge out of my hiding spot nearly overcomes me as my head pounds angrier than the wound on my thigh.

"You're not going to let me go, are you?" Jesse says, his face pale. "If you use me to torture Savannah—"

"I have never, and will never, have any desire to torture that girl."

His words are brisk. Sharp. My hands shake as I absorb them.

He's not lying, I think to myself. *Lying isn't something this man does. Not when the truth can be even more shocking.*

This man brought me water when no one else did. He freed me when no one else did. He's been by my side—not trying to protect me like Jesse would have, because he knows I'm capable of doing that myself—but constantly supporting me and egging me on. He wants me to win, for some reason.

"Guards are coming," Marcel says softly, his head tilting.

"How do you know?" Jesse asks, his voice cracking.

Marcel raises his hands and waggles his fingers. "You have not yet realised what I can do, have you?"

Jesse says nothing, but his lips thin. *Finally*, Marcel says the words I've been waiting for.

"You will leave here with the Hover and with information on the condition that you will protect something for me and take it to

Melanie Beckett. You will promise not to hurt this thing and you will protect it with your life knowing that, ultimately, I'm giving it to you because it will help you win the little wars you seek to wage."

Jesse takes a moment to swallow these words, and I watch his face twitch a little as he tries to sift through it. The offer is more than fair, but only because I know what the offer is. I, too, would question it.

Which is why I'm surprised when he holds out his hand so quickly and says, "Deal. But only if you promise to return my sword."

Marcel's head tilts before he responds. I can sense the guards, too. Many of them.

"I told you, Hayes," Marcel purrs, "I have no use for beaten metal."

I did wonder why he brought the sword with him when he wasn't wearing it earlier. Maybe it's just to tick Jesse off. Jesse is more powerful when angry. When fighting he thinks less and just gets the job done.

It's a smart play.

The anger pounding behind Jesse's eyes is enough to make my blood heat, but I temper myself, digesting Marcel's expression instead. Before I do, he notices the guards enter the main tunnel leading to our enclave. I slipped past those guards before, knocking them out by hitting my switchblade handle into their temples. I wouldn't be happy about it either.

A soft slip of silver hair glimmers as Amadea peers out. Jesse flashes his eyes to her, as if shocked he hadn't seen her yet.

She slinks around her brother, her fingers knotted in his silver suit. She has discarded her Umbran finery for jeans and a blue hooded jacket. A pink bow ties back half her hair.

Marcel's lips move, as if he's whispering to her, and her hair shifts to brown. It travels from the crown of her head, the pale locks absorbing the silver before our eyes. Jesse looks like he's stopped breathing, but he doesn't fight her when she steps forward and trades Marcel's hand for Jesse's.

I watch Jesse tighten his fingers around hers, nod, then force a smile.

I can practically read his mind: *She may be an Argenti and Marcellus Hart's sister to boot, but she is also just a child.*

He helps her onto the Hover without a word, his lips tight.

The look on Marcel's face is peaceful, but his eyes are hard and his posture rigid. My pulse dances in my throat as I stare at him with a sinking heart. To him, she is as special as Mason was to me. I get it. I know *exactly* how he is feeling.

"Please keep her safe," Marcel says heavily.

Jesse doesn't say anything to that, but he nods and helps Amadea nestle down and hide among the crates of supplies.

"And the information you promised?" Jesse says as he turns.

"She knows everything and more," Marcel says.

Jesse nods again. He pulls himself into the Hover, his fingers white as he grips the steering. Daylight from the tunnel behind him almost silhouettes the man, but I know what his face would say.

He didn't think he would be leaving with information, supplies, and with a girl. He hoped, but he didn't think he would. Not when he saw Marcellus Hart.

Trust him, Jesse, I want to scream. But I don't need to. Jesse is doing exactly what we hoped he would. My fingers tighten around a crate, where a dozen tiny silver disks reflect the light into my eyes.

I squint at them, tilting my head to read the label on the crates. *Explosives.*

I take a careful step back and watch Jesse as he manoeuvres the Hover towards the exit. A part of me wonders how he will pass the guards outside, but I need to trust that he has a plan.

Jesse and Amadea will be fine. Everything will be fine.

I release a long, heavy breath and focus on how to get out of this enclave.

I lean against the wall and hiss as I put my weight on my injured leg. Two guards have entered the enclave. I *would* help Marcel distract them, but by the way he stands with a smirk on his face, I know he has it handled. Besides, my leg hurts.

"Damn," I mutter, peering down at my thigh. My dress hides most of it, but blood has begun dripping down my calf and onto the floor.

I drag my finger over the line of blood, wiping it from my leg. When I lift my head, wincing, my heart stops.

Jesse has stopped the Hover and is staring right at me. He's too far away for me to read his face, but I know he knows it's me. He seems to digest my appearance, his body stiff.

To my surprise, he turns away without a word—letting me go and leaving me in the past because he knows that's what I want. My heart flips, but the ache is a distant, old kind of pain. I loved this man, yet watching him leave doesn't hurt as much as I expected it to. *Weird.*

Behind him, Marcel lights the space up with his electricity, knocking out one of the guards. Jesse's head turns toward it out of instinct.

That electricity lost me Savannah.

He lost me. The day Mason died, he lost me.

Not because saving him cost me Mason's life… not entirely. I have changed. I have shifted from the girl I once was—a girl who would have run back to Jesse.

He turns back to me one last time, as if sharing the same thought. And I look at Jesse Hayes. Really *look* at him. I soak him into my heart and hold him there, and I finally realise I have stopped loving him. He doesn't split my chest the way he used to. Right now, all I feel is annoyed that he isn't hurrying while Marcel is giving him a chance to flee. I turn away, and I release him completely from my heart.

I clench my jaw and steady myself on the crate to prevent myself from yelling out at him to *go*, fingers slipping among the explosives.

My eyes search for Marcel, who now stands among fallen guards, their unconscious bodies breathing slowly.

"Now, Hayes," Marcel shouts.

Jesse surges the Hover from the enclave, here one beat and gone the next. My heart slows as I snag a few explosives from a crate. Marcel turns slowly towards me and I drop them promptly into a pocket of my dress.

"You can come out now, Your Highness."

I roll my eyes, then exit the shadows.

He extends his hand. I watch as his silver eyes take in the blood on my thigh.

I don't take his hand, but I let him catch me as I lean onto him.

"Always bleeding," he says with a half-laugh.

I grunt, but I stay leaning against him. "What did Jesse whisper to you?"

It's only a matter of time before more guards come or these ones wake, but I trust Marcel knows that. He raises his brows as he studies me. I raise my own back, enquiring.

"Sweet nothings—I'll tell you when we get back to your chambers," he says, hoisting me upright and stepping away from me into the tunnels.

I hiss, giving a brief glance to my thigh before lunging after him.

"I hope you have a smart way out of getting us out of here unseen."

Marcel only laughs. "I have a smart way out of getting out of everything."

My chest heats with annoyance, but I use that to fuel myself. My thigh doesn't hurt *that* bad, but I put emphasis on every footfall. If only to make him feel bad for not assisting me.

He's still laughing, as if he already knows. Damned man.

MARCELLUS

The moment I leave Savannah in her rooms, my head spinning like a goddamn planet, a familiar hand lands on my shoulder. I turn and assess the face of the Bloodhound.

She's smiling at me like a predator, as if she can smell Savannah clinging to my skin. I fight the urge to straighten my dress jacket as she trails her stone-cold silver eyes down my body, licking me with her gaze in a feral, hungry way.

She's a beautiful specimen—all milky white legs and curling wisps of carefully styled hair, her lips painted red to match her long nails. She drags them down my arm, claiming me.

"You reek of Savannah."

The corridor around us is entirely empty, but it doesn't give me any solitude. Instead, it makes me want to call for someone, anyone, to disrupt the way she gazes at me.

I grab her arm, squeezing until the hunger vanishes and she buckles at my feet like a good dog.

"Bloodhound," I acknowledge, dropping her hand with a slap.

She pulls it towards her but doesn't nurse it against her chest. By the way her eyes pinch, I know I hurt her.

"Your father seeks you," she breathes huskily.

The acid in my stomach rolls, but I give her a sultry smile.

Please don't be about Dea.

"Wonderful. I love how much he cares for me lately," I respond, turning from Savannah's door. Light hits my suit as I round a corner, my heart slamming in my chest.

He knows.

I fork out the Bloodhound's Magic, sending it sprawling through the castle. Hundreds of scents fuse together, forming a map of people dotting the castle. I narrow in on my father's office and find him there, pacing.

He knows I spoke to Jesse about Dea.

Everything feels cold and empty, the world tilting a little as I glide down the castle with nothing but the sound of my feet slapping stone.

Cece interrupts my cool calm by saying, "You're in trouble, my friend."

I suck in a soft breath, trying to calm my heart.

He knows.

Somewhere behind me, Savannah is in her rooms, likely puzzling over her old lover, Jesse Hayes. Perhaps she is slipping into the hot springs, a smile on her face. Or perhaps she is pacing her room like my father.

Either way, she is oblivious to what is really happening right now.

Armies are converging. Men are invading. My father has spies everywhere, planting them like seeds. Technology is being shipped, ready to unleash. Sector 2 will attack the castle soon, but the truth is they will hardly make a dent. I give them one day before they fail.

As of today, my father and the other Elders will likely start mobilising men.

And still, Savannah is probably in her room smiling or pacing, unaware.

Father knows about Dea.

Question is, did he expect me to protect her, as I always do? Or did he plan on it? With him it's always hard to know.

I suddenly stop, my feet stilling on the stone. My entire body feels itchy and raw, scraping against my silver suit, and I do my best not to fidget as I stare at the door to the office I hate most in the world.

The Bloodhound catches up. She leans against the wall and starts picking at her nails, watching me build up the courage to go inside.

I still have Jesse's sword on my back, I planned to return it to him today, but last minute changed my mind. Giving him the sword would have proven myself an ally of sorts, but I don't need him as an ally, I need him *angry*. At least, for now.

Because when Jesse Hayes is angry, he is his strongest self. Savannah can't be the only person acting for her team, she needs the support, and her friends are her best bet for now.

Show us your hand, Jesse Hayes.

"He's waiting," she says, holding her hand up to the light.

His sword is heavy and bothersome, but I try not to show it.

I don't turn to Cece. The mere sight of her shadow across the ground at my feet is already enough to make me feel annoyed by her presence.

"It's one of my greatest pleasures to subject him to at least one form of torture."

She clicks her tongue. "Shall I push you through the door?"

"Touch me and I will rip those horrid nails from your fingers."

She hisses at me and places a hand on her hip, nails tapping. She looks ready to speak again so I slam open my father's door to make sure she doesn't.

To hell with decency. I'm in trouble anyway.

The smell of honey cakes and hot tea wafts from his office where they sit perched on a table. The way he paces tells me this will be a long, long conversation. The Third Elder snaps to attention, his eyes dark, and I click the door closed behind me.

With a heavy look, he repeats the words I always dread hearing.

"Son, I need you to kill for me."

ↄ

Blood. Fur. A wet squelch as flesh meets wood and the head of the wild thing I just killed gets pounded into a spike. Guards prop it on the wall for me. Usually, I do that part myself.

My all-black clothes soak up the blood, but it's thick all over my skin.

Thump, thump.

The sound matches my shameful heart as I lift my chin and grin at the Argenti. They stand in a line. An entire unit ready for war.

"We are mobilising, son. I need you to lead the movement tonight."

My father's words. Expected, but not ones I plan to follow.

The Argenti are all in EXO Suits fresh from development. They mould to the body and erect forcefields over the wearer's skin to protect them in battle, as well as store weapons and increase speed. They even drive the wearer's muscles for them in case they weaken in a fight.

War machines. Death machines.

I rub the blood down my legs, but it only tacks on the stickiness already there. The Bloodhound kisses the air in my direction. Her Magic has left my bones.

I *hate* getting my hands dirty. I slink past the Argenti, the rows of guards, the sound of cheering. They praise and reach for me but think better of it at the last moment.

It's not because I'm coated in blood. It's because I'm a parasite. I'm power incarnate. A god. They're all terrified to touch me. And yet, despite the attention they lay on me, I have nowhere to go. No one to spill my stories to, no one to share my heart with.

There's not a single soul in this entire universe that will ever hear what I wish to scream. *I wish I didn't have to be a foot soldier anymore. I wish I didn't have to kill. I wish I was good enough to be loved by my father.*

And so, I find a hot spring somewhere in a quiet quarter of the castle. Alone, I sink beneath the water until I feel like drowning.

16

JESSE

The little girl is crouching behind me, struggling to keep the contents of her stomach contained as I swerve the Hover around trees like a madman.

We are hitting the castle tonight. Laurence gave me a brief run-down, but I filled in the blanks myself. My fingers tighten on the steering, my stomach churning.

We're hitting the castle.

That's why Laurence was stationed by the supply stock and why Hovers have been running more frequently between the castle and the volcano. Our people managed to infiltrate the armoury thanks to some of the turncoats from Sector 2. We've instructed more Hovers to bring more supplies over, and we have mobilised our people.

It's why we haven't destroyed the Ocean Train yet.

But why the Elders haven't made a move on it yet, either? It doesn't matter. Not now.

I need to get the Argenti girl across the water and drop the explosives off to Lily so she can plant them along the bridge. The moment our teams cross, Lily will blow it so no Argenti can swarm Sector 2 in retaliation.

I warned Laurence of my plan. *Warned*, not asked.

He's currently sending men to hide boats along the shoreline, under shrubs, within caves along the water, or even just hidden amongst rocky outcroppings on the beach.

Tonight, while everyone's asleep. The Elders won't expect an attack during the Second Night, when Sector 2 is exposed to the frigid temperatures.

That's why the Ocean Train is so busy when I pull the Hover up. Men are already mobilising into the Kingdom, which is why the Argenti girl keeps her brown hair.

I scan for Lily. When I don't see her wild furs amid the sea of black, I look to the trees. Still nothing.

"Did you warn my brother about tonight?" the girl whispers from behind me, her worried eyes tracking the men swarming around the outpost.

She knows? Either this girl is one hell of a spy or she has another power I don't know about. I tighten my hands on the steering, feeling her nervous energy crash over me, and don't say anything.

Chances are, if she knows, her brother knows of our plan, too.

"You might have an army, but as do we," I had whispered it into the bastard's ear out of fury.

It was a callous and stupid thing to say, and his eyes just twinkled as if my agitation was amusing to him. Bile coats my tongue as I manoeuvre the Hover towards the base of the Train platform. We avoided the village, because there seems to be something stirring within it.

People are feeling restless, as if sensing our attack.

"He will protect Savannah, you know," the girl mutters, as if sensing my turmoil.

I turn slowly, body tight, and rake my eyes up and down her lithe body. She shakes a little under my heavy gaze. Her back sinks against the crates and wisps of dark hair leak over her features as she lowers her head, her silver eyes glaring at my feet.

She reminds me a little of Savannah, when I first took her out of Silver Valley in my old Hover. Seemingly scared senseless, but with a fire simmering beneath the surface.

"I hope you're right," I say, staring at her.

An old hurt resurfaces, and I peel my gaze slowly away from that dark hair.

She better be right.

"Hayes, what in ever-loving hell have you done?"

Tamaz's voice is like a gunshot peeling over the heads of our people. I find him on the stairs above my head, where he stands with his fist around a sword.

I ignore him for a moment, taking another second to search for my sister, but either she hasn't made it here yet or she is hiding somewhere, because she's nowhere to be seen.

"Got my own supplies, since the lot of you didn't want to tell me about your plans. The rest is confidential," I reply to Tamaz, barely looking at him as I swing out of the driver's seat. I lead the Hover to the back of the stairs where a ramp has been dug into the stone for lugging supplies up the platform to the Train. The Hover doesn't need to go far, but I don't want anyone seeing the girl among the crates unless necessary, so the Hover will be going up.

"Like hell it is," Tamaz growls, pounding down the stairs.

My fist tightens around the front of the Hover, dust kicking up around my feet as I stop and turn to him. Just in time, too, because he's far too close to the girl.

I take a step towards him and guide him away from the Hover. He only makes it two steps back before he stands his ground, teeth gritting. I don't push my luck anymore.

This man can knock me out in minutes if I make a wrong move.

I'm not too proud to admit that he's the better fighter. And he has a much shorter fuse than me.

It's almost like staring into the eyes of someone I might one day become. The thought makes me shiver as I stare upon his scarred face. A sea breeze dances against us, but otherwise we are wholly still.

A long, dragged breath escapes my lungs and I whisper quietly, "Get all the men off the Ocean Train by nightfall, Tam. Okay?"

His gaze darkens. "You're going to blow the damn thing, aren't you?"

I don't want to know how he knows that. I whip my head around, tracking for eavesdroppers and find… him.

Bile rises in my chest at the sight of Melanie's uncle, the Terran Liaison, as he wanders past me, smiling his irritating little smile.

"Does Mel know?" Tamaz enquires, tilting his head.

Does Mel know her uncle is here? Or about the bridge? I blink, trying to bring myself back to reality, but all I can see is the damn man's face as he walks past me.

"One second," I say and abandon my Hover against my better judgment. "Hey!"

Melanie's uncle stumbles, turning to look at me. All the men around him turn, too, protecting the man. I stare into the face of the man I have spent my entire life hating and say, "One more step towards the Train and you die."

He tilts his head. "No. I don't think so."

Tamaz catches up to me, slapping his hand on my arm. "Jesse. The man is with us."

Like hell he is.

I reach for my sword, which, of course, isn't there, and hiss. Stars, that Marcellus Hart boils my blood. I just want to lash out and hit something at the mere thought of him.

"Good day, Hayes." Melanie's uncle grins and tips his head at me before boarding the Train that will take him to Sector 2… and to Mel.

I hold my tongue, face impassive. It takes everything in me to not throw up or to abandon the young girl in the Hover and run for Beckett.

Tamaz pulls me to face him. "He is one of the Elder's men, I know. But he is also one of ours. He gave us weapons in exchange for passage to the hangars. I let him."

"Why?" It's more a demand than a question.

Tamaz looks deadly calm as he says, "Priorities."

I launch for him. *Like hell—*

"His niece is here, you know," he grunts, slipping his hands into his pockets. My hand is just wrapping around my knife as he says the words.

I blink, forcing myself not to search for her. All I can hear is the sound of my breathing as I digest his words. Tamaz nudges his chin up towards the platform.

Mel's there somewhere with her uncle. *Mel's there.*

"Okay," I grunt quietly, unable to say anything else as I turn back to my Hover, fingers shaking a little. It's unlike Mel to come. Hell, it's unlike her to leave her office.

There must be a reason. *Did she know her uncle was coming?*

Tamaz chuckles. "Careful… she's in a mood."

I grit my teeth and ignore him.

He watches me leave with his hands in his pockets, and a part of me wonders if he sees the girl's brown head when the Hover tilts up the ramp. She's doing a good job of keeping herself concealed through, her small, pale fingers holding onto the crates with a death grip.

When we get onto the platform, it takes me a moment to collect myself. I scan the perimeter, taking in people's faces. The platform has been repurposed for our assault on the castle tonight. Tables are covered in weapons and paperwork, with designated units stationed behind them to tick names off with their weapon and assign them a unit.

The Ocean Train just dropped off a new batch of guards before hurrying back towards Sector 2 to collect more. The new arrivals stand in a hastily organised line, going from table to table to sign in, then receiving instructions before moving on to weapons.

I don't recognise many faces. The most familiar are those who came with us from Terra, but they are few and far between. The rest of them are Umbran guards and turncoats.

I return to the Hover and grip it tightly. As I do, I walk past the brute, Samael, who came with us from Terra. He looks comfortable in his uniform, with that smirk permanently etched into his face. The man winks at me when I see him. *Winks.*

I don't like him enough to wink back.

"Jesse. Finally." Melanie emerges from the crowd, a screen in front of her.

Something in my heart lightens at the sight of her. Her hair is tied into a bun, her slim frame covered in a silver dress that brushes just above her knees, where only a slip of her leg shows before ending in a sturdy set of knee-high boots. Practical, casual clothes. Not quite Umbran, but not quite Terran either.

"Why're you here?" My eyes land on her exposed cyborg arm and, immediately, my stomach sinks. She never, *never*, goes in public without her glove.

She's breathless when she reaches me, her cheeks flushed. Without a word, she grabs my elbow. "Looking for you. I need you."

Your uncle is going to Sector 2, I want to shout. But I give her the chance to say her piece first.

"Wouldn't you usually send a messenger?" I say, my voice barely above a growl. I twist my hand around her waist, holding her like a lifeline. She's not here to attack the castle.

As her eyes water as she glances over my shoulder towards the ocean, I immediately realise this isn't about the assault on the castle at all.

"We're…" She swallows sharply, her body shaking under my grip. I pull her closer, away from my Hover. For just a moment, I forget about the girl among the crates and I narrow my eyes onto the only thing that matters—Mel.

"We've lost Sector 2," she breathes.

No. I try not to let the words eat me alive.

"I mean, we haven't lost it yet, but we will. We've been acting like we had control of the Ocean Train this whole time but the reality is we never have. The turncoats, the people that threw down their weapons… they're not fighting with us."

Her fingers tap on her screen nervously, but my eyes stay locked on her face. My brain struggles to process what she is saying.

"Spies?"

"Worse."

Your uncle, I fight the urge to say.

Instead, I ask, "Jasmine?"

"Why would it be Jasmine?"

My skin puckers, a cold dread chilling my entire body as I finally realise where she is heading. Her fingers are white around her screen and when I glance at the images upon it, I feel my insides crawl.

Security feeds of Sector 2. Every clip has either her or me in it, and every clip also has a turncoat watching us. Always tracking us, always listening. It's worse than if spies infiltrated the Sector. There's hundreds of them.

No wonder the Elders can send their Liaison so easily. They already have control.

"Not Jasmine, then," I say through a clenched jaw. "I just thought…"

She tenses. "Jesse. What do you know?"

I follow her line of sight to the guards readying to attack the castle. It seems pointless to rat out Jasmine here and now, but the urge makes me itch, so I say quickly, "She's been meeting with the people from the base on Silver Island. She requested you give her friends from the Safe Holds clearance to the med ward. I didn't plan to follow up on it, though."

Her eyes snap to me. "You should have mentioned something."

Yes. I should have.

"She did say something," I add guiltily, "about how everyone is so focused on what's inside the Dome and how she's desperate to leave Sector 2 for the castle. A little confusing."

"An enigma, but not the infiltration we are thinking about," Mel says.

"Mason's plan, maybe?"

Her eyebrows quirk. "The one where he wanted to destroy the Dome? I don't think so. Honestly, if she's in talk with the people from the Safe Holds, I'd guess it has something to do with expanding the Kingdom. Perhaps bringing families from Terra over before the Elders decide to blow the other bases up."

My heart sinks a little. Stars. It sounds like something she would do.

"If that's true and word gets out, the Elders will come for her throat. They want to cut ties with Terra, not extend them." My stomach twists and I do a quick double-take to make sure no one is listening before I add, "The Elders got that right, at least. If Terra learns of Umbra, it will get overrun. We have enough problems to deal with already."

Mel fiddles with the case on her tech screen. I can see her pulse ticking in her throat when she whispers, "Yeah, I must admit I can see their logic sometimes. But still…"

I swear I *feel* Amadea squirm behind us, so I reach for Mel, my heart slamming. She tips her head against my chest, breath cascading out of her mouth.

"Does that make us bad people, Jesse?" she asks innocently.

I swallow sharply. "No, I don't think so." *I hope not.*

A group of guards wanders past us, and I feel Mel tense a little.

We need to stop this conversation before someone overhears. Spies are everywhere. Who knows how many guards belong to the Elders?

"The infiltration," I remind her. Code for: *we need to watch our words.*

She nods. She feels hard and frozen under my fingers, as if she's afraid to breathe. I need to tell her about her uncle. And yet… Our conversation already feels dangerous enough.

She looks at me dejectedly and with such pain the likes I haven't seen on her face since the day I met her on route to Silver Valley all those years ago. I can't add to it. I just can't.

"Honestly, it makes sense why the Elders haven't come for Sector 2 yet," I whisper.

"Because they were already here," she chokes out.

I don't need to tell her. Knowing her uncle is involved… it will just add salt to the wound. I can't be the cause of that.

Her body begins to shake. I know she thinks it's her fault.

Mel used to live in a manor by the water, with a large garden and a bubbling hot spring. She had zero responsibilities in her life and no reason to know fear. She doesn't know war, she doesn't know fighting, and she sure as hell does not understand the chaos that goes into mobilising an army.

I need to take her somewhere she can think.

She wilts against me, her face sinking into my shoulder, her glass screen with the security feeds lying flat on my chest between us.

"We will fix this," I promise her.

She doesn't say anything, but I know she believes me. I turn my head slowly to the guards assembling to take on the castle and, suddenly, the beginnings of an idea forms.

"We need to get back on the Train," I breathe, suddenly unseeing. I'll make sure to lead her to a different carriage than her uncle in the hopes she won't see him.

I wish I didn't have to ask her to board the damn thing again. But I have no choice.

Mel untangles herself from me, silver eyes searching my face.

I stare into her eyes, holding her there, and repeat, "We need to get back on the Train."

Her hand slips into mine, tightening. "What about Lily?" she asks.

"I think we can trust her but I just don't know."

Mel shakes her head. "No, where is she? Where's your sister?"

"She was meant to meet us here. Why?"

Mel's hand slackens in my grip. "We need to find her."

I don't ask her why, but I nod.

She turns toward the station. "I will." I reach for her once more, latching onto her hand. "Stay with the Hover."

I say it too quickly. The Train is leaving now, taking her uncle with it. It's awful of me to keep this from her, but I feel like I need to protect her.

Slowly, frustratingly, she turns to face me. But it isn't me who she sees.

Beside us, the small girl flattens herself next to the crates, eyes flashing as Mel and her clash equally furious silver eyes. Mel purses her lips, and the girl smiles a little.

Brave little thing.

Any other girl her age would be in a fit of nerves, being surrounded by so many guards and unknown faces… Not to mention the weight of Melanie Beckett's gaze. Perhaps it's because she's an Argenti and knows she has a power that can rival them all.

"Jesse, what have you done?" Mel asks, her voice impossibly quiet.

"I saw Savannah," I utter, as if that explains everything. The words—the admission—feel empty compared to how it makes my chest ache. *I saw her.*

I shove it down and bury it deep behind a door within my soul where I tuck all my painful memories. And, just like that, the pain dissipates.

Mel blinks at me, as if seeing that flicker of hurt, but she flicks her gaze to the child.

"Do you know who she is?"

The corner of my mouth twitches as I answer, "I have my theories. Do you?"

Mel gives me a look. "Theories? No."

But something in her face tells me she knows *exactly* who is in the Hover.

Mel shakes my hand out of hers and climbs onto it, her feet a little unsteady from the lingering nerves in her body. She doesn't make a move to approach the girl, as if afraid in doing so she will give away her hiding spot. Even so, I can tell she is side-eying her as she sits down before the controls at the front of the Hover.

"I'll stay here with her while you look for Lily," Mel says, and I nod and immediately make to turn away. "Jesse, you have roughly 10 minutes before the Train comes back."

I inhale deeply. "I'm well aware of that, thank you."

I don't give her the chance to say anything else before rushing down the station ramp. Hopefully my sister is easy to find for once.

Hope. I feel like that's all we have these days.

SAVANNAH

There's nothing quite like being bored in a castle.

Frankly, I have little time for it. I quickly need to find something to distract the Elders from Amadea.

After taking a long, frantic pace around my chambers and healing my leg with some *Velox*, I instantly slammed back into action. Jesse's words, Amadea leaving, Marcel smiling at me—all things slide into my many plans. But there's one thing I keep getting stuck on.

Marcel wanted me to see the mystery door down near the cavern of weapons. Why?

I grunt, rubbing my temples. There's only one place in this entire castle that *might* just hold answers. The Elders' personal offices.

I lower a piece of paper down onto a heavy wooden desk. The afternoon sun pours through the open window I used to enter this room, where soft blue curtains dance in the breeze. The Elders have paper backups for everything. Every single one of them was born before or during the 1700's in England, eons away from the planet they are on now. Even though they have access to new technology, thanks to the original Occupants who lived on this planet, habits can be hard to break. Especially when you're paranoid.

Their offices line a secluded hallway, where each door is numbered to signify the owner. The ones on the right side start at three, with the largest office belonging to Marcel's father. Room one, which I'm in now, belongs to the First Elder. Farther down the left side, the rooms go from four to seven consecutively.

Thankfully, the castle is eerily empty this afternoon. I've had hours to rummage around.

Marcel's father's room proved fruitless—all his personal information was blood-protected and all books were locked behind forcefields. Even his holographic screens were dimmed and password-protected. Impossible.

The Second Elder, whose name I now know is George Evans, had absolutely no paperwork in his office at all. The entire place was decked with research benches and vials of colourful liquid. He does his own thing, it seems. Less a politician than a scientist.

But the First Elder's room… I shiver at the sight of the messy space. Papers are practically strewn across his room and a massive revolving sphere holograph of Umbra twirls in lazy circles within the middle of the room. Books have been stacked in corners amid more papers that drift in the breeze, and a spilt ink jar has stained the edge of a map that covers the entirety of his desk. The map details the continent on the other side of Umbra, made entirely of desert.

Sector 3.

If I'm to find information anywhere, my money is on this room.

The Elders haven't bothered me much since I was granted roaming rights, but that's all about to change tomorrow when they execute my mother. Perhaps sooner, if my armies hit the castle. I *need* to find an angle to play. Fast.

I fan through more papers on the Elder's desk. Maybe I should head to that godforsaken door near the weapon cavern. *Something* is in there that Marcel wants me to know about.

I slam closed the cover of a heavy, dusty silver book. Hundreds of Argenti names are listed in it, each with birth dates, family names, and how strong their Argenti blood is. Some of them have been crossed off, with markings next to them like: *TESTED, FAILED, INCONCLU-SIVE.* The thing is massive and not what I'm looking for.

But…I tilt my head down. Slowly, I open the first page again.

"You're an Argenti," I whisper to myself. "Sort of."

The pages are as thin as a fly's wings as I flip through.

I stop when I find my name. Page 34, experiment number 114.

But no. That isn't my name. It's listed under Savannah Laurent. Head pounding, I flip back to the first page.

Property of George Evans and Roman Laurent, the Second and the First of Umbra. It's written in black, splotchy ink in the same hand as every other entry.

Roman. The First. The scientific matter of it *screams* of George Evans, but why does Roman care? I pocket the book.

I can barely breathe as I scan the room, hungry for details. Beneath the books and papers, the carpet is a dark brown that matches the desk. The stone walls are void of artwork, save for one small painting of a planet. Venus? From the Terran solar system? I shake my head.

The room is barren of personality, yet lush with information from a man who may have the same goals for this planet as me. A man I can call on for help if time requires it.

Roman. Another man from Amadea's list.

The First Elder has always seemed domineering and ethereal to me, his skin a warm brown and his eyes so powerful they seem to flash ember with flames. If I didn't know the Third Elder had the power he did, I would have expected the First to be in charge.

He speaks with a stern voice and a power that seems to shine like starlight. He is Umbra incarnate.

And he might be on my side.

"Savannah, my dear," a voice that brings trouble says.

I dart upright, my fingers slipping for my switchblade. The heavy silver book disappears within the folds of my dress as I spin and face the window. A mask of casual nonchalance looks down at me as I take in the silver man crouched in the window.

"What are you *doing* here?" I hiss at Marcel.

He tilts his head at me, the evening sunlight playing in his silver hair as he eyes the switchblade in my grip. He's dressed in black and his hair is wet.

My heart is a ricochet of nerves as I approach him.

He won't tell anyone you're here. He won't… Will he?

"I had nowhere else to go. Admittedly."

Something cracks in his face, splitting up the harsh lines. I look at him long and hard, absorbing him. He stands tall, proud, waiting for me to say something.

I sigh. "You have *such* a thrilling life, it seems."

It breaks the tension.

"I could say the very same thing, little mouse." He grins, analysing me. "How did you climb the stone in that dress, by the way? You could always ask for help, you know."

"Help," I scoff.

He grins, amusement lighting his face.

"Roman usually retires to this room before nightfall to drown himself in paperwork, especially after a day like today," Marcel purrs softly. His body is tense from the effort of crouching.

I raise my eyebrows at him.

"Shall we, then?" Marcel continues, holding his hand out for me.

With a long, reluctant sigh, I take his hand. "We need leverage, Marcel. Something to distract your father from Sector 2, where your sister is now heading."

Despite how damp his silver hair is, his hand is dry and cold. It presses against mine hungrily, as if claiming my touch.

"I know," he says hollowly.

I wait for the swell of Magic to course between our skin, but it never does. I don't think he's ever stolen my Magic without asking.

"I didn't find what I was looking for," I grumble, slipping my switchblade back into its holster before he helps lift me out of the office. He makes room for me by scaling down the wall a little. The Elders' offices are too high up to jump, but there is a balcony two storeys below, accompanied by a large, cushioned day bed. Hoping the book of Argenti names isn't as fragile as it looks, I drop it. The cover splits open as it spins before landing on the cushions with a high bounce.

Marcel watches me toss the thing with a starry-eyed expression.

"My curiosity is on fire now," is all he says.

I roll my eyes and slide the glass window shut behind me. "Good. Because considering you interrupted my snooping, I expect you to help me come up with ideas," I snap. I reach for a new hand-hold before lowering myself down the wall. Honestly, I don't really expect him to. But a girl can try, right?

Marcel watches me, dumbfounded. "I didn't say you had to stop snooping."

I roll my eyes. "You didn't have to. You seem on edge, which means I should be, too."

Without waiting for him, I continue my descent. The stone wall is rough on my hands, scraping at the flesh. I land on the balcony quietly, my dress swishing in the breeze as I retrieve the book. My heart is heavy at seeing such an old, beautiful book looking so tattered on the cushion. Remorse sets in as I pick it up gently.

I didn't need to steal Roman's book, but I really didn't find anything else. Leaving empty-handed hurts.

With a quick glance to make sure the Argenti who owns the room beside me hasn't returned, I slip my satin shoes back on and make my way over to the edge so that I can properly watch Marcel battle with the castle wall. I pick at my nails absently and lean back on the railing, biting the urge to smile as his foot struggles to grip onto each stone.

Eventually, he lands on the balcony with a thump.

"Don't laugh at me," he pants, shaking his head.

"I wasn't laughing." I bite my lip.

"It's all over your face, little mouse."

I tilt my head and purse my lips. "Aw, not used to doing the grunt work? No Argenti around to hold your hand? Poor baby."

He just stares at me, until something like pain crashes over his face.

I swallow sharply, wondering which nerve I hit. That's when I notice he smells a little like blood. A strange pang stabs at my heart, so I divert my eyes and jerk my chin to the door.

"Come on."

He bites his lip and shakes his head at me as he follows. While it's true I don't know which Argenti this room belongs to, I did steal a coffee machine from them last time I was here. I'd probably murder anyone who stole a coffee machine from me.

Doing my best to conceal the book against my chest, I lower my head and walk promptly towards my chambers, knowing Marcel will ultimately follow.

He *knows* what's behind that locked door. Or at least has an idea. I debated asking him then what he knew when we first left the caverns, but sometimes finding information yourself is more worthwhile than stealing titbits from other people.

The castle is empty. The sun has dropped low in the sky and a breeze whistles down the halls from the exposed edges of the castle. Usually the castle is buzzing around this time.

What was it Marcel said earlier?

"Roman tends to retire to this room before nightfall to drown himself in paperwork, especially after a day like today."

A day like today.

I freeze in the indoor courtyard. Marcel stills behind me, his hands in his pockets when I turn to him. *He knows something.*

"Hold this," I say, pushing the book into his chest. He gasps a little from the impact but doesn't say a word.

I'm already walking to the edge of the courtyard, which is several storeys tall and bordered in tall white pillars that yawn open to a view of the front of the castle. My fingers bite into the stone railing brimming the edges.

My heart thrums in my veins. The world is deathly quiet but not void of people.

"Savannah," he warns.

I track the edge of the castle, where a wall of stone cuts through fields of flowers and primed hedges. A wrought iron fence sits open to terraces and gardens, recently squashed from angry mobs. Beyond that, the grounds disperse into a forest that travels down the hill and into the village. Usually those gates are closed, but not today.

It takes me a long moment to discover why.

"No," I breathe, stepping back. My foot snags on a piece of ivy.

Marcel doesn't catch me, but he does slam the book down onto the railing, his face sombre. There, on top of the stone wall, is a snow cat's head on a pike. Blood drips down onto the walls in fast drying ribbons.

"Lily," I croak, my fingers shaking.

"It's been a busy day," Marcel says heavily.

My eyes burn and I take a long, uneasy step away.

"You didn't tell me," I snap.

"I was going to," he insists, "before I found you climbing the damn walls."

"I had nowhere else to go," he had said. He dislikes this turn of events as much as I do.

He slams the book back into my chest with one hand. Winded, I clutch it, mouth parted as I try and take him in through my glassy vision.

Without asking him for details, I send my Silver Magic across the Kingdom in a frantic search for Lily Hayes. It takes a moment, but before long, I am struck with agony. Hot and heavy pain so sharp and absolute that I nearly stumble, crashes over me in waves. Lily is alive, but in *agony*. It's so ripe, my own mouth parts with the makings of a scream before Marcel slaps his hand against my shoulder and sucks the Magic from my veins.

I arch a little at his touch, watching with wide eyes as he absorbs what I'm feeling. It snaps me out of it instantaneously. Soon, all I see is his keen silver eyes, watching me like he doesn't quite know what to do with me.

"She's alive," I gasp a little helplessly.

Marcel drops his hand. I feel the absence of my Magic like a sting.

"Yes."

"She's hurting," I continue.

My pulse jumps in my throat. With shaking hands, I tighten the book to my chest.

"Why don't you ask me the question you've been wanting to ask?" Marcel asks.

A plan or an idea of sorts shines in his eyes, but he appears lost—almost breathless.

It's been a busy day. I have a feeling the night will be even longer.

I blink back to reality, zeroing my awareness on the man before me. The indoor courtyard is empty, but I can't be sure there aren't spies lurking.

I whisper quietly, "What's behind the locked door?"

His silver eyes flash.

I was prepared to explain *what* locked door, but he already knows.

"A few chairs, cushions, a piano," he says, stepping closer to me.

He's baiting me, but I'm beyond caring at this point.

"Tell me now, Hart," I growl.

He angles his face towards me, lip quirking. "What are you thinking, little mouse? The castle will be invaded. We sent my sister away with your ex-lover, yet here you are, scaling walls and stealing books. Do you need my help before my father kills us all?"

I grit my teeth. My veins feel like ice as I lean closer to him—so close I can smell him. Our lips nearly brush and I can taste his breath on my tongue. One move from me and I could either kiss him or bite him.

Marcel notices my agitation and slips a steady hand around the back of my neck. My skin heats under his touch but I don't dare move.

He's so damn close.

It would be so easy to lean into him and capture that infuriating smirk with my own mouth. But I don't. Stars. I only just separated my heart from Jesse. I'm not about to give it to this sadistic, lapdog of a person. If I can even call the man a person.

So, I stand tall. I even lean into his touch a little and smile.

Two can play at this game.

"I'm still coming up with ideas," I say almost breathlessly.

His lips part, as if tasting my words. He hears it as *I have no ideas*, which is the truth.

I stare into those silver eyes, endlessly deep and ancient. Those eyes have seen so many things… Things I could never dream of.

Like murder. Pain. And yet, I give him my most flirtatious smile because now *he* is under *my* spell.

A sprinkle of colour peppers his cheeks when I press closer to him.

"Hmm," he ponders. His brain is whirring, too.

"Why don't you ask me what question is clearly on *your* mind?" I insist.

A shadow of a thought flickers over his face. "Only that I wonder what dwells in the depths of your pretty little head."

He taps the top of my head with his knuckle gently. I don't bristle. I just stare.

My intensity jostles him. He grabs my face, trapping me there. I feel him all around me—the smell of blood, the lingering sorrow.

I gasp a little as I say, "I just wish the world had less pain. I wish the Elders weren't so untouchable. I wish they *looked* at all of us and realised we are important, too. I wish—"

His lips crash onto mine. My body startles, my heart erupting in my chest. But stars, I kiss him back. I kiss him back, and all the sorrow is gone.

He tastes like spring… like teardrops. Up this close, I can smell mud and the sweet perfume of moss overlaying the blood. It smells like the hot spring in my room. His chest is warm, his heart pounding. I push my knuckles hard against his muscles and open my mouth, inhaling the taste of him.

Silver Magic explodes between us, whirring between our lips. It feels like a million little stars exploding.

My head spins with it. I reach for him, knuckles dragging across his cheek, fingers opening—

But then, just as quickly as he leaned in, he yanks away. He takes my breath with him. All of me, actually. He takes every inch of heat and feeling.

With a tiny gasp, my body sways. A gust of wind slams between us, widening the space between our bodies that wasn't there a moment ago. My feet don't quite feel like they're on the marble floor, but words tumble free of me anyway. "What was that for?"

I blink at the sharp bite of my words, feeling assaulted by my venom.

Marcel merely shrugs and slips his hands into the pockets of those hideous dress pants.

"Sweet distraction," is all he says.

I don't want distraction. Right now, I just want clarity.

He blinks at me, drinking in my expression. I don't know why, but something on his face has frozen. He seems at a loss for words.

I speak between clenched teeth. "I was forming a plan. I don't need distraction."

"As you say, little mouse." His lips quirk into utter amusement at the way I'm swaying and the blood rushes to my cheeks.

I need to pull myself together.

Lily is in pain. There's an assault happening tonight on the castle. Amadea needs protection. And I'm just as blind and confused about everything as I was this morning.

Heat continues to rise in my cheeks. Marcel positively beams at the sight, and suddenly dying doesn't seem like a bad option.

"Ugh," I grunt, turning away from him.

For a man who knows the castle is going to be invaded, he seems irritatingly calm. I wonder what his plans are for the night, but I don't ask him. I don't trust anything that would come out of my mouth right now, so I stand and wait.

"I ask you again, Savannah. Do you need help?"

Yes. But I'm not going to ask it when he keeps looking at me *like that.*

He lifts a pale hand and brushes a piece of my hair out of my face. I don't move, but my heart is going wild. Every nerve is screaming, itching to both move away and move closer. I can barely breathe.

"They use the volcano as a weapons centre, as well as a place to power our Dome. It's the energy hub. A place everything is run—a world within its own. But what if something happens? What if we need somewhere to hide?" he says.

"Hart." My voice comes out like a growl.

Argenti riddles and side-stepping answers is starting to get old.

"The Argenti are mobilising, as are Sector 2," he elaborates. "Hiding is in order right now, I believe."

"You're talking about the door," I breathe.

His lip twists slightly. "It's an entrance to one of the many bunkers within the castle."

Slowly, I turn and face him. "The Elders and Argenti would be heading there now."

"Maybe soon. Maybe never. There's no way to tell."

"Does your sister know about these bunkers?" I enquire.

He tilts his head, giving me a look. *Of course she does.*

Something in his face twitches as he studies me, as if he can see the many cogs within my brain turning. Oh yes, they are turning.

"You have to tell me everything you know about them," I add.

His eyes harden, then his lips twitch. He's impossibly close to me, so I take a gentle, almost unnoticeable step back. He notices and his face tightens.

"Why? What will you give me in return?" he taunts, his voice gravelly.

"The castle is getting overthrown tonight," I whisper.

"Mmhmm."

"But it won't be because the Elders are preparing the Argenti to fight back, aren't they?"

His fingers twist a strand of hair behind my air. I feel my face flush as his skin grazes mine, trailing fire across my cheek.

"I adore the level of faith you have in us," he says.

I ignore the urge to hit the damn man. "Spies are everywhere in places like these. My army is probably corrupted, or yours is planning something greater."

"Yours, ours, theirs," he muses.

I look into his eyes and he blinks at the sudden intensity I pin him with.

Touché.

"No, you're right," I say, my heart stammering. "Every army is intertwined, because every person has their own ambitions in this damned place."

"Yes, little mouse," he breathes. He lowers his eyes and watches me like a cat, both unwavering and hungry.

"Every outcome is somewhat solidified at this point. Everyone loses, except one army."

"And which army is that?" he asks, his brows furrowing.

"The Elders, if you'd even call their little gaggle an army. They aren't in play and never have been. They're all just sitting in their rooms watching us play a game of cat and mouse."

At this, Marcel turns his head, as if hiding an emotion. He recovers quickly though and, slowly, as if tasting the word, he repeats, "Gaggle?"

I take a step back and grin as I clasp my hands. "You know what we need?"

He blinks. Once. Twice. "No. Tell me."

I glance down to the cat displayed on the wall. The Elders plot and kill and manipulate, but they will always have a layer of protection shielding them, no matter what happens.

It's time we take that away.

"Chaos," is all I say to Marcel. When I turn back to see his reaction, I watch as a grin twists on his face. My heart lightens with a sick satisfaction.

Oh, yes.

"How did the human race survive the chaos of the Moon Blitz?"

His words almost make me stumble, given how often I told myself to do the same thing.

"We know how to persevere."

My switchblade. My goddamn switchblade. It is a promise. A truth. A way to win this sorry excuse of a war.

"Exactly." I grin. "But can we still?"

The army invading the castle is a good thing.

It will be our distraction for the real battle.

I'm going to keep the Elders so busy with trying to stay alive, they won't even be looking at me, or Amadea, or anything for that matter. Every plan will crumble. All armies will fail. But I will be safe, as will my family and friends, because we know how to survive.

"How good are you at handling freezing temperatures?" I ask Marcel. "You know, just in case my plan doesn't completely work."

I expect him to startle at my suggestion. Instead, a feline smile slashes his features. I'm giving him a game to play.

"I prefer the warmth."

I scoff a little. "If you help me, I'll make sure my plan doesn't fail."

I approach him again, scared for my voice to travel in the castle.

"Always with the doubting tone," he mocks.

I take his hand and shiver at the chill. The casual touch stirs something in me after that kiss—like a deep echo in my soul, rekindling a flame. But I don't have time to address it. Instead, I grip his hand harder and try to distract myself from the feelings spinning inside.

I squeeze his hand so damn hard his fingers go white. He doesn't even flinch. Rather, it seems to fuel him.

He stares down at our hands like it's an anomaly.

I feel the heat again between us. But this time it feels controlled.

"May I ask why?" He says it lightly, in a joking way, but there's something like trauma lining his words. As if he's not used to questioning orders but wants to.

A sheepish smile travels across my face. "We are going to blow up the Dome around the Kingdom. You in?"

He doesn't say anything straight away. When he breaks, a laugh like a thunderclap slashes out of his chest.

"Absolutely."

18

AMADEA

The man named Jesse looks angry and scared when he returns to the Ocean Train platform at the same time as the Train does.

The girl who's been sitting with me reaches for him when he arrives, and I turn my head away to give them a moment.

Melanie Beckett. That is Melanie Beckett.

A long, aching shiver goes up my spine.

"I didn't find her," Jesse whispers, his voice raw. "Something must have happened."

"You don't know that," Melanie says abruptly, wincing up at him with her silver eyes.

Jesse only grunts at her.

People swarm the platform. Feet thump on stone, and I nestle into my hiding spot as much as I can—so much so that my back begins to ache.

Jesse casts a quick look at me before scanning the people. A few of them dwindle by our Hover, their hungry eyes stroking the crates, but Jesse glares at them with eyes of blue fire until they move on.

"Tamaz is coming," Melanie warns him, speaking what I can only assume is the same name of the man who nearly saw me in the Hover earlier.

The overwhelming sense to change my appearance overcomes me, but I don't do it.

I trace my fingers over the crates, fingers raking the wood. Bold, red letters stand out of the one next to me. *EXO SUITS.*

Huh. The Elders have been experimenting with suits that will help their soldiers, but as far as gossip goes, they haven't had time to finish them. Apparently, that's another lie.

"We need to go. *Now.*"

Jesse's voice is panic-stricken as he pushes the Hover up into the Train. The platform must be incredibly busy because Tamaz never reaches us before Jesse and Melanie jump into the Train and slam the door shut.

Darkness overcomes me immediately. I squeeze my eyes shut and let myself tremble, knowing no one can see me. Every part of my body aches, including my heart.

I miss Savannah. Stars, I even miss my stupid brother.

I wonder if they are safe in the castle, considering how many guards the rebellion is bringing across the water. Do they plan to attack the Elders? Are the Argenti safe?

I rub my arms, smoothing down the puckered skin.

A light touches my closed eyelids as the Train powers up. I blink a few times before spying Jesse, who stands by the door of the Train with his hands firmly fisted against it.

Melanie turns to me. In the light, her honey hair glows like a halo, the strands brushing her cheeks as she spins to face me. A wire is attached from her mechanic arm to the door of the Train, casting the lights around the lock red. *Closed.* She's barred the doors.

Melanie Beckett, the infamous hacker.

I blink at her as she detaches the wire and makes her way towards me.

"It's a pleasure to meet you. I'm sorry I didn't introduce myself earlier. I'm Melanie."

I know. We met when your parents were still alive, but I didn't look like Amadea then. She looks at me like we are strangers. I suppose we are.

She holds out her other hand to me. I don't want to shake it, but I've been trained my entire life to do so when offered, so I reach out and push myself against the crate filled with EXO Suits to steady myself.

"Amadea Hart," I breathe, my cold hand slipping in hers. "Savannah sent me."

"Do you know why that is, Amadea?"

My heart is beating in my chest like a bird. I pull my hand back just as the Train surges away from the platform. A breath gets lodged in my throat for a moment.

"For my safety… and yours," I utter.

Melanie purses her lips and twists the wires in her cyborg arm, as if hiding it from me. I crane my head a little anyway. It's exceptional and unlike anything I've ever seen.

But that shouldn't come as a surprise, because Beckett is exceptional herself.

"They still talk about you in the castle, you know." My voice is quiet, but it's easy to hear above the near-silent humming of the train. "The Beckett girl who survived the fires. The Beckett girl who befriended the prophesised. The Beckett girl who figured out how to breach Umbran firewalls from Terra. The Beckett girl who stole Sector 2 from us."

I bite my lip to stop speaking.

"We already know Mel is a legend. This isn't the kind of information we need, girl," Jesse says. He slams his body down onto the sterile seat along the edge of the carriage.

Melanie just watches me, her eyes wide.

I sigh. "I can change my appearance at will," I say simply.

Melanie picks up what I'm trying to say immediately. "So because of that, you know how to hide and spy for information... Is that what you're saying?"

I smile. Melanie smiles back.

"You're not here to spy on us, are you?" she asks lightly, but I sense the tension there.

I shrug. "My father seems to think so."

"But Savannah got involved somehow. Figures."

Her smile increases, spreading across her face.

My heart still thrums in my chest, chaotic and restless, but that smile makes me feel a little safer. Melanie will do everything she can to protect me—for Savannah, yes, but also to ensure she gathers any information I can offer her.

Good. At least I have leverage.

Jesse taps his foot on the floor of the carriage, his eyes glassy. Melanie, without asking if he is okay, takes his hands and eases them out of fists.

"Your friend, the one you were searching for," I say slowly.

Jesse flashes those angry, restless eyes over to me. "What about her?" he demands.

"How well do you think she can endure torture?"

Melanie freezes at that. Jesse doesn't say anything.

"If my father knows about them, they will be taken to the dungeons. I know a back way in and can help you check. But, considering you're both terrified and rushing in the opposite direction of your army, I take it you don't want to be on the mainland right now. You'd best pray your friend can hold up against torture for a few days."

My words slide to halt, and Jesse's eyes grow distant again.

Melanie stares at me with her piercing silver eyes. They're not quite as strong as the Argenti I'm used to, but they're ferocious all the same. She doesn't shed a tear. She hardly even breathes, but when she speaks the next words, I notice a crack in her voice.

"Did Savannah?" she asks.

I frown. "Did Savannah what?"

"Hold up against torture?"

My mind takes me back, pulling me out of this carriage and into the dark, foul dungeons where it was eerily quiet, though never silent. Every day, my feet took me down those spiralling stone stairs, past the heavy wooden door where the space was dark and cold, and the torturer did his job.

He was known for breaking his victims and patching them up again with *Velox*, over and over. He didn't just hurt his victims, he broke their minds, too. He took everything from them: body, mind, soul.

But not Savannah. Somehow, he made her stronger, and it wasn't even because of me. I went in there every day, hoping the sight of me would save Savannah Shaw.

But that girl saved herself. To this day, I still don't know how.

"She never screamed," I say in a daze. "Not once."

Melanie Beckett stares at me, her eyes empty. Jesse freezes, his body rigid.

I wonder if he tried to free her—how long he tried or how badly he wanted to. I wonder if it ever crossed his mind that his friend was being torn to shreds while he gave up hope.

I pull myself to the edge of the Hover, my jeans covered in dust from the road. I push some of my hair out of my face with a huff, stretching my back a little to get rid of the kinks.

"Did you see her getting tortured?" Melanie breathes, still staring at me.

I suck on my lips, my chin lifting slowly. "Kind of. I went into the dungeons a lot. Mostly, I just saw her in her cell."

Melanie swallows sharply, but Jesse still doesn't move.

The speed of the Train decreases, slowly lugging us towards the platform at the other end of the Ocean. I dart my eyes around the carriage, ears perked for sounds. I have no idea what awaits us on the other side, but with these two immobile and distant, I won't have anyone to protect me.

"She's different now," I say quickly, speaking in a voice that makes me sound older than I am. "She knows how to play the great game and how to win. She's stronger because of it. So don't mourn the parts of her that died in the dungeons. Celebrate what she gained."

I don't know why, but I swear I see Jesse's jaw stiffen when I say that.

Does he blame himself for what she endured?

Melanie's eyes start to water as she stares at me, her lips in a hard line. Maybe she blames herself, too. It looks like starlight when an Argenti cries. A glimmer of silver light pooling in the depths of their souls.

I wonder if she has any Magic in her. The Magic is buried sometimes, when the Argenti gene is dormant due to dilution and mixed breeding. The Elders had started experimenting on people like that, which is why we have people in court that aren't Argenti.

I grew up with a girl who could feel the shift in the weather outside of the Dome. She would always say silly things in the castle playroom like "I think it might rain today", when everyone knew it wouldn't with the Dome protecting us.

I knew of another woman—a healer who practised in the castle—who had amazing luck with developing new tinctures. She ended up working with the team who developed *Velox*, because prior to that, we only had *Prius*, a drug that healed bad wounds within days instead of minutes.

And then there is Cece, the Bloodhound. Her ability was weak until the Elders began testing on her.

I shiver, trying to refocus as the Train pulls to a stop. The silence snaps Melanie out of her trance. Immediately, her prosthetic cyborg arm is out and she's attaching a wire from her arm into the door.

I don't stay and watch. Instead, I scurry back into the Hover.

"What's the plan, Jesse?"

His body ripples, his muscles moving as he slowly pulls himself out of his frozen position on the bench. He tightens his fists, untightens them, and then stands.

The lights on the door chime, and we all watch as they turn a muted green.

"Take her to Jasmine for now. I'll send the Hover in after I unload what I need. Tell Mark it has weapons on it."

Melanie chews on the inside of her cheek and mumbles something to herself that sounds a little like *I hate being left out of plans*, before turning and helping me out of the Hover.

"Jasmine doesn't strike me as someone who is good with children. She'd probably rather run away than deal with her," she states, her fingers tucking into mine.

"Good thing she's unable to run," Jesse says with a snicker.

Ah, they're bringing me to the disabled girl. Jasmine James, the fugitive.

My heart skips a beat as she pulls me out of the crates, causing my Magic to swell a little. I temper it frantically, my shoes skidding on the floor as I lower myself from the Hover.

Melanie's eyes flutter, as if sensing my Magic, but she frowns and shakes her head a little. "Can you change how you look for a few minutes?" she asks quietly.

The corners of my lips quirk. "How would you like me to look?"

I can hear carriage doors being opened next to us, then Jesse's heavy breathing as he panics about it.

"*Anything.* Just be unrecognisable."

Melanie's voice is strained, her body tense as she secures my hand.

Without thinking, I let the Magic flood into me and I change into the first thing that comes to mind—the girl who could sense the shift in the weather. I allow freckles to spill over my skin and my hair to turn to straw, brushing just over my shoulders.

The last time I saw her, I was six. So that is the age of the person I shift into.

Melanie's grip on me slackens as my hand grows smaller and, just as this happens, someone outside the Train yanks open the door to our carriage.

"Oh," the girl says, her eyes narrowing as she sweeps them over us and the Hover at our backs. Her fingers shake nervously as she steps back.

"Thank the stars it's you, Andrea. Can you cover for Jesse? He needs to unload the Hover," Melanie says, immediately recognising the girl.

"Most of the guards have left with the weapons on the other side. Did you bring some over?" she asks, her eyes dragging over the crates.

Once you've seen a shipment of weapons, you'd recognise these crates anywhere. *That's* what makes them noticeable. I notice Andrea's gaze softens when she sees me.

"I'm coming back," Melanie says, her eyes pointed as she moves me away. Both look at each other for a second too long, Jesse's eyes warming.

I swear I notice a flutter of panic tingle up Melanie's body at their prolonged stare.

"Sounds great," Jesse says with a smile touching his face. "I wouldn't want to miss the fireworks, either."

Melanie coughs.

Andrea asks, "Fireworks?"

But Jesse just grins and stares at the long bridge behind us.

It only takes me a beat to realise he's planning to destroy the Train.

When Melanie leads me away, my tiny feet cannot take me fast enough.

SAVANNAH

With Marcellus Hart by my side, I can do anything.

Night hasn't fallen yet, but the sunlight is dwindling. The sky is fuchsia as the sunset strokes the clouds above the Dome protecting the castle behind us. The Dome that will be gone within the hour, if my idea works.

I grin, the world around me spinning.

Marcel sheathes Jesse's sword at his back as he exits the Hover we stole from the cavern. After changing into fighting leathers and waiting for the sun to descend, we didn't wait long before leaving the castle.

I stare at him as he twists towards me, the light from the falling sun swathing his silver hair and giving him a halo of colour. He rests his sharp gaze on me, trailing over my body, over my lips…

"I'll need you to help me inside." My voice cracks a little when I speak.

He chuckles. "Again, with the demands, little mouse."

He's not wrong. I've been drilling him with questions since we left. Now I know there are exactly three bunkers around the castle.

I know the Elders will most likely use the one adjacent to the throne room and Argenti and guards will use the ones behind the door in the cavern. The one farther off in the forest will be used by more guards.

I know I have a way to get inside.

And I know I can warn my army and get my friends inside before things grow perilous.

With my Magic, I can feel they aren't in the Kingdom right now. They're milling around Sector 2 in various locations, but the simple chaos of destroying the Dome will cause an uproar around the Kingdom. Even Marcel can't predict what the outcome will be. The only place they will be safe is with me. So that's where they will be.

If all goes well, the Elders will be trapped out of their little bunkers. Let's watch them get their hands dirty for a night.

"I owe you survival, remember?" I answer Marcel.

"I remember. I just don't remember agreeing to being drilled."

Against my better judgement, I feel my lips quirk. "And yet, here you are."

I can feel his gaze on me, not once even turning his attention to the towering volcano ahead. Which is impressive, to say the least. The volcano is a sight to see.

I move to stand under a canopy of low-hanging trees, their leaves bristling in the evening wind. In the nearly-twilight sky, their leaves look a muted sort of grey, the sun not quite touching the lower branches. Without stopping to think, I snap some off and toss a few over the Hover.

Marcel just stares at me, perplexed as he stands back and grins at me like I'm a fool.

It takes several beats and me finally brushing my hands down

my fighting leathers with satisfaction at my camouflage job, before
he finally speaks.

"Little mouse, why are you turning our Hover into a shrub?"

I furrow my brow and spin to face him. "What, do the Argenti
not hide their tracks before a heist?"

"Is that what this is?"

"What?" I ask dumbly.

"A heist."

"Oh." I blink at him. "Well, if you'd rather walk into a super
secure base, coffee in hand and a grin on your face, then be
my guest."

He tries to hide the amusement from his face. "That was my plan,
yes."

Oh.

Well, then. Heat rises to my face. He opens his mouth as if to
taunt me, so I brush past him without saying another word. I can
feel his damn eyes on my back, making my skin prickle.

Of course, he's right. Sneaking into the base will only have the
guards treat us like the enemy. Marcel is one of them—high enough
in rank that if he asked them to all go home early and abandon the
entire complex, they would.

A slight smile blooms on my face when I feel him trailing me
like a cat, right up towards the entrance to the Dome. If I keep this
man in my grasp, the world will be available for my taking. He
could get me damn near *anything*.

The Dome splits into a large, stone checkpoint, with lights
flickering along the apex, illuminating the space above the guards'
heads. All of them bristle when they see us approach, their eyes
wide as they take in the man next to me. Marcel moves past me,
his arms nearly brushing mine as he strides towards the large metal
door. It leads into a room much like the storage units at the Dome
Farms, which are orchards surrounding the Kingdom, safe from the
desert heat under forcefields.

Marcel barely bats an eye at the guards. They're fumbling to let him in before he has a chance to stop walking.

It's easy to school my face into one of boredom—months of being around the Argenti has trained me so—but internally my excitement is palpable. This is so *simple*.

The moment we pass the guards, talk consumes the space. No-good gossipers. There's only so long until word reaches the castle. We just need to destroy the Dome before it does.

"I love a good heist," Marcel teases, striding besides me with his hands in his pockets.

I flash him a dark look. *Jerk.*

He offers me a grin as we enter, his body angling to let me pass before he tempers his emotions back into a façade of indifference. *The Argenti mask*, I've started to recognise it as.

A mask much like my own. I turn away from him with my gut twisting.

The area protecting the plant is massive. The ground is peppered with stone and reedy grass, the space between us and the sprawling metal power plant far enough that it would take at least half an hour to walk. Fortunately, this isn't something we need to do.

The entrance to the door pans out, filled with posts for guards and seats for people to wait for the train to the geothermal plant. Off to the side, behind a thin, glass-paned door, workers huff on cigarettes and laugh.

No one bats an eye as we walk through.

My face has been plastered upon holographs and my name has been screamed from the lungs of every Argenti since my capture. And Marcel is, well… he's the infamous Marcellus Hart, standing beside me practically beaming with importance, his silver hair a beacon to all.

I try hard not to keep my gaze on my feet as we make our way across the metal station. Holographs dangle in the air around us, signalling the next train.

"A train station…" I murmur.

Marcel scoffs. "More like a cattle pen," he exclaims.

It's true. Every worker milling around the station seems beaten and worn down. One man sitting stiffly holds a large metal cup I can only hope is filled with coffee as he pretends not to watch us with wide eyes.

No one of high status approaches us because there isn't any.

These men don't have any power in the Kingdom, never mind the fact they run the most powerful geothermal plant in all of the universe.

Ahead of us, stark against the metal geothermal plant and the volcanic steam hissing into the sky, a silver bullet of a train darts toward us. No rails support it, which would make its path invisible if not for how beaten the ground looks underneath. Like a Hover, it floats, attached to a magnet field beneath the surface.

"It's small," I note.

"There aren't many workers."

Marcel's tone is curt, as if bored with my curiosity. Yet the way his eyes flicker, trailing my face, tells me it's just his façade. He can hardly take his eyes off me, as if my musings are something worth studying.

We stand stonily as we wait for it to arrive and, after a beat or so, he mutters. "I take it that you have a plan on how to—"

"Marcel," I say sharply.

He doesn't bristle, but when he turns and grabs my hand, stroking a thumb over my palm, I notice his him eyeing the station behind me. Everyone is still pretending not to watch.

He sees it. Smiles. Drops my hand.

I remind myself that the fluttery feeling in my chest is because I'm nervous over what's to come and not because I can feel the echo of his thumb against my hand.

"The train is here," Marcel mutters, his voice monotone.

He's not like any Argenti I know, who would be scared at the possibility of the Second Night causing havoc later tonight. No, he's excited. I can feel the static radiating off him.

"Train is here," I mimic, my voice teasing.

I think he rolls his eyes as we board the train after the workers.

Tonight, the castle will be overrun.

I follow Marcel to a hard and uncomfortable seat and hold my back straight as I look out of the window.

Marcel helped me set up a comm on the Hover drive over. By the time we get inside the Dome, Melanie will receive our message. In case it's tracked, though, I need a delay between communication—just enough that Mel will get to me in time.

A soft smile touches my lips, but I quickly banish it.

The comm will only send one word and it will only be received by one computer.

I'm not tech-savvy enough to know how he did it but it didn't take him more than a second, all the while driving the Hover with one hand.

It isn't Melanie-level, but it will do. Anyone could hack it if they wanted to, but the Elders have enough on their minds. Besides, the message isn't exactly incriminating. Melanie will know what it means and will arrive at the castle at the same time we will. *I hope.*

My knee starts to bob and, swiftly, casually, as not to draw notice, Marcel rests his palm on my leg. The movement is soft, but his grip is harsh. I try to catch his eyes, my knee stilling, but he doesn't look at me.

The train moves insanely fast.

My skin itches. It takes everything in me not to bop my knee again.

This plan is so rushed. So poorly thought out. The logistics are all there but everything needs to go perfectly for it to work. If not, Melanie will send herself, my family and my friends into a bunker filled with Elders and Argenti and I will be trapped below the volcano with Marcellus Hart, smack bang in the middle of the Second Night, in nothing but my fighting leathers.

Stars, I should have brought us jackets. Would jackets even do if we get trapped here?

I start picking at the skin around my thumb and Marcel's grip on my knee intensifies.

"Nearly there," he says boredly.

The world around me sharpens, the thick press of bodies overwhelming as they sway in their seats. All rows are filled with men in grey uniforms, in a grey bullet-looking train, darting through a grey landscape.

Everyone makes a point of not looking at us standing out in our black fighting leathers. But they will talk. The moment we step off this train, word will spread.

The volcano grows larger and larger ahead of us, the sight of it the only thing that isn't blurring through the windows. The geothermal plant is some distance from the volcano, closer to the ocean. They need water to make the plant generate electricity by pumping it through metal cylinders under the soil, where the active volcano heats the water, converting it into steam to power their thrusters.

I know a little about geothermal plants from school, but the rest I picked out of Marcel's head on the way here.

"Wouldn't the metal cylinders melt? Surely the volcano reaches a too-high temperature for it to—"

"The metals were founded from Terra. Tungsten doesn't melt," Marcel had explained.

"From Terra? Interesting."

"The Occupants were always fascinated by Terran metals and minerals. My mother had a particular penchant for rubies, the way they glistened…"

"So, was retrieving these minerals in the original trade agreement, when they first contacted the British government in the 1700's?"

"Careful, little mouse, or I'll start to think you're a bit of a history nerd."

"Just answer the question."

"Yes. Although, they never quite got enough from the Terrans to play around with. We used most of them to make this power plant. Granted, the Elders had that idea, not my lovely mother."

The train stops, arriving at our destination.

Marcel's hand slips gently off my knee.

Winding pipes zigzag towards the metallic beast of a plant, where they enter to covert energy for the entire Kingdom. The train stops just before the entrance of the main centre, where a mediocre lip of metal, open to the elements, is laid down before it. Men stand in tandem, departing the train in a clutter of feet.

The world feels thick. The workers' faces are taut, exhaustion not only lining their expressions but hanging thick in the air around the station.

"This place always makes me want to take a large, unsolicited nap," Marcel says, almost mimicking my thoughts.

"The feeling's mutual," I breathe, stretching my body as I stand to follow the workers.

"Perhaps we will get lucky and die—the longest nap in the world."

"Perhaps you learn how to shut up," I respond.

He chuckles.

The station ends nearly as quickly as it begun. Marcel leads me on. There are no check points. No one to stop us. We just walk straight through.

Metal turns to concrete, which turns to a network of cylindrical pipes, confusing machinery, and men working in tandem. We watch the ones from the train check in under a large beam with an overhead Dome that glows blue. They reach out their hands, pricking their fingers against a slim needle, which in turn flashes blue on a screen before stating the worker's name and time on a holographic panel. Some then go off to an adjoining room. Others continue in through to the machinery. Most watch us, where we stand frozen.

"Where do we go?"

"You tell *me*, my lovely rebel queen," he says with a glance at the men.

The strong taste of Magic spreads through the room. None of the workers sense it, but I immediately recognise it as my own, coming from Marcel. He's hunting.

"Find anyone you know?" I ask after a beat.

The Magic whips back towards him, practically winding me as I feel it pass.

"No*pe*," he says, popping the p.

I inhale a long, shaky breath, then straighten. "Alright then. Phase one, let's go."

My feet move on their own accord and my mind begins whirring. The workers are channelling water from the ocean through cylindrical pipes past volcanic heat underfoot, which causes a mass of steam; this steam will then spine a turbine, twisting the rod of generators, making electricity. I have no idea how many generators they have, or how many I need to destroy, but that's what I must find.

I don't want to destroy the Dome entirely and rid the Kingdom of its power. I just need to disable the Dome for the Night. The fastest way to do that is to eradicate the generators, which could then take days to be fixed.

"I thought phase one was getting here?" Marcel mutters from behind me.

We move through the first section of the plant effortlessly. All the pipes here merge—a dozen individual snakes that converge next to each other.

I follow them, knowing they will take me where I need to go.

"I never told you that was phase one," I say absently.

"You didn't tell me a single thing, little mouse. Rather, you bombarded me with questions. I enjoy your efforts to sway me, but I am growing bored of your distrust."

"Oh, stop running your mouth for once and help me find the generators."

My eyes catch on an exit blocked by guards. The tunnel leading down to them is short and dark.

"And here I thought you loved my mouth," Marcel says while batting his eyes.

I ignore him.

After I see the tunnel, I stride on until darkness envelops us. When we near the guards, fluorescent lights dotting the path show us the way.

Marcel's eyes sparkle even in the semi-dark. When I turn and give him a long, drained look, I get the slight impression that his eyes look like stars. I never see so much depth within them unless he is looking at me.

Something in my chest stirs, but I stomp it down.

Not here. Not now. Perhaps not ever.

He sees the resolve in my face. Immediately, the swirling galaxies in his eyes vanish, harden, and focus on the men before him. They've been watching us the entire way down the tunnel, their backs stiff with importance. I don't know why, but that irritates me a little.

I sidle up to them without stopping and cast a slight smile on my lips. They sweep their eyes over me but otherwise don't move a muscle.

"Hello, there," I say with a beaming smile.

One man is young, with soft angles and an irritating little moustache on his face. The other is older, red in the face, and sways a little on his feet. I lean close enough to the younger man to smell sweat and grime across what looks to be an otherwise clean uniform.

"You know where the generators are?" I ask directly, cutting any bullshit Marcel might think to spew at them.

The younger guard blinks at me, eyes brown and bottomless as they flash between me and the Argenti behind me. "Uhhh."

Magic flares around us. This time, it doesn't feel like mine that Marcel is using. It feels harsher, more bitter, as if it wants to choke me entirely. I feel it press around me, squeezing my skull, but I ignore it. Hell, I ignore it with such vigour that I feel myself begin to glower at the younger guard before me. The entire tunnel is ripe with power and rage.

For a quick second, his eyes flash to the door behind him, then they move back to me, racking up and down my body.

The generators are in there. Surely. Well, that was easy. We're ahead of schedule.

I could flirt with him, ask him to let us in, maybe spare his life. But I'm already tired of this game. And, frankly, I'd rather take my blessings when they're given.

"Thank you," I say, lighting up with a smile. "You've been most helpful."

I lean backwards and look at Marcel. "Be a gentleman for me?"

Marcel rolls his eyes. Magic lashes out.

I don't know whose Magic he's been storing. Stars, he could be storing countless people's power inside him until the time is right to let it loose. This man is a menace and threat to society, but he's my menace… for now.

The sweaty old man sways a little, eyes wide as he takes in Marcel's silver hair flashing under the fluorescents. Marcel's smirking face is the last thing he sees.

In one great hump, he collapses. The sound of his head whacking the door behind us rings throughout the space. A jolt of panic hisses up my body at the loud sound. But instead of jumping, the panic lashes up in the form of Magic. It tears around the tunnel and through the walls of the power plant, sweeping across the workers, tasting them and tracking them.

No one I know. No one I care about. And, best of all, no one close to us.

The younger guard starts ringing his hands, sweat building on his brow, and he makes a move to help his friend.

Marcel clicks his fingers. "You're next," he says slowly, tasting the words. "Unless you let us inside."

The guard is just a pawn to manipulate, but it's working. The guard freezes entirely.

I step away from the shaking guard and towards Marcel. Together, we stare at him with eyes filled with Magic. I can feel mine crackling against Marcel, casting a sharp taste on my tongue as I stare down the guard. He's shaking so hard as he faces us, I almost expect his moustache to fall off.

He pulls a heavy key from his pocket. "The g-generator room is in h-h-here."

We both stare at him. Unmoving. Biting his lip, he unlocks the door.

I beam at him. "Why, thank you. Again, you've been most helpful."

With a large gulp, he leads us into the room.

MARCELLUS

"Ah, yes. Stealing from the Argenti. Very nice. Very on brand."

My words fall flat in the generator room, where everything is silent and not at all as I expected. Funny, how in all these centuries, I never once considered coming this far into the power plant. I never once thought about the panic it would cause to remove electricity across Umbra.

Until Savannah. My chest feels warm and heavy as I look at her.

She's leaning over a generator with an explosive disk in hand. Stolen from the cavern, I assume. She glances up at me with wisps of dark hair sticking to her pink cheeks, and smiles.

My stomach does a weird little flip at that.

The room is massive, dark, and illuminated by glowing metals that trace the walls in webs, humming as electricity branches down them. I never viewed our people as an alien species like the Elders do. My entire upbringing was tainted, surrounded by death as the Occupants died. I remember little from before that except for the way my mother loved me.

I was her entire world. Father on the other hand, only cared about the planet. Never me.

So, no, Umbra doesn't seem alien to me, it feels natural. Based on the way Savannah watches the currents of power beat around the room from the generators, though, I can tell this looks alien to her.

I squint down the long room, trying to see it. Nope. The thrumming room and the two-metre-long generators look pretty normal to me.

She drags her finger over the one before her. It's sleek, modern, and identical to the one beside it, which is currently turned off.

Just having one generator in the geothermal plant converts enough energy to not only power the Kingdom twice over, but Sector 2 as well. The second generator is simply a failsafe in case the first needs repairs. Us Umbrans do so love our fail safes. One more generator around four times the size sits at the end of the room with a weird attachment to it. Tubes, tunnels and a set of double doors lies to the side, which presumably stores fossil fuels untouched for centuries.

That one is an anomaly to me. Another failsafe, if you will, never to be used.

A smile quirks on my lips upon seeing it. A light crosses Savannah's face, twisting her lips a little as well. It would give the workers an aneurism if they had to try and make that ancient thing work. It could take eons, which would be such delightful chaos.

"Would it be considered stealing, if I am an Argenti myself?" she asks, chewing her lip as she straightens.

My eyes fall to those damn lips. Kissing her was just another game. What I didn't expect was how it would feel. How my heart slowed. How she kissed me back. How her body leant towards me, the little gasp she made, or the way her lips trembled as she pulled away…

I snap my fingers, startling us both.

"You know what we need?" I declare. "We need a grand exit. I've always wanted one of those fire-erupting-behind-us-as-we-sail-away-into-the-sunset type moments. I feel like that would be the cherry on top of an otherwise beautiful first date."

That gets her attention. She whips her gaze towards me.

"First date?"

I grin, shrugging carelessly. Her lips thin, but there's a sparkle behind her eyes and a flush to her cheeks, as if the idea of dating me makes her nervous.

Ha. Got you.

I drag my finger down the edge of Jesse Hayes's sword, letting electricity crackle from my fingers and over the metal. She doesn't look at the sword. Doesn't look at me. Suddenly, she's much too interested in the explosive in her hand.

"Shaw," I say curtly.

She looks at me, all business. I nestle my feelings and thoughts aside and immediately ready to explain my plan for this. Clearly, she hasn't come up with anything grander than using that stolen explosive, which would honestly just tear apart this entire room and then some, perhaps killing us in the process.

"I will cut the generators and you will set that bomb up outside on the first floor, ideally a kilometre away from the plant."

She furrows her brow, wracking her brain. "Explain."

My skin heats at the intense way she stares at me, twisting that small but powerful bomb in her hand, which is currently set to level five and would send us into the atmosphere.

I let the electricity crackle through my arms as I stroll towards the second generator. She hardly moves as I lower my hand, drawing Magic from my soul and sending the power deep into the mechanics. It fizzles and pops, short-circuiting everything. For a moment, electricity hums thicker and stronger down the webs across the ceiling, overpowering the circuits. With a beat of my heart, I reel the electricity back and yank a cog out of the machine, slipping the piece into my pocket.

"Unless you want to be the one to stick your hand inside a foreign-looking machine?" I urge, a little breathless.

My heart is erratic, and not because she is staring at me with awe.

"We don't need to destroy them," she says in understanding. "We just need to steal a small, hard-to-find part of the generators to make them scratch their heads long enough."

I wink at her.

She shakes her head and tries not to smile. She walks towards me and I walk towards her, grabbing her wrist. Her skin slides against my fingers, clammy as nerves flit through her body. She hides the anticipation well, her body solid as a rock and her face smooth, but when I trail my hands over her fingers, she gasps a little.

Just enough to tell me it's not just the heist making her nervous.

I flick the dial on the explosive, lowering the setting. The last thing we need is a fried Savannah Shaw before the Dome is even down.

Her eyes settle on our hands, her eyebrows pressed together as she watches my movements. She's still frowning a second later, as if her body doesn't quite want to move away from me yet.

Alright, then. A wicked smile covers my lips for a split moment. Barely breathing, I lean towards her and lower a gentle kiss on her forehead.

Neither of us move. Time all but stops working.

Her scent covers me, Magic pouring through our skin. Accidentally, I steal a slip of her Magic before stoppering the flow, embarrassed by the lack of control. I don't steal Magic, not anymore. My lips are tingling as I pull away and swallow sharply.

There are stars in her eyes—a whole constellation of them—as she stares at me.

I tell myself this is just another game, just another way to see how she would react. But I would be lying. Truth is, I just want to touch her, smell her, be near her.

She makes me feel like my lungs are on fire. It's an insane thought.

She huffs, breaking the trace, and I pull back abruptly, realising I was staring.

"By the way, Marcel, you don't need to pump electricity out of your hands to dislodge a part in the generator. The poor thing won't bite back." Her voice sounds rough, but the words come across as joking.

I roll my shoulders, stepping back from her.

She takes that as a sign to turn and bundle the explosive against her chest like it's a shield between us.

I let her walk away for a moment. Just a moment.

"By the way, Savannah. If we get through tonight, allow me to give you a *proper* first date."

Savannah laughs, her head turning back to me for a fraction. It's a soul-shattering, all-consuming laugh, as if giddy at the thought.

Everything inside me freezes as I stare at this crazy girl with hair like the earth and eyes like the stars. My Queen.

"Hart, there is not a single proper thing about you."

I grin, just a little. "Wow, you see right through me, little mouse."

I say it lightly as a joke, but it isn't. That terrifies me in ways I cannot name. My heart, which I try to keep on a tight leash, feels constricted. Nerves flutter around me. I'm all-too aware of how I'm standing, how I'm looking at her, and what my hands are doing.

I'm used to people seeing the masked version of me. Everything else is terrifying. Savannah Shaw is terrifying and I'm addicted.

Savannah leaves the generator room with a slaphappy, "Hello, again," to the guards outside before my world quietens.

I stand still, breathe, and I wait.

I wait for the explosion as my sign to continue the mission and steal a part from the next generator. The sign to return to reality and run home.

21

JESSE

Ocean water laps at my feet, filling my shoes. The leather is worn and beaten, so I don't think much of it until Melanie calls my name and I jolt so aggressively that my entire boot slips on a rock, sending half my leg into the water.

"For the love of all—"

"Savannah!" she interrupts, clambering down the rocks towards me. "I got a message from Savannah!"

I exit the water and turn my eyes up towards her as she struggles over rocks, her cheeks flushed and hair windblown. It's dark here, underneath the bridge on the military side of the Ocean Train. The massive structure looms over our heads, like a dark cloud ready to empty. But even despite the darkness, I can see the massive grin stretching across Mel's face.

Surprisingly, the sight of it causes my heart to lighten.

Savannah. A distant throb hits my heart, but the joy of Mel's smile almost masks it entirely.

"What kind of message?" I ask.

I gently lower the bomb in my hands, artfully placing it between some rocks as close to the water as I am able. I've been placing them around the base of the bridge, as well as near the water. Five bombs in total, all of which are enough to blow up nearly half of Silver Valley. I know this because Melanie's uncle and my mother have used the exact same model to do just that.

The military base will survive, given the layers upon layers of metal and bedrock guarding it. But the world around it? The shore of the island? Yeah, that stands no chance.

It might take us days to dig our way up from the military base, but it's worth it. At least we will be safe.

"Just one word," Mel replies. "*Tunnels.*"

The word doesn't shake me the way it shakes Mel. I stand slowly, brushing dried salt down my fighting leathers, and turn to find the girl tapping furiously on the screen she seems to carry everywhere these days. Her brow is furrowed, a small stress line appearing on her forehead. She's searching for more answers or clues, but that's the thing about hacking—even the most skilled hacker cannot uncover information that is not there. Savannah only sent us the one word, which will have to be enough.

"Did you drop off Amadea?" I ask.

It's difficult to breathe down here, choking on the scent of salt. For many, the ocean is soothing. For me, it's sprinkled in memories.

How many times did Lily and I sneak out of the base to come and splash around in the crystalline water? More than I can count. I can still hear her scolding me for going out too far, and still feel the panic of when a large shark-like creature drifted past the rocks one time. I can still feel dried salt crusting on my skin and the sting of sunburn from when we stayed out late.

"Jasmine said, and I quote, '*tell Jesse thank you for bringing me a*

*friend, because I sure as hell know this one didn't come from you, Mel-
anie. No offense. But also tell him he's a coward for ignoring me. I don't
hate him* that *much.'"* Mel looks up from her screen to glance at me.
"What exactly have you been prattling on about with Jasmine?"

"I don't prattle. She does." I groan. "And I'm not ignoring her.
I'm busy."

"I'm worried about what goes through her head."

Aren't we all?

A breeze flutters Mel's hair as she lowers her head back to her
screen, hiding a soft smile. Something in my chest heats, and it's
difficult to separate the frustration I feel for Jasmine from the way
Mel is smiling.

Since Savannah was captured by the Elders, she has become a
distant part of our lives. Every damn day she fights for us. But I'm
slowly forgetting her.

Every damn day, I feel guilt. Pain. Hurt. But those feelings are
separate to who she is.

I swallow sharply, my hands bordering on shaking as I stand
and stare at Mel.

We need to get away from this bridge in case I set the bombs
wrong and they blow early. But neither of us move. Her silver eyes
scan pages of code—numbers and text that mean nothing to me

"I saw her," I blurt out.

An ache shatters my chest at the sound of my own words. I
didn't want to talk about this nor acknowledge it, yet there it is
tumbling out of me. *I saw her.*

Melanie blinks at me. A flicker of sorrow hangs there. She
knows I saw Savannah, but the admission feels different this time.
She lowers her screen so slowly, I barely see her do it.

I want so badly to touch her; to have her touch me or soothe
me. But fire erupts within my soul, the pain so vivid I cannot block
it out. If Mel touches me now, I might explode.

She sees this. Mel knows me better than anyone.

"Jesse," she says softly.

She doesn't ask me about Savannah or ask me how the interaction went down. Instead she just looks at me with a pain-filled expression and *understanding.*

Why have I been so tentative to bring this up with her? Why have I always shut the pain of Savannah out? This is Mel. If anyone knows how I feel, it's her. It's always her.

"Savannah was never mine to keep," I admit. The admission rattles me, because there it is. The truth.

She was never mine.

Mel's eyes soften and, just like that, the truth continues flowing out of me.

"Most of my life, I have dealt with loss. I never thought I'd find anyone or anything to love again. But I found you, Mel. I found you in the darkest moment of my life. You saw my hatred and my black heart for what it was and, instead of turning away, you tried to breathe life into it. I wish I saw that. I wish I knew what you were doing for me before I relied on Savannah to fix me."

I take a steady breath, my mind dizzying. "I saw her, open and joyful and filled with love, and subconsciously latched onto that with all I had. I squeezed life out of her to bleed happiness back into my own. But at what cost? She became a girl who would give everything for me, a girl willing to give her all, in response to my nothing. Savannah was never mine, Mel. We were on borrowed time—just two people who needed something from each other. And yet, I got the better end of the deal. Because all I ever did was ruin her."

The words stop as quickly as they started. The pounding of waves roars in my ears, fusing with the pounding of my heart. Mel watches me with trepidation, her breath appearing to be lodged in her throat.

I wait for her to say something, anything. Instead, she reaches for me. Why would she want to touch me, after all that? I broke Savannah. Maybe I will break her, too.

Her arms wrap around my torso, her device now abandoned on the rock. She *never* puts her tech down, and it makes my heart swell. It grows and grows and comes close to shattering.

I remain in stasis, staring at nothing, fixated at the way our hearts beat as one. I can feel hers, pattering against me, the same way mine is drumming into hers. Of their own accord, my arms tighten around her.

She's so small and fragile, so warm and soft. She's so precious, so beautiful and whole before me. I cannot hurt her or be her detriment. And yet, I stay, because she is home.

"I am so sorry, Jesse," she mutters against my chest. "You did not… you did not ruin that girl. It is not your fault." I move to push her away, to argue, but Mel grips me like a vice. "We both did," she adds. The words are soft, filled with pain.

The admission sinks me. I squeeze her harder, restricting her need to feel. Sorrow halts her next inhale, but she does not cry. Neither of us cry.

Our hearts slow as we latch onto each other, gripping the other like we are each other's centre of gravity. In a way, I guess we are. We always have been.

"We both did," I repeat, testing the words.

We both did.

⤸

The ocean is still sparkling under the moonlight.

Even from here, in our small rickety boat, as we bop over the dancing surface.

Tunnels.

Mel and I don't return to Sector 2. Instead, we go to Savannah.

I don't usually get seasick—living your formative years next to the ocean hardens a person—but I can feel my gut upheaving with every wave. It's the nerves, I tell myself. Nerves for what is about to happen, for who we are leaving behind, and for who we are meeting.

"Amadea is with Elijah, Jasmine and Mark. Lily is missing. I'm still trying to crack Savannah's location," Melanie says matter-of-factly. "Can you please pass me that?"

I pass her the water skin she points to. She takes it from me, chugging some water before settling it besides her.

"Thanks," she mutters, eyes already back on her screen.

We considered bringing our friends in Sector 2 with us, but with Jasmine injured and Eli in a coma, it would take too long. No, it's better they stay and we keep Amadea as far from the castle as possible. I'd like to see the Argenti dig under layers of rubble to get to her.

The thought is almost enough to make me smile.

"Roughly five minutes," I advise Mel, checking the watch she set on her screen, as if she cannot see it herself.

Five minutes until the bridge blows.

I hope I set the bombs correctly. It's been so long since I've tinkered with Umbran military tech. A bead of sweat tickles down my neck at the thought.

"Savannah's mother is in the dungeons. The Elders haven't been seen since they displayed Lily's cat at the front of the castle. Marcellus Hart is missing. Our military have settled around the edge of the castle. They will attack in 10 minutes."

Wrath.

I lean over the edge of the small wooden boat as my stomach finally loosens. The waves clear away my queasiness, slapping against the side of the boat in a constant beat. I wretch, eyes watering.

"You good? Don't tell me you're seasick."

Melanie's words make the blood rush to my face. I am *never* seasick.

"I actually liked that goddamn cat," I admit sheepishly, turning my flushed face to meet her. She studies me, her lips thinning. Just before we made it halfway across the small gulf between Sector 1 and 2, she finally got complete access to the castle's systems. Still, it's a maze to sift through everything and there's a lot of catching up to do.

Lily's cat.

The Elder's must have caught her if they took Wrath. It's no wonder I couldn't find my sister when I returned. The only other alternative is that she escaped the Kingdom, went back to her other cats, and has lost herself in a bout of mourning.

Please let it be the latter. I don't know if I could survive losing my sister twice.

The boat rocks under us, the sound of water slapping filling the silence. I drift my eyes to the stars twinkling outside the Dome. We are under it now, some-ways away from the biting cold that will soon spread across the island of Sector 2. Not even the flames of the explosion will be enough to warm us if we stayed there.

Besides, I don't plan to be anywhere close when the bridge blows.

"One minute," Mel tells me. She puts her screen down, blacking out the screen.

I try not to count the seconds in my head, but I do. Each one is equally as agonising.

40, 39, 38…

I hope it blows on time. I hope Laurence and his men are far enough away.

19, 18, 17…

I drag my hands down my leathers, then fist them in my lap. My mouth tastes foul from upheaving my stomach, but it's a distant annoyance as we wait, our lungs stretching as we both hold our breath.

10, 9, 8.

The bridge explodes on 8.

If I wasn't already holding my breath, I would have lost it.

Fire ripples across the ocean in a gust of heat and sparks, taking chunks of the bridge with it. The explosive closest to the middle of the bridge goes first, then sets off the others in a rippling effect that takes the whole bridge.

The fire arches into the sky, brushing the Dome, brighter than the stars.

My heart goes berserk as I squint.

I swear I can feel heat lick my face, even at this distance past the Dome. But that can't be. The Dome protects us from wind and fire. The water, however, is a different story. A torrent of wind from the explosion sends waves towards us. Melanie gasps as it pushes against our boat, nearly tipping us over. I reach out to the sides, holding myself steady. At the same time, Melanie lunges for her tech. She topples forwards, swaying dangerously, and I abandon all thought as I reach for her.

The boat tilts as I grab her and tuck her against my lap. I urge our bodies to sway towards the other side, trying to equalise the weight of the boat. Water trickles in, just as the boat slams down into the ocean.

I hold Mel, panting. The sound of the bridge collapsing is quiet compared to the explosion. Chunks of metal and rock slam into the water, awakening the peaceful night.

I don't look towards the bridge. I look towards our Sector.

Rubble coats the island, covering it almost entirely. I swallow sharply, my gut swimming. We are so far away, and yet… *it looks like Silver Valley.*

I laid most of the bombs near Sector 2, as I didn't want to risk going too far out on the bridge and getting run over by the Train, and now it shows. One quarter of the bridge still remains on the side of the Kingdom, whereas the military side has all but vanished.

The whole island is smouldering but intact.

The ocean has surged higher onto the land, the waves cresting against what I can vaguely see is the entrance of the base. That's all I can see from this far. To know more, we would have to go back. But we have a different goal now.

Tunnels.

Mel debated us trying to get there before the explosion, but I wanted to see it happen. I wanted to make sure I did it right. We only have several more minutes until the fighting around the castle commences, which means we need to move. *Now.*

We won't get there until after it starts, but we need to pray we don't get there before it ends. Savannah hasn't mentioned anything about timing, but it's obvious we are to act tonight.

I untangle Mel from my lap, where she is practically frozen, her eyes plastered on Sector 2. She sucks in a quick breath, her eyes focusing, and uncrosses her arms from her chest to reveal her tech. The screen is powered on and running before she's back in her seat.

"Find the tunnels she's referring to and I'll get us there," I mutter to her, as if she doesn't already know. We haven't verbalised this part of the plan, but this is the way we always do things. She absently nods, fingers already moving.

I punch directions into the navigation panel, and the boat hums beneath us, thrusting us towards the castle.

The ocean is still unsettled, but this boat is Argenti-made. The wood is sourced from a variety of sturdy trees around the Kingdom and wired with tech to stabilise us. We rock a little but stay afloat. I grip the metal railing of the boat like it's a lifeline, though. My other hand stays near the wheel, ready to change course or speed if needed.

"No," Melanie gasps.

Her screen falls to the base of the boat with a splintering clatter, and I notice it a second after she does. Ice bites at my skin, dousing any thought.

I gasp, fingers slipping from the railing. Wind blasts against us, carrying the bitter tang of fire and smoke. Is it possible for wind to feel both freezing cold yet scalding hot, all at once?

I turn my head to the sky.

Stars dance above. There's no Dome.

The promise of the Second Night wails around us. We are caught in a gust of ice and wind that pounds against our bodies.

A deep, resounding panic floods my chest, pricking my skin. I lose my ability to breathe properly. Vaguely, I hear Melanie talking next to me, saying the same words over and over.

I don't let myself hear it. Did I blow up the Dome?

I couldn't have… could I? I would never allow us to die without finding shelter throughout the Night.

Stars, what have I done?

Ice travels down my veins, bringing my worst nightmares with it, because the Second Night has made its way to the Kingdom. This hasn't happened in centuries. It's the kind of horror only civilians of Sector 2—military—and Sector 3—desert wildlings—have ever had the displeasure of experiencing. I bet even the Elders have forgotten what it feels like.

"No." My chest heaves in panic, my lungs compressing as I struggle to breathe.

Melanie shakes me, her hair whipping in the icy wind. She's still saying the same words, hoping I'll hear and understand her, but my ears are ringing.

I shake my head. The world snaps back into place with resounding focus, and I latch onto Mel. Her eyes dart this way and that as she tries to take stock of her surroundings. She's over by the back of the boat with me, her eyes on the sky, hair illuminated by the distant fires. I can already see her skin puckering from cold.

"Mason's plan. It's Mason's plan." She repeats it.

Mason's plan? What the hell is Mason's plan?

I trace my eyes past the stars and back over the land ahead. We will be at the Kingdom soon, but not soon enough. What will we find there? What level of panic will the people be in?

Utter chaos. We will find utter chaos.

"The tunnels under the castle," I manage, remembering how the cavern of weapons resembled tunnels. Surely the Elders have a place in there to keep warm? If this was Shaw's doing, then that message was a warning.

Mel locks her eyes on me.

I tighten my fingers, flexing them against the chill biting into my skin. It isn't nearly as cold as it can get. This is only the beginning.

We need to get to the bloody tunnels right freaking now.

"Savannah got rid of the Dome," Melanie gasps, realisation flooding her face.

With shaking hands, I gun the boat and fly across the ocean like hell has opened, because in a way, it has.

PART TWO

THE DOME

22

AMADEA

y lungs squeeze in my chest.

The bridge is gone.

My slim fingers grip the blanket on Jasmine Spark's bed, my legs twisted near where her paralysed ones lay. She watches me like I'm a blessing she didn't expect to arrive, and it makes me anxious. Yet her bed is warm and her gestures comforting, unlike the man next to her. Elijah Brookes just stares at me with taut lips.

Jasmine keeps trying to ask me about the castle exits, fail safes, and for ways to get in and find Savannah. I give her vague non-answers, which just makes her press harder.

"Mark," Elijah mutters. He's still covered in bandages; I don't know why they even bothered to wake him. He needs to be taken to the mainland for surgery.

Jasmine looks at him. He stares back, like they're both holding a secret.

Something to do with wanting to reach Savannah, I'd wager.

Stars, they've been left in the med ward together for who knows how long? Granted, Elijah Brookes has been asleep and in pain for most of that time, but wouldn't that be a perfect cover story?

I squint at them, as if by doing so they will tell me what they're thinking. This isn't the usual way I spy on people.

I remember Savannah's father, Mark, from that fated day in the throne room when his son died, but seeing him up close is a whole new thing. The man appears weak, his eyes glazed and his face haunted. He barely acknowledges any of us long enough to get a word in.

The man is rummaging through the supplies Jesse sent. The girl from the station, Andrea, pushed it in with shaking hands. The crate is full of untested ammunition, guns, EXO Suits, and even bombs.

"This thing killed my son."

Andrea's eyes flash between me and Mark, who has a S.P. gun in his hand, then over to Jasmine and Elijah. Her breathing is even more jagged than mine.

I know the feeling well.

My skin itches from being around these people. I do not belong here, yet I can go nowhere. I'm trapped, and not just because Sector 2 is covered in rubble right now.

"Mark," Elijah says a little louder this time. "Put down the gun."

Mark swallows, his hands shaking. The S.P. gun clatters at his feet.

Stars. That is not *how you put down a gun.*

I leap off the bed, my feet slipping on the ground in my haste. Jasmine chuckles at my panic. Does she understand he's holding an *untested* gun?

"Is anyone else worried about the fact we are trapped under layers of rock right now?" Andrea mutters as she fiddles with the hem of her shirt.

"A small setback," Jasmine answers, picking at her nails.

Mark just stares at the gun by his feet as if it's sprouted legs. No one else responds.

I pull away from Jasmine, rubbing my arms in the hope that my puckered skin will settle. They don't know how to escape the rubble but I do, at least in theory.

"There's a back entrance out of Sector 2 if we have access to 3A."

"The where-now?" Jasmine asks, eyes widening.

I blink at her, and repeat slowly, "There's a back entrance."

Her eyes are sparkling. "Spill, castle girl."

"What the hell is a 3A?" Elijah chips in, turning to me.

Heat floods my face as everyone turns and looks at me. Stars, my skin feels itchy. I still haven't donned my own skin since Melanie dropped me off with them, and I suddenly feel too small for my body. The urge to turn into my mother overpowers me, the way it always does when I feel small, but doing that right now? Yeah, not a smart idea.

Before I can open my mouth to respond, Mark decides to kick the gun across the floor.

I squeal and Andrea practically bolts to the edge of the room.

"Mark!" Elijah shouts, twisting in his bed. He winces immediately.

Jasmine grunts, her eyes vaguely tracking the gun as it spins across the floor, hitting the legs of a hospital cot on the way down the room. My Magic swells around me—an automatic response to danger. Even though changing my skin would not protect me from guns in the slightest, I do so anyway.

Shaking, I feel my hands grow. My hair slinks past my shoulders. Distantly, I'm aware of the shift. Physically, all I can do is watch that damn gun as it settles against the wall ahead.

Mark blinks. Staring at me.

Jasmine squirms into an upright position.

Elijah chokes.

They all stare and stare and stare.

"I'm sorry," I splutter. "I didn't mean to—" My words die on my tongue.

Well, now they know they have an Argenti in their midst.

"Holy mother of all things cursed. And to think I thought Mark was being tortured enough," Jasmine mumbles as she darts her eyes to him. "By the way, if you take another step towards that freaking gun, I will grow new legs and throttle you."

Mark was, indeed, slinking towards the gun in shame. Embarrassment seeps from him as he splutters, still staring at me. His eyes do not leave me, even as he steps back.

There are no mirrors in this room, but a silver tray covered in *Velox* syringes and scalpels sits off to the side of me on a sterile bench. I look at the reflection and gasp at who stares back. *Savannah Shaw*.

"Oh… I'm *so* sorry."

Heat expands across my body and my hands shake as I turn and look at Savannah's friends and family. Her energy is scattered within these people… and I clung to that when I shifted.

I immediately shift into my own skin. Just the usual me, silver hair and all.

"I think I'm going to throw up," Mark manages to say.

"As long as you stay away from S.P. guns when you projectile hurl, I think that's fine," Jasmine says, rolling her eyes.

I narrow my eyes, taking in the girl. She seems so unaffected by Savannah and the memory of her brother's death. I was there the day it happened and saw the way his death broke her. I saw the way *Savannah* broke her. So why is she so okay with it now? Is she so used to pain she's now able to cover any layer of hurt with laughter?

She notices my gaze and I lower my chin, training my eyes on my feet.

"You should probably control that, castle girl," Jasmine advises, her eyes wise beyond her years.

"Okay," Andrea says, still plastered against the wall like a nervous mouse. "Back to the rubble that's covering us?"

Elijah groans, leaning back into his bed.

"3A is the third farthest section of the compound. There are tunnels underground for Hovers to get to the other continent. Otherwise, we can backtrack, circle around the rubble, and head towards the castle. But Jesse will need to have left us boats."

"The other continent?" Mark asks, his voice rough. "Honey, I'd much prefer go to the castle to my daughter."

Jasmine sighs, nestling between the pillows. "I'm with Mark. If she means the barren lands of Sector 3, that could take time away from us."

At this, I nod. "But it would give us the chance to heal Elijah and maybe get you walking again. Sector 3 has medicine. Besides, we don't know what state the Kingdom is in."

"We also don't know what we will find in Sector 3. A bunch of wildlings ready to murder us, probably," she rebuts.

Mark blinks at us both, his face waxen.

But I do know. I've been hearing whispers about them for years. They have surgeons and Argenti with knowledge of the planet beyond our understanding. I'm curious about them.

"Let's just leave this tomb first, then decide," I say instead.

"Grand idea," Elijah pitches in. "When Jaz and I get function of our limbs again and can walk out of here, I reckon we do that. Solid plan."

"Maybe we can fly to the castle," Jasmine says sassily.

Again with the castle. What does she want to tell Savannah so badly?

His comment makes my chest heave. Do they not see the Hover before them? Does he not see the *EXO Suits*? Yes, in theory those suits don't work yet, but we can go wherever we like with the supplies we have.

I scan the room, looking for wheelchairs to carry Jasmine and Elijah, but there's nothing. Usually, Sector 2 is well supplied with medicine and healers—the military are always injuring themselves during drills—but the med ward looks unnaturally empty now. It's almost as if, after Melanie Beckett took over, spies from within started draining supplies from the med ward behind her back. It would make sense; the military can be fickle. And my brother did have spies over here that fled at some point.

I wring my hands and face the only adult in the room.

"Mr. Shaw," I say softly, looking up at Savannah's father in a way that ensures my silver eyes do not reflect the lights in the room. "I would like to apologise to you on behalf of my father, for not only his hand in the loss of your son, but anything else that may have caused your family to suffer. If you take me with you to the castle, I believe you can use me as leverage for your safety."

I don't know why I say it, but it feels right.

His brown eyes flash at me, a slip of momentary panic crashing over his face before he pushes his glasses back up the bridge of his nose. He clears his throat. "My dear…"

I swallow the knot in my throat and look down at my feet.

"How old are you?" he finally asks me.

"By my birth year, or by time spent in existence?" I enquire.

The man blinks at me. Jasmine scoffs from behind me.

Technically, I'm centuries old thanks to cryo sleep, but they don't understand that.

Elijah groans as he tries to make himself comfortable in his bed.

I turn and face Jasmine, transfixed as the girl knots her curly mass of blonde locks into an extremely messy pony. She is older than the face she wears, and not because she has lived on Umbra. No, this girl has Magicked her way into a younger life. I came upon that little titbit of knowledge by eavesdropping on Alexsandre one day, disguised as Evaline. The Elder became particularly interested in the runaway James girl after intel came from Terra that Savannah Shaw had been found. No one really knows her story, but the stuff they say about her is still fascinating.

Alexsandre let it slip that he freed her by aid of one of Lythia May's stones. She used that Magic to reverse her age.

Jasmine James is baffling to me. Every expression she makes is childish and very schoolgirl, as if she lost herself to that mask. Every thought is written on her face. She seems fragile, emotional—an open book.

And yet, there's something ancient about her, as if trauma has weathered her. I open my mouth to ask her how old she is, if only to confirm a truth I already know, but Jasmine beats me to the punch.

"Age doesn't matter on this planet, Mark. As soon as you start to understand that you will sleep better at night."

She's right. *Experience* matters.

"Is that why your people have decided to use my daughter as a pawn? Is that why they think it's okay to torture a teenage girl? Is that why they killed my son?" Mark punctuates each word with venom, glaring at Jasmine James.

She leans forwards in her bed, perching her chin on her hands, and stares at the soft-hearted man. No one answers him. There are no answers to a question like that.

The door to the med ward crashes open. Andrea yelps, darting away from where she stood in the entrance. I nearly do, too.

A girl with matted braids covered in specs of blood and a red face from crying prowls through the entrance. Every sound is heightened as she slinks towards me, her hands in claws and her eyes a laser on my chest. I don't know her, but she knows me.

My heart collapses a little, my feet pulling me across the floor and away.

Something like debris or a strip of metal groans from outside; a sure sign of Sector 2 collapsing above.

I stumble over the leg of Jasmine's bed. Hands shaking, I splay them before me.

She grasps me before I fall, nails sinking into my shirt, her frantic eyes dashing over my face. I hang there, limp and immobilised.

"Where is my brother?" she says, her voice chafing.

I tremble under her touch, my nerves flooding the room. Who? Who's her brother?

Jasmine sighs. "The castle, most likely."

They know this girl. This wild thing.

"He went with Melanie to destroy the bridge. How did you get back, Lily? Jesse was looking for you," Mark asks, looking as if he's struggling to breathe himself.

The girl releases me with a hiss. My heart is slamming inside me as I slink away.

"I lost Wrath."

The admission crumples her. The wild, animalistic side of her splinters, and tears run down her cheeks.

"How?" Jasmine breathes from behind me, her voice soft for the first time since I entered this room. I pull myself to the edge of the bed, trying to remember how to breathe.

The girl shakes her head repeatedly. No words come out, but her misery coats me, waxen and fresh. Suddenly, I don't fear the wild girl. I pity her.

Fear is a fleeting thing on Umbra, anyway. You learn to live with it, or you pass it.

Today, I choose to pass it.

Swallowing sharply, I lean over and brush the bloodied hair from her face, giving her a soft smile. Her wild eyes latch on me, unwavering but a little frightened. It doesn't take a genius to guess my father probably killed whoever Wrath is.

I'm about to say that I'm sorry, but Mark speaks before I get the chance.

"How did you get inside the compound, Lily?" he repeats, crossing his arms.

The girl doesn't respond, but I pull back from her gently and look at Mark. "Isn't it obvious? The only way is through the tunnels from 3A. Anyone who has lived in this Sector can tell you that."

Lily blinks at me and smiles through her tears. A guttural sound comes up her chest that almost sounds like a suppressed laugh. "The little Argenti girl is correct."

"You know how to get there?" Jasmine presses from behind me, as if totally forgetting I explained the way in the first place.

Lily nods at her, turning to the disabled girl with a lightness returning to her face.

Elijah groans again as he struggles to turn under the blankets. And, through broken speech, he utters, "Can someone tell Jesse's crazy ass sister that we need medicine? Like, now."

Lily blinks again, her head drifting to where Elijah is like a cat. With feline grace, she stands and stares at the crates of supplies between us and Elijah.

"I wouldn't go to the Kingdom now, if I were you. It's chaos over there. The boat I used to come across the water most likely went up in flames. Besides, as I mentioned, the little Argenti is correct. We need to leave through 3A, but only if you want to freeze your butts off outside or go to Sector 3."

Jasmine swallows sharply. "My back... maybe Sector 3 can fix it."

"And we need a surgeon for Elijah," Mark points out flippantly, his chin jutting to the boy grinding his teeth from pain.

Andrea stirs a little from the door. "I don't want to go to Sector 3. I'll stay here in case there's people from our army still trapped in the rubble."

Lily shrugs, her eyes suddenly void of emotion. "Stay, then."

I part my lips to speak, then stop. Mark notices, his heavy eyes falling on me, and I stumble back a little.

"What is it?" he demands.

I shake my head, lowering my eyes. Stars, these people are so intense. I miss my brother and the seamless way he can work light and humour into the darkest of moments. I miss his laugh. I miss his protection. Even Savannah, who has suffered worse than anyone here combined, is more pleasant to be around. I miss them both.

"There are EXO Suits in the Hover," I admit, huffing out a heavy breath. "They can help the wearer fight when weakened in battle. You could literally fall asleep in them and still fight if you wanted. They can help Jasmine walk again. As for surgeons, the wildlings in Sector 3 have them. If anyone bothered to investigate our history, you'd know all the wildlings are Kingdom civilians who bailed for a simpler life."

Lily hardens her jaw at my words. Yep, she's a wildling herself. She probably even has friends in Sector 3.

Jasmine notices this, too, and asks Lily, "How come you stayed near the Kingdom instead of joining the others?"

Her answer is curt. "I couldn't leave my cats or my brother. I always knew he would return home one day. I was right."

Jasmine sucks on her lips. The light vanishes a little from her eyes, as if she sees more layers to that sentence than Lily lets on.

I watch in trepidation as Jasmine James pulls the blanket from her legs, swinging her dead weight over the side of the bed one leg at a time. Lily watches in a mixture of awe and confusion as the girl makes her way to her, sinking to the floor and pulling herself towards the wildling. No one helps her. We all watch, as if curious to know if she can move herself.

And then, as Jasmine makes it to Lily's feet, she pulls the girl down to her level. To my surprise, the wildling girl allows it. There's not a second of hesitation before she lithely lowers herself to the ground. The two sit and stare at each other, equally bewildered.

Finally, I admit Jasmine looks her age.

"You remind me of Faye."

I don't know who Faye is. From the way Jasmine crumples her brow, neither does she. But Lily trails a finger down Jasmine's cheek in wonder, as if that was the best compliment she could have given the girl. Whoever Faye was, it's clear Lily loved her.

Jasmine holds her breath. She makes it as close to Lily as she possibly can and says gently, "Promise me something."

Lily doesn't speak as she stares at the girl with a finger frozen on her cheek. Jasmine swallows sharply, and everyone's eyes are on her. Even Elijah has stopped groaning for once.

"Promise me you will help me walk again. In turn, I will give you vengeance for your cat, Wrath."

Lily's hands are shaking a little, her face bleached of colour but for a few splotches under her eyes.

My heart hammers. I can see Jasmine's words for what they are. She isn't asking this because she needs the girl's help, but to give Lily something to fight for, something to distract her from her pain.

"Promise me, Lily."

Lily parts her lips, letting out a small breath of air. Resolution sets in her eyes as she takes in the girl who crawled towards her. The girl who is broken but willing to keep her friends from breaking, too.

Savannah Shaw would be proud of her.

"I promise," Lily finally says.

Jasmine beams, as if the girl gifted her life.

Lily grabs Jasmine softly, as if scared to lose her. "I promise to do all that and more. You will not just walk again, Jasmine, you will *run* the way only snow cats can, with life and passion. I promise you that."

Jasmine quirks her lips. "Well, you got me there. I've always been good at running away from my problems."

From behind them, Mark Shaw snorts.

23
SAVANNAH

The generator room has left me hot and clammy. And not because it was warm in there, but because I can barely believe we managed it.

Not only did we succeed in our mission, but we remain undetected. The bomb I set distracted the guards and gave us cover to flee. A miracle on top of another miracle.

I planned to destroy the Dome, but it hasn't quite hit me that the task has been done. All electricity across Umbra has failed. And, in our wake, the land outside the electrical geothermal plant is smouldering.

I grip the edge of my seat, my head ducked as Marcellus flies us away from it all. The night sky blinks above us as our breath clogs in our throats.

"We will have a few days until the workers find enough hands and equipment to mend the generators," I whisper into the freezing dark, blowing warmth into my hands.

Marcellus isn't made for the cold. His entire body is rigid, his fingers shaking as he manoeuvres the Hover back to the castle.

"I give them a day," he grunts.

We'll see about that.

I have never run so fast in my life. My chest is heaving now, adrenaline pumping. We made it past the train station, feet pounding against dirt and skin aching with cold, before lights began to flicker on around the compound behind us, leaving nothing but the embers of our escape bomb.

It felt like we ran flat-out for 20 minutes before they figured out how to turn on the third generator—a generator with enough power left to activate Hovers and power the castle. Not enough to reignite the Dome, though.

I suck in a deep, icy breath, letting the chill burn my soul. The Dome is *gone*.

My fingers tingle with cold as I tighten my grip on the Hover. I can barely sit still, even after pushing my body to a breaking point from running from the plant. My lungs split with the need to scream, to feel the soil under my feet again, to dance in the forest with glee.

The energy inside me is intoxicating.

"The castle looks beautiful without the Dome," I declare as we part through the trees obstructing the structure. The white-grey stone bleeds into the night like a pillar of light against the stars. Warm, yellow light leaks out through windows, casting a glow on the houses nearest the mountain it crests on. The rest of the village? It has all but disappeared in the night.

The Hover ascends and, from the vantage point, I can see the crystalline river twinkling against the night sky. The twisting snake of crystal cutting through the blackness that was once the village is breathtaking.

"If only it weren't so cold, goddammit," Marcel curses under his breath. His words breathe a cloud of fog around his face. "I do pray we encounter the frontline of your army, or perhaps a panicked guard, if only to give me the chance to kill someone and wear their warm blood like a heated blanket."

I scoff. "You *what?*"

He turns his head to look at me.

"There's that smile."

Despite the rigid form of his body and the way he's begun to shiver, I detect a sizzling ember of laughter behind his tone. I laugh at the expression and he cracks a grin of his own.

Not the appropriate time, though.

Screams shatter around us, followed with words of chaos and fear.

I absorb them, digesting the panic I have caused with a devilish tilt of my lips. I lean as far forward as I can, then stand, taking a position next to Marcel. The wind slaps against me, increasing the horrendous bite of the cold like a stinging punch against my skin. The smile freezes on my lips, my cheeks cracking at the effort. I'm too numb to adjust my smile and Marcel sees it, mirroring it with one of his own.

His warmth is the only comfort on this Hover. I can feel a crackle of heat expanding from his near touch as he slinks his free hand down my arm, torn between gripping my hand and twisting his own around me. I shiver, leaning into him, my heart a pounding mess.

Ahead of us, an army has converged.

It's difficult to see if the army has split or if they've successfully taken the castle. The chaos around us is filled with nobility in gowns screaming and clutching their heads and men in black slashing swords in the air or scaling trees.

A few wiser souls have moved towards the castle emitting yellow light and the promise of warmth. My people are here—the army from Sector 2. At the forefront, trying to ease the panic, is Laurence. I resist the urge to go and tell him about the third bunker in the forest. We're too far and there's too many people between us. The castle might be their best bet for now, though from here I cannot see if they're successfully making it inside.

"Well, here's your chance, Marcel," I say with half-frozen lips.

"My chance to spill blood here will only put yours in danger."

The words are curt. Short.

Oh, so he thinks he can win against this, but I can't? I flash him a dark look.

The bitter tang of his Magic spreads as the Hover continues its final incline. It burns my tongue, but I breathe it in heavily, hungrily. His body is on mine, separated only by our leathers. I never asked if fabric halts the flow of his Magic stealing. It never crossed my mind.

"You want to take some of mine?"

His head tilts towards me, his breath pooling around my face in a warm cloud. I inch towards him, the memory of his lips an agonising pinch. I want to feel the burn of them on mine as he sucks my Magic from me. I want to have *him* on *me*. Everywhere.

His chest shudders and he tears himself away. The Hover sways under us, momentarily losing its trajectory.

I gasp as a tree whips past us. Damn, we could have gone into that.

My heart explodes, my skin tingling from where I dig my fingers into his wrist. Our skin burns where it meets. From cold? From the Magic swirling around us? Hard to say. Maybe the burn is just me. Maybe I am made of fire.

We near the castle, the trees thinning as we crest the top of the mountain where dirt turns to stone. The crowd around us thickens, their screams louder than the wind in my ears. Marcel doesn't slow for them. Hell, he nearly runs over a lady in a blue dress, the flowers in her hair spilling to the stones at her feet as she falls.

"Chaos," I breathe, tasting the word.

Marcel smiles, his own breathing laboured as his grip on me tightens. He may not admit it, but he delights in this, too.

I scoff again, my head spinning as he pushes the Hover to a jarring halt before the door of the castle. The stoned courtyard is a frenzy of people and a chorus of words.

Marcel places his lips against my ear, where a circle of warmth pools down my neck as he speaks. I'm a shivery mess, but my body is taut, my face expressionless.

"You wicked thing."

My pulse increases. I grip the man and sink into his Magic. He does not tear mine from me, but I can feel his all around me. It makes my own flare, sending out darts around the castle.

Melanie. Exhausted and sprinting in the village.

Jesse. With Melanie, freaking the hell out.

Jasmine. Sector 2. Flustered.

My father. Sector 2. Jittery.

Elijah. Sector 2. Hazy and half present.

I swallow sharply, my gut swirling.

And then, *Amadea.* Sector 2, nervous.

Everyone is safe and accounted for. And everyone presumably knows the Dome is gone. Good. I would have liked Melanie to bring the rest of my friends and family with her, but I understand why she didn't. Jasmine probably still can't walk. Besides, the Sector will protect them from the Night.

My heart twists a little.

I tentatively fork my awareness out to my foes to see where they are, too. They are exactly where I need them to be. The Argenti are split between bunkers and the castle, but the Elders are all in the throne room. Alone.

"Melanie and Jesse will be here within the next half hour. They are the only ones coming. Amadea is still in Sector 2," I mutter to Marcel, my face inches from his.

The Hover around us shakes as someone rams against it.

Oh, right. The horde of people.

"For the love of all things holy, will you move us before we get trampled?" My words are sharp as I reach for my switchblade. It's a habit to pull the dainty thing out of its holster and slip it up my sleeve, the blade cupped inside my palm. One movement, just one person to climb our Hover, and my blade will slip out and be on their throat.

Marcel chuckles, a sick, hungry delight spreading across his face. I can feel fire exploding over my cheeks, a storm raging in my heart as I glare down at the disarray of people pressing in against us. Some of them widen their eyes at us; others are too hasty to get into the castle to spare us much mind.

"Of course, Your Majesty."

I suck on my lips, force my Magic to flare and pray the adrenaline will work its way into my stiffened joints. I just need to stay warm enough to make it into hiding. Just long enough to bloody live.

"Let's see what the Elders are up to," Marcel says chipperly. His delight is a wondrous thing, glowing in contrast to the fear below us.

I return his cheer with a twist of my own lips. "Absolutely. You know what to do? You know how to find her?"

His chest heaves with glee. He doesn't need to respond—I know the does. After this, he will go one way, and I, another.

"I will tell your friends about your escape plan. Wait for the signal and then bolt like a Hover on legs. We will wait 10 minutes."

10 minutes to get to my friends.

"Will you be okay, though?" I ask, even knowing the truth. His job is much easier than mine. He will be safe in the bunker waiting for me. The hardest thing he needs to do is convince Melanie to trust him while surrounded by our enemy.

I, on the other hand, must face the Elders alone and make sure they don't enter their own bunker. Sounds simple enough.

He grins devilishly and my heart thumps. When he turns to me, what he says shatters my world.

"When you arrive, say goodbye to Elias Hart for me."

With pleasure.

<h1 style="text-align:center">24</h1>

MARCELLUS

I hate the cold.

I hate it more than the sound of Cece's voice right now, which is really saying something, because she is singing an annoyingly ear-splitting ballad from a piano in the corner of the room. She is beautiful, I suppose, in the same way that Venus Collins is beautiful. All stark lines and cold strength.

My pulse ticks, feeding the hot thrum of my blood. Odd, considering it's freezing. I fight the urge to swing Jesse's sword off my back—the strap and pommel digging into my skin in ways I'm not used to—but the man is mere moments away now. I cannot risk it.

Instead, I fiddle with a tech screen, my fingers sliding over the glass. I never use these things, but a certain hacker will.

"Beautiful, Cece," Morana utters. She's a fragile, thin creature with silver Argenti hair reaching past her shoulders. She presses her hands to her chest, staring at the Bloodhound with the same awe-struck expression as all others crowding around the piano.

It's a distraction, because I've told them to keep the bunker open.

All of them have changed out of the EXO Suits my father instructed them to don tonight. Rows of them now hang in the cloak room at bunker's end—an entire military arsenal. A vast power shift from when I had last seen them, lined before the castle ready for war.

All of them now sit in their finery, sipping on wine and parading about pleasantly, as if the world beyond wasn't falling apart.

A muscle ticks in my jaw. Classic Argenti.

It's cosy in here, like an old Georgian reception room. It's filled with dark wood tables with delicate legs, chandeliers with fluttering candles, oval carpets and a variety of leather and cushion chairs, lounges, and daybeds. It was built at the same time as the castle, is cleaned monthly, but is otherwise left untouched. It's the most dated place in the castle, without a single slip of electricity or tech, save for the reinforced walls and door. I'm surprised the alcohol is cold, but I suppose making us comfortable is the first thing the workers in the castle would have been told to do in an emergency. Of course, there isn't enough room for the workers in the bunker, so the guards have started serving us.

I've always thought this to be a dated, twisted system. But at least the Elders pay their staff, unlike the servants of their distant generation.

I tighten my lips and stare at the door, trying to branch out my Magic to find Savannah. It's running dry. Hell, most of the Magic I swiped is running low.

I need to steal more from Cece, if only to give myself some peace of mind, but she's currently occupied, distracting the terrified Argenti with her high-pitch squeal.

I can only spare enough of her Magic to focus on Jesse and Melanie. They are close.

Truth is, this place isn't easy to find, unless you know its location.

The bunker near the cavern of weapons is made to fit 100 people comfortably but built to house 200 if needed. Currently, there's around 30 guards and 40 Argenti inside, most of us crowded towards the front of the bunker in hopes of catching a glimpse of any newcomers. Occasionally, another few slip inside, shivering against the cold. In a way, I wish there were more. It would make Savannah happy to know enough people have found refuge.

A gust blows from the open door, causing all of us near the entrance to stiffen.

Night has barely fallen. It will only get deadlier, colder, and more frightening with the hour. Even the slightest drop in temperature is hell. We're all so used to the consistent warmth that anything else is frightening. Does anyone actually remember what it feels like to be cold?

Until tonight I hadn't. My whole body shivers at the thought that this can get *worse*.

Ugh.

"White wine?"

I don't jump easily, but the guard's words almost make me startle. I break my stare from the door and blink slowly at the guard standing before me. Cold glasses of wine balance on a tray in his hands. I stare at it, flexing my jaw. Every second I don't answer, the guard's pulse rises. The liquid in the glass starts to shake until a fat drop of condensation hits the tray.

If I had any say in designing this dungeon, I would have made sure they served us dry martinis. But I suppose beggars can't be choosers.

"Hell has frozen over outside, Captain! And you serve us chilled wine?" Cece spits, her fingers stilling on the piano. The room goes silent enough to hear the whistling wind from outside the semi-open door. I lift my attention from the glass being offered to me, seeing another guard holding out sparkling wine for the Bloodhound.

The guard before me buckles more with my dismissal but does not move.

I hang my hands behind my back, tech screen between them, and tilt my head a little.

"The Bloodhound has a point," I finally say.

I don't want to drink until Savannah gets here. One martini would do, but anything more is a hindrance. Drinking mutes both thoughts and feelings, and I want to be able to focus my Magic to track her.

I turn away from the guard, throwing myself down on a plush 1800's chaise lounge at the front of the bunker, absent only because people left it earlier to watch Cece play the piano. It hugs my body as I sink into it, swallowing me and eating away at my frozen muscles. Jesse's sword stabs my back, so I flippantly adjust it before swinging my legs up and laying horizontal on the cushions.

I place the tech screen on my chest, watching the way it sways with each lungful of air.

The guard still stands there with my abandoned glass of white wine.

In a huff, Cece pulls herself from the piano, the seat cluttering backwards on the ground as she stands. She storms towards me as she always does when slightly uncomfortable from the attention of her peers, so I swing my legs off the cushions to make room for her. She swipes her hand over someone else's, taking a glass of wine from it, then throws it aggressively on the floor. No one jumps. No one moves.

From back by the piano, Morana rolls her eyes and reaches over to grab a glass of sparkling wine along with the bottle balancing right next to it. In one long swoop, she downs the glass, then refills it.

"MORANA," Cece spits, feeling her movement with her Magic.

Morana reddens but doesn't return the bottle. "Screw you, Cece."

"Stars' sake, Celestine," another Argenti named Baxter says. He wears his silver hair with a trail of black in homage to Venus Collins.

Morana refills her glass. Cece stands utterly still, unsure what to do.

I whistle for her. She hates it when I do that, but it always works.

The Argenti watch us, as if readying for our age-old argument of her insisting such a gesture is like calling her a dog and me insisting she is one. My favourite occurrence was in front of all the Elders on Moon Day—the only holiday we have on Umbra—when we celebrate our survival of the Blitz. I barked at her because her necklace looked like a collar. She threw a plate of eggs at me.

A gust of wind spirals through the door, biting all of us.

Every single person shivers and all arguments halt.

Without the piano or our quips to distract us, panic evolves in the space again.

They start uttering amongst themselves, slinking deeper into the bunker. A couple guards lower drinking trays and announce they will source warm clothing for us. Somewhere, in this large space, they have clothing for any occasion. If there's one thing Umbrans are, it's prepared.

My fingers shake a little, but I refuse to move from my spot by the entrance.

To my surprise, Cece continues towards me. I pat the end of the chaise, giving her enough room to perch awkwardly on the end. She's wearing a flimsy white little dress with whorls of silver over it, and her whole body is shivering from the cold.

Get a hold of yourself, I want to bark out. But I'm shivering a little bit, as well.

She glances at me, eyes hard. I don't meet her gaze, but I hold a hand out for her in question and she immediately places her long fingers in mine, red nails scraping my skin in a claiming sort of way. A flood of ecstasy zeroes into the Bloodhound as I pinpoint the core of her Magic. Deep inside her, like a separate beating heart, it opens its doors for me. I suck it deep within my own hollow soul, the bitter tang of it intoxicating.

She rips her hand back before I get the chance to take too much. With a deep, heady sigh, I fork out her stolen Magic, sniffing out Jesse and Melanie again. It floats down the halls, slamming into guards and past civilians pounding on the castle doors, until locking in on Hayes.

He's nearly here.

"Marvellous," I coo, pulling her Magic back and tucking it away. "My thanks, Cece."

She narrows her eyes at me in silent question. *Why do you need my Magic right now?* Then she demands, "Does this have to do with the doors being open?"

With a grunt, she pulls her legs up onto our chaise, her eyes darting around the room. A guard comes up and offers her a fur jacket. It takes her a moment to notice him, too busy with sniffing out all the souls around us.

A tick of satisfaction lightens in my gut as she hisses, not finding anything.

Why would she? She probably thinks I'm after Savannah or the Elders, and their course hasn't changed in the last half hour.

The Bloodhound snatches the fur coat off the guard before us, then demands he bring us red wine. The shaky guard nearly trips over his feet trying to get it for her, all while she sniffs around the room, her fingernails tapping on the edge of her seat. I suck in my lips, forcing myself to not yell at her to quit it, but then the guard returns with a blood-red goblet of wine. She grins and the tapping ceases.

I rest my head back on the chaise and close my eyes. Jesse's sword is a pain against me and the tech screen still balances on my chest. I feel like a goddamn messenger right now, but it feels oddly delightful knowing the plan when Cece is so in the dark.

My lips twitch a little as Melanie and Jesse finally make it inside the cavern. They take a great deal of time getting through it and, based on how many guards I can feel around that space, it doesn't take a genius to guess why.

Cece has nearly finished her glass of wine by the time I abruptly stand, swinging my legs off the chaise to stride towards the door.

"Are you mad?" Cece screeches, just as I flick a tendril of Magic I took from Morana earlier today out towards the door. Telekinesis, of a sort. The door cracks open, revealing a wide-eyed, flushed Melanie Beckett running towards me at the far end of the corridor.

She trips a little as I poke my head out.

It's hell out here. My teeth immediately start chattering at the shock of cold. I hadn't realised how warm I was inside the bunker.

"Yes," I breathe back to Cece, pulling myself back in. "But we can talk about that later."

Warmth encapsulates me a little, but the cold spears inside the open door. What seems like half the Argenti behind me hiss and wail, their bodies peeling away from it. The corridor is a chorus of screaming men, slamming feet, and the hissing of the wind.

Beckett tumbles inside, her hair windblown and her lips blue.

She's clutching her chest with her metal hand, as if forcing the air back inside her.

I extend a wisp of the Bloodhound's Magic, prying for a taste of Jesse Hayes. A nerve quirks in my lips as I locate him down at the caverns among a sprawl of guards—some of whom seem to sputter out under my Magic, which can only mean they are dying.

It explains the yelling.

She opens her mouth to say something, but her teeth are chattering, so I save her the effort and say, "Bunker 1 and 3 need to be deactivated." I hand the tech screen over to her flippantly. "And once that's done, you need to trigger the failsafe mechanism labelled *IGNIS 1* as a warning for Savannah Shaw. I'll have wine waiting for you."

Before she has the chance to rebut, I turn on my heel. She clutches at her chest, her fingers shaking over the screen.

"What's *IGNIS 1* code for? It isn't in any files on the mainframe."

One of Evaline's nightmares.

I turn languidly and click my tongue before flashing a dazzling smile. "Deactivation comes first, unless you want to see Savannah lose her upper hand."

She glowers at me, just as the sounds of yelling halts abruptly. Hayes is on his way. I shove my hands in my pockets, ignoring the nerves tightening in my stomach.

The girl doesn't move. She's frozen in place, much like all the Argenti before me. I sigh and turn around dramatically. "Well, Beckett? We don't have all night, hacker princess."

She grunts and starts tapping on the screen with a muttered, "Self-righteous pig."

Cece opens her mouth to say something, but I raise a finger, stopping her.

"I'm saving us right now, little dog. If you irritate me, I will chuck you outside the moment Beckett closes the door."

She shoots venom at me as I sit, her eyes slitting. She's taken up more room on the chaise. I kick her, sliding her over. If the glass in her grip were not so well-made, it would snap in her hands. In part, I expect her to throw it at me in a huff, but she's too cold to move.

The yawning pit of heat swirling in my gut threatens to spill when Hayes makes it to our bunker, his eyes flat and hard. His fingers shake around a knife, still wet with blood. He wipes it down his pant leg at the same moment our eyes crash together.

An Argenti behind me growls.

I raise my hand, warning them, and Hayes gives me a firm nod. I nod back.

I spread my Magic towards Savannah, who is now at the entrance of the throne room. My blood boils, the pit of anxiety in my stomach turning into a steady tempo, threatening to make me hurl. I've never been so worried for someone's life before.

Jesse grabs Melanie's sleeve, coaxing her towards the warmth.

Their bodies seem to move in tandem, like two blended souls. His eyes soften as he takes her in, and then his brow furrows when she shakes her head at him. He leans over her to ask something, then pulls his stormy eyes back to me.

I smile as he notices my sword. Time seems to slow between us, but I refuse to be the first one to break. It's easy, staring Jesse Hayes down when your mind is with a free-spirited girl up by the throne room. I let the scent of Savannah Shaw soak over me as he glares at me.

"This is a crazy task!" Melanie splutters, banging the tech screen against the light-up panel by the door. A wire from her metal arm is already connecting the door with her screen.

It's damn near impossible, is what it is, but Melanie's father invented these doors. He invented most every security system on the freaking planet, which is why Savannah called for her aid tonight.

"The faster you work, Beckett, the faster this Night ends," I say absently, tilting my head back on the couch.

A guard comes and offers me a glass of red wine, but I hardly notice it. Or him.

I hardly notice anything around me.

How can I, when I'm with Savannah?

25

SAVANNAH

"Knock, knock, anybody home?" I call out in an annoyingly cheerful voice.

I can practically hear the Elders seething beyond the door. I followed my Magic to find them in the throne room, but it doesn't change the fact I could be walking into a trap.

I slam my fist against the wood separating me from them.

This goddamn heavy door is the last thing between us and the tunnel leading towards their bunker. But I also know they will allocate a team to restoring the Dome before resorting to hiding, which means I have time to thwart them.

If they let me inside this stupid door.

My heart skips at beat. No one from Laurence's army have made it this far into the castle yet—no, they're spreading out through the dungeons first. No one would think the Elders are stupid enough to hide out in their throne room.

I roll my hands into a fist and pound on the door.

The sound vibrates around me, spilling past their hushed voices. It causes them to pause their discussion momentarily, then they continue their chatting, ignoring me. I clench my numb fist and pound again.

The frigid air in the hallway tears into me. I can barely breathe, barely focus, as I reach out and lay my hands against the door. Without Marcel here distracting me and keeping me warm, I'm afraid I'll go insane.

Elias Hart.

The Elders go by numbers for two reasons. First, to keep anonymity. And second, for power. Names have power, no matter how anyone argues against that.

I was safe, once upon a time, as Savannah Shaw. But then my name was spread across the galaxies and associated with the prophesied. Now, my name will forever be a walking curse.

The same way Elias Hart will be to the Elders.

I lift my hands off the wood, huffing. "Helloooooooo."

I think I hear someone trip and stumble beyond the doors. Their voices are hushed. Panicked. No one answers the door.

If Marcel were here, maybe his stolen Magic could whisk it open. But Marcel is down in the caverns, securing the entrance for my arrival. My heart twists a little, nerves spreading down my fingers.

I will see my friends again. Soon.

I can taste them already. Their panic and fear is thick on my tongue as I keep my Magic locked on them like a permanent tracking device.

I grit my teeth and finally scream, "Elias Hart! I request an audience!"

Everything on the other side of the door falls silent.

I hear my own screaming heart pounding in my ears, the fire in the lanterns along the walls crackling, and the sounds of panic from civilians and our armies alike as they cascade in through windows. I need them to open the door. *Right now.*

I need to stall them until Melanie locks them out of their bunker.

I pick at the hanging skin around my nails, resisting the urge to give up and flee as another gust of cold wind smacks into me. But then, miraculously, the door opens.

My feet stumble on the carpet as the heavy wooden door creaks on its hinges, its weight dragging towards me.

"Savannah Shaw," Elias Hart says with a smile. The light in the throne room cascades over him; a shattering aura of stars around his auburn hair. He strokes the sword at his belt, as if hoping the cold metal will coax warmth into his skin. I tilt my head at him and inhale deeply.

"Hello, Elias," I purr. I throw every ounce of venom into those sweet, awful words.

Before he has a chance to change his mind at letting me in, I stride into the throne room. I bring my Magic with me, forcing it out of my body in great heaves. I have no way of knowing if the Elders can sense it, but in case they do, I need to set up the scene by blinding them with it. That way, when I send out waves of it to check on Melanie, it will go undetected. My grandfather, Alexsandre, shuts the door behind me with a shiver. He swallows sharply, drinking in my face. My grandfather is as bright and silvery as the moon. Argenti blood has been injected into his pores. If anyone, perhaps he will sense my Magic.

I stride evenly into the room, not letting the cold night disrupt my lithe movements. The Elders, however, are shaking. Stars, these people look cold. Evaline has a thick fur coat draped around her shoulders, hissing against the ground as her body moves of its own accord. The old one, Eleanor, is practically rattling in her bones. Chilling wind from the ornate windows cascade through the room, dancing in my hair. It causes me to shiver in my leathers, but for now it's the smallest threat in the room.

There's no Argenti in sight, but the Elders are a danger in themselves.

I caress their bodies with my Magic, tasting them. They are familiar enough for me now to get a general idea of their emotions—panic, fear, irritation… those are the dominating ones. It's hard to isolate them to get an individual reading.

I should have been focusing my efforts on tracking them more, instead of honing all my thoughts into friends in Sector 2. *Stupid, Savannah.* I am half blind now, not being able to absorb them entirely. It takes a decent amount of strength to lock my Magic both on them and Melanie simultaneously.

"Your guards are doing a god-awful job at keeping the revolution from storming your gates, Elias," I utter. He winces, his thunderous eyes shuddering at the repetitive use of his name. Good. I intend to keep using it.

"Your army… you…" He prowls forward. Pauses. Checks himself. I watch as he smooths down the front of his navy coat with trembling hands, his breath fogging before him. Then he lifts his gaze to me with a cool expression. "What do you want, Miss Shaw? Another bedroom? Bragging rights?"

My Magic pulses, but I do not bristle.

Evaline shudders, tucking herself so deep within her coat that she nearly disappears.

I drag my gaze over them and the throne room. It seems large when it's this empty, their voices and scuffling bodies echoing with the space. The Night consumes it.

It feels like we are trapped in a constellation. The walls scream of light and space, oozing over our skin. I tilt my head up and see real stars beyond the half-transparent Dome. It's rather eerie.

The dais is empty. Without the Argenti and guards lined up along the perimeter, I can see the walls of the throne room. Blindingly bright, tall white pillars tower up into the ceiling, with painted silver whorls and detailing etched along the white walls between them. Somewhere, there's a hidden door to a bunker.

As I scan the walls, I only give half my attention to the Elders, tracking to see if anyone notices my inquisition. It will only take one movement, one mishap, for one of the Elders to slip and reveal its position to me. I don't even need my Magic if I focus on their expressions.

But these people are too well trained. There is one thing I notice though, and it's enough for a small smile to slip past my mask. Evaline, Alexsandre, and Roman—the Sixth, Seventh, and First—all stand huddled together in a stiff semi-circle. A certain flightiness erupts from their beings when I train my Magic on them, telling me what I already know.

They're my allies, of a sort. I will not leave this room without them. And, lucky for me, they already appear to be a unit.

I twist my arms over my chest, forcing myself to breathe evenly. It's an effort to maintain composure in this cold, but I've experienced worse than this. The memory of real, earth-crushing pain follows like an ache. This cold is nothing compared to that.

I just need to school it.

"I have something you may want, Roman," I say strongly, stroking him with my Magic.

Roman bristles, somehow managing to keep his stern composure despite the tremors of his body. Evaline, on the other hand, flashes him a look as panic flares her nostrils. *More flightiness.* I can't really identify it further than that.

Roman's lips part. As the First and the one who carries the most poise during official meetings, you would think he would be in charge. Hell, I almost thought he was when I first met the Elders. But no, it's clear he isn't.

"Ah, so it's bragging rights," Elias says, cutting over whatever Roman intended to say.

I stop myself from rolling my eyes.

He continues. "Tell me, Miss Shaw. Did my son willingly help you destroy the generators, or have you finally mastered the art of manipulation?"

So, they know Marcel came with me. Of course.

But it isn't that which makes me bite back, "You tell me."

His eyes darken as he rolls the ring with his family crest around his finger.

Tell me how far your security stretches, Elias. Tell me. I would love to know.

I can feel Melanie huffing over the controls down at the bunker. She seems anxious.

I let my Magic slip for a second as a flash of rage explodes from Elias, snapping me back to the present. *Stars, get a grip, man.* It vanishes as fast as it appears, as if he somehow managed to immediately put a stopper on his emotions. Odd. But not uncommon in the castle.

He doesn't catch onto my jab. But that's okay, I didn't really expect him to.

I turn back to Roman. "Tell me who my father is."

The room stills. *Irritation, nerves, anticipation.*

Blood pumps through my body as I stare at them, both igniting from the cold and the anticipation. Truth is, I don't need to know who my biological father is. My mother slept her way into some Elder or Argenti's bed long ago. And that is that.

Mark Shaw is my father. He doesn't need to share my blood for that to be true. But this man has a book filled with Argenti experiments, names, and birth dates. If anyone would know my real father, it would be him. It delights me to watch him bristle at the question.

"You're trying to distract us, Miss Shaw. It's all over your face," the Fourth mutters as he picks a long thread out of his otherwise neatly pressed jacket. I turn towards Elias Hart's lapdog, taking in the plain man's features, dragging out the silence intentionally.

I never got around to breaking into this man's room, but suddenly I am curious.

He's the only one I know nothing about—no name, no insight into his ambitions, nothing. On the exterior, he is a nervous, jittery man. But what is he beneath that?

"The same way fear is lined all over yours?" I rebut, hoping it hits the mark. It doesn't. The Fourth continues to work on his shirt, seemingly bored. He shakes a little from the cold, but he stands so close to Elias Hart, I'd wager he believes they are safe. I turn away from them. "Enlighten me, Roman."

I don't tell them that I have Roman's book, tucked safely away in my room.

I don't need his information. But I need *him*.

"You didn't come here to talk about your linage," the man finally says. "Be a doll and help us fix the power grid so we can save the village from perishing tonight. Unless, of course, there is a point you intend to make first?"

My heart clambers in my chest. No, no. We're jumping the gun. I resist the urge to shake my head at him. We are cutting to the point too quickly.

My Magic clings onto Melanie. *Resolution. Anxiety. Surprise.* It feels like she's getting close to figuring it all out. I just need to stretch out time a little longer.

"I've been digging throughout the castle recently," I admit, changing directions.

Elias Hart purses his lips. Ah yes, he knows I've been stealing from his Argenti.

I smile. "Yes, yes. I stole a few things. But you know the most precious thing I stole? Can you take a guess?"

Rage. There it is again. This time I see it flashing the same time my Magic flares out. Elias Hart is seething, his fingers shaking next to his sword.

"Savannah," Alexsandre says. The word sounds exhausted, but there's hidden meaning there. He says my name like it's a warning.

Eleanor, the Fifth, sinks to the ground with a heavy sigh at the mention of my name. She is turning blue from the cold already, when the Night has only just begun. Elias glances at her, a stab of worry knotting his auburn brows. That split-second insight into his humanity does nothing to grant them sympathy. It just makes my heart explode with agitation, worry, and fear. It cleaves a hole into my chest.

If Eleanor is struggling, they will go into the bunkers soon.

I can't allow that.

George Evans, the Second, moves towards Eleanor just as she darts her eyes to the side of the throne room, right under one of the white pillars. There, the silver art is muted, as if worn down by fingers.

Blood roars in my ears. *There. The bunker is there.*

"Your daughter," I say loudly.

I stole your daughter, you worm. Look at me.

Elias slowly turns his head back to look at me instead of Eleanor. Just in time, for the woman bristles and chokes, her eyes still darting towards the bunker entrance.

"My daughter isn't here," Elias says thunderously. "Our priority are the generators."

"You won't outlive the repairs, Elias. It's too late for that. Instead, think about who you can save tonight. Or rather, who you can kill tonight? Not your daughter or your son. Only I can do that."

It suddenly dawns on him. "You have manipulated them both."

I shrug at him flippantly.

In the caverns beneath us, Melanie acts in haste. But up here, all urgency has died.

"My daughter?" Elias enquires, circling back. "Where is she?"

"Amadea told me you intended to make me kill my mother."

"How much of her loyalty to me have you thwarted?" Elias says. Cracks line his perfectly masked face.

I let loose a little scoff. "You and I are on the same team, Elias. Umbra first, always. Haven't you noticed that yet? I would like to protect your people as much as you right now, so you should consider working with me."

He rebuts, "If I remember correctly, you wanted to kill you mother."

"If *I* remember correctly, I didn't ask to be the one to do it."

His eyes burn mine. I glower back. To my surprise, he looks away first.

Elias smirks. "Amadea has thwarted you. She's been feeding you knowledge, trying to tie our people together. I see. Is that how you managed to destroy our generators, Miss Shaw? By picking her sweet little brain?"

I shrug. Let him think what he wants to think. Maybe he's wrong. Maybe he's right. It doesn't matter, so long as I drag this out as long as possible. Melanie is nearly there.

I release a heavy, suffocating breath, which clouds around my face.

"Let's go to the dungeons, then. Give me Venus Collins," I say, my face now aching now from the cold. It's hard to speak.

Any moment now. We are so close.

"And why would we do that?" Roman says, taking a step towards Elias, his posture regal and his head still held high. But his hands are shaking a little.

For a second, the cold gets the better of me, slugging my brain, and I respond, "She's more important than you think, and she will die in the dungeons. We can—"

"*Why* would we do that?" Evaline repeats, obviously done with my prattling. Her keen eyes are watching me, trying to battle the pain of the cold. *What are you planning?* her eyes seem to ask.

I breathe evenly and assess the threats. Who can I kill? Not Elias. That's a tall order.

The Fourth, definitely. He's too much of an enigma which means he's better off gone. Eleanor, perhaps. She will cause a stir. A second of pause from Elias.

George Evans I should leave as his brain can be of use.

My Magic pulses. A wave of heat stabs into my chest. At the same time, an earth-shattering bang erupts from behind the Elders.

Finally.

I duck, covering my head.

Eleanor screams.

A large pillar near the door breaks in two. In slow motion, I watch the stone crash over the floor. Eleanor screams as a section of the roof falls and George jumps towards her, yanking her out of the way by the arm. It pops out of her socket, which makes her scream even more.

Elias dashes towards the bunker, leaving everyone behind. As he moves, a section of the roof falls on George. The sound of his bones crushing draws out in slow motion.

Craaack. A million pieces of him squashed against the marble.

I lay my cheek against the floor, forcing the sound from my head. It stays there, echoing.

Craaaack.

The cold marble bites into my skin, so I coat myself in Melanie's thoughts. She's happy. So uninhibitedly, profoundly, happy. I soak in it, digest it, let it fill me.

My fingers squeeze around my switchblade. I forget the sharp edge sits in my palm and, immediately, the blade sinks into my flesh. I barely feel it. I'm cold enough that everything is numb, anyway. If anything, the icy bite of the metal is more painful than the cut.

Elias chokes, stopping his dash away to stare at the rubble atop George. Eleanor is still screaming beside him.

I pull myself to my feet with effort, my joints screaming. My body is stiff. The icy metal of my switchblade still rests against my pooling blood as it drips onto the marble. *Drip, drip.*

I have 10 minutes now to get to the bunker. But I already lost my window.

"What was that?" Elias half-screams.

I grin at him, the giddiness inside me utterly intoxicating. "You're too late."

I study the door to the bunker. The bomb didn't touch it, which is precisely what I wanted. I want them to see that door—see what could have been—and delight in their panic when they realise Melanie Beckett just locked them out of it.

The bomb was simply my chance to escape, not that I took it.

At least I'll get to see the look on Elias Hart's face when he realises he's about to die.

I get to watch him lose. Even if that means I do, too.

"Remember, Elias. We are on the same team."

My words are surprisingly loud in my ears.

Alexsandre grabs Evaline's hand the moment his eyes latch onto my face. He sees the senseless smile shattering my face, and he bolts.

Evaline gasps, tripping over her coat, but she follows. Eleanor screams as she reaches for them, but they don't turn back. When faced with death, the Elders fight alone.

"You *witch*," Elias Hart roars.

I smile. "Umbra first. Always."

He lunges towards me, yanking the sword from his belt. I just stand there and smile, for he's already dead.

That's when the next bomb goes off.

26

SAVANNAH

I'm falling.

Down. Down. Down.

Skin shredding. Hair ripping. Blood streaming.

I hear Elias Hart calling my name, but he's gone. We are both dying.

The castle floor vanishes from under our feet and we fall with it. Rubble and rock rain down on us like an exploding moon as another of Evaline's bombs go off.

The castle is whirring past me. It bruises, hits, breaks. And I keep falling. Down. Down. Down.

I want to scream, but the wind has left me. I don't feel pain, though. It rings against me, shredding my body, but I'm numb to my senses. I just close my eyes and pray.

I send one last whisk of Magic towards Marcellus, feeling his warmth. With me, just as he was in the dungeons. Then I sink within myself.

Everything that was once Savannah Shaw vanishes for yet another moment.

Until I become nothing but skin and bones.

JESSE

"Melanie, now! Please."

I drag the girl inside the bunker by the skin of her teeth, my fingers knotted in her clothing. She hisses at me, adamant to wait outside, but eventually relents.

The Second Night is death incarnate. But it's not the promise of death that frightens me, or the way I lose feeling in my fingers. It's the sight on Mel's face. Her lips are blue and her teeth chattering as she shakes against the wiring in the wall. She fumbled as she worked, and I've never seen Mel fumble before.

It makes my goddamn heart fall to my feet.

I recognised the moment she finishes her job—years of watching her work has taught me a few things—and I begged her to come into the bunker. She disabled the entrance points to all the bunkers except ours, locking out or in everyone who knew about them.

Cold air gusts in, ripping over the guards' skins. Argenti... and Marcellus Hart. He stands in the sterile entrance, a warm light from an overhead generator light flicking against his silver hair and my sword still strapped to his back. The man watches me like I'm a game to him, his lips quirking as I unravel before him.

"Don't cry, traitor guard. Your only job was getting your sorry behind inside this room because Savannah seems to still care for you. And oh! Look! The door is wide freaking open."

He gestures to let me pass.

A muscle ticks in my jaw.

His stupid words and his stupid tone heats something deep within me, and the moment Mel grunts from the ground inside the bunker, I launch myself towards him.

"You piece of—"

Marcellus steps back casually. Mel's freezing metal arm grabs me. "Jesse Ian Hayes, NO."

There's already a knife in my hand. I hold it steady, hovering between us. It's warmer inside the bunker, but still cold enough to pucker my skin. We're running out of time. Savannah should be here soon, though.

The bunker is large but feels small from the people crowding here. All of them are my enemies, yet none of them make a move towards us, too busy shivering.

I keep my knife in the air, the temper slowly oozing out of me.

"Get in, Hayes," Marcellus says, his tone hardening with frustration. "And Beckett? Close the door. I'm freezing."

He doesn't look it. He just stands there with his pale hands in his pockets, his shoulders relaxed and eyes scanning the bunker as if bored.

"Savannah—" Mel starts, standing behind me.

"I said close it, Beckett. Savannah still has roughly 11 minutes to get here before I'm going to force you to lock the door. But she'll make it."

11 minutes.

And just like that, the temper returns. I hiss, my body surging, and Marcellus takes another step back.

"We will wait as long as it goddamn takes. We are *not* locking her out of his room."

Marcellus just grins. "She's a big girl, Hayes. She knows what she's doing. I'd wager she's smarter and stronger than even you know. We decided on 15 minutes, so it will be 15 minutes. I trust her choices… do you?"

My body feels like it's in a stalemate with my mind. Heat rushes my limbs, but at the same time, everything inside my head freezes. I want to trust her. I want to trust *him*. But all I really feel like doing is ripping my sword off his back and plunging it deep into his black heart.

Anger swirls within me, but a few Argenti behind Marcellus have started to stand, their silver eyes cutting through the dim room. I need to sit down. We need to close the door.

Damn. If I attack this man, my enemies will kill me here and now. But if I close the door, the room will warm up and the Argenti won't be shivering back there.

I grunt loudly.

"Lock the door, for stars' sake!" a particularly terrifying female Argenti yells from the edge of the room, her strong arms locked around her legs in earnest.

Mel doesn't respond, but I can hear her closing the door behind me. Her tech screen has been placed on the ground up against the wall.

Marcellus turns his back and joins the other Argenti. When he turns, my sword flashes in the light and my whole body goes rigid.

That insufferable, pompous, self-righteous—

"Jesse," Mel mumbles. "A hand?"

Seething, I tear my eyes off my sword and turn to help her.

The wood groans against the concrete floor as she strains with the heavy door. I shove my hands against it and together, we close it. There's still a metal door to cover it—protection that will seal the bunker from the inside—but I will not allow anyone to touch the damn thing until Savannah arrives.

No one seems inclined to. Yet.

The Argenti have started pouring glasses of blood-red wine, handing them out among each other. Marcellus meets them, sweeping his pale fingers around a crystalline glass and sipping at it as if it's a habit instead of a choice.

The sight makes me want to hit something. How dare they sit there drinking wine while Savannah is currently running against time to make it inside?

A guard hands Marcel a fur jacket, his arms bundled with more of them. I cast my eyes around the room and realise all Argenti and even some of the guards are wearing them.

I step back, ready to follow Marcellus back into the weird cavernous bunker, but Mel stays still. She angles herself, making sure to block the door.

Stars, our fighting leathers are so cold. What I wouldn't do for a jacket.

Her chattering teeth reduce to a gentle shake of her body as warmth slowly returns, but my entire body still aches. I'd wager hers does too. Past the unlocked door, frigid air still seeps through the cracks, but it's nothing compared to what it was.

"Lily," Mel utters, realising the people have stopped watching us. Her eyes are imploring, but I find it hard to give her my full attention.

I'm torn between watching her and watching Marcellus, who has now handed his wine over to another Argenti. Unlike the others, her hair isn't silver, but a glowing red. Not ginger or honey-gold, but red. And her eyes… those eyes of molten silver are like death as they slash into your soul. She watches me as I watch Marcellus, her body shivering but her chin high.

My body shivers as we make direct eye contact. My entire goddamn body rocks and I lean against Mel's shoulder.

Marcellus throws his feet up on an ottoman and a different
Argenti there makes room for him. For the first time since entering
the bunker, I realise how extravagant it all is. It's not just the wine.
Stars. The entrance we stand in is sterile, with metal and concrete
slamming from floor to ceiling, but the space ahead is covered in
tapestries and carpets, lounges and ottomans, bars and beds. There's
even a piano.

There aren't just pitchers of wine to go around, either. There's a
circular bar with food and drinks and an ice well that a guard dips
his hand into to fill his whisky glass.

I want one. I pull myself off Mel, but her hand grips the crook
of my elbow.

"*Lily*," she repeats.

I sigh. "What about her?"

"The Second Night. We don't know if she made it to safety."

My heart falls. Everything is cold again.

Melanie stomps on my foot. "She's out there alone."

I turn to the door. Melanie stomps on my foot *again*.

"Quit it, Mel. I heard you."

Her composure is even, her shoulders relaxed, but I see the
tension in her jaw. She's nervous now, which is in stark contrast to
how happy she was when she overrode the codes on the bunkers
moments before.

"I'm not asking because I'm concerned about her, Jesse. I'm
asking because you met her during a Second Night before. Would
she help Tamaz and Laurent survive the Night?"

My answer is simple. "No one is strong enough to survive the
Second Night unless they're willing to lose something of themselves."

She looks at me as if trying to figure that out.

"Savannah better be. I have a bad feeling she may not make it."

I recall what Amadea told us about how Savannah isn't the

same person she once was… but how much more of herself can we ask her to sacrifice?

If it's even possible for my heart to drop more, it does. It absolutely shatters.

"Mel—"

"S-sorry. I'm just scared, I guess."

So am I.

"Let's get a whisky," I stay instead, pushing myself off the wall.

"*Jesse.*" Melanie sighs, exasperated.

The guards part for me like I'm a disease, but the Argenti stand still. In fact, the Argenti on the edge of Marcellus's chaise *sniffs* me. I glare at her, but in doing so my blood runs cold.

Next to her, Marcel traces his finger down her arm like a caress.

I shake my head, eyes lowering for a moment to collect myself. It feels clammy the farther I trek into the bunker, and not because of all the bodies pressed around me. The cold sweat from our dash into the castle has now settled on my skin. Yuck.

I lower a steady fist onto the edge of the closest bar. It's a little strip of wood circling a support beam in the bunker, covered with quality bite-sized delicacies, and surrounded by bottles of liquor and pitchers of iced water. I immediately reach for the opened whisky, surprised at how my hands begin to shake a little as I work open the lid.

I sense the Argenti behind me, but I don't hear him until he speaks. "Your girlfriend is terrified and you abandon her for a drink?"

"Rack off, Hart," I pipe. My voice is an octave too loud in the suddenly quiet room.

Everyone seems to be holding their breathes. It's hard to say whether it's because of me or the still-open door.

I chug some of the whisky. *Damn. This tastes expensive.*

When done I lower the bottle back on the counter with a sharp clunk. Marcellus doesn't even flinch. He just rests his hip against the counter and trails his long fingers down the polished length of my sword.

I stare at it. He stares at me.

"Fight me for it," he suggests.

I inhale a deep breathe. He knows I shouldn't, but I want to. *This is all a game to him.*

Marcellus smirks as I take another chug of whisky. It burns my throat in such a satisfying way, washing away the ice in my veins and replacing it with a heavy ache.

"That's not a fight I will win," I admit. He blinks at me, processing my words. "Care to just hand it over, instead?"

Marcellus sucks on his lips, debating. When he smiles, I swear I can see his canines. "No. I don't think I will yet."

Without sheathing the sword on his back, he rips the whisky from me and departs. Ember liquid sloshes over my shoes, staining the concrete floor. I stand immobile, my heart frozen as he walks away from me, singing over his shoulder in a happy tune, "Three minutes!"

I stare at how easily he turns his back on me, unafraid of me tackling him.

Collecting myself, I reach back over the counter, searching for more whisky. There isn't any. Just clear spirits and wines. With a great sigh, I retreat to Mel with a bottle of red wine and a couple of chicken and grape sandwiches instead.

"Careful, sugar," the Argenti on Marcellus's lounge says to him as I pass. Marcellus is splayed at her feet, letting her twist her fingers through his silver hair. "That one looks like he can hold a grudge."

I tighten my jaw, resisting the urge to look back at her.

"Oh, you'd be surprised. Hayes let's all the best things go."

I stumble. I *actually stumble* at that, my hands almost dropping the sandwiches. But Melanie moves over to me and rips them out of my grip.

"He didn't let Savannah go, you buffoon! He let follow her destiny! Sometimes letting the person you love go is stronger than holding them back."

My chest constricts. Mel is wrong about that. I never gave a damn about destiny.

I blink what I think is a tear out of my eye, causing Mel to swim before me. Mel, my sweet Mel. She doesn't know how I slowly started giving up on Savannah. She doesn't realise that I lost her way before Savannah ran away.

I wonder if Mel knows that I never actually, truly loved Savannah Shaw.

How could I? I was broken from the start, and Savannah was always everything I despised about my life. She had a family to go back to. She had a future to grow into. And worst of all, she had Umbra.

I only had Mel to run back to. I open my mouth to tell her this—to tell her she has always been too good to me, too loyal. Melanie Beckett always saw the best in me and chose me over and over, despite the horrible things I have done.

I never actually told her how much I love her for that. But the moment my mouth opens, the girl shoves a sandwich into it. I choke.

"You are *not* saying anything to him. Not for the rest of the Night."

The tears now pricking in my eyes have nothing to do with the thick emotions in the room. I cough. The sandwich looked nice, but I can barely taste it.

"I wahsnt gaing doo."

The Argenti next to Marcellus looks like she's torn between laughing at me and snapping at Mel for what she said. But she lands on a careful middle ground, withdrawing her hands from Marcellus's hair to say, "Was it Savannah's destiny to be cut up into little teeny pieces by Venus's hand? Or was it her destiny to get blown to pieces in the throne room?"

I blink, forcing down the last of my sandwich.

Marcellus beats me to it. "Oh, the Bloodhound doesn't mean that, Beckett. Breathe. Eat a sandwich. The Night is long and I'm already weary of the two of you."

Mel doesn't eat her sandwich, but she doesn't lash out like I want to. She just drifts back to the door again, her fingers picking a piece of chicken out of the artfully made triangle of bread in her fingers.

Marcellus sips at the whisky then goes back to lounging at the Bloodhound's feet.

"I don't understand you, Hart," Melanie says, resuming her position at the door.

"No one does."

The words almost sound sad.

I notice the guards have drifted back to the edges of the cavern, barely visible except for the gentle way the shadows move around the walls. They never intervene in the quarrels of Argenti, that's public knowledge, but to run and hide? Pathetic.

I move to lift the bottle of wine to my lips, pathetically staring at them all as they stare at me. Once upon a time, I could have been one of them.

"One minute!" Marcel suddenly calls.

Mel jumps a little. The wine stops on its way to my mouth.

She isn't here. Savannah still isn't here.

What was it Marcellus said earlier? *I trust her choices… do you?*

No, I don't trust her choices. Stars, I barely trust *her* anymore. She cares so much about this planet now, she practically glows silver. Her face, when I last saw it, was not her own. Would Savannah still protect Mel and me if it meant losing Umbra?

Stars, would she even protect *herself?*

Melanie's hands are shaking. I put down the wine and grab her fingers. She's squashed the last sandwich between them, the grape juice dripping down her wrist. I squeeze them until my fingers are covered with them, too.

"I shouldn't care if she makes it," I say quietly.

"But you do," she says.

"I do."

Melanie swallows. The cold from under the door is making her teeth chatter. I want to grab her to her chest, pull her to me.

BANG, BANG, BANG.

"Marcellus bloody Hart, you absolute stinking idiot!"

Savannah!

Melanie's eyes flash to mine. She jumps away from the door, fingers reaching for the handle to yank it open. Savannah is here.

Marcellus is still laying on the ground at the Bloodhound's feet, but he's grinning from ear to ear, the whisky swishing in the bottle as he holds it in the air. "10 seconds, Shaw!"

"We have. Stopped. Counting." Melanie pants, her words splintered as she works at heaving the door open. I move to help her and, together, we get it open.

Snow trails inside. Freaking *snow*. Flurries of it spiral around Savannah's head. Her skin is blue, the side of her cheek red from blood, blending into her hair like red icicles. Her switchblade is in one hand, a sword in the other. There's so much blood.

I step back, eyes widening. The long black sword dragging across the ground has a man's frozen hand still attached to the handle.

"Oh, *stars*," Mel gasps.

Savannah doesn't even look at us when she enters the room. I realise she planned for us to be here and she likely already knew we made it, but to not even acknowledge us before making her way to the Argenti casually draped at the Bloodhound's feet?

Melanie grabs her tech screen. I grab Mel's shoulders. And in perfect time, too. Because three other people enter the room. I don't know their names, but I know them.

The eldest comes first, carried in a man's grip. The First and Fifth Elder. Lydia May's mother, the Seventh, comes after.

Simultaneously, every Argenti stands and bows. Even Marcellus.

"We decided on 10 minutes." Savannah is fuming as she catches Marcellus just before his knee hits the ground. She slaps him across the face. "I was—"

She stops. Something clouds over her. I vaguely see her knees buckle, but she forces the pain away and straightens. She was what, exactly? Ready to sacrifice herself again?

Everyone watches her. Even the Elders.

Marcellus swipes his fingers across his forehead, as if making to push back his hair, but the motion causes him to heal the welt on his face. *Stars, that man.* He could end me in seconds if he wanted to. What *can't* he do?

I begin rattling in my bones next to the open door, and I take a step back from them all, tripping over the open bottle of wine I placed on the ground. The bottle shatters, red wine spilling over our feet. Great. Now my feet smell like a mini bar.

"Morana, dear?" the Seventh Elder says to a lithe silver lady with a shaking glass of sparkling wine in her hand. She artfully places the stemmed glass on a marble table and knots her hands in front of her. Then her fingers start to glow and she pushes outwards. The door behind us slams shut in one easy push.

I frown, my body still shaking. If it was always that easy for them to close it, why did they watch Mel and I struggle? Unbelievable.

Mel seems to think the same thing, her cheeks heating, but she immediately hides the embarrassment by turning to the door and locking it. The seventh Elder watches her work with a keen sense of fascination. I don't immediately know why, but I have the feeling she knows Mel… from before her parent's death.

"My father?" Marcellus asks Savannah as he stands to meet her height. He doesn't look at anyone else anymore, just her.

"Probably alive," Savannah says on an irritated breath.

"Barely," the First Elder says with a regal calm as he lowers the elder lady onto a daybed, causing all the Argenti around it to scatter. "Someone get Eleanor a chamomile tea with a tablespoon of honey."

Several Argenti rush to get it, including the Bloodhound.

"Good girl, little mouse," Marcellus purrs to Savannah, making me feel sick to the stomach. He drifts his hands over her cheek, as if moving to heal her. To my surprise, she leans into the touch for a second before ripping herself away.

She drags the big sword towards him. "I brought you his hand."

It clangs as she drops it on the floor. The hand is still gripping it, the knuckles stiff but not yet frozen. The impact loosens it and it slaps against the concrete.

Marcellus reaches down, slipping one of the many rings off the finger with a tentative look. He doesn't put it on his own hand. Rather, he looks at it oddly.

The Bloodhound returns, victoriously balancing a cup of tea for Eleanor. She goes unnoticed as she kneels before the lady, her head bowed. I only notice her because I try not to listen as Savannah begins to speak.

"George Evans, the Second Elder, is dead," Savannah calls out to the room, filling their keen ears all they need to know. "We are luckier than most in this bunker. The Third and Fourth Elders weren't so. They fell when a bomb hit the throne room. If they survive their injuries, we can only pray they have the strength to survive the Night, alongside the civilians who love and care for them."

Wow, the passive aggression in her voice is teeming. Marcellus matches it with a smirk.

He lifts his father's sword, hand and all, and places it on a table at the front of the bunker, where we can all see it. "Your debt to Umbra has been paid, Father. Our thoughts are with you for your safe return."

They're both wildcards.

"Rest easy, my children. Eat, sleep, pray! We have a long night ahead of us," the Seventh says, her coat hanging a little off her shoulders as she addresses the crowd. She trembles a little but holds herself steady, which is impressive.

Savannah shows no emotion, but I vaguely hear the sarcasm

as she says, "Time to pray!" before grabbing the bottle of whisky Marcellus left on the floor and taking a long drag.

Marcellus laughs in her ear, his arm encasing her back. He's practically hugging her as the two of them disappear deeper into the bunker, sipping at the bottle.

I turn back to Melanie, glowering. Her eyes are scanning the room a little nervously.

My body heats. Not because Savannah left with Marcellus, or at seeing how close they seem to be, but because she didn't even glance at me. At us. Did she ask us to come to the castle because she wanted to protect us? Or because she needed Mel's help and knew I could get her here safely?

I grind my teeth, but Mel doesn't have time for my emotions right now. She grips my hand and stands on her toes to speak into my ear.

"Jesse, look."

Unable to fight my curiosity, I turn, expecting to see Marcellus and Savannah giggling together. But there, leaning against the seat the Bloodhound vacated, is my sword.

As if Marcellus had always intended to give it back.

SAVANNAH

"Tell me how you did it," Marcellus asks lightly, his fingers spinning his father's ring. It was on his father's wedding finger. A part of me wonders if the Occupants knew about marriage, or if it's just something his father wore for show. It feels too personal to ask about.

"What *I* did? Nothing." I lift the bottle over the glass tumbler glass, gripping the crystal of with a stiff hand, my body trembling.

I'm not supposed to be here.

I wait for the anger to show and try to look strong. Instead, I feel empty. Lost.

I should have died in the throne room with Elias. It feels wrong neither of us did.

My entire goddamn body still aches from the cold, and the slap of the heat inside the bunker only makes it worse. Only, it isn't the cold that hurts right now, but the absence of it.

The numbness was better. It's not right, to sense the pulse of Silver Magic and feel high on it. It's wrong that I overthrew the Elders tonight. Stars, it feels wrong that I *liked* it.

When Elias Hart came for me, another bomb went off, which I didn't expect. We both fell to our deaths. I didn't see him land—I didn't even feel myself land. I just knew I was dying and couldn't be saved.

I didn't *want* to be saved. The cold felt like an embrace.

Ribs broke as I fell down what must have been at least 3 storeys. Muscles tore as bits of the castle caught and interrupted my fall. Something in my skull was shaking so bad that I couldn't hear, and my vision was blurry. If I were a normal Umbran, I'd be dead. Alas, I'm Argenti, and I survived it and felt everything. Then there was Evaline, shivering with snow drifting onto her hair from the open sky where the roof of the castle once was, holding her hand out to me.

"Come, we must go to the other bunker now. And you must present yourself to be strong so they let us all inside, in case the enemy has taken it."

Let me die, Evaline. I didn't say it. I just stared blankly at the ceiling and let tears well in my eyes.

"No, you're not staying here. Stand."

So, I stood, then they half-carried me. It hurt, but my blood was beginning to freeze and I was already drifting away. I didn't care enough to worry about the way I couldn't walk. So, I just let them drag me.

When we made it to the cavern they found me some *Velox*, which healed my body but not my mind.

I was gone. I lost Elias. Even Alexsandre was nowhere to be found. But when Roman lowered Eleanor on the ground and put a sword on my back, I realised I couldn't be reduced to this.

I saw the entrance to the dungeon ahead of me. I felt something stir. And, better than that, I felt Silver Magic. It was a panicked sort of flare—a spreading of power in a dire attempt to protect themselves. They would not be doing that in the bunkers if they knew they were safe.

We decided on 10 minutes, and yet the door was still open by 15.

I didn't wait for the Velox to finish healing me before striding towards that door. *Hart lied about locking it. He waited longer than 10 minutes.*

Now, Marcellus brushes hair from my forehead. The Velox is still powering through me, though I'm not fully healed. He must have taken a healer's power, too, because he can feel it. I swallow sharply, my body stiffening. His fingers drift down my neck, fingernails dragging down my skin.

"Don't use that all on me," I say emptily.

"My stores are already nearly empty, Your Majesty."

I tighten my jaw, fighting a rebuttal. His Silver Magic cascades over my body. I breathe in heavily, letting it soak through me.

"You didn't plan on coming into the bunker. If you had, you would've been here at the 10-minute mark. Thank the stars I told your friends 15 minutes, or we could have lost you. You wanted to give up and die tonight, little mouse. I can see it all over your face. You need to learn how to mask your thoughts better if you wish to be a ruler."

"You contradict yourself," I say, leaning into him, my eyes burning into his own. "I wish to be a ruler, yet want to die and give up before that even happens?"

"That is the way it tends to go, I'm afraid."

I sink in submission. He is right. His hand moves over my torn clothes, brushing pockets of skin through torn fabric. They pause just under my ribs, where he grabs me.

Pain ricochets and I gasp, nearly shattering the crystal glass in my hand.

"Evaline knew about the bombs, as you said. Smart of her, to plant them. Who knows when you will ever need one?"

Marcellus lightens his grip on my ribs. When he removes his hand, all the pain is gone. "She set off the second one, I'm guessing. Nearly killed you. In the panic, you used my father's sword to cut off his hand?"

I straighten. Something about that declaration makes me laugh. "No."

Marcel smirks. "Sure."

"She ran out of the throne room because she knew the impact of the first would set off the second bomb. And the third. And the fourth. It took me a moment to realise, but when I finally did, I understood we were both dead."

"Both?" he asks, but he already knows.

"Your father and I."

"And yet here you are," he purrs. "Fifteen whole minutes. What a success."

As if he is proud of me, he leans forward, grabs my cheeks, and places a gentle kiss on my forehead. It does something to me, that simple gesture. But because the whole room is watching, I pull away and distract myself before I say or do anything stupid.

Stars, he infuriates me!

He could have killed them all by waiting those extra five minutes. Why? Why is he so happy about it?

I slam the empty bottle down on the table, getting a few nervous looks from Argenti around me, and lift the full glass to my lips. It's almost laughable that *they* fear *me*, when together they could kill me easily. It must be because I am cosy with their greatest killer—the son of Elias Hart.

"You almost killed everyone in here by extending the bunker closure time. That was foolish. As for me being alive... I fell with your father. Broke a few ribs. The only reason I got away was because

Evaline, Roman, and Eleanor made it down to my level when the bombs went off and pulled me out."

I wish Alexsandre had come with them. My grandfather is a great many things, but a coward isn't one of them. Yet, he helped Eleanor, then ran.

It's what most people on Umbra do. Every person for themselves.

"And my father's sword?"

"I was ready to die. One of the others did it, then strapped it to my back. I nearly didn't make it to the bunker and didn't have the heart to tell them it should have locked us out."

"Aren't you glad we didn't, though?" someone's voice that isn't Marcel responds.

Beside me, I sense movement. I turn just in time to see Jesse Hayes slam his body against the bar and reach for my whisky. My switchblade drops and I stab it in front of my glass, barely missing his fingers.

His eyes lift to mine. And I stare into his.

I wonder if he saw the kiss? The angry way he looks at me tells me he probably did. That, or he's just mad at me in general. Perhaps both. It's hard to say with Jesse.

Still, I stare at the man I once loved and smile, happy he is safe and alive. He isn't mine to protect anymore, yet that is all I will ever do. I'm glad he came to find me, because I could not approach him in a room full of Argenti. Mel and Jesse need to stay away from me so long as I'm holding the power the Elders granted me by handing over Elias Hart's sword.

"There's another bar over there." I gesture to the far depths of the bunker.

I take a long sip from my drink. Marcel does, too, as if copying me.

"Are you okay, Savannah?" Melanie asks, drifting over to me. Her hands are white knuckled around a tech screen, as if she's forcing herself not to touch me.

"No," I admit, "but I'm glad you guys are."

"Are you?" Jesse asks, his jaw tight.

I sigh. Take another drink. "Yes, Jesse. I'm glad you're safe."

Melanie fiddles with her fingers. She isn't wearing her glove any-more and doesn't quite seem to know what to do with her hands. I offer her a gentle smile, my heart soaring out to her. I want to hug her so bad but I can't here.

Everyone is watching. Listening. Tracking me. I can't afford to show my hand.

"Do you think Eli, Jasmine, your father…" Melanie trails off, as if basking in regret for leaving them.

It was a wise decision, though. I fork my Magic out before answering, double-checking they're alive. This time, I find some-thing different. Something that lightens my chest.

Lily.

"They're together. Eli, Jasmine, Dad, and Lily." *And Amadea.* But I don't say her name, for fear of being heard.

Jesse's mouth pops open at the mention of his sister, and Mela-nie beams, the news hitting her like a truck. "Are you sure?"

I wiggle my fingers in the air to demonstrate my use of Magic. "Yep."

My heart lightens at the utter love pouring from them. It makes my body tingle so much, it's painful to not openly share the joy with them.

I turn my back on them and drink. *A lot.*

Marcellus tenses beside me but nothing shows on his face.

"There's another bar over there," he says peacefully, repeating my earlier words and pointing to the one I gestured at, his voice venomously sweet. His eyes drift between us all, and I know he knows what I'm feeling. Somehow.

I can't allow myself to share any joy right now. Not with them. They will start asking me questions, and I won't know how to answer, then soon the entire goddamn room will know everything about my friends and how to use them to get to me. I would rather die.

Melanie grabs Jesse, as if getting it, and yanks him away with a grunt.

Marcel drags his hand down my leg, gripping my knee. And he whispers, facing the bar, "You need to learn how to mask your thoughts better if you wish to be a ruler."

I reluctantly hiss back, "I know."

His laughter fills my ears as we turn back to our drinks.

AMADEA

We didn't have to find the wildlings of Sector 3. It turns out they were scouting for us while we waited out the Night.

The hours drag by as the Second Night drips to a close.

Tick, tick.

There's a small, analog clock across the room three beds down from us, where Jasmine sits grunting at it. Every frustrated sound she makes has Lily smiling at her from besides me. I wonder where she found the ancient thing—I miss being around people who know how tech works.

Tick, tick.

The air is musty, metallic, and the distant humming through the walls tells us all we need to know about the air. The backup generators are working overtime.

The time on the clock is wrong, having been chucked in a drawer for so many years.

Mark sighs loudly, withdrawing a syringe out of Elijah Brooke's arm. He found a storage room, filled with things like medicine, clothes, and even drums of white paint.

They're the only ones not watching the clock.

"Melanie," Elijah mutters just once. Then he passes back out due to the pain.

Jasmine groans. She tries to busy herself by running her fingers down a thin glass screen imbedded into the wall, trying to get security feeds up, to no avail.

Tick, tick.

Ugh. I flatten my fingers against Jasmine's bed, where I sit perched awkwardly at the end. My brother is out there in the freezing cold, doing stars knows what, and I'm in here counting against a clock.

"Okay," Jasmine says, throwing up her hands. "This is pointless. We need to get to the castle somehow, find Savannah, and talk to her."

"We will freeze," I murmur absently.

"We spoke about Sector 3," Mark advises.

This entire Night has been spinning in circles. I inch closer to Jasmine, my voice low, yet loud enough for everyone to hear.

"Tell me why you want to go to the castle, Jasmine."

Her blue eyes briefly flash to mine. "To kick ass, obviously," she says flippantly.

I suck on my cheek, feeling itchy. There's more to it than that, but she averts her gaze, afraid to voice her ideas. I glance to Elijah instead as he groans again.

That boy probably knows what she's thinking.

"He needs proper medicine," Lily grunts pointlessly.

Mark sighs loudly, as he clatters a dish of medicine on the bedside table by Elijah's head. "Yeah, he needs painkillers," he says, flicking his finger against a filled tube, causing a droplet to swing against my cheek.

I rub my palm down it, eyes half on Mark and half on the cat girl.

"Okay, nearly time," Jasmine mutters.

Tick, tick.

It is so *not* nearly time. The worst of the Second Night has only just passed. If we go outside now, we would be reduced to shivering, hypothermic messes. My fingers ball in the sheets, my teeth clamping together as I resist the urge to scream.

The room feels hot and entirely too small. Andrea went to sweep Sector 2 for survivors, claiming she was going insane in here in the med ward. I had half a mind to go with her, but I can't risk leaving. What if they all decide they've had enough of waiting and go to 3A without me? I told them where to go, how to get there, and what to bring. They don't need me, baggage as I am. Why save an Argenti girl? We are, after all, their enemies.

Tick, tick.

I wish Jasmine would stuff that clock away.

Elijah mutters in his sleep, which I suppose means he's not in a coma.

"*Melanie,*" he says, her name like a prayer.

My heart squeezes again. I wonder if he knows she's in love with Jesse Hayes? I purse my lips, trying to read the man's pained face, unsure if it's from the unrequited love or the injuries at his back. Probably both.

Lily catches me looking, her eyes flickering. "This circle of people feels downright incestuous sometimes," she remarks, her fingers stretching in the air as she pops the aches from her back.

Jasmine scoffs.

Lily smiles a moment, then it drops off her face again.

"Any luck with the security feeds, Jasmine?" Mark asks. His shoulders are heavy as he pulls back from Elijah, and something flickers in the muscles on his face. This man never smiles. It's as if laughter has all but bled from his world.

I don't blame him, really. Like Savannah, he was forced into a life he never wanted. He lost the life he built for himself and looks to be broken beyond repair.

I squeeze my hands against my lap, pushing the palms against my jeans. The fabric scratches against my legs. I can't say I prefer them over my usual dresses, but I've worn more hideous things before. Dressing in a rucksack while pretending to be poor once was the worst. It smelt like snow cat urine.

"No." Jasmine huffs, letting herself roll back onto the bed. Her legs get knotted under her, arms shaking from all the weight she was keeping on them. "I'm not Melanie, okay? Freaking hell. Never thought I'd wish she was here right now, but here we are!"

Mark grunts. "Maybe answer *without* the attitude next time?"

Jasmine grinds her teeth. "Well maybe if I wasn't a broken goddamn doll, I would be more chipper!"

"Maybe it's about perspective," I interject, unable to bite my tongue.

All of them train their eyes on me, Lily included.

"Oh, and what have you lost, little girl?" Jasmine snaps. "You Argenti always prattle about how annoying and pathetic we lower class are, but have you *ever* considered what it's like down here in the muck?"

Her face is red, eyes blinking rapidly. The words cut something in me, but I don't respond. Only a fool would respond, even though I wish I could tell her she's wrong.

All Umbrans have lost something or someone. We are no strangers to pain.

"You," Lily says, turning her eyes on me. "You have lost."

More than you know, I want to say. But I don't, because they will never understand if I tell them I lost my childhood. I lost my innocence and identity before either could fully form. Most of all, they will never understand if I told them I lost my mother. Why would these people care if I told them I have memories of the Occupants getting burnt alive?

A loud ping echoes through the room, saving me from answering.

Mark jumps, striding across the room to where Jasmine has planted herself under the clock. On the screen, words start to unravel.

I can't read them from here, but Mark fills us in. "Hello, survivors. We have heard your sections of the Ley have been disrupted and have come to escort you to safety on behalf of The Fated. Kindly evacuate all personnel to the discharge point." He stands for a moment, his body freezing, and then turns to face me directly. "What does that mean, Amadea?"

A coldness has seeped through my body. Somewhere outside, the world is still brisk and deadly, yet here they are. I wring my hands against my jeans, stand slowly, and transform my hair into a muted shade of blonde. The eyes I change, too, making them blue. It's enough to hide the fact I'm an Argenti.

With shaking fingers but a heart made of steel, I say, "Sector 3 has found us. I suggest we go to 3A now."

Only the clock responds.

Tick, tick.

30

SAVANNAH

"The flurries look like sleet," Melanie says with her back turned. "The Night is warming, so the snow is calming."

Jesse grunts and clenches his orange juice. It's all the guards would allow him.

My muscles ache from sitting at the bar for hours with Marcel, but I straighten at her words. A few Argenti have drifted off to sleep, while others play cards or engage in light conversation. All the powerful players have stayed alert.

Behind me, Evaline has plucked several ladies from court and have gotten them to feed her information. She seemed to pick at random, which makes me think they are her spies.

Next to us, Roman has assembled an armed force, his face set in a cold sort of focus. He's going to send them out when the Night ends to scope out the damage. No one knows what they will find out there.

No one, it seems, but Melanie Beckett.

I smile against the rim of my glass. Alcohol has long been forgotten, and I sip at chamomile tea much like Eleanor had before she drifted off to sleep. The Argenti love that woman. It's a beautiful sort of respect.

"Lily?" Jesse dares ask Melanie. Her head is over her tech screen, where feeds scatter across it. I can't see what they show from here, as she's hiding it under a coat she got from a guard and pressing herself against the corner of the bunker. Still, she sits close enough so I can overhear. Tactical, as always.

"Nope. But our friends are on the move," she says. At that, she glances up at me, then Marcel. "With others."

I swallow sharply and nod briskly. Melanie sucks in her lips and turns her head back to her screen.

Others? That's the part I don't get. I brush my fingers against Marcel's.

He's barely spoken, except to ask me to share my tea with him. When I poured him some into a small porcelain cup, he merely smiled and said, '*Thanks*' before placing it in front of him and forgetting about it. Every now and then, he twirls the cup in a circle on the table, as if his fingers are trying to remind him that it's there.

I wish he would say what he's thinking.

I lower my chin into my palm. The waiting part of this plan is the worst. I wish I had something to do, like Roman, Evaline, or Melanie, but anything I want to do right now is dangerous. The world is watching me right now.

I'm just so *bored*.

Melanie gasps a little, then stashes her screen into her lap. I fight the urge to turn and face her, trying to not draw any attention to her as her eyes start darting around the room.

She nudges Jesse. He grunts at her.

"Please, no. For the love of— ouch." He swears.

I bite back a laugh. She pinched him, her eyes narrowed in a way that says, *do what I say you goddamn baby.*

And, of course, he does. He stands slowly, quietly, then walks over to us.

I lift my head, eyes batting in confusion. But he isn't looking at me.

"Ley Lines," he says gruffly to Marcel. "What do you know about them?"

Marcel rolls his shoulders slowly, like a snow cat waking from its slumber. His face is empty save for a small muscle ticking against his lip. He tries his hardest to hide it as he flexes his fingers and reaches for his cold cup of tea.

I tighten my hands around my own, heart hammering.

"What's it to you, soldier boy?"

Their eyes don't meet, but I swear I sense a pulse of Magic dancing off his pale skin.

"Soldier," Jesse starts, his mouth slightly open. But he shakes his head. "Never mind. What do you know of it, Hart?"

Marcel's eyes twinkle a little as he turns to him. "Why? Does your lady wife over there have a sudden urge to learn our history?" He mocks a gasp. "Dare I say, she doesn't know it? And here I thought all Argenti spawn grew up being spoon-fed the atrocities."

Jesse growls. "Don't be an ass, just answer the question."

I blink. Jesse's eyes flick to me briefly, unfeeling and slightly unhinged in his fit of irritation. His sudden anger jostles me. I never realised how prone to fury the man can be, because no one ever attempted to get a constant rise out of him the way Marcel does.

The only time I've ever seen this kind of fire from him was when he was locked in a fight with bloodshed all around him. It's when he is his most authentic self, in a way.

The realisation is a little unsettling.

Marcel just leans back in his chair, unbothered by it, and links his hands behind his head. In a mocking way, he begins to word-vomit carefully selected nonsense, though I greedily cling to every word.

"Umbra is a beautiful place, is she not? The power we get from her core channels through the bodies of her greatest creation—the Argenti children. We are extensions of Umbra itself, powerful and miraculous in every way. But what makes us powerful, Hayes? Is it because Umbra chose us? Or perhaps because the people chose us?"

He winks at Jesse, rustling his feathers just because he can. "I was one of the first. Do you know how old I am, Hayes? These eyes have seen many things. Many wonders. I suppose that's why a great deal bores me these days. I like to be delighted, but it's hard to delight me. My father hates how I crave it and how I occasionally vanish in pursuit of it, hunting for new knowledge and secrets of our planet. But what is a year to an Argenti? What is two, three, four years, to someone who has seen centuries? He loves my presence, my dear father, but allows me to satiate my curiosity sometimes."

It seems like Jesse is seething. The man can barely keep himself still as he knots his hands in front of him, trying to force himself not to lash out at Marcel.

Ley Lines.

Marcel knows. He told Jesse he knows, yet the man doesn't quite seem to understand. Jesse just stands and waits, as if expecting more information to follow. Does he not realise the amount of information he's been given?

I look at Melanie, whose eyes have narrowed. A few Argenti stopped to listen to the speech but grew bored midway. Marcel is known for his gloating tangents, and I guess it takes a trained ear to hear them for what they really are.

Fact-spitting, information-grabbing layers of code.

"My chambers, as soon as we're out of the bunker," I say, glancing between Jesse and Melanie. Only Melanie keeps my gaze. Jesse just sighs, as if finally realising the information he asked for was lost in translation.

Melanie smiles. Nods.

My eyes flicker to the front door where Roman has begun assembling guards.

I grasp Marcel's hand. His fingers are cold and still, yet a wad of Magic crackles against my skin. I don't know what type of Magic he's been using, but he's still doing it.

I fight a long shiver, twisting my fingers through his. Melanie sees and understands.

This man is mine, and his information is mine. We will continue this conversation later.

Marcel cracks a wide, devilish smile.

Ley Lines. Stars. I'd heard the words before on Terra, but it's more a myth than anything widely proven—veins of power that twist through the earth, or something to that effect. Is it possible Umbra has such a thing, as well?

Better yet, can I infuse this into my plan?

"And now," he remarks, "we wait for the flurries to sow."

We wait. Only then will I get to speak freely with my friends.

My heart cracks a little, but I bury it.

I turn back to my tea. And wait.

31

AMADEA

They don't have faces or eyes. How will they see through the snow?

This is my first thought. The second?

"What if Andrea forgets to search a room and people get stuck in Sector 2? What if the generators run out before we return?"

My voice is barely coherent as we navigate the cold Night, our small party surrounded by men dressed in long outfits covering their faces.

The generators won't run out because everyone in Sector 2 can leave once the Night ends. They can disable them during the days until returning inside the Sector and switching them back on for Nights. If they do that, they have weeks.

We made it possible by leaving 3A open and painting arrows towards the exit with the tub of white paint left behind in the storage room in the med ward—Mark's idea.

Andrea is inside somewhere, finding survivors. It's a big job for one girl, especially as she doesn't know Sector 2 well. She hasn't seen the plans or heard people in the Kingdom whisper about secret rooms.

My heart thumps, which has nothing to do with the wildling face I stare at. They found us as we emerged from 3A. We are in their custody, though I'm not yet sure what that means.

They lead us through the snow, the crisp air biting through the layers of thermal and snow gear Mark insisted we wear. It felt silly, being donned in so many layers. But the moment the door to 3A groaned open, I was grateful he was so adamant.

"Oh, nope, nope, nope." Jasmine starts squirming in the arms of the wildling carrying her. "I'm a summer girl, I'm not going to—"

Her words are cut short as the wildling takes her outside. Mark goes next, his teeth chattering and cheeks red. Something heats in my heart at how he rolls his shoulders back, straightens his body against the chill, and tries to put a calm face on for us.

The cold of the open hallway is *nothing* like stepping outside. The world hits me like a slap.

My body is shivering underneath the layers of clothes, and Lily comes up next to me and places a gentle hand on my back.

The girl is dressed in more furs than thermals, her eyes thinning against the cold wind tumbling towards us. She doesn't bristle like the rest of us, but for some reason that doesn't give me the strength I suspect she hopes it does.

My feet slow for a moment, tripping over a little from the cold.

Wildlings form a wall, blocking us from heading back in. The dimmed corridor is humming with a deep red light, basking our faces and making us appear haunted.

Elijah is pushed past us in a glass capsule attached to wires and tubes on the sterile pillows they've laid him on. Snow catches on the glass as they push him outside, floating like a Hover. I've never seen a device like it, which is unsettling to say the least.

The Kingdom is supposed to be the hub of all technology, yet here are the desert wildlings with glass cases that drift like a coffin, pumping green liquid into the arms of the unconscious boy.

"Is that from a *Tenere* tree?" I ask one of the wildlings beside me.

The shade of green closely resembles my memory of the *Tenere* sap that kept me in suspended animation for over 200 years. My cocoon was built from the tree sap itself and had a life of its own. It felt like its heart beat along with mine in the same way the core of Umbra swells into my palms when I harness Magic.

But this tank? It doesn't feel like that. Besides, the only people who knew about harnessing the sap for *Tenere* trees in such a way were the Occupants… right?

Lily stiffens and cocks her head, taking in the capsule as it drifts away.

A tall wildling leans forward a little when he walks, and grunts, "Keep moving."

They carry supplies with them—including our offerings from the Hover Jesse stole from the Kingdom—and I can't help but feel we are a prize being shipped back to their fortress.

My gut feels like it's at my feet but Lily coaxes me and I follow obediently.

The red light behind us illuminates the ground outside of the military base. I always thought the land outside Sector 2 felt like a graveyard, but it's more extreme at Night. The wind tears at my face, threatening to rip my hood and my earmuffs off, but Lily grabs my neck and holds my head down against the gust. The wildlings seem unfazed, drifting through the gale with their cloaks snapping like wraiths in the night.

"Wh-e-ere are w-we g-going?" I chatter to Lily.

She lifts a gloved hand past Jasmine and Mark and over Elijah to where a long, flat slip of glass covers the ground. It looks a little like one of Umbra's desert millipedes, complete with divots and legs. Except the legs look like gliders.

"Sand digger," Lily mutters, "with ocean gliders."

I have no clue what that means.

"Is it s-safe?"

Lily sucks in her lips, either in uncertainty or to mask her trembling, before saying briskly, "My cats hate the sound of them."

I squint at her through the gale whistling like a war alarm as it plays in the air, howling past the rocky terrain. It makes it hard to walk as it pulls at our skin, our clothes, our hair. I miss the comfort of buildings and trees around us, my heart suddenly aching for home. I wrap my arms around my chest and Lily notices, tightening her hold on me.

"My cats can't reach me here," she says so quietly her voice nearly gets lost to the wind. It sounds like goodbye as the wildlings pour us into the sand digger.

The sand is supple at our feet, shifting and hissing under our footfalls in contrast to the solid ground closer to the Sector. The sand digger's rear is the only part breaching the sand, where a yawning door with a flapping red curtain whacks around in the wind. The rest of our party goes in before Lily pulls me inside with a quickly drawn breath—as if she's trying to gasp down a lungful before diving underwater.

The sand dagger is quiet save for the sound of wildlings taking off their gear. Men and women alike hang them on hooks the same texture as the glass-like exterior of the sand digger.

I shake a little in Lily's grasp, dragging my eyes around the circular thing. Down the digger, metal bracelets like rivets intercept the glass all the way down to the control room, where a semi-circle of lights flicker. The only other thing breaking up the glass is a strip on either side for the ocean gliders, as Lily called them, which extract and drag us down into the ocean. As the digger starts, we can see all the sand scraping up against the surface and the edge of the ocean yawning open before us.

Mark kneels onto the floor and grips his head with one hand.

The other, he balances on Elijah's floating coffin. A wildling lowers Jasmine down next to him, gently positioning her legs on the ground right above the glass.

"I'm going to be sick," Mark says with wide eyes as we descend.

Jasmine wails in agreement. Her fingers splay on the glass as she tries to wriggle towards the metal section Mark is on.

I don't blame her. I struggle towards the digger's side, morphing my body into the wildlings' clothing where I don't feel like the ocean can swallow me.

Only Lily stays still, her eyes glazing as she keeps them locked on the wildlings instead of what's below her. But her pale face gives her away.

The sand glider is near silent as it pushes us through schools of fish and coral, then deeper into the depths. The wildlings stand against the walls, their eyes alert and narrowed. They are all different ethnicities and races. Most are around the age of 30, with youthful bodies from the Umbran air but skin marked from years of living in the desert. Their eyes are hardened and their hair bleached. None are Argenti.

"What do you want from us?" I ask timidly.

Several turn to look at me, while others head down to the control room. I count nine wildlings before training my eyes on an olive-skinned man with long, braided hair. He doesn't answer me, but a lady with mouse-brown hair beside him says, "A loaded question, little one."

Lily leaps on it. "Tell us about the Ley Lines."

The olive-skinned man responds, "Not yet."

Jasmine, still prying away from the glass ground, wails again. "I want to *go home.*"

I angle my head at her. Where is Jasmine Spark's home, I wonder? Surely not the castle she is always mentioning?

Mark swallows sharply and gives her a hand, to which she shakily reaches for.

"Then tell us who The Fated is," Lily counteracts.

"You do not know?" another wildling asks, this one a man with dark hair and a metal leg. I blink at the leg, my stomach twisting.

"Savannah," I breathe, answering Lily. It's got to be.

Mark's eyes dart toward us. "What about my daughter?"

I flinch. As does Lily. A handful of wildlings from the control room turn, smiling.

Jasmine regains her composure enough to say, "Yeah, if you start talking smack about my friend, you're going to learn just how scary I can be. Even without legs."

But sprawled like that, her eyes wide and chest heaving, I nearly laugh. She's the least terrifying person I have ever met.

Now they know who they have in their digger, trapped, at the bottom of a blackening ocean. My stomach churns at the possibly of what they might do to us now. The urge to change my features prickles under my skin, but I clamp it down.

Lily looks at me. I don't meet her eyes and instead catch Jasmine's gaze. Her face is pale, but not from the digger.

We all know the lore of Sector 3—every child on Umbra grew up hearing about it. The wildlings are a special breed of Umbrans who fled the main continent during the Blitz. During the rebuild, they stayed there, claiming some sections of greenery had survived and offered them as much sanctuary as the slip along the Kingdom. Rivers veined few and far between, and most of the greenery reduced to tough desert shrubbery.

Many people died off quickly. The Elders tried to offer sanctuary, but they never took it. Instead, they offered to trade with the Kingdom. Plants, food, spice, and medical herbs for a portion of technology the Elders shipped out from the weapons centre. Just enough to survive.

The Elders didn't give the wildlings much, but the wildlings gave plenty. It was enough for them to be classed a Sector, due to their input, but more importantly, it was enough for the people in the Kingdom to leave them alone.

The stories said they are an incredibly spiritual people.

They don't use their weapons for death, but for innovation and worship. They actively practise to date, praising the original Occupants of Umbra and the land we were given.

Arguably, they know more about the planet than any other Sector. The fact they have an interest in us and 'The Fated' should probably be concerning. All of this goes over Mark's head, though, and he sits waiting for an answer.

Eventually, one of the wildlings obliges. "We are servants of Umbra and believe The Fated will help restore the planet to the peaceful home it once was."

Jasmine releases a long breath.

"You said you're here on her request. Are you in contact with her?" Lily asks.

The girl with the mouse-coloured hair simply says, "Yes. She is one with the Ley."

Huh? I glance at Lily, wondering if she got that. The girl looks at me and shrugs. Even Jasmine is frowning.

Mark opens his mouth again, but I hurriedly speak before he has the chance to spill any more of our secrets.

"The Fated currently resides in the palace with my brother. She sent me to these people for protection from the politics and what I assume was the plan to destroy their Dome."

Carefully placed truths, spoken in a way to heighten their importance and align with the morals of the wildlings. "We are a collection of the weak—her friends and family wounded from the ongoing tensions. We come to you peacefully, with crates of recent Umbran tech, in the hopes you can shelter us and return us to our strength."

The wildings closest to me smile. Even Lily gazes over at me with a level of pride.

The courtier in me is glowing as I step forwards on slightly shaky legs. Jasmine moans as I step on the glass, as I hoped she would, and some wildlings turn to face her.

"The boy needs surgery and the girl beside him clearly cannot walk. What of the man kneeling next to them, and the wild girl on your left?" the olive-skinned man asks.

Who I am to them is immediately clear: a courtier from the Kingdom who turned and ran. It's exactly who I want them to see me as.

"The man is the father of The Fated, as he earlier declared," I say, trying not to wince at the information being spilled. "He hails from Terra, and was thrust into politics he never wanted to be involved in. The wild girl comes from our Sector but escaped her duties years ago. She lives in the desert, much like you."

Lily grins at that. I don't tell them *which* Sector. Let them figure that one out.

As expected, they brush over it, asking the other open-ended questioned I laid out for them. "How does she survive the desert without help of the Ley? Or the technology?"

She answers somewhat proudly. "How does an animal survive the Night? They use their fur, their tough skin, their resources. I scavenge the edges of the Kingdom, picking from them just enough to not get noticed. I eat in the wild and I sleep in abandoned dwellings. It's a simple life. Better than living in the Sectors, wouldn't you say?"

A couple of the wildlings grunt their approval. And it's that which makes Lily's face turn sour and her eyes drop. What was it she said, back in the Sector?

I couldn't leave my cats. Or my brother.

The ocean spins under my feet, waving under the glass. My feet begin to shake a little, but I don't step back. Instead, I cup my hands neatly and try to smile at the wildlings.

What they say next surprises me.

"You are wrong, child, about The Fated's father," the mouse-haired wildling says, her eyes pinning me. Mark bristles a little, but thankfully keeps quiet as she continues. "The Fated was a product of experimental abuse. Her mother, that power-hungry Argenti woman, likes to demonstrate her Magic too much. She was their perfect victim."

My body starts shaking then. My ears start to ring, my fingers itching to cover them to stop hearing the words. But I don't as the wildling continues.

"It was on the eve of one of their festivals at the end of March. Their celestial doomsday festival. We had a delegate in the Kingdom that day."

My heart instantly sinks at how twisted this 'festival' can become.

Some of us call it Moon Break Week. We have it every turn of the year—a week-long period of mourning where people hardly leave their houses, sometimes drink themselves silly, or cast blessings into the river. The anniversary of the Moon Blitz.

It wasn't meant to be annual, but when enough people mourn at once…

Every year I spend the week of Moon Break with Marcel, locked up in one of our rooms—usually his, because I can never sleep well in my bed when plagued with memories of the sky falling—and we order food and play card games on his balcony most of the day. I sleep in his bed and he sleeps on a daybed outside. It's the only week we ever talk about mother. It's the only time we allow ourselves to fully succumb to that sadness.

But there are others who spend that week differently. Most of the Argenti party and drink, spilling their guts over the balconies of the castle. Some of them celebrate it as the day we became gods, while others drink to mourn their parents and to forget the memory of death.

The Elders often join them. Especially Roman, George, Elias, Connor and Alexsandre.

Alexsandre usually mingles with his Argenti test subjects, like the Bloodhound, whose silver blood he has tinkered with over time.

The Fourth Elder, Connor Stearn, usually sticks by my father. Connor is flighty and nervous and his survival mechanism is to stick by the most powerful.

Which leaves George and Roman, the Second and the First.

Being a scientist, George often experiments with his substances. He usually passes out on a daybed, sometimes with the Argenti coddling him.

Roman is all power and regal fury. He's a good man, at times, and has the same ideal for Umbra that Savannah wants, which would make him a powerful ally. But I wouldn't like to know what he was doing while on the drink.

Which is why it doesn't surprise me much when the wildling says, "Roman Laurent raped Venus Collins in the apex room, under the stars, in front of other Argenti. When he was done with her, the Argenti took her down to her father, Alexsandre Collins, for him to play around with her blood. Alexsandre wanted to experiment with bloodlines, and Roman likes to sleep with power. Venus probably would have said yes to both, if they had asked. Instead, George Evans slipped her a concoction. None of them knew their curiosity and experiments would be the product of their downfall. I suppose when The Fated was born with the dark hair of her father and the pale skin of her Argenti mother, they assumed the bloodline experiment didn't work. The Fated passed as Terran, yet her blood is pure energy."

Mark Shaw vomits on the glass floor of the sand digger, and Lily sinks to her knees, gripping her heart in horror.

My legs shake, but I force myself to stand tall. *Focus. Be a courtier.*

All the wildlings are analysing our faces and reading our response.

"You're kidding. You're joking. You're actually not serious," Jasmine says, struggling to find anything else to say between little gasps. Her skin is pale, like she might vomit, too. Especially because the sand digger has begun to climb out of the ocean.

A bout of what feels like sea sickness floods my stomach, too.

The olive-skinned wildling takes a long, deep breath, his eyes tracking Mark Shaw, who is trembling on the floor, his eyes glazing over as he stares emptily down at the fish.

He isn't weak, I wish to say. *You guys are just insensitive and blunt and this submarine thing is making us all feel faint.*

A wildling man from the front of the ship turns and says with a quirk of his eyebrow, "This isn't a joke, broken one."

And the olive-skinned one adds, "We have memory vials to prove it, if you'd like to watch the scene back in real-time."

I almost faint.

This time, Jasmine does vomit.

JESSE

The one thing no one warns you about with wars is how the morning after feels.

The bloodshed, the screaming, even the haze of the fight can be therapeutic in a way. Fatigue is but a memory, pain is but a thought, and the world becomes a blur of colour.

This is something my mentors told me. They all spoke about the adrenaline and the way a man's instinct takes over. They taught me how best to train so that the right skills become the right instincts. But we were never warned about the morning after.

Everything slams into you at once. Reality shakes you from the trance.

Mel squeezes my hand, her prosthetic fingers solid in my own as we make our way out of the bunker and into the annihilation of the outside world.

This is Armageddon, I think to myself.

People from our bunker have spilled out around us. Most have gone into the castle, but some have followed us outside. All the Argenti do is stand and stare, huffing and making silly noises as they take in the dead bodies around the castle. A few survivors, covered in ice and soot, crawl towards them with pleading eyes.

A few are rebels. Most are villagers.

There are many more dead than there are alive.

Bodies are everywhere, in various stages of blue in the snow. The flurries stop as day breaks and tips of golden light shine over the snow-topped trunks of burnt trees and blackened rubble. Behind us, the section of the castle that once housed the throne room has split across the flowers and hedges below.

"Oh," Mel mutters, a tear drifting down her cheek.

Without thinking, I pull her to me, my heart thumping loudly against her head as she buries her cheek into my chest. I hold her tight and don't let go. I can't, even if I wanted to.

Down in the village, manors have burnt down, the flames still sparking into the sky. Fire has scorched the once-beautiful array of flower and fruit trees down in the village.

We stand on a cliff at the edge of the path travelling down to it, the stone under our feet still slippery from the melting ice.

My heart snaps as I take in the wasteland. It reminds me a little of Silver Valley.

"Why would they burn the houses?" I ask. "To keep warm, you think? Hopefully no one was left inside."

Melanie yanks away from me and glares at me hard. "They would *never*—"

"Mel," I interrupt softly, pulling her eyes to mine. "Savannah took down the Dome. These people haven't known cold or fear since the Moon Blitz. To survive, they would do anything."

She puts her hands over mine, lowering them from her cheeks. "No, Jesse. They wouldn't do that. The villagers are kind people. They wouldn't—"

"Do we think Tamaz made it out? Laurence? Our armies?" I

interrupt, noting the way her eyes had started to glaze as her thoughts became sad and dark. I plant the thought in her mind to distract her from self-imploding.

She takes the bait, her eyebrows furrowing. The sight melts my broken heart a little.

A tall, female Argenti comes up behind us at the mention of *armies*, her fingers flexing a little as she takes us in. But she freezes instantly when the sight of the burning village comes into view, her small mouth popping open.

"I don't know." Mel untucks the tech screen from under her coat, but I grab her hand to stop her from doing it here and now.

She sees the Argenti at that moment, too. The woman lets out a long wail, and a guard and two other Argenti come rushing over to look at what she is seeing.

I hang my arm over Mel's shoulder. "Let's go."

She tries to respond, but all she manages is a short inhale of air, her breath catching on a sob. She forces it down before it comes out, but her eyes look hazed.

It undoes me.

Melanie's home is a nightmare. Not all gone, like Silver Valley had been, but the beauty of it has long since vanished. To make matters worse, the Dome still isn't back. Once the dust settles and the people realise the Night can still return… A cold, angry chill climbs my back.

Together, we walk back into the castle to Savannah.

I recall what she had said the day she decided to follow through on the prophecy—the day the Elders bombed Silver Valley and Savannah promised she would bring the fight to their planet in retaliation. I will never forget the promise of death in her gaze when she stared deep into my eyes and said, *"I want to make them pay."*

Mel releases a long, exhausted exhale as we dip back inside the castle.

I want to make them pay.

At what cost?

SAVANNAH

I warm my fingers against a cup of coffee, fresh from the machine I stole from an Argenti. A distant part of me wonders if they made it through the Night as I lavishly sip at the decadent foam, my heart happy.

It's a small distraction from the world of hurt that awaits outside my chambers.

The moment Roman cranked open the bunker, spilling out his team of guards, worry had begun to nag at me. No one knew what to expect of the world beyond.

"I sent the Argenti down to deal with the fires, but the stupid fools are scared," Marcel says from my balcony.

"Mm," I mutter in response. I took one glance at the fiery wasteland from my balcony and then ran back inside. It instantly reminded me of Silver Valley.

I did that. *I* brought fire to their village and killed innocent families.

How am I better than the Elders, if I did the exact same thing that they did to me?

"Can you hear that? The world is so quiet," Marcel says softly.

I've never seen him look so contemplative. His eyes are heavy when he turns to me.

Your fault, your fault, your fault.

He turns away then, towards the doors. And my Magic feels it the same time he does.

Melanie and Jesse are making their way to my chambers, treading slowly as if unsure where to go. They must be using a map on her tech screen.

"Anything else I should know?" I ask, my eyes heavy as they meet Marcel's. "Before they arrive?"

He shakes his head slowly as he lowers himself onto my bed. "I sent the Bloodhound to look for the Elders while that moron Hayes was questioning us before. A reserve of Magic from Venus. Last bit I have. I figured it'd be worth it, because if they survived, the Bloodhound will now know."

I breathe in deeply, then let it all go. With hands close to trembling, I place my coffee on the bedside table, fighting the urge to lay down next to Marcel and go to sleep, like none of this has happened.

Your fault. Everything is in flames, and it's your fault.

Marcel pats the bed next to him. "Want to get into bed with me?"

I snort at the unexpected words. His mouth twists a little, savouring my reaction.

"I'm good, thanks," I say sharply. "I have better things to do at the end of the world than reduce myself to sleeping with the bloodthirsty Marcellus Hart."

"Glad to hear it," he says, his ankles twisting on top of each other, dirtying my bed. "Marcellus Hart would never want to sleep with a girl who actually *likes* him."

I throw a pillow at his face.

Knock, knock.

"Sav?"

My heart immediately grows heavy again as reality seeps back. With a fluttery breath, I reach into my pocket, gripping my switchblade and flaring my Magic as I make my way towards the door to let my friends inside.

Jesse takes one long look at me, his face dark and lined with a weird mix of anguish and anger, but Melanie at least offers a smile as they tiptoe inside.

"We don't have long," I say by way of greeting.

Jesse sucks in his lips, then goes to stand by the door, his arms crossed.

Melanie just flutters past, her fingers shaking a little as she withdraws the tech screen from under her coat. "I know. The Argenti from the bunkers are startled from what's out there and aren't quick to act right now, but it's only a matter of time."

"Silly fools," Marcel agrees from my bed, his eyes on the ceiling. He looks much too comfortable there. "The lot of them."

I twist my switchblade around in my palm, if only to give myself something to do while I hurriedly mutter, "I'm sorry for my distance, Melanie. I'm sorry for not being there for you. Before you get whisked out of this room I just want you to know that I've never taken my sight off you. My Magic, it—never mind. Just know I'm still here for you, always."

Her eyes are glassy when I look up. Marcel has sucked his lips in, as if to refrain from commenting. I can almost hear him say, *"Royalty never apologises for the sacrifices they have made, either by themselves or others."*

Instead, it's Jesse who says, "Just like you were here for the villagers whose Dome you decided to blow up?"

I turn and look at him, unsure what to say. But my heart is racing.

"Ah, cool it, Hayes," Marcel says, saving me from answering. If he were anyone else, he would comment on my sacrifice and explain away the choices I made and how they were for the best. But he is Marcellus Hart, and he isn't known for his patience. "I thought you were here to learn about the almighty Ley Lines, or was that question only raised because your cyborg lover had a burning question for me?"

Melanie throws the tech down right on Marcel's ankles. The man yelps as he darts upwards, his nostrils flaring in shock. Magic expands through the room. Jesse draws his sword.

Before anyone has the chance to fight Melanie's battle, she says sternly, "Shut the ever-loving-hell up, Hart, before I slam this over your pretty-boy face."

The Magic in the room gets sucked away. Marcel tilts his head, analysing Beckett.

"Pretty face, huh?"

"Not after she's through with you, big boy," I chirp.

He turns his predator eyes towards me, glinting over my switch-blade, then down over the way I've angled myself towards Melanie. He curls his lips, raises his eyebrows, then resettles in bed.

"It's lucky I've never had a thing for blondes, Beckett," he purrs.

Something hot expands in my chest.

"She wasn't flirting with you," Jesse snaps.

Marcel closes his eyes. "Neither was I."

A thick tension fills the room as we all stare at each other. Melanie looks at me and raises a brow. I huff loudly, tossing my switch-blade onto the bed near the tech screen and planting my butt down beside it.

The clothes I'm wearing from yesterday suddenly feel itchy from dirt, so I peel off the top layer of my fighting leathers, down to the dirtied singlet, and kick off my shoes.

Both Jesse and Melanie just stare at me.

"Care to share your findings on Ley Lines?" I ask Marcel without turning to face him. "Because our friends in Sector 2 have just breached the shores of the desert wastelands on the other side of the planet."

Melanie blinks at me. Jesse turns from me, his eyes meeting hers enquiringly.

"How do you know that?" Melanie breathes.

Frustration prickles under my skin. *An irrelevant and side-tracking question.* Again.

I drop my shoe on the ground and wiggle my fingers at her. "Magic," I say, almost rudely. "I keep tabs on everyone."

She blinks at me, and I return to pulling off my other shoe.

Before Melanie or Jesse have the chance to comment, Marcel finally speaks, his eyes still closed from where he lays behind me.

"Ley Lines are veins throughout the planet—areas of land closer to the core. These points increase Argenti power, and each Sector is built on one of the strongest points. The Elders were drawn to its powerful energy, but they're not Argenti, so they don't know its full capabilities. My father seems to have zero clue about the Leys. That's all I know," Marcel says.

I thump my other shoe on the ground. "Is this why I learnt my Magic so fast when in the dungeons? I just assumed it was boredom and survival instincts."

Melanie fiddles her cyborg fingers, her eyes flickering a little.

"The Ley was the real reason, but your perseverance made it possible," Marcel explains.

Jesse and Melanie exchange an obvious look. Neither of them knows what happened to me in the dungeons and, truthfully, I don't really want them to.

I watch Melanie swallow sharply, her mouth opening, but I pull myself off the bed and tear past her so quickly the air gets knocked out of her before she can speak.

"I need another coffee. You guys want one?" No one answers. I turn on the machine, eyes darting to them one at a time. "Anyone?"

Marcel still lays on the bed, his eyes closed. "Long black."

I flick the switch on and watch the black liquid drop into a teacup, scenting the air with the most magical aroma made to man.

Jesse coughs. "Gross."

Marcel opens his eyes and gives the man a long look. "Your weak male ego and need to comment on other people's elite choices of drink speak volumes about your tiny, little—"

I cough, then mask it by saying, "Oh, stars, just leave him alone and drink your goddamn man-juice."

The sound of rattling ceramic fills the space as I put the coffee on the table. "'Atta girl."

I turn to make myself a latte. "Now tell us about the Ley, Melanie. Where did your question about it come from?"

She watches me as if in a trance. When the last drip of coffee falls into my cup, she says, "The message pinged from the med ward on Sector 2. Our friends know about it."

Jesse frowns, as if this is news to him as well. His fingers twitch a little against his sword. He looks long and hard at Melanie, until a faint blush creeps on her cheeks.

I pick at a hangnail, waiting for more.

"If they are with the wildlings, I'd say it came from them," Melanie adds.

I nod a little, coming to the same conclusion. Thoughts and plans spin around in my head. I don't have a clear route for how to win the political war on Umbra, given the variables.

"So, if we want to use force, we fight on a Ley and learn how to draw more power from it, hoping our enemies aren't going to do the same thing," I mutter, then bristle when I realise I said that aloud.

Marcel slurps loudly from his coffee.

"Not a good plan," I hastily add. "This isn't about us versus them, it's about worming our way inside and plucking the pillars of their power out from the roots."

"Is that what last night was, then?" Jesse asks flatly. "A way to pluck away power?"

"It was a way to remind everyone of their morality. To topple the power structure, we need to unsettle those who have been settled for too long," I say, sounding stronger than I feel.

Your fault. All those deaths are your fault.

"It was slaughter, Savannah. Or have you not looked outside yet? Have you become so comfortable in your pretty rooms with coffee machines that you can't see the pain and suffering you caused outside?" Jesse yells.

I hadn't realised he'd taken a step towards me until his face is near mine, red and angry. None of the love he once felt for me is there on his face. I squashed it, squeezed his heart, and watched it bleed dry between my fingers.

And the worst part? I would do it all again.

My heart splinters as weeks of aching pounds in my chest. I stand strong and let myself feel it. No one interrupts us until Jesse finally calms down and steps back.

Marcel claps slowly, breaking the silence. "*Wow.*"

"Shut up," Melanie and I say to him at once.

"Is there a way to get a message to our friends?" Jesse says coldly, his anger sputtering out as he steps back and turns to Melanie. "I wish to go home."

Melanie shakes her head and he sighs.

"You should stay here in my rooms for now. I will find elsewhere to be," I tell them.

Melanie picks at her sleeve, her eyes soft as I take her in. We share a gentle smile, full of sorrow. "Thank you," she breathes.

"What's the plan with the Ley?" Jesse asks Melanie, clearly done with speaking to me.

I turn to Marcel, seeking an answer from the one person who may have them. He just raises his eyebrows, as if expecting the same from me.

I give a curt smile. He gives one back.

While Melanie fumbles for an answer, Marcel grabs my switch-blade and starts fiddling with it out of boredom. Neither Melanie or Jesse turns to look at me again, and my heart cracks with each second. I didn't know it was possible for it to crack even more.

It's a little hard to breathe, knowing I've lost my friends—their trust and patience.

But I did the best I could. I am *doing* the best I can.

Stars, I'm so tired.

"Our friends are with Sector 3 now, and wildlings know all about the Leys. Hopefully Jasmine or my dad are smart enough to ask the right questions. We can only hope and pray that what they learn might aid in bringing peace to Umbra," I say slowly.

My skin feels itchy. I hate hoping and praying.

"Or…" Marcel muses, his eyes glinting as he pulls himself off the bed and to my side. "We do something else. Something *entirely* more fun."

He looks at me.

I look at him.

All the frustration leaks out of my chest, and I grin.

34

JESSE

Marcellus's idea of 'fun' is a goddamn nightmare.

No, scratch that. It's so embarrassing and stupid, it's going to get me killed.

Hours later, we're now standing around the smouldering remains of the city, surrounded by almost all Argenti and hundreds of angry Umbran survivors.

And there's Savannah, standing by a podium with a small microphone in her palm, grinning like a madwoman. Marcellus is by her side, levitating the corpse of his father.

Marcellus Hart's freaking father. Or rather, a fake version of his father.

We don't know where Elias Hart is yet. He could still be alive, or perhaps he did indeed get squashed under a pile of rubble when the side of the castle rained down.

Somehow, Marcellus has a small well of Magic that enables him to change people's appearances at will. I can only assume he took it from his sister, Amadea.

Damn, I hope the poor kid is okay. She was mine to protect, after all.

"Elias Hart is dead," Savannah announces as everyone stares at her in mute horror. "Thanks to the armies and Captains of Sector 2." She holds a hand out towards me now. "This is Jesse Hayes, one of their Captains…"

Suddenly, all eyes turn to where I stand at the front of the stage.

If I were a lesser man, I would pee my pants.

Melanie watches me, her face expressionless. She holds her composure well, her shoulders straight despite the flush on her cheeks. She's downright embarrassed to be here, too.

Anyone can be in this crowd. *Anyone.* Our armies, our side, our people… Or theirs. Hundreds of loyal Argenti around me make me sick.

"We need to speak to them before anyone else gets the chance to," Savannah said just moments before.

"They will hate us if they know we are the sole reason for all the deaths," Marcellus had added when I told them for the thousandth time how insane they are.

"Maybe they should hate you," I'd replied.

They shoved me onto the stage after that.

Now, I stand beside Savannah, Marcellus, and the three Elders from the bunker. The old one, Eleanor, yawns heavily from behind me, as if ready to take a nap.

The Seventh Elder—a lithe woman who seemingly had time to change into a sparkling red dress—grabs my hand in hers. Where my skin is hot, hers is cold. The space between our skin feels like a warzone. I want to pull my hand from hers, to wish I didn't have to touch her, but instead I kiss the top of it in front of the hundreds of people, as instructed.

My blood boils as everything in me fights the urge to pull the sword from my back and slash it across her neck. These rulers are the root of all our problems. *They* are the reason Umbra is broken. *They* are the reason why its people are all bloodthirsty.

It's beyond me why we can't just kill them.

Savannah purses her lips at me from the podium, as if reading my thoughts. I fight the urge to kill her, too, in the moment.

Who even is Savannah Shaw, but a puppet of Umbra?

She is nothing like the sweet, soft girl I met in Silver Valley. Umbra has broken her.

I sigh a little as I pull back from the Seventh Elder.

Every eye is on me. A kid covered in blood near the front of the stage is shaking and glaring at me as I accidentally meet his eyes. Lythia May's ethereal mother cups my hand between both of hers then gracefully lowers it.

"I regret to say," she calls out, "that my bombs in the throne room were the reason."

Now, we have Savannah, the prophesied; Evaline, the Elder; and finally… me. Just a Sector 2 military figurehead. The people won't know who to blame or turn to.

The crowd stirs as a few people shout.

I just want to fall into the stage and vanish.

Mel stares at me, her silver eyes molten, and I focus all my attention on her.

Savannah addresses the yelling crowd. "The loss of the Dome teaches us this: we are *all* in this together. No one is entirely untouchable and no one is better than the next. We can all die as easily as we were born into this world, and we can all suffer. Even the Elders, even the Argenti."

Every soul in the crowd is taken in by her, their bodies trembling and their eyes wide. Everyone, even the Argenti, look worse for wear today. But there's a soft rage that burns in the eyes of the people. It fuels my own as I stare at the prophesied girl with the chocolate hair, standing behind the podium in her bloodied fighting gear, her hair a mess.

It's intentional, I realise, for her to remain in her dirtied clothes.

The regal Elder steps forward, his skin glowing under the pounding sun, offset by the white suit he chose to wear. *The man looks like a walking domino in that suit.*

He places a hand on Savannah's shoulder in a subtle way of dismissing her from the podium, which hardens her face a little, then he lifts the microphone to his mouth.

"It seems we've all become rather soft as a society, since being gifted this oasis by the river, sheltered by engineering. We've been fed the lie of our immortality, when the truth is we are anything but. Remember this, when you clean up your homes and bury your loved ones. Remember the loss, remember the struggle, and remember how blessed we are that we made it out. Praise Umbra!"

What the ever-loving hell has Savannah been feeding this man?

Melanie's eyes burn into mine, catching my attention again. She looks flabbergasted and rightfully so.

"*What the hell?*" I mouth to her when no one is looking.

Her lips crinkle at the corners.

"Praise Umbra!"

"Umbra!"

"For Umbra!"

Civilians start to call out. The Argenti all seem to sway on their feet.

During the shouting, one woman manages to call out, "Give us back our Dome!"

I search for her. It's the only smart thing any of them said. Savannah notices, too, pursing her lips. Roman cuts off the mic, stepping down from the stage. But Marcellus isn't done having his fun yet.

He drops the body of his lookalike father, smacking it across the stage. The sound is splitting, the wet slap of flesh cracking through the din. He swipes the mic up from the podium and switches it back on, grinning.

"Anyone in this crowd heard of Ley Lines before?" he speaks out.

The blood drains from my face.

Mel nearly drops her tech screen.

Savannah takes a deep breath and, from how close she stands by Marcellus, the sound catches a little on the mic.

"No?" he taunts, his teeth flashing as he smiles. "No one?"

The crowd is dead silent. And then Marcellus turns back to me.

"Hayes, come here."

My feet stay planted on the stage. Mel's eyes flick towards me, then Marcellus, then to Savannah, pleading.

"*Hayes*," he singsongs.

The sound of his voice heats my blood, ripening the hatred in my chest. My fingers twitch to my sword. As I do so, I notice Savannah shifting her body, her fingers cupping under her sleeve. I recognise the movement because I was the one who taught her that.

Her switchblade is in her sleeve, and she's glaring at me to not cause a scene.

I do anyway. I pull my sword from my back and hold it up against Marcellus's throat.

My feet have moved me across the stage where I ease the metal a little into his throat. Behind me, the Seventh Elder starts to make her way towards me. All the Argenti under the stage have tensed, too. I'm about to have death rained upon me if I don't lower my weapon.

But he's just so, so *vexing*.

"Good boy," Marcellus purrs, and I realise I've obeyed his order. He lifts his hand, wrapping his fingers around the metal of my sword, and pulls it away from his face. I keep my hold on it, but I don't put strength behind it, because the sight of silver blood welling around his fingers causes my mind to mentally freeze.

Is this man insane?

He uses my temporary distraction to hoist my sword out of my grip and toss it into the crowd. It plunges towards Mel, and my heart backpedals. It lands at Mel's feet, where she hisses at Hart.

He just wipes the blood between his hands and raises the microphone. "Hayes here asked me that same question last Night. Can you believe, while the world was going to absolute shit, *that* was the question on the forefront of his mind?" He chuckles. "I know what you all must be thinking. '*How does a brainless little military man have the mental capacity to be asking the right questions?*' I know, I know, it shocked me, too. But alas, I've been doing some thinking myself since then and it turns out the answer is beautiful." He steps back, the entire crowd seeming to hold their breath as he passes the mic over to Savannah. She grabs it, angling her sleeve so the switchblade sinks out of sight, then she smiles at the crowd.

She *smiles.*

Mel picks up my sword and holds it against her chest alongside her tech screen.

"Ley Lines are veins of power that run throughout the soil of Umbra—places where Magic touch closer to the surface. As far as we are aware, the strongest lines are on all the Sectors." She lets the words sink in for a moment, her eyes gently scanning the crowd.

My gut churns watching her, because this girl is otherworldly. *This* Savannah is a leader. A queen.

She is everything Mel has always wanted her to be, and everything I have always hated about Umbra. And yet… I can't help but admit that it suits her. Even if I hate it.

Marcellus gently watches her as she surveys the crowd.

My stomach flips, because that isn't just approval, satisfaction, or pride that she is playing the person he expected her to play. No. That's goddamn love right there.

It strikes me. Not because I'm jealous but… shocked.

Savannah lifts the mic again and I can practically see Marcellus glittering with joy. The anticipation is rolling off him in waves.

"The Dome was a tragedy, as Roman eloquently described. Thank you for that, Roman." She levels him with a look that makes him seem small. "It has united us in ways we have not been since the Moon Blitz, but that is but a blip in our story. The Leys are the next step. We stand on a powerful energy hub and, with it, we can grow to become something more."

My mind melts as I stare at the queenly woman before me, wearing her blood-tattered clothes like a goddamn crown.

"As of today, the Elders have invented a way for *all* of you to access that Magic. As of today, the Elders standing behind me can attest that we are *all* Argenti. It's in our blood and science can magnify it. We can alter everyone," she says. "Just imagine the power we would all have here, in contact to the Ley. Imagine the good we can do for our planet."

The whole word stills. The Argenti gasp. The Bloodhound steps forward.

Suddenly it all clicks in my head.

Melanie looks at the Bloodhound and smiles. She has already reached the same conclusion, her mind working faster than mine.

The Bloodhound is a known project of Alexsandre Collins. Hell, Alexsandre Collins is a known project of Alexsandre Collins. For years, the man has been experimenting with Argenti blood. He's turned his complexion silver and white, but because of the lack of Occupant gene in his body, he never amassed the ability to use Magic.

The Umbran people, however? No matter how small, they all have *something*. The Bloodhound is living proof.

Everyone is quiet, as if trying to figure it out, too. The Elders begin to retreat, their eyes flashing towards Savannah and Marcellus. That's fear in their eyes. Utter fear.

But Marcellus is grinning, enjoying every second of the confusion.

Savannah too seems to be floating on a separate plane.

Marcellus claps then, the sound ricocheting through the mic. Silver blood drips down his wrist as he calls out, "So, who wants to be turned into an Argenti first?"

AMADEA

By the time we make it back on land, the shock of what the wildlings said about Savannah's biological father has subsided for all but Mark.

The man is still reeling, and Jasmine's doing a not-so-good job at trying to comfort him.

"It's fine Mark, your ex-wife is evil anyway." Followed by, "I'm sure she would have slept with an Elder even if she wasn't drugged."

Mark gives her dark looks at each comment, which causes Lily to scoff.

I stay by Elijah, my fingers brushing his glass coffin as they lower it out of the sand crawler and into the desert. I look down at his waxen face instead of staring at the sand, which is blinding us all in the sun.

It's late morning, and we are all fighting fatigue.

The bright light makes a headache slash through my skull.

Never have I been so jealous of a boy in an enforced coma. I wonder if this is how my brother felt watching me in cyrosleep while he fought day after day to rebuild our home, slaying never-ending demons so that I could wake up to a peaceful world.

Magic flares under my feet, my concentration waning. Everything inside me wants to give in and embrace the power.

"The walk isn't far, little one," a wildling says, misinterpreting my frown.

I nod and blink against the glare as I try for a polite smile.

"Now *that* is a desert fortress!" Jasmine exclaims. Mark is carrying her, and I think I hear her slap him gently before saying, "Do you see it, Mark?"

She squeals in delight. The man doesn't answer, peeved as he is to carry her. He just grunts a little, still out of it.

I squint through the sun to spy what Jasmine is seeing.

She's right. It is an impressive desert fortress.

The breath huffs from my chest as I struggle to take it all in. It's made of grey stone but years of desert winds have chafed it down and covered it in sand. A few wildlings brush it away from above, brooms in their grasps, and they stop and stare as we approach them. The fortress barely meets my waist—which is saying something because I'm still in my own body save for my hair colour. Windows branded into the stone peer down into a labyrinth beneath.

They live underground.

Lily's breath hitches. Her body seems tense, her knuckles white as she grips her furs. She is helpless without her snow cats here.

I wonder if she's more nervous than she lets on. I know I am, being here without my brother.

"*Stars*," I gasp.

A wildling unit pushes in around us, urging us to an entrance that looks like a stone cave. Around it, desert shrubbery hisses in the wind, and a critter runs over Lily's feet. She doesn't even flinch. She's too transfixed, staring at the cave as if it's grown an extra extremity.

I duck my head to enter, which is silly because the entrance is tall, but my heart is hammering too loudly in my ears and I instinctively keep my chin low.

Lily stops behind me. The wildlings press on her, trying to push her forwards.

Mark frowns as they move supplies in waves. Jasmine's EXO Suit flashes past me.

"I would like to stay outside," Lily says simply.

"No," a wildling responds, grabbing her arm.

That's a mistake. She flips a knife out from her furs and holds it to his throat. Lily doesn't know this, but the Argenti tell stories about her on the mainland—the wild girl who tamed the demons of the north. The Snow Cat Woman.

Leave the safety of the Dome and she might have you for dinner.

There are many civilians who ran from the Kingdom into the wild, but there's only one that tamed the Cats. Mix that with her Hayes heritage as the daughter of the infamous pilot, and, well, safe to say you don't say 'no' to her. Ever.

I step backwards and hit the cave wall. It's strangely warm behind me, as if it's been resting in the sun for hours. A reed of desert foliage that climbs the interior of the cave tickles at my cheek as I tilt my head to watch.

Stomach twisting and breath catching, I focus all my willpower on not shifting my features. A weird swell of Magic seems to want to jump out from under my feet. It's like I have to shove my entire soul against it to win out.

"I'm staying here," she says in a low voice.

A few wildlings have stopped to watch, but none have moved to attack her.

"No," the wildling says again.

Next to Lily, Mark huffs and tosses Jasmine on the ground. No one looks towards the girl except me, even though she yells at Mark to help her back up.

He walks forward and rests a hand on Lily's, encouraging her to lower the blade. "No friendships are made by slitting throats."

She looks at Mark but doesn't lower the knife.

"They tell stories about the wildlings on the other continent. A part of me has always been curious," she says, more so to Mark than to the wildling at knifepoint. "But if I go into those caves, I fear I will never come back out."

What does that mean?

Jasmine, still sprawled on the sand at their feet, yelps. "Oh my god, there's bugs."

A large desert critter, as long and thick as a finger, with several legs and a mouth like a leech, slides over one of her immobile legs and sucks at her ankle.

"Lily, help!" she screams, her words shrieking down the tunnel.

Mark bats an eye, his body freezing at the sight of the thing.

Lily sighs, lowers the knife from the wildling and grunts.

"For the love of all—" She pauses, sliding her knife under the bug and flicking it away. "It won't kill you."

"It was eating me," Jasmine protests. Her cheeks are noticeably red.

The wildling ducks his head and walks into the cave at the reprieve. Some follow, but others stand at the entrance, their backs blocking the exit. Lily sees this and sighs heartily.

"Don't even think about fighting your way through them, Hayes," Mark declares. "If you're anything like Jesse—"

"I'm nothing like my brother, thank you very much," she snaps.

Oh, how I wish that were true.

She slits her sapphire eyes and glares at the poor man.

I swallow, the sound loud in my ears, but no one turns and looks at me. The scent of Magic seems to be swelling now, prickling my skin. I sigh as it ripples over my pores, shifting my skin the slightest shade darker.

Lily turns and sits on a rock meters away from the entrance. "I'm sitting here until you all return, then. Mark?"

The man grunts. "Don't ask me to choose."

"He loves me more," Jasmine says, her eyes still on her ankle where the bug had been. It didn't even break the skin.

Mark flinches a little at the words.

Pushing his glasses up the bridge of his nose, he says to Lily, "I have a boy here in a coma. A boy whose parents I was friends with. A boy who took part in a hunt for my daughter. A boy who nearly died for my family. And, yes, there's Jasmine, too. She will need help with the techsuit."

"Hey, you've known me since I was a baby," Jasmine says. "Where's my anecdotes?"

"I don't know you. I have absolutely no idea who Jasmine Spark is. You are not the girl I knew. If it weren't for the person you've become, my family would still be whole."

No one breathes. Not even Jasmine.

I think I see her eyes watering a little, but she just juts her jaw and stares at him.

Lily opens her mouth to speak, but Mark holds up a hand.

"I will see you to your techsuit simply because I will never forgive myself if I see another person suffer while my daughter has done nothing but fight to keep us all alive. But don't think I'll forgive you for what you did to my family."

Mark turns down the cave without another word, his back hunched.

At that point, Jasmine starts to cry.

SAVANNAH

"We need to find your father," I say, pulling Marcel off the stage with me.

The man is grinning. Magic vibrates from his body in waves he cannot control. He's intoxicating as he turns and smiles at me, his silver eyes piercing into my soul.

"Yes, my dear. I couldn't agree more. Let's go hunt."

And the mouse becomes the cat.

We launch past the startled faces of Roman and Evaline and into the frenzied crowd.

Above, the sound of ships drones out the chaos of the crowd. The pilots must have been on standby, and now rush to save the Elders trapped on the ground. The world is on fire around us. People scream and Argenti flare with Magic as they try to keep the people at bay.

The Magic just causes the crowd to cry in joy. It's a beautiful thing.

Roman grabs Evaline and hoists her over his solid shoulders, his usually calm eyes shooting rays of hatred at me as they rush towards the landing ship. *Cowards.* I flash him my prettiest grin and turn away.

The crowd presses in as people try to grab us in confusion and happiness. All want a piece of us. All want to touch the girl and the Argenti who brought them the promise of power.

Marcellus grabs the shoulder of an Argenti man, tearing him towards us through the crowd. "Baxter!"

Baxter yelps and shrinks into his silver robe. Marcellus shakes him, the movement more intense because of the crowd pressing into his shoulders.

Fear fills the man's eyes as he lifts his head. Then he flees.

But Marcellus needed only to touch him.

Magic flares, and the crowd is thrown back on an invisible wind. Bodies tumble against soil and, through it, I spot Mel reaching for Jesse's sword and her tech screen, blasted from her body by the gust.

I gesture her to follow us.

Jesse jumps from the stage and lands in our circle. "Savannah, what the actual—"

I hold up a finger, shushing him. "Follow me."

We run, dipping into the burnt trees around the village. The castle isn't far, and there's a clean-cut road directly towards the castle. The problem is the people following us.

Many linger, running after their Elders.

I pump my legs, pushing myself towards the castle. Magic spears up towards me and I dig deeper, reaching into the earth.

I know what it is immediately. Pure power; easily accessible. The Ley Lines, like the weaving webs of metal magnets in the soil to make the Hovers float.

As I reach for the net of strength underfoot, lightning hits my veins.

I see all of them. Civilians and Argenti hunting us, the Bloodhound at the forefront.

"Marcel?" I pant as I run, the breath wheezing out of me.

He's just ahead and barely breaking a sweat. "I know," he says, a beam of light flashing in his eyes. "But first, can you find me the Bloodhound?"

"Behind us."

Jesse catches up to us as I speak, his eyes flashing with concern. Marcel notices the look that crosses between us.

Melanie.

She isn't as trained as we are. I slow, my mind fizzling with Magic. Marcel sighs heartily as I do so.

"Get the Bloodhound. I'll wait for Melanie," I tell him.

I press my hand into Marcel's, our skin hard against each other. Magic spreads, flaring between our bodies. My heart kicks up a heavy tempo that has nothing to do with being out of breath. The boys are breathing normally, but they weren't trapped in a dungeon recently.

Jesse glances down at our hands, his eyes contemplative, just as someone bursts through the trees. There's still some fruit on the high-hanging branches and, as Tamaz drops down, they dislodge and rain down on us.

Jesse jumps aside, his sword rising.

Marcel is gone from our side as if he faded from existence.

I lift my hands in front of me, wishing my Magic were better in combat. But it's okay, because I still have my switchblade in my pocket.

"I don't know whether to trust you, Hayes," Tamaz grunts, his scarred face peppered with soot.

"Ditto," Jesse says.

"Laurence has a ship we can get you to. But the idea of watching you get swallowed by the Umbrans you riled up almost seems more exciting," he says.

Melanie is close. She's running hard, but there's several men around her. No one stops her, because she wasn't onstage with us.

We're in trouble here, and I send a silent prayer that Melanie takes a different route towards us. I take in my surroundings. We are in the orchards I stumbled into the day I escaped the dungeons. Ironic, that I would be captured and killed here.

"And you," Tamaz says, turning to me. "You've turned out to be quite a problem."

The sky blazes with ships. I spot three and track them with my eyes, but it's difficult from under the trees.

The Elders are safely on one of those.

Jesse says, "She isn't the reason for the Dome, Tam," as if defending me is a habit.

I roll my eyes, looking Tamaz dead in his cold ones. He has a sharp, polished knife in either hand, poised to attack.

I ignore that and tell him, "Nah, I am actually."

Tamaz lunges. Jesse moves to help me, but Tamaz has always been better.

He knocks Jesse in the temple with the butt of one knife while easily sidestepping Jesse's slash. I watch as he tumbles to the ground unconscious.

I barely have time to breathe before Tamaz pins me to a tree.

His blade bites into my neck. My legs are pinned with his, his other knife at my gut. I slash with my switchblade, but another man from behind the tree grabs my arms.

Civilians converge around me.

I recognise many from the base and Silver Valley.

The brute I stole the switchblade from emerges from the trees, glaring at me.

"We lost over half our army to the cold last Night. Laurence's entire squad is dead, too, thanks to the fires people set to keep warm. Your army, Savannah. *Your people.*"

"Where is Laurence now?" I manage to ask.

"Leaving you behind. Hunting the skies for the Elders as they fled. No thanks to you."

I don't fight them. I simply stare as tears well in my eyes.

His knife pierces the skin at my stomach and I lose feeling in my hands from the strength of the other man's fingers.

"So, kill me," I plead. "I'm dead, anyway."

That causes something to flash across Tamaz's face.

The knife in my gut withdraws, but then pain crashes his features and it returns with more fury.

I sink deep inside myself to the place where the world is hazy and nothing matters. My mind vanishes, leaving nothing but my body behind. It feels right. Comforting.

Except the last time I was being picked apart piece by piece, I had Marcellus with me. All I have now is Jesse unconscious on the floor and Melanie somewhere in the trees, running in circles trying to find us.

I sink into my Magic, finding Marcel.

My heart lightens. Something inside me returns… then vanishes again as I realise, he isn't moving. He's standing utterly still, somewhere inside the castle. The Bloodhound is next to him and…

I shake my head, trying to forget about who he is with.

Why isn't he coming to help?

"You know what you cost me?" Tamaz asks. "My daughter."

I return to myself and crack a little at that admission.

Lucille. Oh, stars. She was a wonderful lady who introduced me to Amadea, fed, and housed us. Despite her fears, she not only gave me hope but gave me Tamaz and his army.

I open my mouth to say sorry, but it doesn't feel nearly enough.

When I don't speak, Tamaz slides his knife across my stomach, cutting out skin. It isn't enough to spill my guts, but it's enough to freaking hurt.

My Magic wavers. I try and move my fingers, but they have lost all feeling. My switchblade is probably on the floor.

At my feet, Jesse stirs, and I watch him in vain.

"Kill. Me." I pant.

I can almost hear Marcel saying, "*No, little mouse.*" But he isn't here like he should be.

My head drops, tears falling down my face, and I suddenly realise an awful truth. I've come to rely on him too much. He is my safety net—the man who gave me water in the dungeons and showed me the exit to escape. He has been by my side ever since.

What would it mean, to live a life with Marcellus? To fall in love with him in the way I think I have been?

Right now, it would be futile. Right now, I could only ever really give him half of me.

Because I've grown comfortable in giving up and relying on others.

"*Good girl,*" someone purrs. It comes from within my mind, and I don't know if I'm imagining Marcel's words or if it is actually there. "*You don't need me. You are Savannah Shaw, usurper of Umbra, Queen, little mouse and fierce hunter. Stop using me as your crutch and start fighting.*"

Jesse's eyes flicker as he wakes. The brute pushes Jesse's face with his shoe, but it's too late, because he has already stirred. As he jumps to his feet, I push forwards, slamming my head into Tamaz's and yanking my hands free.

The motion makes his blade sink into my stomach and the other skitter across my neck, but he tumbles back, surprised.

I spin around the tree until I face the other man and swing my leg up and into his groin When I turn, Jesse is already pulling his sword out of someone's back.

Tamaz. The shock on his face is mimicked in mine as the man

falls forwards. The sight makes Jesse gag a little, his fingers shaking. I watch in a trance as his sword drops.

"Jesse!"

I turn to the sound.

Melanie. She breaks through the trees, her eyes wide and her chest heaving.

She looks down at Tamaz, just as I look down at the sword at Jesse's feet. My switchblade has fallen by the tree, and I watch lazily as the brute, Samael, reaches for it.

Tamaz's army don't move. They simply stare at us, frozen.

The smell of Magic is ripe in the air, but I don't question it. Not as Samael's slimy hand wraps around the mahogany handle, covering the word *perseverance* with the soot from his fingers.

I slam my boot into his wrist, making the man yell.

Melanie looks at me but doesn't even have time to open her mouth before I free my blade from him and drag it straight across his throat.

"You should have died a long, long time ago. I hope you realise that," I breathe, my voice as heavy as the air around us.

Jesse gapes, looking at me like I've grown an extra head.

Samael's mouth bubbles. Blood creeps out as he tries to wretch and swear at me, dying slowly and awfully. I force myself to look at every second of it, because if you kill someone, it's the least you can do.

I killed someone.

"Savannah?" Melanie prods.

Slowly, once Samael has stopped breathing, I lift my gaze to hers. The world around me has frozen, Magic pumping every which way. Tamaz's men struggle towards us as if wading through water, their bodies immobile.

Magic.

"There's an Argenti near," I finally speak, my voice feeling separate to me.

Jesse exhales. Before him, Tamaz's body has smeared the ground red.

Clarity returns to my body and suddenly my gut is throbbing. The world feels hot as Magic thumps at my skin. In the distance, people are talking and shouting, quickly turning into a mob.

And then I hear Marcel's voice again and decide he's definitely speaking in my head. It makes sense, because when I fork my Magic out to him, he's with both the Bloodhound and my mother.

"We found the Elders."

I can sense the Argenti near us, throwing out waves of Magic. It's clear she's only doing it to help herself.

I thrust my switchblade into my sleeve, wincing at the pain in my stomach, then throw my Magic back out to Marcel, locating his position. The Third and Fourth Elder are near him.

I don't know if it will work, but I try reaching out to Marcel's mind.

"You didn't come when I needed you."

I hear him chuckle. The sound is warm and affectionate and full of the thrill of a good challenge.

"You didn't need me, though. I thought you may need reminding of that."

I grit my teeth and stare at the tree I was pinned to. I both want to strangle Marcel and thank him for the compliment, but instead I settle on saying, *"Heading your way now."*

I try to force him from my mind, not that I have the power to do so, but he senses the sentiment and retreats.

"Come on," I say roughly to Melanie and Jesse. "I found the other Elders. They're in their rooms in the castle."

37

JESSE

The sight of Savannah strolling the castle like a woman scorned, her palm flat against the bleeding spot on her stomach, makes me feel a little sick.

But I must admit, as terrified as I am of her, I'm also a little proud. She used the combat skills I taught her exceptionally well.

I rub my temples, my head throbbing. *I killed Tam.*

Melanie slips her hand into mine, as if out of habit. It's not something we normally do, but when she squeezes, I squeeze back.

The walk through the castle feels haunted, each of my steps feeling heavy. Savannah seems unbothered, though. She drifts through like a wraith.

I nurse my wounded heart and fight the urge to fall into Melanie's arms. She keeps giving me a look, like she can see the weight there. She doesn't comment, which I'm glad for.

"Ready to meet our enemies?" Savannah singsongs, suddenly

spinning. Despite the lightness in her voice, her face looks clouded. Dark. She looks like she's about to cry or scream or slap someone.

I wonder if that man was her first kill?

"Didn't we just do that?" I counter, unable to hide the pain in my voice.

Melanie slips her hand out of mine, catching a vague look from Savannah, and sets her shoulders.

We're now in a numbered hallway. The castle is bright and hot as the daylight rolls in, but this hallway looks dark and ominous. It doesn't take a genius to guess these are the personal chambers of the Elders.

"I hope you have a plan," Melanie says, stepping forward.

Savannah nods, leading us to a room. "I have a hundred plans. But so does everyone in this Kingdom. Let's see if we can make any of them happen."

Yes, because that's reassuring.

I reach for Melanie again, clambering for her hand. My fingers brush her metal ones and I hold them as hard as I can, knowing there is no way to break her even if I wanted to.

Savannah leads us through a door labelled 2.

I hold my breath and can't help wondering if it may be my last.

38

MARCELLUS

I prop my feet up on George Evans's desk, wondering if he is spitting at me from the afterlife, and put on my most dazzling smile for Savannah.

She glides through the room with a frown, immediately spotting the Bloodhound, picking her red nails near the window, followed by Venus, where she is nailed to a post.

My father, bound against the Fourth Elder, Connor Stearn, is also in the centre of the room, gagged and glaring at me.

"My favourite little group," I declare, sipping from a porcelain cup of Eleanor's favourite tea: lavender and rosemary. A distant part of me wonders where she is, but I used the dregs of Savannah's Magic to find the Bloodhound.

The people in this room are the only ones that matter right now anyway.

As Venus groans, Savannah's eyes immediately latch onto her, narrowing. The woman is worse for wear, covered in grime from the dungeons and drugged-up on a bunch of random vials I plucked from the Second Elder's lab. The entire room is filled with vials and syringes, code and research. I didn't really have time to ask what did what before shoving them down her throat and nailing her to the same post Savannah had been once upon a time. I did it out of spite, but I felt empty doing it. And now, seeing Savannah struggle to stand, I wonder if it was a good call.

"Catch," I say, lowering my tea and tossing a syringe to Savannah. *Velox.* She grabs it and thins her lips. I expect her to immediately deal with the injury at her stomach, but I guess I shouldn't have been surprised when she addresses me first.

"What will you do with her?" she asks.

I took Venus from the dungeons and practically carried her up to this room. The Bloodhound laughed the entire time, the sadistic excuse of an Umbran that she is.

She was the one who found my father. Connor and Elias had been watching the chaos unfold outside, no doubt plotting their next steps as they waited for their soldiers to return.

I intercepted that.

"Well, if I remember correctly, you were assigned to kill her. But if you'd rather not, just say the word," I tell her, picking up the tea again and taking a long drag. It's still too hot but it does wonders for my dry mouth.

"I'd rather not," Savannah says.

Hayes visibly sighs in relief behind her. Odd, that. The man would be no stranger to seeing his enemies die.

I shrug, leaning back in my seat.

"Why am I still here?" Cece huffs, slapping down her hands and turning from the window. I can distantly hear the crowd outside, but I attempt to tune them out as she glares at me. Her eyes shine with a residual thrill at being found by me, yet there's hatred at being kept away from the fun.

"Because at this very moment," I say slowly, fighting frustration, "you are the most important person in the world."

Cece tries not to let it show, but a flash of satisfaction beams on her face.

"Shucks, Marcel," Savannah teases, tossing the empty *Velox* into a syringe bin by a research desk. "And here I thought I was your favourite plaything."

My heart kicks up a gear and Magic buzzes at my fingers at her voice. I let a smile bloom on my face, uninhibited. "Your head is growing too big for your shoulders, little queen."

"Oh, shut up already," Hayes groans, slipping his hand out of Beckett's, his eyes heavy on the bound Elders on the floor. "Stop flirting. We have bigger issues."

I tilt my head to the array of vials on a research bench against the wall.

The Second Elder was a fanatic, obsessed with science. His office is sterile and filled with glass, colourful liquids, research benches, notes and labels. And by the window is an invention he never planned to create: The Bloodhound.

That was all Alexsandre.

The thing is, I don't need to pick Alexsandre's brain when the information is right before me in the form of my father. Two birds, one stone.

"Get it out of him," I say to Savannah. *"I think you'll enjoy it more than I would."*

She smiles and angles her head at me, curious as to why I'd say that.

Truthfully, I have no desire to torture my father. In fact, I think very little of him these days. His weakness disgusts me.

"And my mother?"

"Are we finally calling Venus Collins mummy, now? Don't tell me you've forgiven her."

"Never. But that doesn't change the fact that I'd be murdering my own mother. I don't know if I can do that."

I understand completely. As little as I care for my father, a part of me wonders if I could bring myself to end his life. Luckily, I have Savannah.

"A vial," she announces, her voice shattering the room. Everyone turns and looks at her. "One used to alter Argenti DNA. Tell me where to find it, and I may spare your life."

My gagged and red-faced father stares at her blankly. Melanie, to my surprise, reaches over and pulls down his gag.

"You should probably answer. I just watched her slit a man's throat outside."

Surprise drifts through me and something electric fills my stomach. I want to grab Savannah and absorb her mind. I want to know how, why, when. She never fails to undo me.

My legs swing off the table, my grin popping as I open my mouth.

"You slit someone's throat?" I throw out to Savannah. The words pull at me, growing heavier as the Magic wanes. *"Please tell me who."*

Savannah smiles and rolls her eyes, not looking at me.

Heat pounds through me. I watch in rapture as a curtain of her hair falls over her face, my heart absolutely squeezing. There's no Magic in the room, but I feel *alive*.

Usually, the absence of stored Magic freaks me the hell out. But right now, all I can see is the hair I want so badly to push behind her ear, then lift her chin so she looks into my eyes.

She's ignoring me entirely, which makes my heart roar louder. I let it as I stare at her.

"No?" she asks my father.

He stares at her with the hatred of a million suns but doesn't say a single word.

She sighs. Swallows. "Okay, then," she says quietly.

She completes a lazy circle around them. Connor Stearn

is watching her, his body shaking. He's always been a nervous little bird.

Savannah kneels to his level and looks him deep into his eyes.

"I don't know you, but I do hope you have lived a somewhat fulfilling life," she whispers. "Thank you for the years of servitude you have done for this planet."

I watch in utter disbelief as she slips her switchblade from her pocket and slides the blade deep into the Fourth Elder's throat.

Melanie gasps.

The Bloodhound hisses.

"You little bitch," Cece spits. I hold up my hand as she prepares to storm towards Savannah. She bristles but, surprisingly, listens.

Sometimes it rattles me how tight a leash I have her on. All it took was making her believe I loved her. The thought makes me sick, but I stomach it like I always do, and focus on Savannah. She's shaking a little as she wipes Connor's blood on her already dirty pants. The Elder sags, but he's still bound to my father at his back.

Elias is currently freaking the hell out before me. I feel the blood drain from my face as his eyes meet mine. He opens his mouth, then seems to think better of it.

I tighten my jaw, burying my years of hatred for the man until I feel indifference. I wonder what my mother, an Occupant, ever saw in him. I wonder if he used to be a better man.

"Now," Savannah says evenly. Her eyes seem distant though, as if she is lost within her soul. "Ready to speak?"

Elias says coolly, "You are not an Elder or an equal. I owe you nothing."

"Better," Savannah says. "I missed the sound of your voice. Now, ignoring that slight, can you tell me which vial you asked Alexsandre to use on the Bloodhound?"

At this, Cece gapes. She digs her claws into the desk at my feet, bending the supple wood. "Wow, really? Is the little bitch here for good old me?"

Savannah doesn't look at her, but Melanie does. Silver wrath floods in her eyes, and I quickly look away. But Jesse sees the look and watches me closely. It makes my skin crawl.

I lift the cup of tea back off the saucer and take another drag of the herbal liquid.

"I should have killed Venus years ago," Elias manages, showing the first true signs of fear. A bead of sweat drips down my father's forehead, tracking through the dirt on his face.

Savannah grins at him. "True."

Elias says nothing else.

Savannah, clearly exhausted, lifts heavy eyes to mine. The usual spark in them is gone as they drift past me to Cece. "Do you know which vial?"

She laughs. "Of course I know."

My father breathes heavily as he squirms on the floor. He won't escape them. He made sure I always had the best tutors growing up and I *always* paid attention.

I can tie a knot like no other. I wonder if he ever cared to learn that about me?

"Show me," Savannah demands.

"And why would I do that?" Cece snaps, drumming her fingers on the desk.

I swing my legs down and stamp them on the ground. The girl hisses as I pin her against the wall. I stare into her hateful eyes and say coolly, "Show her."

The Bloodhound, a woman feared by many, trembles under my fingers. I release her, and she scurries over to the research bench.

Melanie uncrosses her arms. Her gaze is etched with concern as Savannah drifts over to Cece, plucking a vial from her fingers a second after she lifts it. "Perfect."

The Bloodhound is seething.

I walk around the desk, leaning back onto it, and pat on the counter. Like an obedient dog, the Bloodhound comes and sits. She looks up at me with longing eyes. Pitiful.

"How does it feel, Father?" I say coldly.

From the side of the room, Venus snores. Her head rolls as if waking from a dream, then drops again. Jesse recoils from his position closest to her.

Savannah hardly notices, to my surprise. As she hands me the vial, the sun from the window shines through the blue liquid. It swirls inside, tossing as I spin it.

"It's unfinished," my father declares, squirming against the floor again. "You've never been smart enough in the ways of medicine to figure them out."

The jab touches a nerve.

"You'll never be like me." He used to say it to me as a child. I believed him and became someone better. Someone stronger.

"No, but I know someone who is."

Finally, I turn to Melanie. The girl hasn't said a word since she entered the room, but when she looks at me, I know she can figure it out.

Amadea has always known a lot about Melanie Beckett. I never quite understood how, but I am grateful for the knowledge. The sweetest fact being the cleverness of her mind. Beckett is both a hacker and a medic, trained in many fields.

On the latter, I hope she has stayed vigilant.

Savannah laughs loudly, which makes my father flinch.

Jesse reaches over and grabs Melanie's hand, who takes a deep breath.

Melanie finally speaks, feeling the pressure of our eyes. "Okay, Savannah. Not going to lie, I'm a little lost. Start from the beginning."

And so, Savannah tells her our plan… parts of it, at least.

AMADEA

Jasmine is put into the EXO Suit several hours later by the wildlings. All of its weapons were stripped and the forcefield mechanism disabled, reducing its capacity to simply allow her to walk. The joy of walking once more hasn't quite hit her yet.

Sector 3 is a whole new world, but I hardly see any of it.

We quickly realised the wildlings don't like outsiders. We are only here because of our link to Savannah Shaw… or so they say. There seems to be more to it than that.

I sit at the end of Elijah's bed in a small, cave-like room. He's just come out of surgery and his back is rapidly healing from a strong dose of *Velox*. Jasmine paces back and forth next to me, trying to get a feel of her new legs.

The room is dimly lit and sand seems to get in everything. A curtain hangs over the threshold, and I can hear everything happening outside. Voices, singing… even someone slamming metal together as they work on constructing more EXO Suits down the hall.

Mark is nowhere to be seen.

"The end of the world is near, and I'm stuck here in a freaking cave," Jasmine says.

I hold my hands up. "Savannah can look after herself."

"Noted," Jasmine says. "That's not to say she needn't have help. If the Argenti have suits and S.P. Guns, who knows what else they have? Besides, Savannah just destroyed the Dome like it was a casual Sunday. What will they do to retaliate?"

I chew on the inside of my cheek. Jasmine is right. My father will not go down easily.

"Add Netsils to that," I say.

I rack my brain for anything else I know about the Elders' inventions, but truth be told, it only became a recent passion of theirs to make war materials. The Netsils were first, centuries ago. But it wasn't something they steadily worked on.

Until Savannah.

Jasmine stops her prowling. "What's that?"

Her breathing is laboured. I think she already knows.

"A bomb. Netsils are implosion devices. Evaline invented them way back. They were tested in space, but…" I sigh. Those tests were the result of the Moon Blitz, which I shouldn't really be sharing with a scared girl who has nothing to lose.

Her words are flat as she realises it anyway. "Evaline May was the reason for the Moon Blitz. The reason the Occupants died."

"No, her bombs were."

She shakes her head. "Far out."

Rubbing her temples, she resumes her pacing, muttering occasionally.

I look at the door, nervous about anyone overhearing. It's been wildly speculated that war testing was the reason for our second moon to implode. The debris scattered around our planet and rained down death. The world was thrown off its axis, the ocean crashed tidal waves onto the shore, and fault lines splintered… it was chaos.

The Elders survived because they were in a spaceship, staring down at the mess. The rest of us—the Occupants and the first Argenti—scrambled to survive.

I wonder how much of this the wildlings know. They're guarding our room, but they're distracted with Mark right now. He watched as they worked on Elijah's back then stormed back outside to rejoin Lily.

I could go with him, but the wall of wildlings posted outside our door makes my pulse quicken. They know things about Silver Magic that I do not, and I can't help but wonder if they noticed the slight change in my skin tone as their Magic got the better of me.

"Ugh," Elijah moans, waking from his slumber.

Jasmine misses a step in her suit. It's a pretty metal thing that hugs her body as it shifts, moulding and coaxing her muscles. It covers all but her fingers and her face. I can tell she hates the look of it.

"Eli!" she exclaims, scrambling for him.

They didn't give him gauze after surgery. They simply placed him on his stomach and propped his head sideways on the pillow as if he wasn't worth their time. There are no blankets, just one plain pillow on his stone cot. He doesn't even have water or food.

The wildlings are doing the bare minimum.

"Where's Melanie?" he croaks, his throat bobbing as he tries to turn.

The skin on his back is healing as we speak, knotting and moving around the puncture wounds from where the wildlings dug metal out of his skin. I wonder if it hurts.

"She's safe with my brother. We are in Sector 3 right now," I say when Jasmine doesn't answer.

She crashes to her knees, feet failing her, and waves her

hands in front of his face to get his attention. "Dude, look at my ugly armour."

He squints at her as he pulls himself from the threadbare mattress, wincing as he does. "I thought you couldn't walk?"

"Still can't, but this helps. I want to see if there's a way to cut it at the waist so I can wear a pretty dress over it and still look human," she mutters wistfully.

Elijah, only half listening, twists his head to look at me. He has a soft face, full of innocence and youth, but it's hardened in a way that only Terrans' faces are—crinkled at the edges and dulled at the eyes. His large, calloused fingers scrape the mattress as he hoists himself up, towering over me.

"Who are you?" he asks plainly, his brown eyes thinning.

I smile politely and straighten. "Amadea Hart. Savannah sent me here to keep me safe."

He analyses my face, my body, my hair. Magic tries to crackle at my skin, making my muscles itch, but I sit still.

"I was in Sector 2," he says. "I thought I was safe there. You said this is Sector 3?"

"We're hopefully leaving soon. It stinks like dust here," Jasmine spurts.

I shoot her a long look. Elijah just blinks at her.

Sighing deeply, she tries to explain why we are here in a way only Jasmine Spark can. "They hate us, but they love Savannah. They fixed your back and gave me a suit."

He turns. Stares at her. Stars, the girl is *exhausting*.

I plaster a smile on my lips. "It's been a weird few days but I fear it will only get weirder. Would you like me to catch you up? The wildlings of Sector 3 look like they plan to keep us in this room for now, so I think we have time."

Elijah grunts, twisting the pillow into his lap. His back is still healing, but he fights the pain, curls his legs under his body, and swallows sharply as he sits. The dim lights that line the roof cast half his features in shadow, but I can still see him trembling a little before me.

"Tell me about all that later, new girl. Please just start with what you know about Melanie Beckett."

Well, then. How do I tell him she's in love with another man?

Jasmine sighs profusely, then struggles to clamber onto the small bed to join us. And because she takes a while, I take a shaky breath and begin.

"Okay, I think in order to explain what I know properly, we should start go back to the day she met Jesse Hayes, and how meeting him changed everything."

The day she fell in love and the day the war on Umbra began.

Elijah holds his breath, and I tell him a secret I've kept for years.

40

JESSE

I watch in a trance as Savannah tells us about the vials.

If what they said in the village is true, can they really turn Umbrans into an Argenti? Like, right at this very moment?

I stare at my shoes, crusted with dried mud. The polished stone floor is peppered with blood from where the dead Elder spat moments before death. I don't glance up, not even as the Bloodhound stares at me, her eyes drilling into my body.

"Celestine is second-generation Argenti but was born unconnected to the source of Magic. It wasn't until they started tinkering with her blood that she connected to the source deep within her. Now, she is one of the most feared Argenti for what she can do. I'm not going to pretend to know the technicalities of how such a thing was manufactured, but I do know it has something to do with this," Savannah says, pointing at the vial of blue liquid rolling in Mel's prosthetic hand.

As Melanie turns it, the wires in her wrist bend. She still has fresh skin grafted over the metal, and for once doesn't try to hide it.

She purses her lips. "We're going to need Argenti blood and lots of Magic."

Savannah immediately holds out her hand.

Melanie just stares at her. "Not you," she mutters. "We don't know anything about your blood. We need him."

All of us turn as she points at Marcellust, who slurps from his cup of tea.

The Bloodhound angles her head at him. *She looks a little like Venus Collins in the way all evil Argenti look like Venus Collins.*

I've heard stories about how she relishes in a hunt. How she likes the feel of blood on her fingers and how she finds joy in the kill.

I never knew she was a bottle experiment.

She watches us all as if this is news to her, too. But from the way she sits on that damn table like a golden trophy, it's obvious it isn't.

Mel sighs when Marcellus ignores her, turning back to the lab. "Another way, then."

She works quickly, her hands shaking a little as she places down the vial. I don't know how she does it, and I stare in absolute awe as she scours pages of research, finding the right papers in less than five minutes.

Savannah watches from over her shoulder, absorbing every-thing. I can tell it bothers Mel, but she doesn't comment on it. Not as Savannah hands her paperwork and vials and slips into a helpful role in a matter of seconds.

The Bloodhound watches, too, her fingernails tapping. She looks like she wants to kill Savannah.

"Tell me what weapons you have invented, Elias," Savannah mutters without turning.

At my feet, the Elder with auburn hair just stares at her back. His eyes are like disks, drinking her in. My skin crawls just watch-ing him. He's like a starved animal.

"Hart?" Savannah says.

Marcellus bristles, but she isn't talking to him. Elias responds, "Not my speciality, Shaw."

"Hmm." Distracted, she points to something on the table. "What about that one, Elias?"

He doesn't answer.

But Mel makes a noise, reaching for it.

Elias squirms. With Savannah preoccupied, he turns and drinks me in. In fact, he holds his head high. He doesn't even look at his son or the girls playing with medicine. No, his eyes are all for me.

It takes a solid beat before I suddenly twist out of the shadows at the end of the room and demand, "What?"

He smiles at me. From the desk, I vaguely sense Marcellus's attention on me.

"Out of everyone in this office, you are the most ordinary," Elias tells me.

Heat thrums in my veins. I stare at the way he gives me a soft smile and feel the earth shake under my feet. Without catching a breath, I step back into the shadows.

The Bloodhound beams.

"Oh, calm your panties, Cece," Marcellus says. "Remember the day my father tried to kill you for sleeping with me? Yeah, he hates you, too."

She snaps her teeth at Marcellus tauntingly.

"Give Celestine a weapon or something, son," Elias commands. "Let her free me."

Marcellus doesn't comment.

Savannah swallows loudly.

"Don't worry, my dear," Marcel coos at her. "He's just trying to rile you and insult Cece in the same sentence. We only give weapons to the ordinary. How else would our guards protect us?"

"S.P. guns," the Bloodhound spits.

But Marcellus isn't looking at the Bloodhound. His eyes are all for Savannah.

And still the Bloodhound looks at the man longingly, as if waiting for approval. Elias was all but forgotten the moment Marcellus opened his trap.

The Bloodhound is only loyal to Marcellus Hart. Noted.

I try and catch Mel's gaze to convey this, but she's too busy frowning at the lab table.

"Venus, my sweet thing," Elias purrs.

I jump as she groans beside me. I was too busy staring at Mel's back.

Nerves flutter down my spine. The last time I saw the woman this close, we were rescuing Elijah from the Safe Holds back in Silver Valley. Then, she was a regal, untouchable woman. She didn't even have access to Silver Magic there, but here, where she should be at her full potential, she is a prisoner.

She rouses slowly at first, then all at once. Her head darts up, her body arching against the pole Marcellus nailed her to. She hisses, "You stupid, worthless piece of—oh."

She notices Connor's limp body before spotting Elias, who doesn't once look at her.

"Oh," she repeats, seeing Savannah Shaw.

Savannah leans back, eyeballing her mother. "Morning," she mutters, then turns back to her work with eyes as cold as the Night.

I stare at Venus from my position in the shadows. It takes her an entire round of the room, drinking everyone in, before she finally sees me.

"I demand you to free me, or I will kill the one you love."

Her voice makes me lean harder on the filing cabinet I'm perched against.

"Oh, yeah?" I say, rubbing my head. "You and what army?"

She turns away from me. "Celestine, child. I order you to free me."

"Tried that," Elias bites.

The Bloodhound just lifts her chin pointedly. Ugh, I could

sucker-punch that Argenti. She's *enjoying* having more power over Venus and the Elder right now.

"Beckett's uncle has a team on Umbra that communicate with me." Venus continues to speak to Elias. "Where are they? My Magic isn't reaching them."

I smile deeply as laughter threatens to spill.

"Mel," I say from the shadows, twisting one of my ankles over the other. "Have you been keeping tabs on your uncle, by chance?"

Mel drops something metallic, which skitters across the workbench.

"I'm sorry, what?"

Savannah's lips thin as she analyses my expression. I keep it void of feeling.

"No," Venus gasps, pulling against the nails in her hands as if it doesn't even hurt. "No, that's not necessary." And then, with a panicked quiver to her voice, "Elias?"

The Elder sighs, twisting in his restraints to look at her. She buckles under his stare.

Marcellus slams the teacup onto the saucer in delight. "So *that's* what the second drug did. Bloodhound, get more of that red liquid with a large stopper. It shuts off people's Magic."

Venus's fingers shake. Melanie's head turns towards us.

Elias still stares at Venus. The woman sinks low, sweat beading on her brow under the weight of it, her face all twisted. I angle my head at her, drinking in the light freckles scattered across her pale skin and the gentle fingers curled above her head. Even with the silver eyes dulled and painfilled, she looks a little like Savannah. For the first time, I can see the girl I once loved in her evil mother.

The Bloodhound lowers a bottle onto the table next to Marcellus. He reaches for it, eyes twinkling. "Thanks, pup. Now, Savannah, ask your friend to hurry up pretty please. It's getting hot here so close to the window."

Savannah sticks her tongue out at him. A smile small brushes his face.

"You traitors need to free me so I can send teams to continue working on the Dome," Elias says over his son at the mention of 'hot'. "I was sending word out before you grabbed me. We will all die here tonight if you do not allow me to do my duty to our people. Is that what you want, my son? Do you really want our people to suffer?"

Marcellus picks at his fingernails. "They think you're dead, Father."

The room freezes. It's not news to me or anyone who was down in the village, but we all watch as Elias bristles and Venus pops her mouth.

She sidles her legs over to me, tracking them through blood. I watch them with narrowed eyes. She's reaching for the dead Elder for some reason.

"Not that one, Beckett," Marcellus says with a click of his tongue. He doesn't lift his eyes, but Melanie freezes upon opening a file of notes. How this man knows what she's looking at without directly looking at her is frightening.

He gives off casual indifference, but as I analyse his countenance, it's clear the display is intentional. A small muscle ticks above my left eye.

"Enough!" Elias yells. "Celestine, put your pride and lust aside and do your duty to your planet. Free your superiors."

She clenches her fists, nails digging into her palms. "I am an Argenti just like Venus. I'm *sick* of the disrespect—"

"FREE ME," Elias screams, finally snapping, his body trembling.

Mel drops a file with a bang, jumping a little in the air.

Savannah lowers a hand on her shoulder.

"You are not even close to coming up with a drug that will suffice. Free me, allow me to restore the Dome, and I will personally send Alexsandre to make you a vial." His words are rushed and panicked, his tanned skin flush with sweat.

The Bloodhound hisses, her fingers denting the wood as she flexes. Her body looks poised to strike, but it's unclear if she means to go for Elias or Savannah. Which side is she even *on*?

Venus lifts her chin, a little smile on her lips. Her foot brushes the dead Elder's pocket, straining against the nail in her hands.

Marcellus smiles. He ignores his father and sighs.

"Cece, my dear? Stop stressing." He slides his cup of tea towards her, freshly refilled. She blinks at him, body stilling. "Eleanor has excellent taste. This tea really calms the nerves."

She stares at the tea as if it's poison, unused to the unexpected kindness.

From the other end of the room, Melanie sighs and flattens her hands on the table, oblivious to our conversation.

"Any updates, Mel?" I ask from the shadows.

"We need Argenti blood. The more powerful the Argenti, the more powerful the vial." Mel's voice dances through the room as she straightens and drops a pile of paperwork on the bench. Savannah swipes the blue vial before it can roll off the table from the impact.

The Bloodhound snorts, drinking her tea. "Guess I'll be the only one blessed enough to be the Bloodhound then."

Venus slips her toes inside the dead Elder's pockets. Maybe it's the drugs in her body, but she doesn't notice me noticing. I peel from the shadows, sword in my grip, and swing the thing down in a long arch.

"Watch your aim," Savannah says as I swing.

Metal pounds against stone, shooting sparks.

Venus's scream clambers through the space, ricocheting off the walls. Elias leans forward, wincing. Blood seeps over stone, licking against my dirty shoes.

I stare at it and think of Tam.

"Stupid boy. Stupid guard."

"Good aim," Savannah applauds.

The Bloodhound peels herself off the desk and darts towards me, spurred by the action.

Blood streams from the stump in Venus's leg. The dismembered foot still sits inside the Elder's pocket, right near a knife he'd concealed there.

I should have taken it, because Elias uses the commotion to grab it with bound fingers.

I only have eyes for the bloodthirsty Argenti aiming for me.

I duck her.

Just as Marcellus intercepts, almost panicked. "Celestine! Come back to me, my dear."

The Bloodhound stops a moment, ready to pounce. Her silk slippers slide in the blood trailing over the stone. Venus whimpers below her.

"Ugh!" The Bloodhound groans and reaches down to wrestle the knife from Elias. "If I die because of you, Hart, the world will hear about it."

Her words are dripped in venom and lust, and I'm not sure if I appreciate or hate her when she whips around and glides back to the Argenti man still perched lazily against the desk.

He smiles. "I'm sure they will."

Elias writhes, but no words come out of him as he tries to free himself of his bindings. I wait for him to start spinning bullshit or to beg for freedom again, but he doesn't. He's just a weak, terrified man.

Marcellus claps his hands together. "I'm growing bored. You ready, Beckett?"

When she doesn't respond, Savannah hands him the vial and says, "She's ready."

Mel shakes her head. "No, I told you. We need—"

Marcellus grins like a madman and takes the blade from the Bloodhound, spinning the feeble thing in the air. Celestine watches it in a trance, not even mad.

"It's okay, Mel. We got blood."

So fast I almost miss it, Savannah tosses Marcellus an empty vial that he catches with his free hand.

She doesn't even look at him. She's looking at her mother, who's still sobbing and carrying against the floor, the stump of her leg spurting blood.

The silver colour fuses with the red of the Elder's, and all of us stare in shock as Marcellus walks over and grips Venus's stump.

The woman's shriek is deafening. I lift my hands to my ears, covering the sound.

"Let me go!" Venus screams.

He digs his fingers into the wound I created and gathers the liquid in the vial.

"Release her, son! This is barbaric!"

"You're only saying that because you're frightened of what I can do with this," he says, dropping her leg with a wet smack. As he holds the silver liquid in front of his father's face, he stares deep into the eyes so alike his own—a mirror of each other's, save for the silver. He lifts his father's chin, forcing him to look at him. "You are the barbaric one, Father."

"I am a ruler," Elias spits.

"No," Savannah says. "You're a coward."

The Bloodhound laughs at that.

Marcellus dips his chin. "A coward who deserved to die centuries ago. Alas, this is not your moment. Instead, you will become a spectacle. Just like you always dreamed."

He turns his back on the man and hands Savannah the silver vial. The Bloodhound follows him, plastered to his back.

"I made you a monster, my son. I admit that."

I almost miss the second Marcellus's expression changes. The Bloodhound doesn't, though. She flexes her fingers, stepping back from him. Savannah gasps a little, but her troubled eyes seem almost expectant.

Melanie screams, "No!"

Marcellus grips Celestine's face with a splayed hand and tips his head back as if drinking. The other is holding a blade's edge deep against her throat.

She's writhing, screaming, as blood pools out of her mouth. Marcellus groans, absorbing every lick of her power.

"I can't use my Magic! I can't use my Magic!" She's babbling it around the blood as panic flares in her eyes.

The tea he gave her, I realise with sickening clarity, *he spiked it with the vial that stops their Magic. And now he's drinking her raw, and she cannot fight back.*

Savannah turns away, her eyes blinking against silent tears.

"You're stealing all her Magic!" Mel screams. "You'll kill her!"

"Ahh," Marcellus groans, his eyes rolling. They thrum with power.

The Bloodhound stumbles back, crashing against the desk. The teacup falls and shatters on the ground.

Her eyes are unseeing.

"He's giving you what you asked for," Elias says on a breath, eyes wide as he stares at his son. For once, he doesn't look afraid. He looks at his son in awe.

All at once, Marcellus drops the Bloodhound. Her body crashes to the ground.

"Give me the vial," he says with power lining his eyes.

With shaking hands, Melanie takes both vials from Savannah's hand and gives them to Marcellus. Savannah seems frozen, staring at him, her chest heavily rising and falling. The room feels thick with static, as if the Leys under the castle have come alive.

If I can feel it, I can only guess what Savannah is feeling right now.

Marcellus grips the vials in both hands, pouring one into the other, then closes his eyes.

The static in the room feels like it's about to combust.

I tremble as I step back and slam into the cabinet. Venus is whimpering at my feet, her head lolling as she tries to steady herself both against the pain and the static in the room.

Marcellus pours every drop of the Bloodhound's Silver Magic into the vial, then holds the thing out, shining and silver, towards Mel.

She stares at him, unable to move. Strands of sweaty, buttery locks have fallen in her face, and her lips pop open. No sound comes out.

"Take it!"

She does not. Her fingers start to tremble, but her feet remain planted on the ground.

"Is this the right way to make it, Beckett?" he asks when she doesn't say anything.

She closes her lips, tightening her jaw. Her prosthetic arm spasms.

I want to reach out to her, push her hair back from her cheek, but I, too, am frozen.

"Daughter," Venus moans. "Savannah."

Savannah ignores her, but at the sound of her name, she jolts out of her trance.

I watch as she takes a deep breath, filling her lungs with what must be Magic. She takes one careful step towards Marcellus and grabs the vial, her motions steady.

"That isn't... that's not..." Elias is fumbling, shaking his head.

"It is," Marcellus declares. "Everyone in this room helped make it, Father. Except you."

"Because it's *wrong.*"

Savannah holds it out to Melanie. "You were born to be this."

Melanie's silver eyes are alight in the streaming sun. She doesn't flinch or shrink, she just stands tall and breathes in the sight of her friend. "Savannah..."

"No one will force you," she quickly adds.

"Although we will all strongly urge," Marcellus mutters quietly.

Melanie takes a long, deep breath, and reaches for the vial. "I was born for this."

It's her eyes—so warm and gentle, and full of knowledge and determination, that get me. I know those eyes so well I could paint them in my sleep. They drew me out of the darkest hour of my life and gave me a new home and purpose.

Melanie Beckett's eyes, which have always shone the silver of an Argenti, just like the Bloodhound, before she turned.

It's at that moment that I know what I must do.

I lunge forwards, my body swaying as my sword clatters to the floor.

"Mel!" The scream rakes deep in my throat, and my soul is left behind as I reach her, because I know I am already too late.

She tips the vial down her throat in one brisk motion.

I fall at her feet just as Marcellus says on a shaky breath, "Congrats, Beckett. You're the new Bloodhound. Now, *go and kill*."

She turns to look at him with eyes that glow with the rage of a thousand stars.

The eyes of death.

The eyes of a Bloodhound.

SAVANNAH

She looks at Elias Hart for what he is: human.

Not an Elder. Not a villain. Just a man desperate not to die.

Melanie stares at him and smiles with violent Argenti eyes.

The empty vial slips from her fingers, shattering on the floor. The sound makes me flinch and step back. I pull my hand to my heart, trying to still it.

"Mel," Jesse gasps as he stumbles.

Melanie doesn't notice as her cyborg hand drags, metal on metal over the counter, the nails of the prosthetic scraping until they meet the handle of a scalpel. The container it was in tips over, spilling an assembly of pens, among another tools.

I step back once more, trying not to show my shock.

"Mel. Mel, look at me," Jesse pleads. His voice is low, raw, and aching as he holds himself up against the wall, his sapphire eyes like obelisks.

Melanie does not. Melanie is gone.

What have we done?

She strides towards Elias and tilts her head at him. I can feel her tasting the sweet pleasure of Silver Magic all around us.

Magic covers her skin like a cloak, as if she is tearing it from the very walls of this castle, sucking it from the Ley under us and moulding it.

The air feels cold with power.

"Mel, please," Jesse tries again.

Vaguely, I sense Marcellus watching me, his eyes intense and prying, his chest rising and falling as he takes in the monster before us. I don't give him what he wants. I don't even look at him as I fall to my knees.

Because when Melanie tilts her head, Elias copies her.

Silver Magic pounds over him. The sweat dripping on his brow seems to stop and the rapid rise and fall of his chest eases. He tilts his head, exposing his neck.

She doesn't say anything as she looks at him.

What have we done?

"Mel," Jesse croaks. "Mel."

The scalpel drives through Elias's exposed neck. Hot, red blood drips down his front. The Magic melts away and, as the man crumbles, reality comes back to greet him.

He thrashes, eyes bulging, the sweat deepening on his brow. He looks with panicked eyes towards his son, but the man is beyond words. Blood spills from his mouth until his head lolls, slapping down to his chest.

Melanie just watches, frozen in time. She watches him die with a keen fascination.

A sharp breath shudders past my teeth as I watch the blood

waterfall to the ground. It's red and vibrant yet muted compared to the wicked silver sheen of my mother's blood.

When I finally turn to Marcellus, our eyes crash, equally wide with shock.

Elias Hart is dead.

AMADEA

“When I grew up in the castle, my only company was the whispers of others,” I tell Elijah, my holds folded in my lap and my voice low. “I never had friends because there was never another child like me. My mother died during the Moon Blitz and my brother kept me in cryosleep. There are trees on Umbra called *Tenere* trees, the sap of which is ice to the touch and can envelop a human body and freeze their cells. I didn’t dream or feel pain. But I had horrid nightmares and fatal injuries when I woke centuries later. It was soon learnt that I…”

I swallow, my eyes darting to the curtain at the end of the room. I let some Magic pour over my veins, shifting my form slightly to reassure me.

“I was powerful,” I whisper. “Children my age either feared me, wanted to be me, or hated me. I had no friends. Not even my tutors. And my brother disappeared for months or years at a time on occasion."

Elijah, his eyes wide, blurts, "I'm sorry, but what has this got to do with Melanie?"

I clench my teeth, refraining from huffing.

Jasmine bats him on the shoulder then leans forward on her palms, now weirdly splayed out on the bed. Her round eyes have never been so interested in me.

"Because," I say, trying not to sound annoyed, "I became a good spy. My brother trained me as soon as he could. I was only six, but I was there the night Melanie's parents were killed. I was pretending to be a staff member in her manor when I heard some of the nobles talking about their plan to take out the Beckett family. I barely got out. And Melanie… she saw me as I ran outside. She tells everyone there weren't survivors, but there was me."

"No way. That's actually so cool. You're a badass, Dea," Jasmine says.

"She watched Melanie's family die, Jasmine. I don't think that's as cool as you think it is." Elijah scoffs, but the appreciation is behind his eyes, too.

The next words I speak are the hardest things I've ever had to say, because I have never, *ever* admitted them before. I held this damn truth to my chest like admitting it would get me killed. Only, now I don't think it matters that much.

"I was one of her contacts for years. I was Melanie's best informant. Of course, she is an exceptional hacker and there's a great deal she can find out herself, but I was the one who helped her find Savannah. She never told anyone she had access to Umbra when she was on Terra, but she did."

No one speaks. They just stare. And stare. And stare.

My heart beats wildly in my throat, but I force the next words. "She doesn't know who I am, of course. She always thought I was a girl who worked in the castle. I have always wondered if maybe she thought I was lying about that, too."

"Holy mother of—" Jasmine starts.

"Jasmine, don't swear in front of her, she's a child."

"Nuh-uh. She's not a child, she's my idol."

I fight the smile creeping across my face. Jasmine stares at me like I'm the stars and the moon, and when Jasmine looks at you like that, it's easy to forget how to speak. She's downright ethereal, despite how annoying she is.

"Wait, wait, wait," Jasmine rushes to speak. "You said you were six when Melanie's parents were killed, but if this is your actual body, you look eight now."

I smile again, but it's without feeling. Jasmine has seen the world and the galaxies, reversed her physical form to a younger body, lived a brand-new life, and done a million things I could barely dream of doing, yet she is so closeminded. I'm a *shapeshifter*, for heaven's sake.

"I'm the youngest pure-blooded Argenti in Umbran history, but I am not eight years old," I admit quietly.

I sound childish when I say it and, truth be told, I do look very young for my age. But for some reason my face grows hot at the insinuation that I'm *that* young.

"Melanie lost her parents and her arm in the fire when she was a teenager. She went to Terra quickly after that. After the fire, I found her in the med wards making herself a new arm. My father had heard word of someone breaching the Umbran database. He was confused, since the Becketts were dead and their daughter was training to be a medic under the strict care of her uncle. He sent me to check. I used the same face as the one I wore the night of the fire, and she knew immediately. I told her to cool off on the hacking, and she told me she needed to escape her uncle.

"He beat her when she didn't listen, locking her in her rooms when he caught her sneaking out to the med wards to work on her arm… stuff like that. So, I spewed some lies to my father, and he promoted her uncle as the Terran Liaison. What we didn't expect was that her uncle would take Melanie with him."

Elijah releases a long, heavy breath. He's fuming a little, his cheeks red, but he stays quiet. Jasmine has started picking at rogue pieces of metal sticking out of her suit, losing interest at the direction of my story.

"She was a broken girl when I knew her, but the day she met Jesse Hayes a spark grew in her chest. That man is *everything* to her, but I dare say she will never admit it, because he was broken himself and had fallen in love with Savannah at some point. But they're a power unit, those two. Melanie became a force. She got better at hacking, and she found a way to reach me on Umbra. She picked up her parent's work and started hunting for Savannah. I guess the rest is history."

Jasmine holds her hand out, staring at her nails. They are chipped and worn, but surprisingly clean. She picks under them from her spot on the bed.

"She only found Savannah because I moved to Silver Valley, where Sav found my Lythia May necklace. She's not really the god you make her out to be."

I shake my head, jostling my brown hair. "She is, because the prophecy needed someone to help get Savannah to Umbra. '*The chocolate-haired princess will sail from Terra to take over the throne and neutralise the destruction of our planet*', the prophecy said. But for that to take place, she needed a way home. She needed a powerful, loyal Umbran friend."

Jasmine sits upright, her face reddening. "That was *my* job."

Elijah grunts, his face a little pale. "Jasmine, no hate, but you kinda have no right to say that after everything you've done."

She whips her head to him. "After everything I've done? After the family I lost and the many years spent living a lie and changing my entire life? All that, only for you to say I have no right to have a say in any of this?" Her body is shaking a little, her curls bouncing around her head. "I am Savannah's best friend, not Melanie Beckett."

What does this girl have against Melanie, anyway? My chest feels heavy with fatigue, my skin crawling from this conversation.

"We're not undermining what you did. But you must admit that Melanie was there when Savannah needed her most." I squeeze my fingers together, trying not to fall off the bed from the effort of inching away from her.

"Maybe you only care about Melanie because you feel like, through her, *you* made a difference to Savannah and the prophecy. But you were just a contact, locked in a castle."

I let Jasmine's words drift around me, unbothered by them.

Elijah swings his legs over the bed and puts his head in his hands. The room seems to get a little darker as does.

"I think we should get Elijah more medicine," I murmur.

"He's fine." She pats his exposed back. It's healed now, but he still doesn't look great. Jasmine pulls back, lowering her chin back in her palms as she stares at me innocently. "Savannah only came to Umbra because she fell in love with Hayes. Just admit it, Amadea."

I really don't care about that. Magic pulses at my fingertips as footsteps sound outside our room. I freeze a little as the curtain to our room flutters, but I hold myself steady.

"Melanie and Jesse are endgame."

Elijah rubs his temples, his eyes squeezing. "Guys. I was there, okay. She lost Silver Valley and said she was going to Umbra to make the Elders pay."

That isn't how life works. I don't want to say it out loud, because they're both glaring at me, and my stomach is flipping because the sound of people speaking behind the curtain have hushed. But Savannah has been prepped for this so much longer than they know. The bombs were just her breaking point, I guess.

If it weren't for Melanie bringing Savannah to the base on Silver

Island, sacrificing her tools and her time to aid Savannah's wishes, and standing by her and supporting her when she needed it most… I daresay it would have taken a great deal longer for Savannah to choose to come to Umbra, explosion or not.

But they're both staring at me, so I suck in a breath and mutter quickly, "I think we should catch Elijah up on what has happened with the Dome and everything—"

"Oh, no." Jasmine slaps the bed, her face red. "You spill out this story about how Melanie is great and powerful, but she isn't. She is no Argenti. We are all just human beings trying our goddamn best. I want to fight, too. I want to help my friend again, okay? I'm trying to find a way to make up for my mistakes, but no one is giving me any chances to, whether that be because I'm crippled or because they hate me."

Or because you're constantly whinging about bugs or busy flirting with Jesse's sister? I want to say. All I do is arch an eyebrow.

"We didn't mean…" Elijah sighs. "Geez, Jaz. Not everything is about you, okay? We're both healed now, so we can do stuff again. I promise we'll find something meaningful to do for Savannah. But in the meantime, chill out about Melanie. You hate her because you think she took your spot at Savannah's side, but she didn't do that. Melanie's a good person."

The curtain behind me sways, as if the wildlings are listening. No more footsteps. No more voices. I reach for my Magic because it's the only shield I have.

A shadow drops behind the curtain, tall and dark.

Jasmine freezes. Elijah still has his mouth open, mid-speech. I hold my breath, Magic pulsing, but it's just Mark. The curtain is pushed aside, revealing a dozen wildlings behind him, their faces all covered. The man looks tense as he scans us.

Eventually, he settles on Elijah and smiles.

"I hope you're right, because we just got news from the wild-lings. Melanie has become something else. She rounded up the

Elders at the castle." He turns and looks at me slowly, his face soft and eyes wide, if a little flighty, behind his glasses. "She killed your father, my child. His head is spiked on the walls, rotting in the sun."

43

JESSE

I 've never seen Mel like this and that's saying something, because I know this girl as well as my own soul.

She is pure power. Pure strength.

The sun is hot on our backs, melting my skin. I let it. I let the pain crash over me.

"Mel…" I breathe. "Mel, look at me."

I've barely been able to breathe since the medicine slipped down her throat. Not since she turned to me, not as Marcellus told her to "Go and kill", not since she killed Elias, and not since Savannah stepped back against the lab table.

I am undone. Something inside me is broken.

Because it wasn't Marcellus's idea for her to slash his neck, nor was it his idea for her to drag the body to the castle walls. She tore down the head of Lily's cat, Wrath, and replaced it with the Elder's head, leaving it there for everyone to see.

"Mel," I beg, my words trembling. "Melanie."

The Argenti emerge first, standing still and staring. Her buttery hair floats in the breeze, glistening in a way that is not quite silver but not quite human. Her eyes glow like stars. Her entire body is immobile, the mechanic arm for once not twitching at her side.

She is the bringer of death.

The square slowly empties as the Argenti slip away, making their way towards the cave full of S.P. guns, EXO Suits, bombs, and Hovers. They are preparing for war.

Savannah stands at the front of the castle, her hand over her heart and Marcellus by her side. No one is around to see her empathy or to see her exhale loudly.

"I think we got the calculations for the medicine wrong," she says, but it's just background noise.

All I can process right now is the woman bearing the face of the one I knew so well. I reach for her hand. "Mel."

Soon, the villagers come. Men, women, children, even men from Sector 2 all come to the wall to stare at the severed head of their Third Elder. Melanie stares back at them, not saying a single word.

"Melanie Adelaide Beckett, please look at me."

Her eyes stay frozen on the crowd. She doesn't even bristle as I take her hand.

There isn't a single moment in my entire life that I have felt the earth shatter beneath me as I do now. My entire heart and soul falls from my feet, and I suddenly wish I had never met the girl before me.

I wish I never snuck onto a shuttle to Silver Valley as a boy.

I wish I had died with the rest of my family.

Because the moment I met Melanie was the moment I signed myself this fate.

And have lost the only girl I ever truly loved.

AMADEA

"How did it happen?" Elijah asks Mark the moment the wildlings let us out of our room. They blindfold us as they lead us through more tunnels, the occasionally flickering lights branding the outside of the dark cloth.

"They fused some concoction of chemicals with Umbran plant matter, Magic, and Argenti blood, and fed it to the girl in the hopes of turning her into a pure-blooded Argenti."

"And did it work?" Jasmine asks as she stumbles in her EXO suit. It encases her feet, and each footfall sounds like metal cutlery hitting stone.

The sound of Mark swallowing loudly is our only answer.

Eventually, the wildlings take off our blindfolds, and we are all too awestruck to keep speaking anyway.

I ball my hands in front of my chest and nervously rub the

dust off my hands as they lead us down row upon row of winding tunnels, each one looking the same as the next… sandstone walls, throbbing lights, and rooms obscured with curtains. It's hard to know if we are travelling up, down, or across, as they lead us on.

I keep peering up at their faces, but they are hidden by their veils. The only person in our party that stays missing is Lily, which is jarring.

This world under the sand seems like a place woman like her would thrive. It's so separate from the world I grew up in—so at one with the nature around it. It's an extension of everything Lily had tried to build for herself outside of the Dome.

A part of me wonders if her refusal to come inside is because she worries she will fall in love with the place and will end up living away from not only her snow cats but her brother.

When they lead us through a curtain into what appears to be a menagerie, that thought only increases.

"What stinks like horse poo?" Jasmine asks from behind me. When she finally sees where we are, she mutters, "Oh."

The wildlings have carved out a large cavern with translucent ceilings that flood the place with natural light.

A man grips my shoulder, yanking my frozen feet forward as we head down a winding path which snakes around animal enclosures.

Mark's jaw hangs upon as we skitter past what appears to be a natural watering hole where large water birds with gills interwoven among their feathers splash around chasing fish.

Piscators. They used to populate the rivers near the Kingdom. An Argenti who had a way of understanding animals trained them to hunt for fish. They all but vanished from the waterways when that Argenti died.

"I didn't even know there was a third Sector until the other day, and now you're showing us all this?" Mark gapes, his glasses sliding down his nose a little.

I don't know how, but a comradery has formed between our

little group over the last several hours. Mark stands by me protectively as the wildlings all rake their eyes over us. And Elijah does, too. His hands are in his pockets, his chest rising and falling rapidly.

His stance is relaxed, but I think he'll be ready to move if anyone touches a hair on any of our heads. Then there's Jasmine, doing a wild job of looking down at the wildlings, her wide eyes hard and distrusting.

She's never looked at any of us like that.

"Not to mention healing Elijah and giving me legs again," Jasmine says, her sandy-blonde curls bouncing as she takes in the menagerie before turning back to look at them, her lips set. "What's up with that, anyway? Why do you care?"

"A trade," a female behind us says. "You brought us tech from the Kingdom and we gave you what you needed. That is our form of currency."

Jasmine snickers. "And here I thought you cared about us."

Elijah touches her shoulder in warning.

A wildling ahead lowers his face coverings, his hands marked and calloused from years of grisly work. My heart startles when his onyx eyes go straight for me.

They pick apart my soul, as if he knows my father is an Elder… *was.* I push away the feeling of Magic surging under my feet and stare back.

"We live a separate life from one you were brought into," the man says. I blink at him, recognising him as the man with olive skin from the sand crawler, his long braids now pulled back from his face. "We made a deal with the Elders centuries ago to remain undisturbed."

"I don't understand," I interject, my fingers trembling as he analyses me. "Why are you bringing us to your home if you want things to stay that way?"

The man smiles, his eyes alight. "A good question."

Another wildling comes into our field of view—the man with the metal leg, also from the sand crawler.

"As we understand, you are what remains of The Fated's family. Each of you is someone she loves dearly. And, as we discussed with Mark earlier, the reign of Elders has come to an abrupt ending last Night."

I bristle, my words an octave above a breath when I say, "What?"

Mark reaches over and shields me, his eyes softening at the worry in my voice. He doesn't touch me, but I feel his protection all around me, covering me from them.

My eyes glaze a little at the notion of it. My father has never stood by me like that. Not even Marcel, who has spent his entire life protecting me, has ever felt the need to hide me from people. Why would he, when he knows I can hide myself just fine?

But this, right here, is something else. For whatever wild reason, Mark seems to believe I am innocent enough to protect. I fold my arms over my chest, clenching my heart.

"They still have time to reclaim their seats," the wildling continues. "We have reason to believe a handful of them survived the Night and that The Fated won't be quick to kill them." This one is a woman I don't know. She lowers her cowl, analysing us with copper eyes.

A large mammal whinnies behind us. Desert horses.

I try and stop myself from turning to look for them. *Fortis pellis mammilia* was what the Elders wrote in their journals about them, which was just another way to say a strong, skinned mammal. Now, we just call them desert horses. They have tough skin, like lizards, with brown fur over their backs to cover them from the sun. In a way, they do look like horses, or camels, aside from the lizard faces.

They're innocent, harmless creatures but I've always found them terrifying.

I recognise the sound of their whinnies from the time Marcel took me beyond the Dome to a Dome Farm and made me ride one. I hated every second of it. The enclosure for the *piscators* is too green and filled with trees for nesting and waters for fishing, blocking the desert horses from sight. I lean against the gold railing where a forcefield also meets my back.

"This is all good and dandy," Jasmine comments, trying to kick what looks like either a stone or a piece of animal dropping away with her foot, "but why did you take us to the smelliest place in your sand dungeon?"

"A small price to pay," a woman ahead of us mutters.

Mark runs his hand along the gold railing behind me, his eyes thoughtful. "Can we perhaps discuss what you want from us, then?"

"We want what we have always had," the olive-skinned man says. "Privacy and immunity from Argenti affairs. This place was built as a refuge for people to escape. There are many who didn't want to live under the Elders' rule, who decided instead that they would brave the elements of the planet to live a free life. This place is for those people. This is our stronghold, a centre point, and a haven for travellers and runaways. We've existed here, thriving off the planet, for centuries. The Elders let us do our own thing in exchange for half of our supplies—be that food, knowledge, and all our reaping of the planet."

The covered woman interrupts, her voice tinged with panic. "Let's just say we had a deal with the Elders. Anonymity. Now they're all dying off, we fear for our relationship with the Kingdom."

I study the solid way they stand and the scent of fear coming off their bodies. These people are full of apprehension and nervousness. If I were to wager, there's a lot more to their Sector than they have showed us, but unless I join them completely I doubt I will ever see it.

Fair enough. None of us here can strike a deal with them, but by being closest to Savannah, we could get her the message and put in a good word.

Politics are never ending. So, I give them what they want.

"Help us get back to the Kingdom and use your men to free anyone who may still be inside Sector 2, and we can promise to put in a good word for you with The Fated."

Jasmine turns to me, gaping. Mark just chews on his lip.

"I dunno about you guys," Elijah says, speaking for the first time since entering the menagerie, "but I'm a little curious about what Sector 3 can do to help us in the Kingdom."

All the wildlings tense. Even Jasmine notices the insinuation and rolls her eyes.

"We each left the Kingdom and our old lives behind for a reason. We certainly don't want to go back and fight their wars for them."

I can't pinpoint the speaker amid the wildlings around us.

"We won't ask you to fight," Mark declares. "Savannah wouldn't want innocents to lay down their lives. All we ask is that you help those who may need it and keep your doors open for anyone who may want to run."

The man with the braids nods his head. "Of course. As we have always done."

The other man adds, "As long as doing so will not get us involved in any squabbles."

"We can promise to try," Mark answers softly.

All of them watch him carefully and uncertainly.

With a deep, hearty breath, I shoulder my fear of staying ambiguous.

"I have people in the castle who will rain hell down on anyone who dares to come for Sector 3. You can trust that."

A bold promise I can never be sure to keep. But they seem to take it.

A couple of them murmur under their breath.

The wildling with the metal leg nods at some of his friends behind us. "Kent comes and goes from the Kingdom often; he will organise your travel arrangements back."

A man with a concealed face nods. *Kent.* He takes a friend and they disappear into the menagerie. A chorus of animals chirp at them as they stride past. The desert horses carry on louder in the background.

Elijah watches them go with wide eyes, absorbing the sounds. I wonder how startling it would be for him to see so many new animals. Perhaps I would look like that, too, if I visited a zoo on Terra. It's an impossible feat now that the Elders have cut all ties to the planet.

"Oh!" Jasmine suddenly exclaims, jumping upright. "I have another condition."

Elijah starts at the sudden announcement. I swear I hear Mark groan.

I hide my own irritation and smile at the girl, as if on board with her declaration.

"Ley Lines," Jasmine adds, making herself look important. "Can you tell us all you know about them? I have a feeling Savannah will want that. I can come with one of you privately if you'd rather keep the information secret. I'll be happy to bring it to her personally."

"I can lend you my journal with all my personal findings," the man with the braid says. "The Leys are no secret of ours. All the Argenti know of them, in a way. It's a planet-based power they can access by birth right."

I swear he looks at me when he says that. The back of my neck heats, but luckily, no one else notices. The desert horses whinny again, making me twitch.

Jasmine grins. "Excellent. Your Fated would be happy with that. Anyway. Carry on."

Elijah glowers at Jasmine.

I think back to what she spilled in the room earlier. *"I'm trying to find a way to make up for my mistakes, but no one is giving me any chances to."*

The edge of my lip twitches a little, and Elijah gives me an exasperated look. I return it with a small roll of my eyes and, in that moment, I decide I like Elijah Brookes. He's the kind of friend I can imagine playing tag with around the castle. Someone to laugh at my jokes. A kind of friend I never thought a person like me could have.

It makes me think of Savannah's brother, Mason. They both had the same glimmer of light in their eyes, the same broken innocence, and the same look of childish adventure.

Mark wraps his arm over my shoulders, as if reading my thoughts. "If that's all then?"

A few of them lower their heads in acknowledgment. Jasmine just rubs her hands together, smiling. She leans toward the wildling who promised her his journal, watching him hungrily as he takes his leave from the menagerie to retrieve what was promised.

The desert horses whinny again, as if sensing we are leaving. Magic swells at my feet as my heart does a little slap.

"Alright then," Mark smiles. "I would like us to go back to the Kingdom, to find my daughter."

His arm tightens around my shoulders, which I'm thankful for, because a wildling has just started staring at me again. Sweat lines my hands as I wipe them down my jeans.

"The water passage is narrowing, so you will take that route on foot. We have clothes and water, but the trip to your shore is a short one, so this is just customary," the wildling with the metal leg tells us.

As Kent returns with a desert horse, my knees buckle. I don't even really watch as the wildlings start handing us clothes, to absorb the heat of the sun, and water, to give us strength.

"How far are we from home?" Mark enquires.

"Several hours. This part of our home is closest to you. The reason it took longer for you to arrive via sand crawler was merely from precaution."

They took a detour here. Smart.

But really, I don't care. Because the horse is now staring at me.

"If you follow Kent, there is an exit on the other end of the menagerie. He will guide you back to Sector 3. I've already sent someone to escort your other friend to meet you with the horses. Lily, I believe you call her," the man explains.

I'm still staring at the desert horse's pointed face and flashing tongue. I still remember the way its grisly hair felt against my legs and the sound it made when eating a desert mouse on our commute to the Dome Farms.

Nope. I would rather die than sit on that thing again.

Mark notices, his face softening. He reaches for my hand.

"The beasts are safe," Kent assures me. He still wears his hood, but his light voice sounds friendly. I give him a watery smile, my heart accelerating.

I want to run and call for my brother, or slink away and hide. Instead, I douse myself in Magic and take a deep breath. The Silver Magic dances over my skin like a fog. I sink into the comforting feeling and look away from the beast, letting Mark guide me forwards.

Kent leads our group through the menagerie, past all the animals. I can barely see, because the horse is following us.

A wildling hands Jasmine a journal, his fingers shaking a little.

I don't know how, but when we step outside, I somehow find the strength to shoulder my fear and let Mark hoist me up onto the animal, my legs trembling the entire time.

Stars, screw this. I never want to step foot in the desert again.

SAVANNAH

"Let me help you, Daughter," Venus mutters as we plop her on a bed and let the *Velox* course through her body. I didn't want to save her. Frankly, I considered letting her bleed to death in the Elder's office. "Let me go."

But there's been enough death for one night.

Marcel went to the volcano with a team of Argenti to repair the damage to the Dome. Melanie was pulled back into the castle by Jesse and locked up in Amadea's room, so I now sit on the edge of my bed, nursing a fresh cup of coffee. I stare at my mother while medics begin to work on her.

I'm on Evaline, Roman and Eleanor duty. I can sense them on a ship circling the castle, but I couldn't help but take a detour to visit my darling mother first.

Sweat beads down my brow from the hot day, and I wish I made the coffee iced.

I take a lazy sip from it. "You once said that you're one of the loveliest gems of Umbra. Do you still think that's true, Mother?"

She's shackled to my bed. The *Velox* healed the skin, stopped the blood flow, and erased the scars, but it didn't regrow her foot. If medicine could do that, Melanie wouldn't have a metal arm.

I wonder how my mother would feel about being a cyborg. I tilt my head at her, analysing her face. It's full of grime and her hair is a mess. Those cruel silver eyes are narrowed at me, and she spits a little as she responds.

"Then give me a bath. Free me from my ties. My people need me."

I slurp my coffee loudly. "Why?"

"You killed Elias Hart. They will be retaliating."

"Nah. Marcellus is on my side and he controls the Argenti."

As she tilts her head at me, I can almost hear her say, "*Is that what you think?*"

One of the medics bristles as they pack the medicine into a neat little bag. The second one waits by my door, unable to leave us fast enough. I barely even acknowledge them. I probably should, but I also don't want to take my eyes off my mother for a split second.

"Free me, Savannah. Let me help you win this."

Her Magic is still kept at bay from the drugs Marcel forced down her throat. I put the red liquid on my nightstand, right next to my array of ornate ceramic cups. The moment my mother slips into my head with her telepathy, I will make her a coffee and shove the stuff back down her throat.

"You also said the last gift you will ever give me was freeing Elijah Brookes, back when you so delightfully tortured him in the Safe Holds."

She leers at me with eyes in perfect reflections of my own. Only, hers are filled with hate.

I take another sip of coffee and wait for her to answer.

"Things change," she finally bites out. "Let me free."

"'Remember, the Elders always win,'" I singsong, quoting her again.

"Things change," she seethes, but she doesn't say it like she believes it. Her body writhes against my covers.

"Perhaps," I muse. "But you do not."

She thrashes some more, pulling at her bindings.

I feel the need to squirm like her as Magic cascades over my skin, pricking my nerves.

The weight of my switchblade is heavy in my pocket. I changed out of my dirtied clothing while the medics worked on my mother, bathing quickly as the *Velox* I took worked through my body. Then I donned jewels and a pretty yellow dress that offsets the golden hues in my dark hair. A promise of sunlight, much like the blistering heat outside.

My mother stares at the fabrics as if she wants to pry them from my skin.

"There is one way you can help me, though," I tell her.

She stares deeply at me, her eyes now obelisks, as she tries to comprehend my pleasantries. I'm so different to the daughter she thought I was. I can see it all over her face.

An annoying flea, she thought I was. But now my mother *fears* me.

She thrashes some more, silver eyes shining. I try not to wince at the way she's smearing dirt and dried blood all over my bed.

"Elias Hart died with little to no fight. I would like you to tell me why."

And there it is. The sinking feeling that hasn't escaped since Melanie cut off his head. It isn't going away, because a man like Elias Hart does not succumb that easily.

Why spend the entire Night hiding and licking his wounds, knowing my people were safe inside his bunkers? He had something else at play. Even in death, this man haunts me.

I can just feel it.

"Oh, you think yourself so cocky. So proud. My dear, has it every occurred to you that the villains in your story are just men? On Umbra, we are seen to be untouchable, but we can all die as easily as the knife turns. In death, we all find our mortality. The question is, will you be able to stop it?"

A threat. I almost drop my coffee as my heart sinks to my feet. As I stare down at my mother's wide silver eyes, my body begins to shake. I place the coffee on the nightstand, fingers twitching for my switchblade.

The Elders always win.

"Melanie's uncle… he's one of many addicted to the taste of power. But he will never get it. That can make a person dangerous, unless you know how to control it. Have you considered that maybe the Elders are doing the same to you? Operating still, doing what they always planned to do, while you blow up the Dome and kidnap your helpless mother?"

My mother writhes as she seeks a better angle to glare at me. And, suddenly, it all ticks into place. Elias was a petty man. He wouldn't have spent the night hiding.

Instead, he would have hunted for a way to best me. And what better way to do that than to end me the same way I tried to end him?

I stand, my pulse climbing as the realisation hits. "He's going to blow up the castle."

My mother is silent for a moment. "Now, why would he do that?"

I fork my Magic out to my friends, sensing if they're still alive as panic overcomes me. "Elias Hart is going to blow us all up, isn't he, Mother? You wanted to help, so answer me!"

Her eyes flash. "Free me first."

I do not.

"Savannah!"

I hurriedly gather up a few supplies, stumbling over my dress in a panic.

"Daughter!"

I spare her a glance. Magic tears from my body in search of my friends, my father… everyone. Over and over. Even with the medication preventing her use of Magic, my mother feels it. Her teeth flash, grinning at me.

Yes. Alert them. You don't have time, anyway, her eyes seem to say.

I have no clue what it means.

"Remember the first fires, Savannah? Remember the deaths you caused?"

The bombing of Silver Valley. The first blow Umbra ever landed on me.

I pause at her tone, my fingers frozen around the red medicine as I pick it up.

"What are you saying?" I ask.

"Free me."

"No."

She cocks her head at me. "Then run to your father. Tell him how the Argenti are evil. Show him what you've become, Daughter. And maybe, just maybe, he will blame you when the missiles launch on his home."

Remember the first fires, Savannah?

"Impossible." I all but stop breathing.

"Not impossible. The Elders invented faster ships. You didn't know that one, did you?"

I nearly drop the medicine, but I somehow make it out of my room.

I run and I run, all the way to Melanie Beckett.

AMADEA

We collect them one by one.

Men, women, children... we lead them to the shore as we go.

Kent takes us, the embers of Sector 2 drifting on the winds behind, as we stand down by the currents near some boats still intact after the bombing.

I stare at the lapping waters separating the Kingdom from where we stand. Tunnels of smoke drift up into the sky; plumes of death from the Night before.

Somewhere out there, I'll find my brother. Better yet, I'll rid myself of the desert horses.

My pulse flutters a little as I hear my horse navigate the wreckage to avoid the water.

"I give you our memories, Amadea Hart."

The sound of my name makes me spin and gasp.

He called me Hart. How long have they known?

Kent approaches in full garb, probably sweating under all those clothes. Between us, he holds a draw string bag, waiting for me to grab it. My palms start to sweat, and it takes everything in me not to rub it down the coarse material of our desert clothes.

I turn to Jasmine, whose wide eyes dart between me and him. She's squeezing the book about the Ley Lines against her chest. Elijah, too, looks uncertain. But it's Mark who grabs the bag and places it into my palm. It's heavy, filled with clinking glass, and I try not to drop it.

"She thanks you," Mark says.

"And I thank you for the peace you are due to bring our lands." Kent's words are raw, almost like a plea.

Lily pats the hind of the desert horse she rode and clicks her tongue. The beast rears, whinnying, and makes haste towards the desert. Apparently, there is a slip of land between the island of Sector 2 that connects with the desert continent, which we were all unaware of. The water laps at the desert horse's feet the entire way.

Never again.

I grip the bag to my chest and nod at Kent. He nods back and pulls himself onto his steed. Survivors from Sector 2 gape at him, their breathing uneven.

We don't have many yet, but we will. We'll save as many people as we can.

"*Per aspera ad astra.* For Umbra."

Kent's words do something inside my chest.

I whisper. "For Umbra."

The man tightens his fingers on the reins and turns away from us. He sails like the wind, smoothly making his way through the wreckage. The survivors part for him like a splitting sea. They clamber down the rocks, through stray bits of metal and stone, their bodies in various stages of hurt. I watch them with a heavy heart and take a shaky breath.

"You guys go," Lily suddenly says, swinging her way down to us. "To the Kingdom." Her knees bend as she lands before us, absorbing the impact.

Jasmine blinks at her, nearly dropping the book, her EXO Suit making her movements look uncanny. "Not without you."

"I have to go to my cats."

Jasmine's lips thin, her body stiff as she searches for a rebuttal.

Lily smiles, her face warm. And, for the first time, Jasmine looks strong and brave.

With my heart ticking in my chest, I smile as Lily slides her fingers through Jasmine's curls, their eyes locked in such a way it makes me look away.

Elijah turns to the ocean, grinning like a madman. And, from the corner of my eye, I see Lily brush her lips over Jasmine's. Both stand tensely, as if the world has come to a stop.

Then I fully turn.

"*Per aspera ad astra,* Lily," Jasmine mutters on half a laugh.

"Go what you came to do. I will find you."

The ocean lulls against stones. Mark clears his throat a little, busying himself with preparing a boat. A few of the Sector 2 survivors we found stand back, wary as they watch us. But Andrea, at the front, guides them down reassuringly.

"Find me," Jasmine answers shakily.

Lily tugs on a braid by Jasmine's hair—one of many she wove throughout our trip. We all shared horses. I rode with Mark, Elijah with Kent, and Jasmine with Lily.

Lily braided hair the whole way, as if to settle her nerves. And Jasmine, with a gentle sort of peace on her face, busied herself by reading the book about Ley Lines.

Jasmine touches her hand, stilling it in her hair.

"As fast as I can," Lily assures, then pulls back with a smile.

We follow her to the shore, watching as she swallows hard and climbs into a boat.

I reach for the boat myself as Jasmine bobs up and down, her hand waving at Lily.

"Give them hell, Jasmine!"

Elijah barks out a laugh; the first real joy I have heard from him.

With glowing eyes, Jasmine reaches her hand into the sky and shouts into the heavens. It's less of a war cry and more of a wild release. The sound is pure ecstasy and delight, and my chest raptures at the sight of it.

That girl is a glimmering star. All life. All passion. As if she finally has something to fight for.

I hold my hand to my chest, squeezing the bag Kent gave me.

"Ready, child?" Mark asks me, his hand on my shoulder.

I nod, smiling at Jasmine.

I'm ready.

JESSE

"Help me!"

Savannah crashes into Amadea's room, her hand on her heart.

I take one look at the panic on her face, the flushed cheeks, and the switchblade in her palm, and immediately jump from my seat. The silly pink chair almost topples over, which startles Mel. She is sitting cross-legged on the floor, her back to us as she stares out the window.

The summer breezes dances in her hair and over the light blue dress she wears, and pushes the smell of her perfume towards us. She was captivating before, but she is utterly ravishing now as an Argenti. Her beauty is terrifying.

"What is it?" I demand Savannah.

Mel doesn't turn, but I can sense her listening. She hasn't

acknowledged anything since Elias's head was spiked to the castle walls. Not as I guided her inside, not as staff bathed and dressed her, and not as I grabbed her hand and repeated her name.

Melanie Beckett is all but gone.

The thought is like a sucker punch to my chest. I look at her, and all I want to do is throw up my recently eaten breakfast of oats and berries. I want to cleave out my chest. I want to scream and pace—anything but look at the girl I just lost.

Instead, I stare at Savannah while she rushes out, "We need to find Evaline. Now."

I cast my feelings aside and focus. "Why?"

Savannah crashes to her knees, her pretty, yellow dress spilling across the ground like liquid gold as she drops a backpack in front of her.

"Because I messed up, Jesse. All I have ever done since moving to Silver Valley was mess up. Jasmine was right all along. I should never have become the prophesied. I should have stayed home, finished school, and lived a simple life. Instead, I got my home bombed, my brother killed, and myself locked in a dungeon for stars knows how long. I lost everything. I'm so alone and so sick of fighting and so frightened. I have no idea how to beat the Elders because I'm all the way here, on Umbra, while Elias Hart sent ships to Terra to destroy the rest of the bases—to destroy what's left of me. And I can't... I can't keep getting people killed. I can't keep fighting."

She's the cleanest I have ever seen her since landing on Umbra. Her soft, curling hair is pulled back from her face, and her cheeks are bruised but rosy. Her shaking hands drop her switchblade, the word *perseverance* clattering on the ground as the sunlight catches it.

The fight is quickly leaving her.

I walk towards the girl, lift her chin, and say with resolution, "You haven't lost everything. You still have us."

She shakes her head. "I lost you the day I told you that I loved you."

An old ache grips my chest and I ask her a question I wish I had asked sooner. What right did I ever have to be scared of talking to her about this? What right did I have to not patch things over?

"Did you mean it when you said it?"

Her eyes glaze over. "I thought I did."

I pull my hand back, nodding. "It's okay. I understand."

And I mean it. I sunk my claws too deep, holding onto her because I thought I had nothing else to hold onto. It reached a point where we would both walk away bleeding, eventually. And maybe, just maybe, Savannah was doing the same thing with me.

Argenti fire lights her eyes with Magic as she lifts her chin. "You do?"

"I do."

"I loved you enough to choose you over my brother, so I suppose that's something," she admits.

And my heart wallops. *Yeah, I know.*

And you had every right to hate me for it.

Mel is a statue behind us. I want to reach for her, to go to her, but I don't. Not now.

"You were just trying to keep us alive," I acknowledge. "And perhaps I was, too. Perhaps we are the same person, Savannah. We are both protectors. And maybe we mistook that for love."

She picks at the skin around her fingers. "Perhaps."

Twin flames, destined to find each other, but destined to fall apart.

The pain in her eyes is one I know too well. The feeling of despair. Of losing everything.

I must remind her that the light hasn't died yet. It's all around her in the still beating hearts of the other stars—her family. She need only look to notice them. It's something that took me years to learn.

"Call Marcellus. See if he knows a way to stop the bombs from reaching Terra," I offer, giving her the only answer I can think of.

I don't trust the man. Hell, I don't trust anyone except the girls in this room. But Savannah trusts him in ways I will probably never understand.

I do know one thing though. Marcellus is Savannah's Melanie. He gave her something to wish for in her darkness hour. Perhaps that's what it means to find your soulmate.

I turn to Mel, reaching for her, but she is still lost to me. I walk around her, grabbing her chin, and kneel. Her silver eyes, so fierce and unfocused, slowly meet mine.

"Wake up, Mel."

For the first time, I don't beg. I just hold her and I wait. No tears leave her eyes, no sorrow, yet mine are full of it as I lower my lips to her forehead.

I press them there, breathing her in. Somehow, it's that which makes her stir.

Melanie lifts her hands, grabs my face, and stares into my soul. "No, Jesse."

She lowers her head to mine, touching my forehead. She's warm and cold all at once, the wires in her hand scraping against my stubble. Electricity fires against my skin... Or maybe that's just me and my firing nerves.

She sinks her head onto my shoulder, breathing in. I swallow sharply, my fingers trembling as I hold her. I support her like she has always supported me.

My anchor.

"No, Jesse," she repeats.

And this time, the inflection feels different. The words make me step back, blinking. I make to pull away, but... there. Right there. A softness to her face as her lips quirk and her eyes melt.

Melanie. *My* Melanie.

I know that look. Right now, she means business.

Savannah is fiddling with her switchblade again, watching us with distant eyes. She hasn't called for Marcellus yet. Not as she waits for us to collect ourselves. It speaks volumes, because Terra could be exploding right now.

Instead, she watches us. Her family.

Mel turns her head slowly towards Savannah, and says just one sentence.

"Tell me what you know about Silver Magic."

49

AMADEA

The moment we cross the ocean again, I feel it.

The Ley Lines.

I grip the satchel of memory vials in my fingers and try not to squirm. The rocking boat is just begging to tip me over. I try and keep myself from throwing up, but even though it's tight, my stomach is empty. We nibbled on food on our journey here, but it was hard to focus on that while sitting on a horse.

"The Kingdom looks like it was beautiful once," Elijah says with a sigh.

It was. I try to tell him that, but I'm not me anymore. I've changed my skin, my face, my hair, into someone I never dared shift into. An Elder.

"Again, like we practised," Mark says.

I glance at the man's soft eyes and encouraging smile.

"It looks a little like Silver Valley did," Jasmine croaks.

Pain slashes across Mark's face so I begin speaking to distract him. I repeat my pretty little speech until my body is trembling and the Magic of the Ley is unbearable.

Mark turns to look at the land ahead of us. Waiting there is an army of my people.

I'm almost home.

"Is it supposed to be so hot here, still?" Elijah asks.

It's true, the sun is near blistering.

"Not for long," Jasmine breathes. "Look."

I feel it before I see it. The Magic in the earth shudders at the wake of it, because all the Argenti along the shore gasp and shout, awakening the Ley. The sweet scent of Magic is nearly enough to make my skin shift, but I grit my teeth and hold on to the face I wear.

The boat nearly topples. Vaguely, I'm aware of the men behind us yelling in delight.

Because there, across the sky, a vague shimmer leaks and spreads, cascading over the entire Kingdom. The temperature eases and the sun sways a little as the forcefield solidifies.

Jasmine jumps up and flaps her hands. "The Dome is back!"

MARCELLUS

They emerge from the river, wind-torn and covered in sand.

I stare into my sister's eyes, noting her silver hair and stiff posture. It's only when I look closer that I realise it's not her own skin she's wearing but Alexsandre's.

The truth is her eyes never change. The colour, the shape—that's all someone else's. But the sheen, the way they widen whenever she looks at me and the way they soften when someone falls for her disguise … that's all her.

With a trembling heart, I step towards her, making to grab the bag in her hands, curiosity getting the better of me. The gentle breeze around me sways, cool and pleasant.

"Wait," Jasmine announces, her blue eyes glittering.

Everyone heard her silly little declaration about the Dome being back, and the army behind me snickers a little when she speaks. She doesn't seem to care.

I smile at her. She's the only one not in desert rags, her blonde hair braided back and windblown, much like how the wild Lily Hayes wears her hair.

Gone was the broken girl I met in the castle with distant eyes and broken legs. In her place is a blonde warrior in an EXO Suit. Granted, they stripped her of weapons, but she holds herself in the suit better than any Argenti. Her movements are fluid and strong, as if she was born to wear the greatest piece of tech known to mankind.

"Waiting," I answer with a smirk.

The Argenti press in. They're in EXO Suits, too, except theirs are laden with weapons.

I came from the geothermal plant and accumulated a variety of Argenti along the way, plucking them from the village where they were being hunted. The villagers took over, taking power where they could. There are more of them than the Argenti and, for the first time, I think they realised that.

The Argenti fell back to the castle and prepared for war before I came.

I didn't want that to happen but, stars, the sight makes my blood sing. The power we possess is disturbing, though rather beautiful. Besides, it wasn't me who guided them here. Baxter saw their boats first and the consensus was that we all go and guard the shore.

"We have something to say first," Jasmine tells me.

I brush my hand into the open air. *Still waiting, broken girl.*

My sister lifts her head in her guise as Alexsandre.

"The coalition of the Elders ends today," my sister says in a poor imitation of Alexsandre's voice. "It ends with the severing of class and Sector. The wildlings from Sector 3 have reminded us what this planet is all about. Umbra is a place of Magic, of immortality. It's a haven for humanity. This will never be achieved by bloodshed. We cannot live in utopia by building over bones. It will never suffice."

Pretty words for a little girl.

Savannah's caregiver, Mark Shaw, smiles at my sister.

I tilt my head at him, making a point of dragging my gaze over his fatigued body.

My girl to protect, not yours.

He doesn't bristle once, so I smile. He smiles back.

Impressive, for a Terran.

The men from Sector 2 look uncomfortable. Most of them are what remains of the army meant to storm the castle. Even more drift over as we speak. Villagers, children, injured Umbrans… even some of our guards, holding S.P. guns of their own.

The entirety of Umbra faces the Argenti—faces us.

"We do not stand as an army, I assure you," I tell my sister. "We are just survivors with fancy armour."

Amadea knows how to read between the lines of that, though. My father trained the Argenti for death. It is what we will resort to if required.

Mark surprises me again. "There is more to life than just surviving," he says gently.

I turn and stare at the man who is weak and aged from the many years lived on Terra. He might still meet a fatal end, due to the contamination in his lungs. Yet he stands before me, glassing twinkling in the sun, looking so self-assured.

Looking so… so… Savannah-like. My heart does a weird sort of whack.

"Is that so, old man? Tell me more, then."

Jasmine reaches for his hand, her head high. He stiffens but grabs it.

Then Elijah reaches for Jasmine's other. My sister follows as Alexsandre, until they are all linked.

I tip my chin. "Cute."

The Argenti behind me are stirring.

"I'm just a man trying to survive, so this might be a selfish ask," Amadea says with Alexsandre's face. "Help me escort all survivors to the castle, where we can tend to the wounded. Argenti, if you can use your skills to scout out survivors, I will be most grateful."

The words are clipped and almost begging. Very un-Elder-like.

But many of the Argenti seem to buy it. They squirm, their muscles stiff in their suits. Then something miraculous happens. They all turn towards me, waiting for my answer.

The breath stills in my lungs. I turn, feeling the full effect of Magic spilling into the sky. I taste it, welcome it, yearn for it. I look at them, one by one, taking in their faces.

I know them all. Their names. Their families.

And they know me. They look at me as their leader.

I ignore the tingling in my fingers and shove my hands deep into my pockets, then clear my throat. "Very well, you heard the man. Go and do what the Argenti were born to do, I guess. Protect the innocent."

A few nod. Others just stiffen their shoulders. But at once, the Argenti fall back.

I watch in earnest as they disperse on my order. It's like I'm the newest Elias Hart.

51

SAVANNAH

"They're here!" I yelp, jumping to my feet.

Jesse is working hard at trying to translate code. Melanie is still half-present, half-gone, pressing fingers down into my mother's skin in a morbid sort of way. We've been trying to get more information out of her, to no avail.

Venus tries to lash out, snapping her teeth. Then she stops and starts laughing.

Melanie tilts her head at Venus. Not a moment later, I watch in perplexity as Venus's eyes fill with fear and she inches away from Mel, the laughter dying on her tongue.

A million emotions and reactions repeat as she takes in the new Melanie. It's too much for my head, but I don't try to understand it, because there, below the balcony, is Marcellus leading my father to the castle. Behind him, her head low, is the small body of Amadea

Hart, her clothes hanging off her as if she recently shifted out of a larger body.

I resist the urge to call out for them but, as if in response, my father's eyes lift towards where my balcony and he sees me anyway.

"Jesse, any luck?" I ask frantically.

He's tapping away at Melanie's tech screen. Sweat beads on his brow, the anxiety visible in every tense arch of his body as he sits cross-legged on my floor.

"I'm not Mel," is all he gruffly says.

Melanie pokes my mother again, her eyes blinking languidly. Magic is pushing and pulling, ebbing and waning around her. Stars, it's distracting. I press my fingers to my temple to block it out.

She settles among the silver stains of blood on my bed and looks at my mother.

"Tell us about the missiles."

Venus blinks as sudden fear and panic floods her face.

"You cannot stop them. Evaline sent the Liaison before the Dome was destroyed, and the pathways between planets stretches longer by the day. You see, the Elders are not evil, they're practical. We cannot have any survivors on Terra. And now, our remaining connections to Terra will be gone before the next Nightfall."

I blink at my mother. Even Jesse lifts his head, eyes pinched.

"How did you get her to say all that?" he asks Mel, who sits smiling on the end of the bed. "She's never been that forthright with information."

I know even as he asks the question. *It's her new Magic.*

It falls like a shroud as Melanie frees her, and my mother begins to squirm, her eyes darting between us. Her lips thin. "How *dare* you."

"I'm sorry. I'm done now. If you answer us truthfully from now on, perhaps I won't have to do that again."

The door to my room swings open. My body jolts at the noise, but a small girl peeks her head through, her silver eyes searching.

"Dea," I gasp.

She leaps, throwing herself into the room. I don't bother holding myself back as I launch towards her, pulling the girl into my arms. My heart squeezes and all the pain and worry leaks from me as I hold her and breathe in her scent. She smells like the desert, which is off-putting, but under all that is Dea.

She buries her head into my chest.

"I'm so glad you're okay. I'm sorry sending you to Sector 2 didn't go to plan."

She pulls back. "Plan? Nothing is ever as easy as a simple plan."

I cough a little at that.

Marcellus leans against my door frame, one ankle folded over the other, and takes me in with glistening silver eyes. I lift my gaze to his, staring back.

Heat pounds between us, filling the empty space. We don't say anything, but the words are all there.

Until Melanie Beckett opens her mouth and breaks the spell. "Marcellus. My Magic. It's not that of the Bloodhound's."

He narrows his eyes, taking the girl in. "Hello, Beckett. You look more yourself."

She doesn't, though. Her hair looks much too pale, her skin is like diamonds, and her eyes are silver and sharp. She stands a little too straight, her head a little too high.

Jesse sighs.

Melanie ignores us all and continues. "I can alter their instincts."

Her Magic swells through the room then. My own peels out with it, echoing in response. I feel my father, Jasmine, and Eli seconds before they enter our room. Jasmine, walking once more, pounds through the entrance, nearly shoving Marcellus with her shoulder.

Her blue eyes widen and her braids swing as she beelines straight towards me, almost dropping a heavy book she carries in her arms. "Sav—"

But my father beats her to it. He storms into the room like a man possessed and throws his arms around me, tucking my head against his chest with his large hands. "My sweet girl," he murmurs.

I hold my breathe against his cheat, trying not to cry as the rapid sound of his heart thrums against my forehead. We never embrace like this. It's just not our style. And yet… it feels familiar.

"Hey, dad."

I don't want to move.

But Melanie isn't done speaking. She's lost herself again, stuck in a void where only Magic and logic can reach her. I let my father hug me, but I'm busy listening to Melanie.

"It's almost like reprogramming someone's source code. I can override their original instincts, any reactions they may have been born with, until their response becomes something I wish it to be." She lowers her hands and studies our new visitors. Elijah looks into the vacant soul of the person she has become and loses himself, stumbling in the entranceway. "When someone holds a weapon to your neck, the natural response would be fight or flight. But what if someone reacted in a way where they felt no fear, and their core instincts tell them to tilt their neck to the side and accept the blow? What then?"

Marcellus inhales deeply and reclines against the wall. His voice is deep and feral when he answers. "That's how you killed Elias Hart."

Oh, stars.

"Do not repeat that ever again." Jesse lunges to his feet, throwing one of his knives.

It sails through the air towards Marcel's head. My head skips a beat and I jump forwards, but Marcellus whips sideways and the knife impales in the half-open door.

My father gasps.

Marcel chuckles and pockets the knife like a prize. "Hello to you, too, Hayes."

"Don't worry, Jesse," I say. "The remaining Elders won't kill her for that. No one will. They probably all think I did it."

I feel the weight of many eyes on me when I say that. I blink away my emotions—still holding Amadea behind me like a shield—and trying to centre myself. Jasmine grabs my hand.

"Melanie killed him?" Eli breathes, swallowing sharply.

From behind me, my father grumbles something under his breath.

Melanie turns her soulless eyes on Eli and smiles. "Apparently that is my nature now."

Jesse shakes his head a little. Eli looks like he wants to weep.

Melanie just gives a humourless smile. "I, too, thought I'd assume the Bloodhound's Magic or perhaps something closer to hacking. It's ironic, though, that my soul reflects something even worse."

She clears her throat, which is the most human thing I've seen her do since turning, before staring out of the window.

"All those stupid lessons from my mother about brain anatomy… I never cared. Who would have ever thought such a thing would apply to me? Funny, that."

Jesse lowers the tech screen to the ground, his face waxen.

Melanie doesn't see as she slowly walks towards the balcony, her eyes on the sky as if her mother is up there looking down at her.

But she must feel all our eyes on her back.

"Lift the screen back up, Jesse," she says without looking back. "You will need it to blow up the control room."

He smiles and looks at me.

We both pray Melanie is still in there somewhere.

52

SAVANNAH

Jasmine is pacing. Back, forth, back, forth.

Her new legs give her gusto but she's still squeezing her book to her chest.

Apparently, the only way to stop the bombs from reaching Terra is by cutting them off at the source. Melanie has been in the control room only once back when she was a child on her father's work trip. It's the zone where they control all security, located in the geothermal plant under the volcano, in a tall above-ground chamber.

"There's a catch," Melanie announces.

Jasmine lurches, catching herself against my vanity.

"The only way to destroy it is manually. We can't override the systems fast enough to stop the ships, so we must get inside and set off a *Netsil* bomb."

My heart sinks to my feet. From the looks of it, so does everyone else's.

"Someone will have to die," she adds slowly.

My heart stills. But not from fear. From resolution.

I take in a long, shaky breath and look into the eyes of everyone in this room. Everyone I love. Everyone I've been fighting for. My soul is whisked away from my body, my thoughts buried deep. I sink deep into that happy place where nothing matters.

"Okay," I say.

Turning, I look at the sun high in the sky and close my eyes. The Dome is back, and stars, if it isn't beautiful. *Umbra* is beautiful.

With my back to my friends, I utter the words that have haunted me since the start.

" *'The chocolate-haired princess will sail from Terra to take over the throne and neutralise the destruction of our planet.'* "

Everyone watches me with narrowed eyes. Jasmine is the first person to get it. She launches toward me, stumbling faster than the EXO Suit allows, just as I step forward and say, "I was born for this. I'll set off the bombs. It's nothing I haven't done before."

It doesn't scare me, even as I turn and memorise their faces. Instead, it gives me a weird sense of peace. A peace that is immediately disrupted as Jasmine shakes me.

I breathe in the sweet, flowery scent of her as she rocks me.

She smacks my cheek. "Look at me."

I push her off. "I was born for this, Jasmine. Neutralise the destruction. End the killing."

Her eyes darken. "Just because you were some sort of morbid bottle experiment of some very messed-up leaders does *not* mean you have to do this."

Some sort of morbid bottle experiment? What?

Before I have time to puzzle that over, Marcel says, "You're not dying, little mouse. Not on my watch."

My father jolts. A full body movement.

Suddenly, the man understands. He lurches for me, as if to grab me back into another embrace. Raw panic crashes over his face as he storms over, his glasses toppling. "No way in hell—"

"Perseverance, little mouse," Marcellus reminds me.

A nerve racks down my body. I fumble for my switchblade, my heart empty, as if the word has long been forgotten. With a shake of my head, I hand it to Jasmine.

Jasmine swallows, opens her mouth, closes it. Her eyes are wide and flashing. But she slowly shakes her head.

I've already died, Jasmine. And I will gratefully do it again for the ones I love.

I open my mouth to say the solemn words, but Marcellus moves towards me, twirling Jesse's knife. The last thing I see is him lift the pommel up before I see nothing at all.

I sink to the ground as darkness envelops me.

ꕥ

"I would really appreciate it if you untie me," I grind out through my teeth.

Marcellus clicks his tongue. All too proud of himself.

They've tied me to the railing on my balcony under the gentle sun after Marcel knocked me unconscious. The soft breeze tickles my cheeks as I stare at my friends inside, all of them avoiding my mother who is still on the bed.

"Or get me a coffee. I would like that, too."

Jasmine is pacing again.

Ugh. My head.

Jesse's tinkering with that godforsaken tech screen like it will spit out a miracle.

I wriggle against my bindings and wince as the fabric cuts into my wrists. They tore it from the linen of my bed, and I can feel spots of dried blood where fabric chafes against skin.

"We don't have time for this." I say, huffing.

Marcellus finally tears the tech screen from Jesse's fingers and slams it against Melanie's chest. His eyes are filled with cold rage. She turns to him, as if waking from a slumber, then looks down at the screen.

"Don't make me ask again," Marcellus warns. "Figure something out, Bloodhound."

Jesse hisses. "Melanie. Call her Melanie."

Marcel's lips tighten and he gives a strained smile. "Melanie. Whatever."

Amadea has folded herself onto my bed by my mother, using a dampened strip of bedding to wipe her forehead. She seems calm, but on closer inspection, she is anything but.

My father looks at his ex-wife with dark, stormy eyes. It looks like they've been lecturing her about the ships.

"Just let the Terrans die, for stars' sake," Venus says, bored with our theatrics. "What happens when they start to blab about us to the rest of Terra? What happens when their people flood our planet, hungry for immortality? Let them die and cut the issue out by the root."

Mark fumes at her, his lips tight. They don't say anything to each other, but the tension is painful. So many unsaid words and unsaid questions, piling on top of each other until neither one can breathe.

My gut twists whenever I look over, because for some unfounded reason, I cannot escape the thoughts that long ago, my family included both parents. My sweet father, my confusing mother, and me… a small girl with enough Silver Magic to destroy them.

I turn away, blinking yet more pain from my eyes.

"Just let me do this," I shout.

Everyone ignores me but one. My soul, freshly breaking, hunts out the one person who always knows how to free me from my own personal torture. He kneels before me, trying not to show the thoughts on his face.

Marcel doesn't touch me. He always waits for a small sign that he's allowed to. I gesture for his hand, cold and soft, and he exhales loudly when he places it on my cheek.

"Take my Magic. Find the Elders. You're closer to their minds than I am," I say. "Maybe they know something."

He looks like he wants to say something, but instead he just nods.

"They don't," Melanie calls out to me, her tone flat.

We both ignore her.

Marcel takes only a lick, then he drops my hand. He forks out the Magic, searching for the familiarity of their minds. A jolt hits my system as it happens, and it suddenly occurs to me that I'm the last Argenti left with any sort of power to track.

"They're circling above in their ship. They're frightened. I think they know we have taken the castle." He lowers the Magic, trembling a little. "Only Roman appears morbidly intrigued by it all."

Amadea freezes a little at the mention of his name, then stares at me as if I know what she's thinking. I don't.

Jasmine stops her pacing. "Oh, god, Savannah. Don't trust Roman. You won't believe what we heard." She wrings her hands as she enters the balcony, and I sigh. More politics incoming.

"Later, Jasmine," Mark says, moving from the bed. "Tell Savannah about the book."

"No. Untie me first, talk later."

They ignore me.

Jasmine places the book on one of the daybeds with trembling hands. "It's filled with a lot of nonsense. But I can catch you up to speed."

I think I see Melanie roll her eyes at that—the most Mel-like expression I have seen her make since turning Bloodhound. My chest thumps, and Elijah grins from behind her.

Jesse doesn't even notice. He's busy striding towards Jasmine, grabbing her book from the daybed. He opens it at a random page, leafing through it. His eyes pinch.

"It looks like one of the original Elder's journals. Like the ones your uncle kept in his study on Silver Island. Mel, look."

He walks over to Melanie, still pouring through the pages.

She doesn't look. Not when Jasmine pipes up again.

"It's not all from the Elders. It consists of clippings from many journals. There's one paragraph on page 67 that was translated from the actual words of an Occupant." She points to it, gesturing Jesse to flip, which he does. "Anyway, my point is that Umbra is fuelled with power—an energy of sorts that floods out from the core of the planet and into the soil we stand on. The Ley Lines are veins, like a volcano in a way, that connect directly to the source. According to page 32, all of us feel it, not just the Argenti. The Occupants were one with Umbra, like servants of the planet. They seeded the energy. The Argenti can only connect to it when they train themselves to, and the ability of what they can do varies depending on the individual mind of the person. BUT!"

She leaps a little in excitement, her eyes darting. "It doesn't matter. We have all been so caught up in our own power that we haven't stopped to realise what we can do here together. The castle is right on an energy source. We can band enough Argenti together and expand the Kingdom."

All of us stare at her. Venus even snorts a little.

"How does this help us?" Marcellus asks as he lounges against the railing at my side.

Elijah pops his head out, his gaze troubled. "Because Mason Shaw was a genius. Mason came up with the idea to bring Umbra back to its former glory."

Melanie's hands begin to shake. She lets out a weak, "What?" and steps towards him.

Mark clears his throat. "No, he wanted to blow up the Dome. Remember?"

My heart stills. I think Marcellus notices, because his silver eyes roam my face as he moves closer.

Venus looks towards me, her eyes on fire. And she laughs. And laughs. And laughs.

The sound rings endlessly, popping in my skull. Eventually, her laughter dies.

"My children, both so inventive. You didn't know, did you, Savannah?"

My lungs are burning as I try to breathe. *No. I didn't know my brother wanted to blow up the Dome.*

Marcellus chuckles. "Nice memorial."

I fight the urge to kick him, but my feet are tied. "Jasmine," I say between my teeth, "get to the point."

She sighs heartily, holding up her hands in mock defeat. "If you stopped for a moment and paid attention to me, Savannah, you would have seen that I've been trying to help you from the start. It began with the idea to blow up the Dome and ended with a plan to teach the Umbrans how to survive the desert. I told him about the Dome Farms and the safe houses outside of the Kingdom. He had the idea to extend the Kingdom, grow more plants, more shelter, and bring more people to Umbra. There were many weak spots in his ideas, but the ideas were founded on something special."

I didn't realise my eyes had started watering. It's just so… *Mason.*

Tears fall down my face, slapping on my lap. Marcel inhales strongly, as if understanding the emotion for my sibling.

"The first time I've actually seen you cry," he says on a low breath. I let him wipe a tear away with his finger as he adds, "All those days of pain and nothing touched your heart. Nothing except the love for that little boy."

Mark, not looking at us, nods. "Of course, the blowing of the Dome would have also served to stir panic and distract from our arrival on Umbra. Seems Mason was right about that, at least. I wonder, sometimes, what we could have prevented had we entertained that plan."

His eyes meet Melanie's, but we've lost her again as she grapples with her new Magic, pushing and pulling it around her in waves. A trauma response. I had the same reaction when I was tortured.

I swallow the heaviness from my throat. "Please, untie me. Every second we waste here is a second closer the ships get to Terra," I say weakly.

Marcel sucks in his jaw and stands with his hands in his pockets.

"Dea, speak to Jasmine about the Ley Lines, learn as much as you can. Savannah's brother was many things, but a fool he was not. I think it's due time we find a way to make the rest of Umbra liveable and, frankly, I think the Ley Lines can help with that. Especially if we find a way to convert all the Commons into Argenti. We can make it happen before the next turn of the century."

Without missing a beat, he turns to Melanie, his silver eyes meeting her own.

"And you, my new little Bloodhound. Remember yourself. You were hacker first, Argenti second. Find a way to stop the ships from reaching Terra."

Melanie bites her cheek.

Jesse stands behind her, sword at the ready. "It's *Melanie*. And she said there's no way."

And then it hits me. I lurch a little, eyes flashing. *It's so obvious.*

Everyone turns and looks at me. Even my mother, who must crane her head on the bed.

"No, Mel. Forget hacking. Be the Bloodhound instead."

Marcel's eyes crinkle as he grins at me, perplexed.

I scramble a little as I fight against my bindings. "You're going to tell my mother how to stop the ships. And then you're going to Magic her into blowing up the command centre."

Melanie blinks at me. Her metal arm spasms.

Jasmine frowns, as if trying to make sense of the plan. But quickly, her mind seems to resolve on something.

She kneels before me, grabbing my hands. I let her lower her head on my shoulder. It feels familiar, her warmth, and I instinctively sink into it.

"I love when we are a team," she mutters happily.

Elijah looks at us with a deep, troubled gaze. I meet his eyes, trying to make sense of it, but he dips his head and moves out of sight.

Marcel claps. "Alright, you all heard your orders. Chop, chop."

Jasmine leans over and pecks me on the cheek before jumping to her feet, fluttering inside like a little dancer to where Amadea waits. For a moment, my heart lightens.

This could work.

"Good job, Your Majesty," Marcellus teases. He wraps one ankle over the other as he leans against the balcony beside me.

I fight a smile. "Shut up, Marcel."

"Never, my dear. Talking is what I do best."

He spins Jesse's knife between his fingers, unable to fight the twinkling of excitement in his silver eyes. I tilt my head up, trying to get a good look at him. My pulse is alive, and Silver Magic flows through me like a wave of nectar.

He strides inside with a wink, slapping the knife against Jesse's chest as he passes him. "Want that coffee now, little mouse?"

Jesse grabs it, glowering. I roll my eyes at them.

"I just want you to untie me."

He flashes me a dazzling smile from around the corner.

"Not a chance," he says as he turns to make my coffee. "Cappuccino?"

53

JESSE

"Hate me, if that's what you want. Hate me until my name haunts you in your sleep. But please, don't stop me from doing this," Jasmine begs me.

Savannah's plan is bull. But this feels even worse.

I can barely breathe as the girl stares at me, her blue eyes filled with tears. She's asking me to help her die so that Savannah will not.

"*Please.*"

What about Lily? What about us… your friends?

Stars. Why am I the one holding her fate in my hands? I barely even like the girl.

I left Mel tucked against the daybed, staring into the abyss, and grimly followed Jasmine outside. It's late afternoon, but Savannah fell asleep and Amadea curled at her feet with the Ley book in her small little lap.

It's now or never.

Melanie needs me, but if I stayed while she was still and unmoving, I'd regret letting Jasmine slip away, helpless and alone. So, I did what Mel couldn't do.

I followed Jasmine, Marcellus at my heels with a curious expression on his face. It almost looks like he's fascinated by my grief, which is disturbing.

I don't know what to say. What to do. What to think.

Not as I pass her the tech screen. Not as she shakily takes it. Not as she smiles and leans in to hug me.

"Thank you," she breathes into my ear.

I don't push her away, like I once would have. We are both stiff and at odds with each other until she pulls back and releases me from the torture of her affection.

"*Thank you,*" she says with a soft, grateful smile.

I watch the girl go for the final time, her blonde curls dancing in the sunlight as she exits the castle. There's a small bounce in her step that I haven't seen since Silver Valley. Something in me begs to run after her, to ask her to change her mind, but I know I can't.

Even Marcellus steps out of Savannah's rooms and looks deep into my soul with those frightening silver eyes. "Let the girl do this. For Savannah."

I almost hate the man as much as I hate the girl, but in this moment, I can't feel anything except pain. I know what will happen when Savannah wakes up.

We both do. And it might just be enough to send her over the edge for good.

Even so, I repeat the words, "For Savannah."

The only alternative would be Savannah sacrificing herself again. Jasmine knows this, as we all do. Savannah will wake up to learn that Melanie cannot do what she asked. Her Magic is changing someone's instincts, not their willpower. Venus would never have the willpower to sacrifice herself in the control room.

Marcellus—a man who once tried to kill me—holds out his cold, pale hand. And for the first time ever, I reach for it gladly.

Our skin touches. We shake hands. In understanding, we both smile a sad little smile.

"Come. We should be with Savannah when she learns of Jasmine's death."

I nod. Every movement hurts but I walk back into that damn room anyway.

For Savannah.

THE FALLEN

54

ELIJAH

I always knew I would meet my end on Umbra. My only regret was how little time I had.

"*Eli?*"

I stop pacing outside the staircase to the control centre, where I rode a stolen Hover inside the Dome of the geothermal plant. The frazzled workers ignore me as I stand and stare at the entrance, a little apprehensive to walk inside despite the resolution in my chest. Nothing can reach me. No one can stop me.

Except…

I turn away from the staircase, panic gnawing at my chest, and stare in horror as Jasmine slinks out from the shadows of the facility. Her hair is still in the braids Lily gave her, twisted into elaborate coils. The sight of it makes me sick to the stomach.

"Jasmine." My tone is empty. "Go home."

My heart flops as I grip the *Netsil* bomb I stole in my fist.

She squeezes Melanie's tech screen between her fingers and uses it to flap wind against her face. Some of her blonde hair now sticks on her face from sweat. She must have run from the train that carried her here.

I didn't waste my time with it, instead stealing a Hover from the castle and darting directly through every checkpoint until I made it to a hallway inside the facility that the Hover couldn't fit through. A few workers stopped and shouted after me, but most of the checkpoints were unmanned due to the worker shortage since the Night. No one came after me.

"Absolutely not," she insists. "We spoke about this."

Many times. We spoke about this many, many times in the med ward.

We find Savannah, tell her about Mason's plan, and make it happen at any cost. Any cost. Even if we need to die to do it.

I can't shake the feeling that Jasmine wasn't talking about my death but hers.

"Nah. This is different, Jasmine. Go home to Savannah and Lily. They need you."

A worker looks down the hallway, his mouth moving against a comm at his lapel. I rub my sweaty palms down my pants and take in my surroundings, suddenly feeling flighty.

The *Netsil* feels like a brand in my grip. Jasmine, taking no notice of it, strides towards me with her eyes glassing over.

"Savannah never needed me. I needed her. Today, that changes."

I suck the insides of my cheek. "Just go home."

She flaps the tech screen in my face. "You weren't the one assigned to this. I can get us inside the control room."

"Okay, fair." She beams, as if winning. But I add, "Let me inside and then leave."

"No. Jesse sent *me* to do this."

The air sucks out of me and I step backwards, my eyes roaming her face.

"I don't have time for this," I say, grabbing her hand and yanking her up the staircase. She yelps a little, her eyes wide as I lead her away from prying eyes. "Jesse is a dick. That's all there is to it."

Our feet pound on the concrete and lights slam down on our skin.

"No, Jesse knows that I will do anything—*anything*—to make it up to Savannah. Eli, stop." She pulls me to a halt and catches her breath. "I was meant to die many years ago, you know. I was caught on Umbra. Alexsandre, Savannah's grandfather, gave me a second chance so I could help his granddaughter. But I made the mistake of loving her. My selfishness messed up everything I had with her. I can fix all of that now. I finally have a way to fix it."

"By killing yourself?" I demand, my cheeks hot.

She sticks out her chest stubbornly. "I'd like to think of it as a redemption. I will happily die for Savannah Shaw, just as I was happy to die all those years ago for the prophesied princess. I was always meant to be here to do this. Please don't talk me out of it."

Her words are strong. But she stares at me with her large, glistening eyes, her lips trembling a little. The sounds of workers bustling around, combined with the humming facility, echoes around me as I try to find a retort and fall short.

Instead, I say, "Only if you promise not to talk me out of it either."

My voice sounds like a death chime.

She gasps a little. "It's stupid for us both to die."

"There's nothing left for me here, Jasmine. I just want to be with my parents."

My heart shakes and splinters with those words. *I just want to go home.*

I fight back the urge to cry. A painful thickness clogs my throat as I say, "I can't sit and watch more families on Earth get blown up the way mine was."

She's trembling as she stands before me, gripping that tech

screen against her chest like it will force her heart to steady. I swallow the tightness in my throat and banish the pain. Just as I have been doing every single day since Silver Valley was destroyed.

Fire raining from the sky. Broken bodies in the street. The fallen stones of my mother's store. Trees, once so full of life, blackened and raging red.

Never again. I will not sit still and wait for the worst to happen.

The sound of someone's voice spirals up the staircase, calling out for us. This time, Jasmine notices. I watch her blink back to reality.

Then, the firecracker of a girl I once knew with laughter and life in her soul, pushes away the pain and exhaustion that has plagued her for months, and reaches out her hand in resignation. Both of us are set in this. So, I guess both of us will see it through. I step forward, gripping it in my own.

I grip her hand so hard it hurts.

"Together, Eli?" Jasmine asks.

"Together."

SAVANNAH

I wake up to someone shaking my shoulders. "Savannah! Savannah!"

I lift my hands to my face, rubbing my eyes. My eyes dart open, staring at my fingers. Marcel has untied me.

Groggy and disorientated, I swing my eyes over my friends. They're all standing over me, gripping the balcony, except for the small girl still shaking my shoulders.

"Oh my stars, Savannah!" Amadea is half-gasping, half-sobbing.

Melanie stumbles back from the balcony, her hand against her heart, and yells, "Where is Elijah?"

It isn't a question so much as a demand. I leap to my feet as I see the sun above my head. No, not the sun. Flames.

It looks like the volcano has erupted, except it isn't lava streaming down over the geothermal plant facility, it's a vortex of orange death, sucking in on itself with a great heave. It's imploding from within the control room.

I stumble back. Wind thrusts past and over us, eating through the soil, pulling across the sky. The Dome keeps the gust from tearing at us, but I feel it within my soul.

"Where did he go?" Melanie repeats, her breathing laboured. "Jesse."

She slams her fists onto Jesse's chest, who steps into the blows. She pulls for him and her Magic slashes over him, causing him not to fight. But anyone can see it isn't needed. He takes every single punch with sorrow etched over his face.

"I don't know," he mutters. "I don't know."

"Where. Is. Elijah."

The world around me slows. I distantly see Marcel look to me, his expression pinched. Amadea finally releases her sob.

I look past my father, who is dry-heaving against the balcony, and settle on my mother, who is still tied to the bed.

"No."

I gasp and fall to the floor. All the while, my mother tries not to smile at me.

"NO," I repeat, screaming it. Magic slams out of me, spiralling through the village, hunting for the two faces I cannot find in my chambers.

Elijah and Jasmine.

My Magic comes up empty. As if they never existed.

"No…"

I try and stand, but my legs feel separate to my body. Darkness eats me whole as I trip and slam my head against the door to my balcony. Marcel gasps as he reaches for me, but it's too late.

His hands cleave past my head.

And I hear Jesse say to Melanie, "I thought Jasmine went alone."

56

JESSE

After exactly nine punches, Mel collapses, her mouth gaping open as the most heart-wrenching sob I have ever heard leaves her body. She wilts like a dead flower, sinking into me. I wanted Mel back, but not like this.

Not like this.

I lay her gently down on the nearest daybed.

Amadea is sitting on the floor, gaping idly at the fallout of the explosion.

A shaking Mark starts rattling off nonsense. "They made it in time, right? We stopped the ships? Jasmine and Elijah stopped them. Right? *Right?*"

Marcellus, busy with an unconscious Savannah, merely grunts.

We stopped the ships in time. I guess there's that, at least.

Mel's hands rip into my shirt, dragging me down onto the daybed. The thing is only really designed to fit one, but I lay beside her all the same, cupping her head against my chest.

She's frozen against me, her mouth still open. No sounds come out except for the occasional sob. I drag my fingers through her hair, twisting her honey locks in soothing patterns until the last sound of pain escapes her body.

Our hearts beat as one, thumping against each other.

Marcel carries Savannah inside with a groan. Mark lifts Amadea from the floor. And I just stay with Mel, trying not to crack open.

Yelling, swearing, and spitting erupts from inside. It sounds a little like Mark, his voice raw and angry. I block it all out.

The sounds drum into my skull, but they aren't loud enough to cover my thoughts.

I think I just sent Jasmine to die for nothing.

Why did we lose them both? Why did we have to lose *either* of them?

The guilt shreds at me, yawning open in my chest until it hurts to breathe. Suddenly, I wish I had more time with them. I wish I put aside my petty hate and got to know them. Elijah, always so annoying and hovering, was one of the strongest people I had ever met.

He never let his misery show.

How did I manage to miss that he may have been dying a little inside? How did I think that him losing his family could have been any less life-altering than when I had lost mine?

And Jasmine… Frustrating, moronic Jasmine.

"Hate me, if that's what you want. Hate me until my name haunts you in your sleep. But please, don't stop me from doing this."

"I don't hate you, Jasmine," was what I should have said. *"I don't hate you at all."*

I did, for a time. But can I hate a girl who spent her entire goddamn life fighting for the one person she loved?

The sight of her soft, helpless smile as she turned and left for the last time will haunt me until my death. I may just spend the rest of my days trying to atone to that girl for the misery I caused in her life.

Hours later, Mel stirs against me. The sun is setting on the horizon, battling against the fumes still wafting from the volcano. Bright and orange, like an inferno. My body aches from the small daybed, but I force myself to stay.

"Why did Elijah sacrifice himself?" Mel quietly asks against my chest.

I don't know where the others went, but it doesn't matter.

"I don't think he did," I admit. "I think he just realised he had nothing to live for anymore."

"I know the death of his parents haunted him, but I didn't think it was quite that bad."

I look down at her, shuffling so I can tip her chin up to look at me. Her silver eyes are reddened and ringed with pain. The soulless Argenti that had taken over is now buried down deep.

I hold her gaze, staring into her soul. "It's always that bad," I say. *We all just have different ways of dealing with it.*

Her face hardly moves as she says, "I didn't even get to say goodbye."

Her voice cracks on that last word. I grab her shoulders and press her into my chest. She hiccoughs, burying into my shirt. Against my better judgement, I place a soft kiss on her brow.

"You would have never let him go."

She huffs, her body tensing. "Is this supposed to make me feel better, Jesse?"

"No. But it's the truth." I try to keep my voice light, but it's hard. "You're not as heartless as you pretend to be, my love. Despite what you want for Umbra, you would give everything up if it meant saving the ones you love."

That undoes her. The sobs she's holding back finally break, and she's gushing tears against my chest. "*But I never got to say goodbye.*"

I have nothing to say.

I just hold her tighter, and together we ride out the sunset.

MARCELLUS

Savannah finally stirs around dusk.

I only notice because the mattress under me shifts. I had carried her into my chambers, all the way down the halls, her head rolling against my chest.

Amadea stayed with Mark, watching over Venus.

Both Mark and Venus had begun yelling at each other when I left, with Dea cowering in the corner, trying to coax them both down. The poor girl looked terrified, but I didn't have time to reassure her.

I slap my hand against my mattress. Still warm, but no Savannah.

I gave her drugs to help her sleep, but clearly, I didn't give her enough.

I swing myself out of bed, swearing. "For stars' sake."

I search for her with some of the Magic she gifted me.

Down the hall, heading towards her rooms. She's fuming.

"Not good," I mutter to myself, throwing on a shirt to cover my bare chest. I doubt her father would be happy if I strolled in there wearing only pants. "Not good."

I peel out of my room, nearly slamming into a group of Argenti.

I don't look at them. I don't even waste Savannah's Magic trying to read who they are. But Morana's familiar voice calls, "Marcellus! The Elders landed their ship outside the castle perimeter. What should we do?"

Nothing, you fool. Move.

I shoulder past her, my head pounding.

Savannah makes it inside her chambers, so I ru n.

I bump into more Argenti, all in the halls of the castle chattering amicably. Something is happening. The Elders are making some sort of stand, but I can't go out there without Savannah. Not now. Not like this.

"Savannah!"

Mark's voice crashes through the open door, and I spin the corner, spiralling inside just as Savannah swipes her switchblade through the air and casts it deep into her mother's heart.

Venus sputters, her silver eyes flashing. "Daughter..."

Amadea is screaming. Jesse is regaining his feet on the balcony, his sword at the ready. But there is nothing to be done. Underfoot, Melanie's Magic surges up through the Ley, crashing through the room.

It doesn't meet Savannah. She stumbles past Jesse, trying hard to get Savannah's attention. I cock my head at her. *Interesting. She needs eye contact to use her Magic.*

Savannah twists the blade in her mother's chest. "For Jasmine."

Her voice is lethally quiet. Through the Magic I have trained on her, I can feel the emptiness in her mind. All the rage is gone now, buried deep within.

Her mother splutters. "You killed men on those ships, Savannah! Both the Liaisons..."

The blade drags up through Venus's chest.

The woman arches her body. Her mouth is wide open, but no sound comes out except the gurgling of blood.

Amadea covers her ears and squeezed her eyes shut. Melanie cries out a little, but Savannah is beyond caring.

A few Argenti come into the room behind me, panting. Taking it all in.

"For Elijah." Savannah yanks the blade out, her eyes cold.

Baxter mutters something from behind me. I sense him raise his Magic, but I hold out a hand, asking him to stop. To my surprise, the Argenti listen and fall back to the hallway.

"You are… the villain… of this story," Venus gasps.

Savannah quickly shuts her up. With one last slash along her mother's throat, she says, with lethal quiet, "For Mason."

Venus gargles blood. The silver streaks through the air, hitting Savannah's cheek. The last breath she takes is a brutal, spluttering sort of thing, until she folds and collapses on the bed.

Savannah, unseeing, rises from the bed. Eventually, her eyes meet mine.

Despite it all, I'm not afraid.

I swallow sharply, my pulse firing as I take in the magnificent creature that is Savannah Shaw. Terran and Umbran, Argenti and Common.

Melanie makes it around the bed and catches her eye. It's only then that Savannah catches her breath. I step between them, covering Savannah's body with a snarl.

Melanie blinks at me, then places a hand on my chest. "*Let me help her.*"

I flash her a grin. *Thank you, you idiot.* I use the contact to suck out her Magic.

She yelps and slams into the protective force that is Jesse Hayes. He pulls out his sword towards me in silent promise, but I'm already turning from them, sighing around the sweet taste of Beckett's Magic.

"Her death was owed to me," Savannah whispers.

Her words captivate me as I turn to find the cool, calm returning to her as she takes in the Argenti in the entrance. There's maybe a dozen of them now, and they all stare at her with wide eyes.

"*Argentum Mortis,*" one of them whispers.

"*Argentum Mortis, Argentum Mortis, Argentum Mortis.*"

It turns into a breathless chant. *Silver Death.* Argenti killer.

She is the usurper princess they were told to fear. She takes a step towards them, covered in silver blood, and they all stagger back.

I hiccough, rolling my eyes at them. Mark, trembling by the door, glares at me.

I spot Morona in the crowd and point my finger at her. "You were saying something about the Elders landing their ship, Morana?"

The gentle Argenti woman trembles, nodding her head.

Savannah stashes her switchblade in her pocket. "Time to end this."

They bow and part, making way for their queen.

Argentum Mortis.

AMADEA

I run after Savannah, my chest cleaving, and grab for her elbow. Slick, warm Silver blood meets my fingers.

She turns and focuses dead eyes on me. I let out a helpless little breath.

"Dea?" Savannah says when she sees me.

"The Bloodhound was your sister," I spurt, sidestepping all formalities.

I had wanted to say it since arriving. Celestine was the child of Venus Collins and a second-generation Argenti, born without a slip of Magic. Like Melanie, she always showed promise. Unlike Melanie, she didn't deserve the power she was ultimately given.

Savannah stumbles and reality crashes over her face. "What?"

My brother releases a long breath.

Congrats, Beckett. You're the new Bloodhound. It meant more than Savannah realised at the time. Melanie, the sister that Savannah chose, was built to amass that kind of power.

"I need you to know, family isn't who you're born to, it's who you choose." I keep my words shallow. "Here."

I thrust vials at her and, before she can say anything else, I turn and run.

I run and I run down the halls, past Argenti who call my name, and out onto a grassy field. Somewhere in the distance I think I hear a snow cat scream.

I sink into the burnt grass along the road where there used to be flowers and focus on my breathing. In the sky above, the stars are dancing. They twirl and spiral in a world where nothing matters.

I tilt my eyes up to them, focus, and breathe.

59
SAVANNAH

I stand in what remains of the throne room in the light of the setting sun. The Argenti swarm around me, watching with curious eyes as I shakily make my way to the First Elder's seat and open the small bag of vials Amadea handed me.

The Bloodhound was your sister.

Marcel's body is tense as he tries to read my mind. I'm not entirely surprised by what Amadea told me. Cece always looked like Venus Collins in ways I could not describe. Just because she shared the same blood as me does not change anything.

I only have one sibling. And his name was Mason Shaw.

I attempt to control my breathing as I stare down at the crowd of powerful beings dressed in the mechanical silver of their EXO Suits.

My heart feels empty and raw, but when Marcel places his hand on my shoulder, sitting on the stairs at my feet, I suddenly feel strong. As I sprawl over Roman's seat, the Argenti regard me as if I'm their saviour. Odd, because moments ago they were terrified of me.

Fear is strength. Death is power.

I reach into the bag, rattling through glass.

"Savannah, forgive me," an Argenti murmurs, "but the Elders are moving to the castle. We intercepted their comms—they want access to their rooms to send a signal to Terra. Something about the ships that never made it."

A fresh pang rips through my chest. I shudder a little, shouldering it, and look towards the Argenti known as Morana.

"Evaline is brave to power on with that, considering I lost two of my people in order to stop those ships."

Whispers circle the room, some of them slanderous. I can't tell who it's directed at.

Marcel takes a vial with the words, CIRCA 1830, THE MOON BLITZ AS SEEN BY ELANOR PUGH, written on it.

"What do you mean by that?" Baxter asks as he shoulders through the crowd.

I lift my chin and smile, but there is no warmth or happiness in my face, so the expression feels empty.

"The Elders decided to kill all the Umbrans on the Terran base. My friends, Jasmine Spark and Elijah Brookes—two people who were never shown a scrap of kindness from this planet—gave their lives to save your people."

Outrage flares through the room.

"Enough!" Marcel declares, huffing. His dangerous eyes greet mine, filled with hidden worry, and he gently folds the vial into my fingers. Just for mY ears, he adds, "Go hunt for the information my sister wants you to see. I'll deal with the Argenti."

He stands on stiff legs, his eyes sweeping the room.

"Follow me."

SAVANNAH

CIRCA 1830, THE MOON BLITZ AS SEEN BY ELEANOR PUGH.

The ground shifts, rocking the very foundation of the planet as the ocean cleaves through the continent with the next earthquake. I turn, looking into the silver eyes of the tall, ethereal creature, his fingers soft on my cheek as he attempts to soothe me. The love cascading through my chest is eternal and filled with raw agony. I didn't breed with them, like the others, but that touch makes me see why they did.

I sob a little against his gentle hand, feeling pain for the loss of his planet, since the creature doesn't understand the meaning of the feeling.

Our ships roam the skies, darting past scrapes of the moon. Evaline's idea. To be safe in the sky.

I was their mentor and I trained them well. Almost too well. Roman. George. Elias. Connor. Alexsandre. Evaline. They were mine to protect on this mission to Umbra, and now I feel I must protect the pregnant Occupants. The lovely creature before me helped me place them into the roots of the Tenere trees to protect them in cryo.

Among them are as many children as I could round up, yet they slumber against their will. None of them wanted this.

"They refuse to board our ships." I sob as I look down at the sleeping faces in the bellies of the tree's bulbous roots. "How do we know that cryo will protect them?"

It feels as though even the trees cannot save them now.

The tragedy of losing a moon could take years to recover from. Anything could happen.

They don't understand that. They have never lived with pain or death.

The sight of their world shattering has only added confusion to their minds. Children were something they were excited about, as it's incredibly difficult to breed on Umbra. But saving those children? Why would they, when they've never had to survive anything?

And so, I stand, protecting them while my friends roam the skies for a safe place. Evaline's ship stays near, egging me to join her. But she doesn't yet know about the children. She knows we experimented but has no clue how successful we were.

"Eleanor," the creature says, testing the words. And then, in a sing-song voice, he begins to speak his own tongue.

It's like a sad song. A ballad for death.

I sink into the tree behind me; its soft hide is like skin, rubbing my flesh. The ground is quaking, and from the volcano we stand on, I can already see the ocean pouring over land. Fissures break through the large continent, snapping it in half as the planet is thrown to its side, the smaller of our two moons already a halo twisting around us in the sky. The ocean extends what was once a small lake within the centre of the planet, ripe with vegetation and trees. Not even here, among the equator, are we safe. Some rubble breaks through the atmosphere and streams down, pounding into the soil.

"Eleanor," the Occupant says again, this time in a cry.

I've never heard these beings cry.

Agony is thrown over its long, angelic face, and the sight of it is enough to break my own heart.

"Home." I speak the word in their tongue.

Umbra. Home.

Vanishing beneath us.

CIRCA 1850, THE INTITATION OF THE BASES AS SEEN BY ROMAN LAURENT

"Elias, your spies are plentiful enough. Your direct involvement in this cause will only prove a disruption," I advise the man.

This island is perfect—just offshore to the newly settled New Holland. It's close enough to the roots of England, should our people wish to board ships with the colony and return home. But that isn't the intention. We need to eliminate ties with England soon, because the greedy minds of the colonisers will never stop hunting us if they discover the wonder of Umbra.

And yet…

"Our children are scared, Roman. We have only just regained the manpower necessary to test the science of the forcefields, and our castle is still just a concept. There's only so long I can expect the Argenti children to live in tents along the shore of the only inhabitable place on-planet. We need something more. More people. More houses."

Our wonderful creations, the Argenti: A departing gift of the Occupants.

We didn't realise what they were at the time. But a few years ago, our silver children began preforming miracles. We lived on our spaceships for many years, fleeing the tragedy of Umbra, and came home to find a few of the Occupants had survived.

No, not Occupants. Their children.

Our children.

Apparently, Eleanor knew the experiment was a success. More than we could ever dream.

I turn to Elias Hart, whose eyes are wide as he takes in the beauty of the island. It's lush and thriving in a way that Umbra hasn't since the damage of the Moon Blitz.

"Tell your spies to stop the hunt. While it's nice to know what our people are thinking about extending to Terra, we need to make people believe it. The Argenti listen to you, so perhaps you'd better go home."

"And what of Terra?" he implores with a soft smile.

No longer Earth, but Terra. Not our planet or our home, just a scientific advantage.

"We have sacrificed enough people already to build this base. Let's start with what we have."

He nods. It's practical yet there's too many variables. "And if the message about Umbra leaks?"

I smile at Elias Hart. "I'm not the one who decided to start calling us Elders, Elias."

"It's better that the people turn to you. You're double the man I am. And as the First, I believe that choice now rests with you."

I look at the man admiring the island—at the years of hardship that balances on his shoulders—and feel fear for the first time. The idea of establishing the Elders was so we could get things done and more efficiently issue orders to rebuild our home. It was never meant to be a display of power.

Even so, as I stare across the island so beautiful and ripe for the taking, I decide I want that power.

"We are in this together, Elias. All of us."

CIRCA 2000, THE BIRTH OF THE FATED AS SEEN BY KENT MAY.

The screams of Venus Collins as she gives birth to what will be The Fated Usurper of the Elders was as damning as the day she became pregnant.

I wasn't there when Roman Laurent drugged Venus and pinned her to the bed, but my sister, Lythia May, was forced to watch as her friend was brutally experimented on. She told me everything about it. That is my curse.

I'm a special sort of Argenti—I can make people's memories disappear. And so, they tell me their horror stories, in hopes I will erase them.

I got sick of it and made them forget me instead. Everyone except my sister, Lythia May.

She found me in Sector 3 the day Venus went into labour and told me to come.

I told her no.

"Help me to understand, Kent!" she pleaded. Over and over.

"I gave up being an Argenti for your people, Sister. I choose the planet instead. Join me before news of this birth gets out. And for the love of Umbra, never bring it up to anyone again."

My sister, I now realise, was never good at listening to me.

"Just please come. I think her birth will change everything for Umbra. You say you choose the planet? Well, this is it. Come with me and maybe I will join your cause."

With a heavy sigh, I followed her reluctantly into the birthing room, disguised as someone other than Kent May.

On a bed draped in satin and covered in silver blood, Roman Laurent plucks a babe with grey eyes from between the woman's legs. She's howling as she comes into the world, her mouth wide.

I almost drop the medical tools at the sight of the girl who could change everything. But Sector 3 do not want anything to change. Not this way.

"Beautiful, loud, marvellous little thing," Roman Laurent coos. "Do you know what you have created, my child?"

Bile sweeps my stomach and I force myself to stand still as I pretend to be an Argenti on duty to deliver this babe. Across the room, trembling, the other nurses are whirring around doing their job. Not once do they look at me. I used my Magic to make them forget me. A small pang hits my heart, but the memory of these people's affection is one I have already forced myself to forget.

Just as I will make everyone forget this child.

Between sobs, Venus utters, "She not only carries my blood, but a transfusion of all the Elders' blood."

My very bones chilled at that.

"I wonder if her hair will run silver or brown. If my child is the girl of your prophecy, May, she will look Terran but will have the full abilities of a pure-blooded Argenti. That would be a rare type of power to behold. Don't you think?"

My sister trembles as she touches her friend's hand. "If she's the girl I saw, she will end Umbra."

Roman shakes his head, smiling. Curiosity is more dangerous than fear.

He holds the babe to his chest and turns from the delivery room. "Thank you for the part you played in this experiment, Venus."

I follow him out, Magic already cracking at my fingers.

Lythia May was right. This is the change we have been waiting for. Yet she was also wrong, because this babe will live an awful life. It's unfair to sacrifice the Fated in this way. She needs to be forgotten before Roman ruins her and ruins any chance Umbra has of change.

Sector 3 told me not to dapple, but outside, the uprisings are already beginning. They wonder who this usurper child could be. And if they discover it, potential war will ensure.

I must make them all forget.

I must make Venus believe her child is nothing special.

And I must make all the Elders forget their involvement in this.

To save my sister and to save our planet.

Maybe one day, they'll remember some of it.

I tear myself out of the last memory vial, gasping and panting. What the ever-loving hell was that? The half-filled glass tumbles to the ground. My lips are still wet with the sticky stain of the memory as I swallowed it. My heart misses a beat and I scramble off the throne to lunge for the thing before it rolls deeper into the rubble.

"Don't shatter!" I scream out to it, my fingers scrambling. I tuck it into my palm, my heart pounding. "I need you," I gasp.

Hardly able to operate the drawstring of the bag of vials, I lower the thing back inside, my entire body trembling.

"Roman Laurent is my father," I breathe.

My. Father.

I shake my head repeatedly, refusing to believe it. Somehow, I carry the blood of all the Elders. Another type of experiment, I assume. Did their Terran blood turn mine from silver to red, overpowering the gene from all the infusions? Did the experiments eliminate the genes from my mother, forcing me to have Roman's dark hair cascading down my back?

How does that even work? What does that even make me?

Then I remember Kent May's memory and realise… "None of the Elders know."

No one else knows except for Sector 3's people and Amadea.

Perhaps she knew before the vials? She's a spy, after all. She could have learnt this much sooner.

I stand, reaching for the switchblade still crusted with my mother's silver blood, and stare out across the empty wreckage of the throne room.

"What does this mean in relation to your list, Dea?" I mutter to myself.

My father is on that list, along with Evaline, my grandfather, the original Bloodhound, and Marcellus. Some of them, I'd wager, are not on my side.

And then, like a giant pang in my chest, I understand.

"You coy little girl." I laugh. "I can't believe you."

Because Amadea, despite her gentle eyes, has always been a spy. She knows things. *Awful* things. And I'd bet my life on the fact she knew Roman was my father. Just as she knew Celestine Collins was my sister.

Amadea's list was not of people I could trust or even people who wished the same things for Umbra. It was a list of my family and hers.

All people to save, bar Elias Hart. She wouldn't have known whether I'd like to save Celestine or Roman. How could she have? I didn't know them at the time.

Now, my question is who Evaline really is. Not to mention how I am connected to Lythia May.

The sun splashes orange over the clouds and, from where my brother once stood, I almost feel he is with me.

Just as they all are. Mason. Jasmine. Elijah… The people of Silver Valley. Even the Umbrans who lost their lives in the Night.

How many more will be added to that list? How long will we keep fighting, keep trying to kill each other, in the desire for power?

"I wish it wasn't up to me, Mason," I say to the stars. My throat tightens up, and I heave a little as I force down a sob. My legs fold in on themselves, making me sink from the throne and into the rubble. "I don't want to wear the crown."

I wish I never took the role of Usurper, the Prophesised, The Fated.

I wish I wasn't Savannah Shaw.

"I want to stop fighting, Jasmine," I say to the sky, feeling the weight of her all around me. "I wish I could go home, with you and Elijah, to Silver Valley. Walking down to the beach with a coffee in our hands, fighting the cold as we take Mason for a sunset swim. I just wish… I wish I were dead, too."

A piece of rubble tumbles as someone enters the small slip of an entrance left at the front of the throne room.

"No, you do not."

I turn and look at Marcellus. Pain is riddled over his face as he takes in my tears and the switchblade in my trembling hands. Slowly, he steps toward me until he is kneeling on the steps at my feet.

I let him take my face in his hands and watch with a slowly beating heart as he kisses away my tears. I feel the touch of his skin like an explosion. His fingers run through my hair, down my back, over my yellow dress and down to my fingers.

Magic swells between us, but neither of us use it. Not as he leans forward and kisses me, long and steady.

"No. You. Do. Not."

He says this between breaths, his mouth a mess of heat and longing as he soaks me in. My soul reels back into my body and something stirs in my chest with each word. I let the switchblade and the vials tumble to my feet as I reach for him.

I kiss him like it's my last day on Umbra. I kiss him like I might actually deserve him.

My shaky hands wander over his chest over the soft fabric and past the grooves of his tense muscles as he yanks me closer to him. I move them to his back, pulling the man into me, until we are flattened against each other so intensely I cannot breathe.

I arch backwards, my eyes briefly soaring over the stars and the dancing lights that rain down on us. He pushes me against the throne, one hand on my back and the other cupping my throat, his mouth wandering across my shoulder.

I need him closer. I need to feel him against me, over me, under me. I need him everywhere.

My equal. My Marcel.

"Be with me," I pant, pulling him up on Roman's throne until I am straddling him and kissing him again. His teeth grab my bottom lip, his silver eyes hungry.

"Just be with me."

The words are hard. My thoughts are even harder, especially as he abandons my lips and kisses a trail of fire down my neck and over the scars adorning my skin.

He manages to say just two words. "My Savannah."

And then I am truly, absolutely, gone.

61

JESSE

"Jesse, my uncle is dead," Mel says as her fingers rapidly drag over the large tech screen.

We broke into Elias Hart's office moments after the death of Venus Collins. Melanie has been hacking through his firewalls ever since.

"Venus spoke the truth," she adds, sinking back against the creaky seat.

A part of me already knew this. The last time I saw him, he was going to Sector 2 with instructions to get to the hangar. He was leaving for Terra.

I place a hand on her shoulder and hold her tight. It's enough to make her release a long, aching breath.

"You're finally free from him," I tell her.

She turns to me, half-Argenti monster, half the girl I love, and mouths, "*I know.*"

She doesn't look sad. She looks relieved.

"I hadn't seen him in so long. Part of me wonders if, since Silver Valley, he was trying to avoid me by busying himself with aiding Venus. And I'm glad. But at the same time, I wish I had the chance to rub our victory in his face," she mutters.

Our victory. Is that what this is?

She pulls back from the screen and rings her fingers, the metal of her prosthetic glistening against the human hand.

"Should we go and see what Savannah has to say to the Elders?" she asks.

I purse my lips and study her face for any insinuation for how she is feeling. Barely a day ago, she killed Elias. And now, in the wake of Jasmine's sacrifice and Elijah's death, it's hard to remember that monster ever existed.

Something flashes in her eyes as she waits for me to answer. But honestly, I don't really have one.

"I don't really mind, Mel. I'll do whatever you want to do. Always."

Umbra stopped being my home years ago. I stopped caring for anything or anyone the day I decided that. Yet here she stands— the girl who reminded me that some things are worth living for. I'll follow her to the ends of the universe and into my own grave if that is required, if only because I'm terrified of what would be left of the world if she wasn't in it.

Melanie Beckett is my home, my family, my girl.

"I think I want to stay here."

And so, we stay.

She busies herself with programming and unravelling information about the Elders' ships. Apparently, the Elders have a hangar somewhere at the back of the castle with one lone ship inside it.

An escape plan.

In a castle this vast, I guess I shouldn't be so surprised.

It's an older model—one of the first that came to Umbra and one of the only ships that made it out in one piece after the Moon Blitz.

It's the same ship that hovers in the sky near the front of the castle where Savannah and Marcellus make their appearance and stand united. Around them, all of Umbra has congregated. A mass of fighters and families both healthy and injured have joined to watch the assembly that may just decide their future.

Melanie gasps and pulls me towards the balcony, her fingers trembling in my own.

A large ship is humming and blowing heat across the destroyed courtyard. Out of the open hatch, Evaline makes her way towards Savannah. From up here, we cannot clearly see our friend, but it's safe to assume she is by the edge of the castle. Evaline's gentle face looks haggard, even from up here. Her lips tighten as she regards the united front of citizens and Argenti, most of whom are in EXO Suits.

The sight of those suits sends a long pang through my chest.

"I know," Melanie breathes at seeing the hurt on my face. "I know Jasmine forgives you."

"I sent Jasmine to die." I gasp. "I killed Savannah's oldest friend."

She turns and looks at me, her face hard. "No. You made sure she got the job done. The girl would have gone anyway, even without your help."

"I gave her the tech screen that you coded to get her inside the control room, Mel," I bite back. "I gave her a clean path. I even told her that you wiped the security cameras, which gave her a clean shot into the damn base. I gave her all the tools for her to kill herself."

"You gave her the equipment *I* provided you to help her stop an unnecessary massacre. I worked hard on that coding, Jesse. Me. If you think you're responsible for her death, then maybe I am, too."

The words freeze me to my core. I inhale a long, trembling breath and lower my eyes.

"No, Mel. I shouldered that so you didn't have to."

"That's not how this works. There's not one lone person who could have stopped those ships. We did it together, all of us. You, me, and Jasmine. Even Elijah, though I question whether he was there mostly to die or if there was some other motive."

I don't know how, but I swear I feel a power crackling inside her from where our skin touches. I doubt she's using her Magic on me, because nothing within my rotten soul feels any different than before, but I feel the Magic all the same.

We are all Argenti.

We can perfect the drug we gave Mel and build a race of people who could do wonders for this planet. And maybe, just maybe, with the help of the Ley Lines and our ability to combine Occupant DNA and science, we can restore Umbra to its former glory.

The idea is chilling.

"He sacrificed himself, Mel," I urge. "He probably did it so the other bases on Terra would not suffer the same way his family did. He did it to end a cycle."

She presses her lips together and shuffles her feet. "He was always so good at not showing how broken he was."

Weirdly enough, I don't feel a single shred of hatred when I say, "He did it for you, because he loved you."

She pulls her palm from my grip and wipes it down her clothes, hiding the fact that she's shaking. My entire body is tingling with the need to touch her again, but I let her stand back and smile at the memory of Elijah first.

"He was a good soul. I hope he found his family again."

A soft smile touches my lips. "He did," I say, assured of it. "And honestly, isn't it beautiful that he didn't have to do it alone?"

Mel cracks a smile. "Oh, stars, imagine the last thing you see before you die is the face of Jasmine Spark." She lets out a soft peel of laughter.

It's ill-mannered to speak poorly of the dead, but I laugh, too.

"Horrendous. I'll remind myself to plant extra flowers on Elijah's grave."

Mel, a little giddy, shakes her head and giggles. "He deserves a whole orchard."

"At best."

"We will build graves, wont we?" She furrows her brow as the thought crosses her mind. "Down by the ocean at the forest edge, where it looks like Silver Valley."

I grab her hands again, unable to stay away from her any longer. "Yes, my dear. We will make graves for all of them."

The smile she gives me is dazzling. *Intoxicating.* Not even the stars shine as bright as Melanie's eyes as she looks at me, staring right into the depths of my soul. The truth is right there in those eyes, just as it's always been. I know now, why she busied herself in work all those years and why she held herself back from Savannah so much when we were together.

Her eyes, wide and honest, shine with the greatest love.

Melanie is in love with me. And I'm a damn fool for not realising sooner.

Suddenly, the Magic between us is crackling, like a whole-ass forest fire between our souls. I tremble as I hold her hands, folding into the burning feeling. I want to bridge the gap between our bodies and stop the irritable heat.

She smiles, as if she feels it, too. She lifts her shaking prosthetic hand and lays it on my cheek. My breath stills as she flattens her fingers against my skin.

"I think something is happening below," she whispers upon picking up on the sounds of the crowd. But I'm not ready to look down yet. I'm not ready to let go.

"They don't need us," I say.

And I do the one thing I should have done years ago.

I kiss Melanie Beckett.

62

SAVANNAH

"Feeble, aren't they?" Marcel asks me.

I look at where he has propped himself up against the castle wall, his ankles crossed casually. He rubs his hands together to keep from touching me.

To hell with that. I stubbornly reach for him. His soft skin melts over mine, gentle and familiar. When his eyes lighten, he winks at me. Someone snorts from behind us, and I force myself to pull away.

"You intercepted my fleet to Terra," Evaline says over the whirring of the ship. The Argenti stopped them from breaching the castle, so they flew their ship into the gardens instead.

I sigh. Back to reality.

The sunset is still bright above our heads, as if the dead are watching over me.

I say with a voice stronger than I feel, "I stopped a massacre. As soon as you surrender your vessel, I will send men to the remaining Terran bases to bring all Umbrans safely home."

The Argenti around us straighten as if pleased by that. *How weird.*

Evaline sees this and quirks her mouth.

I fold my hands carefully over my yellow dress and tilt my head at them. *Your turn.*

Roman comes down behind Evaline, his dark eyes raging. "And if the secret of our planet comes out? If the Terrans swarm our planet?"

He is right in so many ways. But he is wrong in many more.

"It's something we will need to prepare for, *Father.* But nothing we cannot handle, considering how well you hid the bases."

The man freezes. He looks over at me, surprised at the declaration.

Does he know, that he's my father? The surprise seems feigned. Perhaps he discovered the truth, as well.

Within the crowd, I spot my real father, Mark Shaw. He narrows at his eyes at me and I can almost hear him say, "*Tread carefully, Daughter.*" But screw that. I haven't done that since landing on Umbra and making my way through their godforsaken desert. Screw careful.

I didn't die then, so I won't die now—not with all of Umbra at my back.

"It's too volatile!" Roman declares coolly as he looks over the Argenti surrounding me.

Fine. We can play.

I roll my eyes at him. Marcel mutters something joyfully about how entertaining it is to see Roman bristle.

"The ships we dispatched to Terra were sent for a reason."

Yeah. To kill your own people.

The Argenti look furious at that comment. The Commoners, too. They all have family and friends on those bases that their leaders tried to kill.

Marcellus yawns loudly behind me. I just hold my hand out,

palm to the sky, and turn to my father, Mark. He comes over immediately and places the book I gave him—Roman's tome of Argenti names—upon my exposed hand.

Idly, I comb through it, ignoring the conversation Roman is trying to coerce me into. The worn paper flutters in the breeze like wings as I leaf through the pages.

When I reach my name, I slam it shut and throw it at his feet.

"Know what this is?" My heart feels dark and cold as I look him down.

Argentum Mortis.

"Where…" He clears his throat. Everyone watches like our conversation is a scene they can't look away from. "Where did you find that?"

"Your chambers. Before the Dome Night, when you were busy prepping for war and murdering innocent snow cats. It has my name on it. December 31st, 2009. Page 34."

One of the braver Argenti slinks forward, picks it up, and combs through the pages until landing on my name. He looks up at me, eyes imploring, and says, "Savannah Laurent. Experiment 114, labelled under SUCCESS."

Argenti and villager alike begin to stir.

"Not only do you Elders plot to kill your subjects on Terra, you experiment on Umbrans you are tasked to protect out of sick curiosity. How many more of us to do you plan to destroy just because you feel like you can?"

The people shuffle closer to me. Some look at me in awe. Others look at Roman with hatred. A large knot has formed in my throat, but I refrain from clearing it and steady myself.

"This is a book of names! A collection of human experiments! The Elders have been running tests on their subjects since the Moon blitz. Many of these subjects never again saw the light of day. I am one of the few survivors."

Marcel steps forward, running his hand down my arm as he

passes. All the Argenti look to him like he's a god when he opens his mouth.

"The Elders have lived with one fear their entire life: death. The Moon Blitz shattered a once perfect world and ever since, the threat of death hung over them like a shroud. Sending ships to Terra to blow up the bases was an act of fear. Do we really want this to be our legacy? To blindly follow a group of old, crazed fools?"

The people start to mutter among themselves. Even my father wipes his forehead.

"So, you two think *you* deserve the crown?" Eleanor says. It's the first time she has directly shown agitation towards me.

Evaline adds a little hesitantly, "We did everything to protect our people. In return, you're trying to turn them against us."

She sounds a little sad as she says it.

"You sent a fleet of destruction to wipe out our people. How many Umbrans have family on Terra, do you think?" I muse.

A couple heated shouts follow at that.

Roman tightens his jaw. Alexsandre opens his mouth to speak his piece, but I hold up a finger. He stops, his mouth open.

The sight makes Marcel chuckle a little.

"I was told once that it's hard for someone with Argenti blood to bear children. However, thanks to the help of Sector 3—who are very powerful, by the way—we have proof that the Elders handled this by forcing the Argenti gene onto otherwise Common people." I point to my chest. "I didn't want that for myself. I never wanted this. I think we all deserve a choice in the matter. Choices always matter."

"That book could have been forged," someone calls out from the crowd.

Roman smirks at a little at that, but I was expecting this.

"Don't believe me?" I raise my eyebrows. "See for yourselves."

Marcellus tosses me the bag of memory vials. There are hundreds of them.

I hold the fabric upside down, spilling them across the stones. "Memory vials."

Shock cascades over Roman's face, followed by a drop of recollection. As if maybe, just maybe, he was privy to the invention of the damn things.

But Kent did a number on the guy. I wonder how much the Elders actually know, though I doubt I'll ever find out.

"The way we're handling the blessing of this immortal life needs to stop. As I said the other day, we are all Argenti! That means we are all equal. We all matter. And we all deserve the right to choose for ourselves."

Mark beams at me proudly. Marcel squeezes my hand.

"We are all Argenti! And together, we will all fix our planet. We faced extinction when the Dome was taken… and maybe that never needed to happen. It was our wake-up call."

Evaline tilts her head and, even through the loud babbling of the crowd, I can hear her ask me, "And what do you propose… *usurper?*"

I finally swallow the lump in my throat. "I'm no usurper. All I have done is bring everyone's secrets to light so Umbra may grow. I say we are all given a choice to become Argenti and establish an equal order. In doing so, we can use our Magic to rebuild our planet instead of destroy it."

The crowd goes wild. People scream my name. I swear I even hear couple '*Argentum Mortis*' shouted throughout the mix, but for the most part, the people seem elated.

All Umbrans have been offered the chance at becoming gods. Better still, they've been offered a voice.

"No more cowering under the Second Night. No more isolating ourselves to the strip of vegetation along the river. No more Elders. No more classism. No more blindly following the whim of our Elders. Umbra, for all of us."

They repeat that last line.

Converting Umbra back to what it was could take centuries, but on a planet that gifts us immortality, it seems like the perfect goal to work towards.

My hands start to tremble as the people debate amongst themselves, calling out and asking questions. The remaining Elders glance back and forth, taking it all in, their eyes wide. But it's Eleanor, the sweet frail woman with a penchant for tea and naps, that lifts herself up from the ground by the ship and makes her way towards me, her lips tight.

The crowd is still calling out chants.

"Savannah!"

"The Prophesied!"

"For Umbra!"

Suddenly, I feel sick. They reach for me like I'm a replacement and stand behind me like guards. But what I said earlier was true. I truly never wanted this.

Marcel looks at me. Deeply. He sees the heat on my cheeks and my frantic breaths, but I look past him, to my father. Mark Shaw is smiling at me. He's proud... yet sad. The crowd around him is screaming my name, over and over.

Is this really what I am to become?

The *Argentum Mortis.*

Usurper. Princess. Prophesised. Fated.

What about Savannah Shaw? The girl who loved her family with all her heart? Who came to Umbra for them? I just want a place to call *home* again.

I briskly turn back to the crowd. "Wait!"

It takes a moment for them to quiet down. My fingers reach for the switchblade in the pocket of my dress, knuckles white around it as I take a deep breath.

"You guys got me all wrong," I admit. Marcel is beaming. My father is beaming. Everyone else just looks confused. "We are among the few lucky people who have been gifted immortality on a planet that is more utopia than it is home. As a result, the Umbrans haven't grown as a people. Instead, you've all spent your lives trying to take *more* from it. *More* power. *More* right to rule. I don't want to be the next person who does this." I look past the Elders and towards the Argenti. "I was never meant to wear the crown, was I?"

Eleanor, amid the frenzy of the courtyard, finally smiles at me, the sight making her face radiate. Mark stiffens as he fights the tears from his eyes. It's his vote of confidence that makes me continue.

"I propose we form a new coalition. After today, we should all be given the choice of what to do for the rest of our lives. After that, we can elect a spokesperson for each field of study. Argenti creation; technology and surveillance; medicine; architecture; agriculture; space travel, and so on. We form a place where everyone has the right to impute their thoughts, and together we band together to rebuild our home. This is what I propose."

Evaline, her hand fluttering to her chest, tips her head. "And what of you, Savannah?"

Am I giving it all up, just like that? Am I handing Umbra back over to the people?

I smile at Eleanor as she slowly makes her way towards me, her grin as wide as I have ever seen it.

And I think to myself... *Yes. Yes, I am.*

"I never deserved to sit on a throne. No one does. Not anymore."

Mark reaches grabs my hand and exhales the deepest breath I have ever heard him take. Eleanor casts her hands on her heart, then offers them to me with a smile.

I wink at her.

All the people stare, unsure what to make of me now. Frankly, I don't really care.

Marcellus swallows sharply. "You heard Her Majesty!" he says playfully. "As of the new dawn, the crowns that have rested on the same heads for centuries will be gone. Umbra will be a place of equality."

Roman seethes a little at that final line, but Evaline and Alexsandre look glad. And Eleanor, her face glowing brighter than the setting sun, finally looks happy.

Mark tips his head up to the sunset casting orange against his glasses, and sighs.

"For living, instead of surviving."

Eleanor finally reaches me and tosses her frail arms around my shoulders. She relaxes into me, her breathing shallow. She has lived so many years here on Umbra. She had already spent a great deal of her life on Terra. Age lines her skin, melting her bones. It's in stark juxtaposition to the Argenti man still holding my fingers in a tight grip.

"*Momento vivere*," she mutters upon hearing my father's words. *Remember to live.*

Tears prick my eyes. As I turn to my father, it occurs to me that I will be seeing his gentle face for a long, long time. For eternity, perhaps.

And that… that is what I want. It's who I want to be.

I'm half crying when I repeat against Eleanor's hair, "*Momento vivere.*"

AMADEA

When I leave the courtyard, I don't expect to find Kent standing under what remains of an apple tree, his hands to his chest. His hood is down for us, his silver eyes devouring me.

"The Fated was what Umbra needed," he tells me as I stand by his side.

Hundreds of Argenti and villagers mill about nearby, chatting and asking questions. No one pays us much attention as we stand under the shadows of the tree as dusk begins to fall. I don't know what to say to the man.

"Thank you for the memory vials" doesn't quite seem to cover it, but I'm glad he is here, representing Sector 3 in a way only they know how to. Anomonously.

"We lost a lot to get here," I reply, my chest empty.

He nods softly. "Some more than others."

I flash him a quizzical look. Loss is loss. Who cares who lost more?

"Your friend, Lily Hayes, joined us," he tells me. "I came here to let her brother know, but I'm afraid I may not be able to relay that message."

Lily joined Sector 3? Stars.

My heart thumps loudly as I turn to him. "I'll let him know."

He nods at me again.

My pain seems to go unnoticed. He smiles lightly at the people around us, taking in each of their faces. And he says more to himself than to me, "You know, I have spent my entire life praying that the Kingdom would return to the ways of the Occupants again. I never thought I would see the day where that would actually happen."

I offer a soft smile at that, taking in the slightly scared and confused faces of our people. "I'm afraid it might take a while before it all settles into place. But the idea is a beautiful one."

"A while, maybe. But it will happen. The people have long hungered for a change and they're starting to see the appeal of this one. Can't you see?"

I can. It's everywhere. In their nervous faces. In the ashy remains of their homes. In the seduced expressions of the remaining Elders. This change will happen, even if it takes a hundred years.

A small child pushes past me, his eyes brushing over mine for a second. I wear my own face today, but all he sees are Argenti eyes. And yet… it isn't fear in his gaze. It's hope.

I smile at him. *Stars,* hope is beautiful.

"I once gave Savannah a list of names to save. Your mother was on it," I tell Kent.

Evaline's name. She's still standing near her ship, taking in the crowd.

"Why?" Kent asks.

I shrug. "She's Savannah's godmother." Kent blinks but doesn't say anything. Not even a thank you. "The Elders aren't all bad. I'm glad that Evaline is still alive," I continue.

"Even after knowing she was responsible for the Moon Blitz?" Kent asks.

I shrug again. "Even after that."

Because she wasn't directly responsible for it. She created the *Netsils*—the bombs that imploded so many wondrous places—but it wasn't her hand that set most of them off. So why should she die for that? Why hold her to just one of her mistakes?

We all make mistakes. The time for killing is over. Now, we rebuild.

The sun is officially below the horizon, and a large portion of the crowd splits to go home. The Elders walk out to Eleanor, where she stands with Savannah, and urge her back into the castle.

I give Kent one last look. "I hope to see you and your people on the day we vote for new representation. I think Sector 3 should have their say. Especially about how we go about using the Leys and how to integrate our lives beyond the Kingdom."

Kent nods. "I would like that, as well."

I give him a soft wave and make my way back home.

↶

"You should represent us for security, Mel," I advise, sitting cross-legged on Savannah's bed two days after.

Sometime overnight she hauled most of the tech from my father's old room and erected what looks like a mini control centre in the middle of her rooms. Savannah doesn't seem to care, though, as she busies herself with unravelling bedrolls along her balcony, replacing the daybeds. Something about wanting to keep an eye on her family until all else settles.

Melanie turns and beams at me, but then shakes her head.

Despite the many screens, she spent most of the previous Night working on grafting fresh skin over her metal arm. In the background, codes have been tracking all online comms throughout the Kingdom so she could keep an eye on what people are saying about this proposed new government system.

She flecks her new fingers at me and Magic cascades around her. "I don't even trust my new power yet. Why give me more of it?"

Jesse leans over her office chair and kisses her hair. "Because you're the best, my dear."

Red blooms across her cheeks. She looks around the room tentatively, nervous that anyone saw. But Mark is busy making his fourth coffee of the morning and Savannah only just makes it back inside off the balcony.

She claps loudly, making all our heads swivel. "Okay, guys, anyone feeling nervous?"

This morning, the Umbrans will vote on whether they want a new government.

If Savannah's proposal is approved, another vote will take place in a week to decide who is to preside over each section of work.

"Why be nervous?" Mark smirks and slurps his coffee. "My daughter is a terrifying badass and I doubt anyone will ever cross her again."

Savannah snorts.

Melanie's chair creaks as she leans over to hide her blush, which is only deepening as Jesse taunts her by trailing his fingers down her back.

"Umbra wants this," I say softly, smoothing down the blankets under me. Savannah demanded I have the bed last night—after changing the sheets, of course. She said she probably wouldn't be able to sleep much anyway.

I don't blame her. She spent most of yesterday chatting with the Elders, as well as a few Argenti, about the proposition for the future. To everyone's surprise, they were on board, with one condition: the Elders get a chair on this new government.

Savannah granted them the chair of History. We don't yet know what it means, but I must admit, it seems only fair.

Marcel didn't like it much, though. He's been out of the castle since.

"I hope so," Savannah absently answers me, her eyes now on Jesse and Melanie by the tech screens. Her gaze doesn't look heavy, though. In fact, she seems glad.

"Any news of Lily?" Savannah asks Melanie. Jesse's jaw tightens at that.

"None."

A large pit yawns in my stomach. I could tell him what Kent said, but the timing feels off. One day, I will go after her and tell her of Jasmine's sacrifice. But not now. She needs to be alone, to shoulder her grief and find her own place in this world.

Besides, she *lost* Jasmine. I doubt she will show her face here for a great while.

Mark folds himself against the wall and clutches his coffee. Dark circles line his eyes, which tells me he didn't sleep very well.

The front door slams open then, jostling him.

"*Stars*," Melanie says.

Savannah smirks. "Annoying when they do that, isn't it?"

"Mel has been less angry as of late, which means less door slamming," Jesse says.

And she goes red again.

When Marcellus pulls into the room, he laughs at our shocked faces, and my heart slaps a little at the sight of my brother, safe and whole.

"The Argenti have given up half their supply of EXO Suits to the villagers. The half that refused have been allocated to do the clean-up work themselves. Everyone with a Suit will work overtime on rebuilding while we figure out next steps," he announces as he strides into the room, Magic vibrating in his wake.

He enters the space and says this like he's been here the whole time.

The corner of Savannah's lip quirks. "I bet they loved that."

He grins and winks at her. "Not one bit. But they're terrified of me."

Jesse rolls his eyes.

Savannah goes to Marcel and straightens his jacket. It's dark blue and utterly ordinary. She wipes a fleck of dirt off his cheek in such a casual way, my heart aches at the sight of it. People have always been afraid to touch my brother, but she touches him as if she doesn't care if he drains her.

"The vote will pass, Savannah. Stop fussing."

"I'm not fussing. And I'm not worried about the vote."

He quirks an eyebrow at her.

She places her hands on her hips, brushing the satin of her silver dress. It's an elegant, regal thing, chosen out of spite. Just because she doesn't want to wear the Umbran crown doesn't mean she can't rub it in the Elders' noses that she *could*.

"It will pass," Melanie affirms as she pointedly tries to ignore Jesse. "People have been chatting a lot via comms. All of it positive. The people want this. It gives them a say and a choice in matters. Something they've never had before."

"And besides," Mark muses from the ground where he's nursing his coffee, "you've already sent the ships to Terra to save the people living on the bases. That was the final stand. The people who have families there love you already."

"I don't want to be loved. I just want to be happy. I just want peace." She sighs.

Don't we all, I think. I loosen my hands around the sheets and crawl off the bed towards my brother.

"Mar, should I go and scout today? Pick up some information on who the people might vote to represent them?"

He places a finger on my chin and wipes a bit of dried drool off my face.

Okay, yuck. I stumble back in embarrassment.

He chuckles. "Nah, rest, Dea. The grownups got you."

"From what I've gathered," Melanie says, "Laurence will be head of Space Travel. Eleanor of History. Me for Security. The villagers are still deciding someone to rep Architecture. Someone from Sector 3 will step in for Agriculture. A villager for Livestock. Mark, you've been in talks for News, if you want that. And, umm, there's Military—Jesse, you could probably have a clean shot for that. Which leaves Medicine and Argenti Advancement."

She looks over to Savannah, questioning.

"Medicine should be given to Alexsandre," Savannah says instantly.

Melanie's eyes flash and she jumps out of her chair to rebut.

Jesse beats her to the punch. "Are you insane?"

Marcel just starts laughing.

"No. He's a scientist, and a damn good one at that."

My pulse increases, but I say nothing. *Definitely insane.*

Melanie exhales heartily. "Next week's problem," she says offhandedly.

But Savannah isn't done. "Marcel should lead the Argenti."

At that, Jesse looks ready to draw his sword. My chest lightens and I smile, turning my eyes on the shocked face of my brother. It takes a lot to surprise him, yet here he is, hands flexing.

"I'm sorry?"

"You heard me," she responds.

I lift my chin. "I agree, Brother. They listen to you."

He laughs. "Yeah, because I suck them dry. They fear me."

Melanie pushes her chair back. "I think they respect you, too. I'll back you."

Mark nods. "I will, too."

He gazes over us, his eyes wide, and folds his arms to stop his hands from shaking. Awe flashes over his face, at war with his disbelief. Savannah flicks his nose.

"Alright, what now, then?" Jesse suddenly asks the room.

All of us, languid and half-exhausted, turn to Savannah.

She beams. "We start living the way Mason wanted. And Jasmine. And Elijah. We bring Silver Valley to Umbra, and peace with it. *Momento vivere.*"

As simple as that. We repeat, as if in a daze, "*Momento vivere.*"

Because that is what immortality is all about.

Living.

SAVANNAH

Our house along the lake is almost like a small cottage, but something about it feels timeless.

The wooden weatherboards are an earthy, faded brown that bleeds into the trees, except for some white detailing hanging off the lip on the roof and the windows. The trees all hang around the house.

I can feel the forest perpetually hugging me, standing off just a short distance from our cottage home.

"It's a nice place, isn't it?" my father asks me.

I stand down by the twisting beast of a lake that glitters under the morning sun, the rocks along the shore covered in a lacquer of dew from the fog. I carry several stones in trembling hands up towards the treeline. Here, wildflowers have begun to bloom, marking the graves of my loved ones.

I lower the stones around the simple wooden crosses that

make their headstones. Moss still covers the branches that I freshly snapped from the trees. It's a beautiful place to rest.

My father hands me my switchblade, the small thing flashing as the metal hits the sun. *Perseverance.*

I smile as I take it. "It's wonderful, Dad."

But he's not talking about the house we built in homage to our home in Silver Valley. He's talking about the world we built and the life we've made for ourselves.

The graves are many, but we keep three out front belonging to Mason, Jasmine, and Elijah. We can visit them any time we want, just by crossing our front yard.

I kneel before Jasmine's and bury the switchblade under the earth by her cross where she can rest with it until the end of her days. We didn't have anything to bury, so the ground remains alive with flowers. All the same, I feel their energies all around this place, cloaking me with their memories.

A slight waver hits my step as I stand back and brush the dirt from my hands. I wish I had the words to say goodbye, but I don't think I need to. They know I love them.

"Come, Marcel will be here soon."

My father reaches for my hand, and we walk back to our home.

Today marks one year since their deaths. I decided they finally deserved a place at our cottage home, here along the river. They have been gone a while, yet I will never forget them. Not once in my immortal life.

I smile at the thought. I spent my entire time on Umbra trying to save them, but the truth is, they saved me. They brought me back to life. Back to what matters.

Umbra never needed a leader or a saviour. It never needed me on its throne.

I'm finally happy. I'm home.

Most of us are Argenti now, save the few that turned it down like my father. And, because of our new coalition, Umbra is already prospering. Many houses are still being rebuilt, but nature has begun to take hold again. Turns out, Melanie's new Magic to manipulate instincts didn't just end with human beings. She can alter plants, too. And while she needs eye contact to command a human being, plants are a lesser life form and don't need that level of focus. It didn't take much for her to convince the weathered trees to resprout and thrive. With help from other freshly-turned Argenti who had a penchant for plant life, Umbra's forest has grown beyond the river. We are taking the desert back, one day at a time.

Just like Jasmine and Mason wanted.

"I'll wait here," I tell my father as we come up to our house. He nods and smiles as I turn towards the rows of rosebushes with a skip in my chest.

Umbra is so damn beautiful now. Thriving in so many ways.

The people just needed a choice, because life sucks when void of them. The Elders didn't see that at the time. But now, I can't say I've had many complaints from any of them. Even Roman, who always exercised his power, seems to be enjoying his new life.

The castle is but a memory.

No one bothered to fix what we destroyed, although the monument stands to remind us of what we lost a year ago. Every second week when our coalition convenes, I follow Marcel up that haunted stone path where our leaders meet in the courtyard under the stars.

But that's as far as I go. Marcel leads the Argenti. Melanie, security. Jesse, military.

I am just… me. Savannah Shaw.

I sit in the treeline and snack on fruit, sometimes with Amadea, other times with Lily's snow cats, who have begun to roam the lands around us once she left them.

Lily is gone. We know she's in Sector 3, but she never visits.

Melanie and Jesse returned to Sector 2 after the leader of Architecture deemed rebuilding the bridge was important. It's a poor execution of what it was, but it does the job.

They seem happy, together, as they have always been. Working hard, as they always will. My friends, as much as they are my family.

I run my hands over my roses, plucking a dead one from its stem and marvelling at all the new buds. Melanie wanted to help me with them, but I refused. They are my pride and joy.

"Marcel's here," my father says from inside.

I lift my head to see him exit the treeline, looking dazzling in white trousers and a silver button-up. My heart does a weird little flop.

He lives with his sister, closer to the castle, but he often visits me.

I didn't want to rush anything. The pain of loss still haunts me—and him. I want to learn how to breathe again. How to live.

But I live for our mornings.

His constant presence is a blessing I never thought I would be lucky enough to count. I yearn for him every single day. I work on the rosebushes, watering or trimming them, and wait for his familiar face to smile at me from the trees.

My father always leaves a mug of coffee out for him every morning. And every morning before his shift starts, he comes. It's the happiest moment of my day until reality steps back in.

"Morning, little mouse," he purrs. "Your collection is sprawling."

The front of our house is peppered with rows upon rows of lush roses. Excessive? Perhaps. But I work the gardens every day, extending them. They are a symbol, just like I was.

A symbol for those I lost. A symbol for the future.

Beautiful, deadly, wild. Just like me.

"Just like Umbra." I smile and fall into his arms. He wraps me into him, the sound of his breathing filling that vacant hole in my heart.

I immediately feel alive. I chose him, just as I chose this house. Everything around me is mine. My home. My future. My family. Because sometimes the best part about life is knowing you have a choice and a good cup of coffee to wake up to every morning.

That, my friends, is the dream.

And, stars, if I'm not living every damn second of it.

THE END.

Featuring:

Jasmine Spark's death

Lily Hayes leaving for Sector 3

JASMINE

I love you, Savannah Shaw. Persevere for me.

That is what I want my last words to be before the bomb goes off—even if Savannah will not hear me from the castle. But even so, it's the testimony I wish to leave behind.

Love. It's the strongest force of all. I want to be remembered for that.

Because I love Savannah Shaw.

Everything I did, I did for her. And I would gladly do it all over again.

"I'm scared," Elijah Brookes utters. His hands shake a little as he stares down at the dark screens in the control room.

I must admit, I share the feeling. It's one thing to say you want to die, but it's another entirely to do it.

I reach for his hand, warm and gentle in my own, my nerves ticking against his. Both of us shake and sweat. I open my mouth to answer him, *"Me too,"* but only a squeak comes out. The room is large, but I feel the walls caving in, claustrophobic like I have never felt.

The control centre is dark, bar a distant blue light humming above our heads. I gently lower the tech screen Jesse gave me onto the smooth metal table in the centre of the large expanse of screens. Reluctantly, I release Elijah's hand and sigh audibly.

The tech screen got us inside—all I had to do was plug it into the door.

There's nothing left to do except ignite the bomb. And yet…

"Do you think it's possible to turn on one of these screens?" I ask Eli apprehensively.

The quivering man blinks at me. Once. Twice. He runs a large hand over the back of his clammy neck. He's a sight to see, dressed in the same clothes from Sector 3, smelling faintly of the Umbran desert. The door to the control room sputters a faint orange light over him, shooting colour every so often across his face. He turns his dark eyes onto me and swallows.

"Why?"

"To see it. To see home," I croak.

Silver Valley.

This is the Umbran control centre… they must have a live feed of our home planet somewhere. I'm no Melanie Beckett, but I suppose it wouldn't be too hard to find… right?

Again, Eli asks, "Why?"

The next words are even harder to get out. "I want to see it one last time. Before we…"

Before we go up in great clouds of smoke. Yippee.

I clear my throat.

He rubs his hands down his sandy pants and says thickly, "I guess there should be an 'on' button somewhere."

His eyes are glassy as he runs his fingers down the edges of the glass screens. Umbran tech isn't like normal computers and I somehow doubt he will find what he's looking for. But I stand back and watch him, unable to do anything myself.

The room around us feels heavy. I can barely breathe.

When Eli comes up empty handed, he almost looks like he's ready to cry.

"Mkay," I say. "It's okay."

Eli sits in one of the chairs lining the desks and puts his head in his hands.

"No, it's not."

I reach for him, ready to tell him that it's alright if he wants to live to see another day. But I don't. He doesn't *want* it to be and we don't have time to argue about morality.

He sniffles loudly, his leg shaking a little. In the pocket of his pants, the bomb hangs heavy, ready to be used. I stare at it, unseeing.

"I still remember the first time I saw Silver Valley," I begin to say, knowing he needs to see the image of his home almost as much as I do. "I was so young, so terrified. My father had just died, and I was sent down to a strange planet with strange people, out of my wits. But then… I stepped out of the transport shuttle and all I could think was, *I never knew a place that could look so green*. I was happy, despite everything."

The memory consumes me, full and ripe. Suddenly, I'm not breathing in the metallic tang of the control centre. Instead, the sweet aroma of morning dew on pine trees, wafting past on a salty ocean breeze, fills my memory. I can see the sun nipping the forest and feel the sand crunch beneath my feet. The forest was thick around the base when I first saw it. Fog spilled down through little slips in the perimeter. Everything felt calm.

"Nothing mattered, for just that moment. I was at peace."

Of course, I didn't stay in Silver Valley for long. My course was set for the mainland and Savannah. I scraped and dragged my way through the forest, too young to drive a Hover and too frightened to get caught. I fell many times in that forest. I still have a scar on my knee, slim and white, from a rock I slipped over during that first commute.

"Silver Valley was the only place I mattered," Eli adds when noticing I'm finished. I tear my contemplative gaze towards where he sits, his fingers brushing against the pocket holding the bomb. "I was the product of its very beating heart—the lifeblood of the next generation. Dad always told me that, but I never quite appreciated what I had until it was gone."

He pauses to clear his throat. "Our family was one of the very first founders of the small village, unaware of the Umbrans already occupying it. Dad was always so proud of that. And he was right that Silver Valley was a life that was made for me. I was so, so *happy*. Everyone was every day. Savannah strives to make Umbra that but fails to see that she already had it in Silver Valley. It…" He clears his throat again heavily. "It was everything to me, Jasmine."

If I were anyone else, I would console Elijah Brookes.

I don't. He needs to vent. To remember. So, I stand back and let a soft breath go.

"I know exactly how you feel."

Silver Valley was to him what Savannah was for me. *Everything.*

He turns his pained eyes on me and forces a lump down in his throat.

"I don't remember seeing Silver Valley for the first time, like you do. But I do remember the first time I saw you come to the Valley, and I suppose that's the same thing."

That makes me forget the thickness in the room. I giggle. "The same thing? What?"

I shake my head at him, the silly boy.

"I was with my dad down by the docks. He told me of this reporter who was due to arrive. Someone thrilled at the prospect of giving life back to the old warehouse. I was there when you exited the ferry because my dad insisted I give Ethan Spark's daughter a warm welcome—something stupid about how we are the same age or whatever."

I squeeze my brows together, my pulse ticking in my throat. "I didn't see you."

He chuckles a little, the heaviness leaving his eyes. "Yeah. Saw my mates surfing down at the beach, so I left after my dad went to greet you lot. He yelled at me that night about it."

When I laugh, Eli stares at me with stars in his eyes.

"Is that why you came up to me at school the next day and asked me to come hang out?" I enquire, remembering well. He jumped when he saw me in the hallway, arms waving a little in a mission to come to me, his white teeth dazzling as he grinned.

"*Oi new girl! Get over here!*" We became fast friends after that.

"I couldn't forget the way you skipped off that damn ferry! You sparkled like sunshine, so happy and joyful. I knew I made a mistake not meeting you, because you're exactly the kind of person that Silver Valley was built for. You, Jasmine Spark, were always destined to be one of my greatest friends."

And it was true. We were. I was just too absorbed with Savannah and he was too much of a moronic boy around his happy-go-lucky friends that we never got the time to properly become the friends we ought to have been.

I lean forward and ruffle his hair. "Ditto, Brookie."

He laughs—the kind of laugh that doesn't exist on Umbra and hasn't existed since before Silver Valley was destroyed. It ignites his face and lights the whole room. Eli always knew how to brighten a room and to make people feel loved and welcomed, but tragedy stole that talent from him.

I miss the old Eli.

"Well," he says, still swallowing laughter, "you ready to do this?"

His hands tighten around the bomb, not quite pulling it from his pocket, but ready if I say the word. I'm not ready. But there isn't really a choice, is there?

I sigh loudly. "Ready as I'll ever be."

He gives me a stiff smile. "Glad you're here with me, Jas."

The atmosphere in the room instantly thickens. This time, I pull a chair over and sit next to him. We both stare at the dark screens in the control room, nothing but our reflection staring back at us. If I were Melanie, I would play some beach ambience sounds. But no. All I get is my own sad face.

"Think of Silver Valley," I offer him as he pulls out the bomb.

His body shakes so violently that the chair looks ready to spill. My heart feels like it's stopped beating, my skin cold. There's a faint ringing in my ears.

Teeth chattering, he turns to look at me. *This is it.*

"Did you know that after death the human mind stays alive for at least seven minutes?" Eli asks me between quivering lips. My leg jerks as I turn and look at him. My skin is prickling, but I don't have the strength to rub warmth back into them.

Would we, considering we will be blasted to pieces? I want to ask.

But I don't. Stars, I don't. I can't even think like that right now.

Instead, I fill my mind with images of Savannah Shaw in Silver Valley: *her pale fingers wrapped around coffee, morning dew hanging from her dark hair as we parade through morning fog, a small but blissful smile blessing her pink face.*

The fantasy settles my stomach, stilling my body.

I lean back into my chair, breathing sharply. "I already know my seven minutes."

My voice is but a breath, but Eli hears it.

"Me, too." His eyes are glassy again, and I know he's thinking of Silver Valley and the happy memories of the beach and his parent's smiling faces.

I reach over and place my hand over the bomb he holds. He isn't shaking anymore.

"Let's do it, Eli. For them."

A soft smile manages to touch his face. "For them."

The next few moments are intangible. All I can register is the faint flicking of the orange light and the reflection of my face on the dark screens.

I close my eyes, envisioning Savannah's face.

It's time to go home.

"I love you, Savannah."

And Elijah Brookes pulls the pin.

LILY

I never thought I would see another person I cared so deeply for die right in front of me.

Yet here I stand.

Cerberus licks my cheek and Amaryllis—the young pup just old enough to run with the others—howls a little into the sky. They don't understand what the roiling plumes in the sky mean or why the Command section of the energy plant is smouldering, but they do know the sight of it is causing me immeasurable pain.

"The girl and the boy are dead. Please, there's nothing I can do," a guard says from behind me, tied to the tree I chose for him. He was one of the first to flee the explosions. Exterreri, one of my more ferocious snow cats, ran him down.

"*Talk*," I had bit out at him, lazily watching the blood tinkle out of his arm from where Exterreri held him.

The man talked instantly. Coward. I almost wish he hadn't.

My fingers rake the ground beneath me, as if by latching onto the soil I can hold myself steady as the world rocks and sways. I can barely see, barely feel, as I watch the plumes of the explosion drift into the sky.

"Find me," Jasmine had asked.

"As fast as I can," I promised.

Not fast enough.

It took a while to assemble my snow cats and bring them across the water. I'm surprised I managed to get a few of those big fat babies to brave that crossing, but by the time I arrived with my pack, patrolling the edge of the castle, it was obvious my friends were adamantly staying inside. The sun had begun to ebb by the time Cerberus caught her trail—*Jasmine*. My heart kicks up a fuss at the mere memory of her.

At the memory of what we could have had.

I lost Faye to an S.P. gun. There was nothing I could have done for her then, but Jasmine? I could have followed her into the power plant and coaxed her back outside, if only I knew her intention was to kill herself in that damn explosion.

I wail a little, my throat tightening with unshed tears.

Cerberus nudges my arm.

I grab him and twist my fingers into his fur. The cat shifts so that I lay atop him.

"Wait!" the guard mutters, still attached to the tree with the rope I use to ride. "WAIT!"

It's too late. Cerberus takes off in strides, my body hanging from his back, fingers twined into his fur. The ground is adrift under me, blurring over the crevices of rocks.

We run until nightfall through trees and crowds of people. Cerberus shows little care for hiding us from the villagers. Instead, he plunges through the crowds with a snarl on his maw. The entire pack follows, close on his heels.

I don't pay them much mind.

I flick through the memories of Jasmine over and over. She was so bright, full of zest and fervour—so different to Faye, yet exactly what I needed. Us Hayes are an intense sort. We need someone to balance our fire and meet us halfway. Jasmine was my balance… or could have been.

Cerberus stops sometime in the Night, plopping me down by a deserted bend in the river. My cats slink out from behind us, wetting their maws by the stream and drinking heavily.

I roll off Cerberus's back, sliding down against a thick carpet of grass, letting the cat get his own fill of water. I don't even remember him coming back up from the stream. I just lay on the grass and stare at the heavens.

The lights in the blackness sparkle and dance; an array of laughter and smiles. I can see Jasmine there, smiling down at me. Faye, too.

I'm sure my brother is knee-deep in the politics of Umbra, using Jasmine's sacrifice to bring about a better future. Perhaps the Elders are finally ready to listen to Savannah. Perhaps the world will finally be at peace.

But I don't care.

I don't belong in the world of politics, death, and pain. I never have.

The grass shifts around me a little as cats move to sleep in large piles of fur, cocooning me as I mourn. It's a quiet sort of comradery.

A soft breeze cascades over our bodies, twisting the braids on my head and the fur on their skin. The grass sings a song, sad and wistful, and I breathe in a long, long, swath of air.

"This is where we will stay," I tell the cats. "In the wild, forevermore."

One of them purrs against my body.

"*Per aspera ad astra*, Jasmine Spark. *Et iterum*," I whisper, closing my eyes. "Through hardships through the stars, and back again."

Back to where we belong.

⤷

"This may be farewell, dear Cerberus," I say softly.

He glances up at me as if he understands me, but I have long since learnt that he does not. It's the body language that he reads. And, standing here at the entrance to the great expanse that is Sector 3, I know he understands.

When I told my friends I may never return should I enter these caves, I meant it. It was not something said out of fear but trepidation.

I'm worried Sector 3 is the place I belong.

But that meant leaving Jasmine behind, leaving my brother and, worse of all, my cats. But they, too, deserve to return home. It's been too long since any of them saw the snowy crops of the North. Cerberus came down one fated Night and found me. We began harbouring more and more stray cats into our midst until we formed a substantially frightening pack—a pack which, at this size, could rival any predator they may face in the Northern Snow Caps.

They are strong. Even the babes are fierce. And they deserve to go home.

Just as I do.

Cerberus licks my hand, warming my fingers. We came during the Night after Savannah made her announcement for Umbra. I was curious to see what would happen, had to ensure my brother was safe before I left. Now, there's nothing left to do except say goodbye and enter the threshold of Sector 3.

The desert above the caves is empty, unlike the last time we came here, but that's not to say that the people of this Sector do not know I am here. Besides, it's much too cold to be outside. A thick layer of fog hangs over the fortress, hiding it plainly from view, but I marked the landmarks to memory.

I can sense them watching.

I turn back to face the cats swarmed behind me, nearly invisible among the icy fog. I wonder if the people of Sector 3 can see them here from the entrance of their caves.

"I'm safe now, Cerberus. You can return home."

The cat just stares at me, as does the rest of them, their snowy coats swaying against the soft breeze.

I take a gentle step back, giving them a watery smile. Somehow, they understand.

I take another step, my boot crunching against the cold sand. The Night is brisk around us, aching against my skin, but it's only early. I've survived worse.

My smile feels tight, and it's hard to know if it's from the cold or from emotion.

"Perhaps we'll see each other again," I offer them.

They just stare at me and huff steam out their maws. I let Cerberus nudge my hand, running my fingers through his curls one last time.

"You'll always be family."

I choke on the final word, so I spin around on soundless feet, dashing away from them. Each footfall against the sand seems to punctuate the fast thrum of my heart, drilling into my head. I run until I'm certain they are not following me.

The familiar entrance to Sector 3 comes up to greet me, the harsh stones biting like cold metal as I hang onto them from support, my chest cleaving with each lungful of icy air.

In the distance, I hear Cerberus howl a keening sound of pain.

"Lily Hayes."

The words are gruff yet familiar.

I give myself one last chance to catch my breath before standing and meeting the watchful eyes of a dozen Sector 3 civilians, all donned in their long cloaks.

Every step I take into the cave seems to echo.

"Hello, again. I'm here seeking refuge, if you'll have me."

One of them breaks from the others, pulling down his hood as he does. When he reaches for my hand, I let him. His brown eyes are new to me, the lines of his worn face unfamiliar, but the warmth in his gaze stretches deep within his soul.

"My dear," he says warmly. "We have been expecting you."

I smile a little sadly. But my words are strong when I respond, "*Ego domi sum.*"

I am at home. At long last.

ACKNOWLEDGEMENTS

This is it, the end of the beginning. Silver Valley, you are my heart and my dreams—the stars that I always dreamt of reaching. And here we are. We made it.

First, and most importantly, I want to thank the person I was at 14. Silver Valley wouldn't exist today if it weren't for the dreams of that young girl.

I still remember the day I called a random hotline for a publishing agency I found on Safari, using my mother's home phone, and the spam calls that followed for years after. I panicked and never called them back but those spam calls kept reminding me for years to keep trying, to keep dreaming. This series is everything that girl would have wanted it to be, and I'm so glad she dared to dream it up.

Secondly, I need to thank my friends and family. To every soul that sat and listened to me talk about this book and dealt with me end-lessly spoiling every plot twist in my excitement. You mean more to me than you can even imagine.

And of course, my amazing team. To my editor, Chloe Hodge, my cover artist, Gab Kell, and the entire team at Author Services Australia—thank you for riding this series out with me. You all mean to world to me.

And no, I haven't forgotten you, my readers! My internet family. Whether you've sent me reactions on Direct Message, tagged Silver Valley in your stories, or watched and read the books from afar—every one of you have made the difference in this journey. I hope Silver Valley has left a mark on your heart, the same way it has for me.

Thank you, endlessly, to everyone who laughed, cried, screamed with me while reading. Thank you, thank you.

But lastly, Savannah Shaw. (Yes, she's a real person to me, no judgement).

My sweet baby child, thank you for enduring the suffering I put you through and for showing me that sometimes a character doesn't have to change to be considered strong—despite how often I tried to give you the crown, you never wanted it! You stayed the same since that first draft when I was 14, and that blows me away. Thank you for being a by-product of my journey as an author.

Thank you, everyone. This isn't the end. Just the beginning.

Happy reading!

See you in the stars!

ABOUT THE AUTHOR

Arabella Rosier is a 26-year-old author from QLD, Australia. Books have always been a part of her heart since the moment she learnt how to read. When she was 14 years old, she read her first big fantasy novel and dream of writing her own. And now, 10 years later, the *Silver Valley* series has come to life. Hopefully it enraptures your soul as much as it has hers.